Dustin Rielly is an Australian author. Following musical pursuits, he studied creative writing and history at the Queensland University of Technology, worked various jobs, and while traveling developed the ideas for his first novel, *Bounding Line*. He lives in Brisbane, Australia.

www.dustinrielly.com

# BOUNDING LINE

## DUSTIN RIELLY

First published by Wayfarer Press in 2024
This KDP paperback first edition published July 2024

A catalogue record for this book is available from the National Library of Australia

ISBN 978-1-7635747-3-1

WAYFARER

Published by Wayfarer Press
wayfarerpress.net

*This book is dedicated to the memory of my mother,*
*Beverly Ann Rielly,*
*who always believed.*

# Acknowledgments

Thanks to my manuscript assessor Tom Flood, at Flood Manuscripts, for his insight, patience, and honesty. Sincere thanks to the first readers, who helped this story immensely—in particular, Wendy Waters for her valued support, counsel, and analysis, Sarah Yates for her critiques and sharing some long writing sessions, and James Lucas, for his criticism and Shakespearean discussions in the late stages. Also, thanks to my creative writing teachers at QUT for their advice and encouragement. My heartfelt appreciation to all those who provided moral support, and friendship, along the way—most of you know who you are—particularly, Ryan Adam, Linnea Carina Lofling, Matt Haines, James Dwyer, and Mandi O'Sullivan-Jones. Damon Rielly, my brother, for his enduring support, enthusiasm, and seeing potential in the craziness. I would also like to acknowledge the valued contributions of my late mother Beverly Rielly for her in-depth reviews of the manuscript, and for always being there. Ian Rielly, my father, for encouraging a work ethic. A special, posthumous word of gratitude for the support and friendship of Tyronne White, for his inspiring pursuit of a greater reality, who read and critiqued an early draft. Finally, thanks to all the people I've crossed paths with in the Brisbane recovery community, without whom this book would not be possible.

# BOUNDING LINE

WAYFARER

Dr. Eldon Tyrell—*"What seems to be the problem?"*
Roy Batty—*"Death."*

**- BLADE RUNNER, 1982**

# THE CROSSING



THE PLANETARY HORIZON BLAZED.

Through the cockpit window, the solar corona darkened, and sank into the ecliptic. Falling away, the abyssal plains of the Levant wastelands were streaming, moving beneath like a shadowy sea of ghosts between my past and future.

Strapped into the co-pilot's seat, I interfaced with Jericho station. 'Control, this is the *Hecate*. We are on final approach.'

A burst of static came over the net. 'Copy that, *Hecate*. You are cleared for synchronization in t-minus twelve minutes, eleven seconds.'

'Copy, Control.'

I stared ahead, willing the darkness to reveal its secrets.

'Passing Dead Sea, we're over Zion,' said the pilot, Lieutenant John Li.

*Zion. Incarnation of the new abnormal. Every time I'm here I feel more suffocated. Perfect place for insane experiments.*

The capital of the world following the Terminal War, Zion had displaced old territorial borders, and the urban sprawl stretched hundreds of kilometers from the Golan Heights in the north to the Negev Desert in the south.

I glanced at the man beside me. Li's weathered face, framed by short-cropped black hair, looked tired. But the quiet strength in his penetrating brown eyes, born of a distinguished career, was comforting. We'd trained for Project Sirius together for a year now.

A controllable gateway to the afterlife was the goal. The prize? Ultimate power: to cheat death, to swim the time stream, to manipulate destiny itself. My motivation, however, was far less grandiose. To understand my daughter's fate. Absolution.

I mentally reviewed the mission once more, trying to still a trembling that had begun in my hands. From the relative safety of the ship, I would mind-link with Daniel Weir, who would soon be clinically dead in cryo-stasis, far below in OriGen Corporation's Zion research facility. Weir's spirit would then leave a perfectly good body, and I would piggyback his consciousness as he entered a naked singularity. A naked singularity was a black hole, but without a gravity field. Meaning you could walk right up and knock on—and theoretically step through—the edge of the universe. Using a revolutionary energy source, the OriGen Corporation was about to create one.

My job was to anchor Weir to this world, allowing him to climb back through the doorway of death, and return to life. The phase-link would bind us across dimensions, and I would experience everything he did, while remaining safely on this side. I was a failsafe, so that if Weir went down, I would—OriGen would—possess firsthand mission knowledge. From the high troposphere, danger to the *Hecate* was mitigated, and if there was a catastrophic mission failure, the ship could evacuate the area in moments. At least, that was the theory. The vessel slowed.

'Geosynchronous orbital plane secured, Control. Altitude twenty-five thousand meters and holding over Zion Temple. Coordinates 31.77° north, 35.22° east,' I said.

'Copy that, *Hecate*. You are cleared for link,' a filtered voice replied over the net.

Li tapped a control. 'Phase-link coded and locked, Control.'

'Copy, *Hecate*.'

'Initiating mind-link,' Li said.

The phase-link with Weir began. I felt a dislocation of self, a sense of going beyond, and in my mind the ship began spinning.

'I'm...' I said, shaking my head, 'entering phase one.'

'Etheric-double isolation, commenced,' Li said.

I felt the familiar tingling as in a seamless merger of human and machine, I web-linked on the molecular level. Stage One of the neurological phase-link provided a physical reference, for a spiritual experience.

My vision blurred. I had to maintain control.

Li glanced at me. 'Focus, Solara. Talk to me about Rebecca.'

My daughter. Had it been seven years? It felt more like seven days. 'You know the last thing I said to her?'

'What?'

I paused, took a deep breath. 'We'd just made it out of Kansas City and were caught in a sweep. Rebecca asked me not to leave her. I'd never leave, I told her.' A prickling grew in my hands and feet. 'That was the last time I saw her. When Rebecca died, I thought—how dare she be taken from me? The same thing when my EOD team were lost, and I signed onto Sirius. I'll show you, I thought. I'll show God...' My vision shimmered like liquid crystal. 'I've always felt I would see her again one day, that it wasn't really over.'

'Five minutes,' Li said.

I relaxed into a meditative state, letting my mind sink into alpha, theta, and felt a page turning deep in my circle of being. Maybe another one would open, if I survived. If one of the participants in a mind-link died before the connection was cut, it could result in permanent brain damage to the other.

'You're cleared,' Li said.

'I'm going in.'

An arcane-like mind interface washed over me in a procession of luminous digital waves, the streaming code like a torrent of stars against infinite space.

'Just come back, Solara,' Li said.

Fading fast, I gave him a brief last glance. 'Relax, John, I got… thi…'

'Phase two, etheric separation,' Li said.

I closed my eyes and entered the Sirius Matrix, warmth coming as my energy rose with a sense of dislocation. Then an undertow of connection pulled me towards Weir, and an abyss of trusting vulnerability.

Li's voice was far away. 'Execute…'

●

FROM THE nerve center of the subterranean Zion research facility, project leader Dr. Neil Andrews was seated like a monk in prayer, immersed in a collective neural interface. His virtual overlay displayed the vacuum matrix, the web of force at the source of the experiment's power. An experimental physicist from Cambridge, nothing in his career had prepared him for the immensity of Project Sirius. A decade ago, the experiment would have been illegal, but the war had ushered in a new, unrestrained morality. Not everyone, though, was comfortable with the new order.

Andrews had never agreed with conducting the experiment in a populated zone; however, multiple redundant containment measures shielded the control room. Ultimately, the chronic arrogance of OriGen leadership had decided the location, and the people on the streets far above were oblivious to the dangerous anomaly that would soon appear beneath their city. But at a certain scale of risk, location became irrelevant. If the experiment was on the far side of the galaxy, it may not reduce consequences of failure.

Andrews nodded at Tori McNash, his second in command. 'Initiate particle acquisition phase.'

'Vacuum tunneling,' McNash said, tapping a control. 'Locked on, stable, initiating collision sequence.'

Andrews was grateful for McNash. Her brown hair was done up in a ponytail, and she balanced a coffee in one hand while interfacing with the other. A cybernetic scientist and physicist from ODSEI (OriGen Deep Space Exploration Initiative), she had a razor-sharp mind, and the ability to see to the heart of an issue.

They witnessed a primal force building.

McNash swiped a holo-control. 'Containing!'

The newly created particles were directed into a containment chamber, a charged cage which would hold the energy suspended. An energy signature blinked to life on the main display, and Andrews knew they had achieved something once believed impossible: harvesting energy from space. The matrix showed a multitude of sparkling lights appearing in the containment cage, only a few at first, but multiplying until the intensity was beyond comprehension. The chamber was at the epicenter of a cosmic cyclone, shining with blinding luminosity.

'We have force unification!' McNash announced.

Andrews willed himself calm. If the energy field became unstable it could kill everyone on the base. 'Ready for the next phase.'

The deep underground facility had been carved into the earth three hundred meters beneath the Zion Temple. A huge cavity, the walls of the control room were dark gray and peppered with jutting, stalactite-like protrusions which engulfed the room in shadows. Three levels of catwalks and workstations were situated around the perimeter of the control room behind reinforced glass barriers.

He turned his attention to enhanced scans of Daniel Weir, whose stasis tube was placed at the perimeter of a safe zone at the edge of the ground floor. His toroidal subtle body, or aura, looked healthy, emanating about five feet outward with a strong flow from his feet to his crown. Following clinical death, induced by cardiac arrest, the separation of mind from body would occur, and the subtle body would collapse to a micro-singularity.

Telepathic signals would begin. In a state of suspended animation, induced by profound hypothermia, the body could survive without irreversible brain damage for up to one hundred and twenty minutes. Weir would then mind-link with Solara. The window the spirit had to enter and return through the portal was a maximum of seven minutes, after that the gate would close. More than enough time to return to the body without incurring disability or coma. Resuscitation was achieved by closed chest cardiopulmonary bypass, post cardiac arrest, and accelerated mild hypothermia. Medical use of nanotechnology and genomics made possible an accelerated intensive care recovery of only several minutes.

Andrews tracked Weir's biodata. 'Initiating cryogenic sequence.'

The temperature in Weir's pod dropped rapidly, and a shimmer passed through the fluid. The solution did not crystallize, but vitrified, becoming solid liquid. Weir's breathing slowed, his movements became smaller and less pronounced, until he was motionless in amorphous ice.

McNash followed live readouts. 'Solution temperature minus one hundred and thirty-eight degrees Celsius, and falling.'

In less than a minute, the freezing process had completed, and Weir lay within stasis like an insect trapped in amber.

McNash continued. 'Minus one hundred and ninety-six degrees, cardiac arrest in three, two, one –'

The high-pitched drone of a flat-line signal hummed out from a monitor as Weir's neural activity ceased, and silence pervaded the room for a moment.

'Receiving medical diagnostics…' McNash said, tapping a command. 'Tissue damage minimal, brain activity zero, nanites on standby for cellular reconstruction, bio readouts… he's gone, establishing telepathic link.'

Andrews interfaced. 'We are opening a naked singularity.'

In a clash of thunder, a churning fireball came into being in the center of the Zion singularity control room. Infinite mass-density in a non-space. Hovering between the double vortex cones of the particle collider, the anomaly seared the pressurized atmosphere of the vaulted chamber with the acrid reek of a blast furnace. Without a gravity constant, the core was volatile, emitting sporadic gravitational waves that warped the space around it. Andrews checked the electromagnetic/anti-gravity fields around the perimeter, which were part of the containment measures.

Stable.

Tori McNash frowned at a display. 'Neil.'

'Yes?'

'We've got erratic surges in the field. The configuration doesn't seem right, there's some kind of unidentified interference. Also, the gate is sucking an unusually high amount of power.'

'Damn.'

Her eyes were troubled. 'Our window's been cut to two minutes, maybe three.'

He turned to stare at the portal, and for a long moment considered its mysterious depths. The absolute boundary of reality. Something was wrong. The facility was tense as Weir and Solara attempted entry. Now the predicted seven-minute window was cut to two. Another attempt would not be possible for days; that was the time it took to charge the energy field.

'Isolate the disturbance, reconfigure the field to compensate,' Andrews ordered.

McNash entered a complex sequence. 'Field array, stable.' She frowned at the screen.

'Are we good?' She gave a brief nod.

'We're committed now, Tori.' He glanced at Weir. 'All of us.'

Andrews re-immersed his mind in the seat of control, and Tori started fading away from his vision as a computer-generated world materialized around him.

●

SPEEDING INTO an array of energy vortices at the origin of nature, I searched for the seat of Weir's consciousness, and arrived at my soul's destination. I was now a point of awareness, and movement was achieved by thought alone. In my spirit's vision, the matter of the singularity control room shimmered along the contours of variant, vibrational fields, which cascaded as if from an unfolding, boundless reservoir.

'I am here.'

Weir's telepathic reply whispered through the ether. 'We wait.'

His separated subtle body was indiscernible until he communicated, and appeared as a localized fluctuation in the field. I focused, and perceived the essence of Weir: a micro-singularity—or wormhole—that appeared as a tiny point of light at the center of the variance. At the core of consciousness, the singularity was theorized as the key to unbounded, continuous memory, generating a phase-link which bonded an awareness to an information network present throughout the universe. This network formed the basis for our telepathy. Sender and receiver shared impressions, imagery, or just a sense of knowing. Through it, we could contact the nerve center via what amounted to a high-tech Ouija board, which translated our thoughts for the technicians.

I grasped the etheric tether, connected with Weir's subtle body in an intimate rapport, and we paused in union. Weir's personality dimensions were as boundless as his ambition, and just as murky, and despite the link time logged together, I had never penetrated the depths of his mind. Life seemed a construct to Weir, a god-driven sculpting of reality he appeared to neither resist nor understand.

The naked singularity was unearthly, hypnotic. A small, impossibly bright star-like object, it was surrounded by a churning pool of warped light and particle collisions which shifted continually through the spectrum. Waves of shadow rippled outward in a dark miasma, neutralized by the anti-gravity shield. Reassuringly, I understood that after crossing over, in theory, I could will myself back through in an instant.

Control phased in. 'You are go for vacuum entry, Archangel. Repeat, you are go for entry.' Archangel was the call-sign of the incursion team.

Weir replied, 'Copy control, we are entering the naked singularity.'

The portal warped violently.

*What the…*

I paused behind Weir. We observed the control room message screen: no alerts were posted, whatever it was hadn't been picked up by any sensors, or wasn't considered important enough to note. Instabilities, although potentially highly destructive, could be rectified by adjusting the controlling energy field that held open the gate.

We moved to the threshold.

'See you on the other side,' I thought.

'You bet, kiddo,' replied Weir.

Time stopped at the edge of the abyss.

*Say goodnight.*

I willed myself into the infinite.

Holding tight to the chord binding me to Weir, chaos engulfed my awareness, and my mind was rolled up into the sub-atomic manifold as I hurtled through a shimmering tunnel and then smashed into another reality.

NEIL ANDREWS monitored schematics. Because of a predicted temporal shift on the other side, Solara's and Weir's return should be nearly immediate. 'Phase link stabl—'

A keening noise began that seemed to come from a great distance. Andrews froze and heard the sound building, building...

'Neil!' McNash shouted frantically. 'Weir's back! But... shit, look at that energy surge...'

'It's Weir—it's coming from Weir!' Andrews yelled. 'Aborting!'

A horrific cry burst over the telepathic transmitter. Scrambling through code in alarm, Andrews checked the integrity of the containment chamber as the grotesque noise reached deafening proportions. Shouts rang out from the personnel, and the control room descended into chaos.

'What the fuck is going on!' McNash screamed, and pressed her hands over her ears.

The energy field spiked, and Andrews felt the blood drain from his face. 'Jesus, Tori, I think something came back through with Weir!'

A thundering roar shook the facility, as if a power had been set loose from its prison and was beating down the door of the living. The surface of the naked singularity exploded, and a concussive, otherworldly blast ripped through the anti-gravity shields, penetrated barriers, and scattered bodies like leaves in a hurricane. Stunned and shaken, Andrews' hands shook as he attempted to get a distress signal away to the OriGen network.

'Unable to deliver message,' the AI replied.

Knocked off her feet, Tori McNash struggled to her knees, gasped for breath. 'Neil… shut the gate.'

Andrews' small hairs rose at the increasing sense of presence, and for a fleeting moment, he had a glimpse into horror: his mind was propelled into a chaotic realm of violent energy displays, primal conflict, and eternal, inescapable emptiness. With a sense of moving at immense speed, he crashed down to the floor, vomited, rolled, tried to stop the scream growing in his throat. Blood gushed from a wound in his head, but he rose, staggered to the shattered observation window. An ominous black void hovered in the center of the ground floor where the fiery naked singularity had been, and riots of light particles sped out from its dark core to spiral upward in a scintillating array.

McNash screamed as an unseen force slammed her brutally up against the back wall like a troublesome insect. Struggling to breathe, Andrews frantically tried to close the naked singularity just as the light particles, now stationary, ignited.

'Unable to terminate energy field,' said the AI.

Andrews saw something come into being around the naked singularity: a wrongness in the appearance of the space in the room he couldn't identify, couldn't name, somehow out of synch with the world. Then came a catastrophic explosion, and Andrews' world went black.

◉

IN THE COCKPIT of the *Hecate*, Li watched the singularity control room descend into chaos. He paused his finger over the extraction control, well aware that ending the link prematurely risked brain damage to Solara or worse.

He punched comms. 'Zion Control, this is *Hecate*—do you read me?' Solara began shaking in her seat, and her phase-link went ballistic. Li hit the keypad. 'Extract!'

'Mind-link terminated,' said the ship AI.

Solara drew in a ragged gasp, but remained unconscious. Her heart rate was rapid, and her breath started coming in short, erratic bursts.

'Fuck,' Li said, tapping Solara's bio-meds. He placed his hand on her forehead, holding it down firmly to prevent injury in case of seizure. 'Doc!' Li shouted.

'Administering nanites, sedative,' the autodoc said.

Biometrics showed countless molecular machines interacting with her system.

Li hit comms again. 'Zion Control, this is the *Hecate!* Come in, over?'

Flat static.

'*Hecate*, this is Jericho. What's your status? Report, over.'

The main monitoring station for the experiment, Jericho operated on the outskirts of the Zion Temple complex.

Li said, 'Jericho, Solara's mind-link is broken, but she's failed to wake up.'

A new voice transmitted. 'Lieutenant, this is Rhodes. Transfer Solara to the *Tempora* now. Then I want your team on an immediate recon of the singularity control complex. Understood?'

The operational commander of Project Sirius, General David Rhodes, reputation was legendary: his arduous rise through the ranks of the US Airforce as a fighter pilot, Wing-Commander in the Middle East campaigns, the Sino-Russian-Arab conflict, the Terminal World War where he'd attained a battlefield commission of Air-Marshall. Li had studied his tactics in War College, and the General's voice always brought calm to him.

'Copy, General,' Li said.

He stayed on comms. The *Tempora* was a MEDEVAC aircraft which provided rapid mobile support to OriGen operations across the region, and had monitored the experiment from nearby. Solara would be evacuated to Jericho. They wanted her safe; that was the reason the mind-link had been airborne. If things went south, she would be able to get away, and Sirius would survive with her. If Weir, still down on the surface, had been lost, she was the mission now.

'*Tempora*, prepare for casualty transfer,' Li said.

'Copy, *Hecate*,' the *Tempora* responded.

Locking on the *Tempora's* transponder, Li hit the thrusters, and the acceleration jolted him backward into the seat. His heartbeat thumped in his ears, emphasizing the now eerily silent cockpit. Through the forward window, the canopy of clouds was broken only by the approaching lights of the medical ship. He glanced at Solara: her eyes remained closed, her angular face bordered by long brown hair was peaceful, her breathing steady, but a slight trembling remained in her hands. The *Tempora* loomed up before him, sleek and functional. Nearing the aircraft interface, Li prepared for linkage.

The *Tempora* transmitted, '*Hecate*, you are clear to dock in ten, nine…'

Ship AI guided the *Hecate* in, the craft met in a snap of hydraulic clamps, and the airlock began pressurizing with a distant hiss.

THE TRANSFER had been completed with efficiency and precision, and Solara was safely aboard the *Tempora*. Detaching from the other craft, Li hit the thrusters. The *Hecate* was linked to his thoughts, like a biomimetic extension of his body, giving the sensation of 'swimming' through the air as he plunged downward in a steep descent.

He neura-linked a command. *'Pass-through.'*

With his virtual overlay linked to an array of external cameras on the ship, the hull appeared to become transparent, granting him 360-degree spatial awareness. He focused on Zion Temple below; from the high tropospheric altitude of fourteen kilometers, the lights of the vast pyramid were a tiny cross of fire in an abyssal void. He punched the turbots, jolted back again as the ship shrieked down through turbulence trailing a blue tongue of plasma, and felt the blood pushed to the back of his head in protest at the g-forces.

He tapped comms. 'Amy, Helberg, meet me at the east temple entrance. Prepare for control room recon.' The unit had been on standby, monitoring the experiment from Operations, and would have witnessed the control room fiasco live.

Static cut through. 'Already on it, boss. See you when you get here,' Sergeant Amy Winters replied.

'Copy,' Li replied.

Li enjoyed working with Winters. They'd served together in an anti-terror unit before Sirius, and she was one of the best operators he'd seen. The youngest of the Sirius team, Amy Winters had a distinct lack of interest in promotion and an irreverent attitude to match. She possessed a risk-willing, but shrewd attitude, although not everyone appreciated this trait. Corporal Alex Helberg was a man who dedicated his life to two things: his job, and his passion for catamaran racing—the deep space type. Crazy bastard. The lights of the temple grew larger, more distinct, and Zion became manifest. A slight jolt shook the *Hecate* when the ship penetrated the barely perceptible City-Shield. A plasma dome confined by magnetic field which arched over Zion, it protected the city from hazardous particles and radiological contaminants released in the war.

'Solara?' Winters asked.

Amy had known Solara since the US exodus, and the two women were close.

'Stable,' Li said.

The ship leveled off on approach, and the *Hecate* was met by several Planetar Interceptors which drew up in formation.

'Lieutenant, I'm Wing Commander Nadav. We'll be your escort,' said the lead pilot.

Although highly unlikely, random attacks upon aircraft from criminal elements on the streets were known to occur. Sirius assets had been given the highest security priority.

'Copy, Commander,' replied Li.

Following the Planetar in, Li scrolled the new objectives across his neural feed. One—recon the base for threats. Two—retrieve Sirius mission data from secure servers, and third—locate and rescue any survivors. In the heart of Eden Sector, the Zion Temple was an immense pyramid-like structure. Looming up ahead, it dominated what had been Jerusalem's Four Quarters area, and its bulk splayed out like a giant boot stomping down on a bygone age. The nighttime sky over Eden was alive, and lights of thousands of sky-cars soared amidst the glittering high rises in a seamless merger with the city blaze. Far away across the city, barely visible, were the power-starved, darkened, outer city enclaves. Mechanus, and Hades. The Planetars turned away with a flash of taillights, and Li veered the *Hecate* down to the tarmac. He thought of the screams he'd heard, just before comms blackout.

*Something came through.*

The craft landed with a thud of hydraulic struts. Releasing his harness, he heard Jericho continue attempted contact with the singularity control room over comms.

They received nothing but silence.

# RECRUIT

$I$ OPENED MY EYES.

Blinded by sterile light. My throat tightened with the sour taste of bile and waves of heat rolled through me.

'Revival, complete,' said an unfamiliar voice.

Voices penetrated my head painfully like a plucked string through my nerves, and it felt like I'd pulled every muscle in my body simultaneously. Jolts shot through my calves, thighs, abdomen, and neck. I heard myself moan, closed my eyes again, and imagery flashed through my awareness: the blinding light of the naked singularity, speeding down a tunnel with Weir, darkness...

'Follow the light,' said a clinical male voice.

'She's delirious,' said another.

Squinting, I saw a light move in a circular motion, and tracked it closely with my eyes.

'No, she's okay,' said the voice.

I made out a figure standing beside the gurney.

'Tell me your name and date of birth?' the voice asked.

'Solara Jordan. February 9, 2077,' I rasped.

More flashes of insight came at random: a face—Rebecca? Shivering. Nothing clear.

'Place of birth?'

'Skye, Scotland.'

'What year is it now?'

'2113… water.'

Someone moved a tube to my mouth. 'Here, drink this.'

Alkaline coolness moistened my throat, and I kept drinking until the straw was withdrawn. My vision adjusted fully, and I saw an OriGen medical suite in which, apart from several personnel, I was the sole occupant. A drip was attached to my hand.

'I hurt all over,' I groaned.

'You're experiencing a physical reaction to the shock. It will pass soon.'

The doctor's name came to me. Shaw.

I frowned. 'That never happened in the training.'

Shaw made a note on his handheld, tapped a command. 'I've given you a strong painkiller. You may experience slight drowsiness.'

'Where am I?'

'You're in an ICU, at Jericho station.'

'What?' I eased myself up on an elbow and my head spun. Intensive care? 'Why aren't I on the *Hecate*?'

He checked my drip. 'Someone will be along to discuss it with you soon. Apart from the pain, how do you feel?'

I considered. I felt oddly euphoric; was it the painkillers? My senses felt more acute than usual, various sounds of the room seemed sharper, and the light was harsher. The incursion was a blank, but this was expected. It had been theorized that once passing through the naked singularity, although minutes, hours, years could pass on the other side, entry and return would only take seconds from this side, the experience beyond the ability of the conscious mind to comprehend. Science Division believed the subject would need to undergo mind regression after returning. Temporal Displacement Amnesia, they called it.

'Solara?'

'I feel the same, but… different. I don't know. Confused.'

'You're doing well. No lasting impairment. Your MRI results show healthy brain activity. Very healthy, in fact.'

'How long have I been out?'

'Not long.'

'Daniel?'

'Don't worry about that now. You're doing well, but you need to get some rest.'

I tried to rise again, but my head spun wildly, and sparkles appeared in my eyes. Shaw eased me back to a lying position, and I noticed my journal on the table beside the gurney. No one knew I would be in the ICU. Someone had placed it there for me. I fell into a restless slumber.

A familiar young face, so like my own, looked back at me from my dreams.

●

LIEUTENANT JOHN LI exited the central pyramid shaft elevator at Sub-Level 7, and entered the singularity complex lobby. In the high, vaulted chamber, the service desk, lounge area, and various exits were silhouetted in dim, amber emergency lighting. Main power was down, and the station should be deserted after personnel had been evacuated. Behind him, Sergeant Amy Winters and Corporal Alex Helberg stepped warily out of the lift. Like Li, they were covered in a flexible suit of dark gray body armor, carried the Shadow 7 Adaptive Combat Rifle, and an array of specialized sensory tech. The weapon could fire either a 90kW continuous laser beam or a pulsed energy projectile; basically, a high-energy stun gun which fired an expanding burst of plasma, causing temporary paralysis. It also possessed the new anti-matter tipped bullet with a six-round cartridge and variable charge. Nevertheless, Li felt naked, and knew the weapons were to deal with any unforeseen threats from this world, rather than the next. Unhinged personnel, malfunctioning machine sentries; whatever had hit the control room had messed with those who had evacuated, and the electrical systems. With surveillance down, they didn't know what to expect. Something had come through the portal they didn't understand, and their job was to secure the control room, so that Science Division could come in and assess.

They fanned out into the silent lobby. Amy Winters' short blond hair framed her tanned, wary face. At five feet six, her build was athletic and compact, and she moved with an air of competent ease. With his hardened, muscular physique, Helberg stood a head taller than Amy, and his steely gray eyes scanned the area cautiously. With a jagged scar between his right eye and ear, Helberg was a walking weapon and wore a perpetual scowl; he was a soldier with the ability to run a marathon and fight a battle after crossing the finish line. There was a rivalry between the pair which sometimes crossed the line into antagonism, but all quips now were absent. Li strode to the ballistic security door which led to the singularity control room.

He neura-linked, *'Open.'*

The door was unresponsive.

Helberg approached, tapped his handheld. 'Circuits are fried. Bypassing,' he said, in his guttural, English accent. After a series of rapid commands on his device, the door ground open with a rush of pressurized air from the interior. He interfaced again, and nine metallic spheres detached from his backpack and hovered in the air. 'Cerberus online. Connecting with resident AI… authenticated.'

The team linked with the drones, becoming part of a networked super organism, and probe-vision came up in a virtual-overlay display.

'Deploy,' ordered Li quietly.

Probe-vision showed Cerberus move forward into the dark passage, one after the other in three formations of three. The weaponized, intelligent surveillance drones would separate and explore the area. Nearing the end of the corridor they took a ninety-degree turn and came to the vault-like auxiliary door.

**CONTAINMENT ZONE 2
MAXIMUM SECURITY: ULTRA
STRICTLY NO UNAUTHORIZED PERSONNEL**

Helberg tapped his feed. 'Singularity control room reached. Outer entrance sealed. No response. Deploying thermal lance.'

Intense, convergent blades of plasma shot forth from Cerberus, cutting into the high-tension steel of the blast door. The surface rippled and after a few minutes a small opening had been cut. The probes moved through, entered a small antechamber alight with a womb red glow. Barring the way was the inner door stenciled with bold red letters:

**CORE**

'Bypassing,' said Helberg.

With an affirmative beep, the inner door slid open. Probe vision went dark and the Cerberus link was cut.

'Transmission lost. Could be interference,' said Helberg, analyzing his handheld readout.

Li walked to the open passage entrance, waited. A minute passed. He'd taken a step toward the opening when one of the drones shot back down the corridor toward them, and probe-vision flashed back to life. Bursting into the lobby, the drone hovered motionless before the entrance and chirped with a series of excited electronic warbles.

Amy read the comm. 'Dense electromagnetic field inside the control room. Limiting signals to approximately ten meters. Cerberus have formed a chain-line from the control room to the entrance to link the transmission.'

Li scanned the dim corridor, and saw another probe hovering just before the first turn.

'We've got a visual scan,' said Helberg.

Li watched silently as the footage came up in overlay. The timer played in the top right corner of the video. It showed the probes nearing the inner core entrance and then passing through into a vast chamber. Cerberus swarmed into the singularity control room and their lights swept the darkness, running sensors through all known spectrums.

Ice encrusted the blackened surfaces, like cold sweat off a living organism. The wall spikes cast moving shadows, as the sequence of imagery played in Li's overlay with a hypnotic rhythm, and then an unsettling vision pearled through the feed. The outline of a human form was seared into the metal above the walkway in the northeastern corner of the control room. In a random, freakish burn pattern, the face seemed frozen in an agonized scream.

'Jesus,' Li observed, gravely.

Helberg frowned. 'If this area's totaled, how the fuck is the rest of the base unaffected?'

'The control room is a reinforced bunker,' said Li. 'My guess… may have been a dark energy burst, which could have hit the control room with limited kinetic effects.'

Amy monitored Cerberus vision. 'Something for our geniuses in Science Division.'

The probes moved down to the ground floor, now a charred crater, and Li felt a cold hand grip his spine.

'What the hell…' Helberg said.

A massive, spherical apparition hovered in the center. The fiery naked singularity was gone, and an anomaly hovered in its place. Blue-tinged and radiant, within its curved boundary were myriad smaller globes, each one filled with a spattering of light. And within each of these were more diminishing spheres, an endless succession of copies descending into its depths. Spiraling around it, suspended and apparently frozen in time, was a vortex of poised, glowing particles.

Li checked schematics. 'It's in the exact location the naked singularity was opened.'

Amy frowned at something odd in the anomaly. 'Activity—'

Static cut through the recording a second. When it cleared, the anomaly had turned the deepest black. A hungry void light could not escape. It flickered a moment before the bluish, fluctuating glow returned.

Li's body hair prickled. 'Could the naked singularity still be open?'

Helberg raised his handheld. 'I'm picking up a faint signal from the bunker. It's Weir.'

Weir's stasis tube had been connected to an escape chute that led to a hard site buried kilometers deep in the earth.

'Condition?' Li said.

Amy frowned. 'Bio-signs are low, heartbeats erratic… cryogenic-trauma recovery is behind schedule. Could be effects of the pod jettison disconnect.' She paused, studied the readout some more, and then glanced at Li. 'He's borderline.'

The bunker was reached through means of a lateral passage connected to the central pyramid shaft. Then a secondary vertical shaft. It would take at least twenty minutes to reach Weir.

'Let's go,' said Li.

He abruptly turned from the blast doors, and jogged across the lobby towards the exit. Without a word, Amy and Helberg followed rapidly on his heels.

HOURS LATER I lay dozing, staring out the window at OriGen's Jericho campus, and the late-night city vista. The gloom of nuclear winter had begun to clear during the last year, and the moon broke through thick clouds, splashing hues of luminous ivory across Zion like the memories washing through my awareness, triggered by something unnamable. The building where Sirius began for me was directly across. At first, I had refused the mission. A year ago, I had been on a mine clearance mission in Hades Sector as part of an OriGen EOD (Explosive Ordnance Disposal) anti-terrorism deployment. Pulled out of operations early, I was ordered to Jericho headquarters for a briefing on a new operation. The briefing was compulsory; acceptance of the mission was not. Unsettled by the odd protocol, I'd left my unit. They'd become my surrogate family after the war. 'I'll be back,' I'd said, 'after I see what this bullshit's about.'

On the outskirts of the sprawling Zion Temple complex, Jericho was comprised of glittering glass and steel buildings on a landscaped campus. After arrival at the meeting location, I was escorted to an upper floor and led down a bland corridor to a door guarded by two machine sentries. Obedient slaves of OriGen, their delicate-looking, humanoid forms concealed lethality. My guides simply stared at the sentries, one of which ran a short-beam signal over my head. Implant scan.

'Commander Jordan, come in please.'

I entered and left my escort waiting in the corridor. The office was sparse and functional, and two men sat on the far side of a large, particle-board desk. A machine sentry had entered behind me and closed the door, then stood at the rear of the room.

One of the men gestured. 'Please have a seat, Commander.'

I sat across from them. Both looked middle-aged, but their relaxed, confident composure, evident fitness, and highly specialized status within OriGen indicated men at the peak of their fields.

The man to the right said, 'Welcome to OriGen, Commander. I'm sorry to pull you out of operations, but the reason will become clear. My name is Ezra Linear.' With an intense face and short gray hair, he measured me with calculating blue eyes. Very deep blue, and very cold. Linear was solid, barrel-chested, and stocky, but looked as if he didn't have an ounce of fat on him. He nodded to his right. 'This is Dr. Neil Andrews from research.'

Andrews nodded. 'Commander.'

Andrews' smile was warm and mirrored his curious brown eyes. Unassuming, lean, with neat brown hair and trimmed beard, he wore reserved checkered attire and possessed a scholarly look; that peculiar 'trained to go along' academic air, I thought.

'What kind of a doctor?' I asked.

'Experimental physicist,' Andrews said.

Linear said, 'I regret the necessity for asking this, but I'll need your core verification code to continue this meeting, please.'

My curiosity was aroused but I felt a flash of annoyance. General identification, acceptable by any government agency, was available with a surface scan, but what Linear was asking of me was much more. A CVC was the unique signature of your nervous system.

'Why? You know who I am.'

'Forgive the intrusion, Commander,' Linear said, seeming to understand my reluctance. He smiled ruefully. 'But this old man has his orders.'

I was under no obligation to comply with any request from Linear; he had no official authority over me. But I understood when I'd been ordered here, an invisible line had been crossed.

'Orders from who?'

'Please?' Linear asked, raising a hand in supplication.

I nodded reluctantly. The machine sentry approached from behind and I allowed it to run a finger along the back of my skull.

Linear received the data on his handheld, studied the readout. 'You have an impressive career, Commander. A marine biologist. Following the war, you enlisted with the OriGen military. After a highly impressive service record you tried out for an EOD team, one of the most respected elite units in the world. You became the first woman to make it, and then went on to command.' Linear lifted his eyes from the display, glanced at me, a glint in his blue eyes I couldn't read. 'Quite an accomplishment. A first.'

I gauged Linear. 'So I've been told.'

Linear continued. 'Numerous commendations. One psych report states "she takes calculated risks", and "at times acts as if she had nothing to lose, and some believe she has a death wish".' He swiped his interface again. 'Your family was lost in the war.'

'Yes, Sir.'

Linear lifted his eyes from the report again, considered me a moment. 'My condolences. We all lost someone.'

I detected sincerity, and nodded in acknowledgment. 'Thank you, Sir.'

He opened a new document. 'This may seem extreme, but before we go any further, I must ask you to sign a non-disclosure agreement. This information is sensitive to the OriGen Corporation. Also, I warn you some of what you hear will be difficult to accept.'

I was familiar with such agreements. They prevented sensitive information from ending up in the wrong hands. The foreboding I'd felt since being separated from my unit increased.

'Let me see it.'

Linear sent the link, and I mentally downloaded the document, opened it in a virtual overlay display. An AI-assisted scan through the clauses revealed nothing out of the ordinary. The penalty for revealing any of the information I was about to hear was up to twenty years imprisonment; extreme, and a sign of the times, but I was not in the habit of breaking confidentiality. Besides, my curiosity was aroused—OriGen was onto something big. I transmitted a unique, encrypted neural pattern, and the code appeared at the bottom of the digital document.

Linear smiled, like a master fisherman who had just felt a bite. 'Thank you, Commander. What you are about to hear is highly classified.' He leaned forward. 'Using new developments in physics, six years ago the OriGen Corporation embarked upon a project codenamed Sirius. The goal of Sirius is to open a controllable gateway to the afterlife.'

The statement hit me close to home. Linear paused, watching my reaction. A thousand questions and emotions churned inside me, but I just shook my head. 'A what?'

Linear turned to Andrews. 'Doctor?'

Andrews considered. 'I'll try to put this in layman's terms, Commander. A recently developed scientific theory of unification has overturned our concept of reality, of who we are. It predicts that human consciousness shares the energetic boundary condition—or event horizon—of the universe, known as the Planck Boundary. A point where, except for what appear as chaotic, quantum tunneling events through this barrier, our investigations until now have hit a wall. Beyond this boundary, lies an unexplored, potentially infinite sea of energy we call the vacuum.'

His claim seemed a contradiction to me. 'Wait—the vacuum? You're talking about empty space, right? How can it be infinite?'

Andrews smiled slightly, then continued in precise, educated tones. 'What I am about to explain may sound absurd. But please bear with me, it will become evident. Einstein discovered relativity by stepping outside our entire framework defining reality, and how we look at time. Before Einstein, time was absolute. Wrong. Using his creative insight, Einstein discovered that time is relative to motion. Through a series of experiments, we have tunneled deep into empty space. We have confirmed a wormhole network in the structure of space is an information superhighway communicating at a dizzying rate. And consciousness is bound to spacetime in a remarkable way: time and memory.'

'So, Einstein was wrong?'

He inclined his head. 'From a certain perspective. But Einstein himself understood he had not achieved a unified theory. It frustrated him greatly. Time, as previously understood—a linear set of information along a specific vector of space—does not exist in unification. Time, we are coming to understand, is memory. Contrary to what our eyes tell us, memory is not stored in the brain; it is not static, but a flow of energy and information across the vacuum field. Humans, as we move through space, leave data on the Planck oscillating field as if encoding a hard drive. This information communicates instantaneously through spacetime, and, we predict—into the vacuum.'

I frowned. 'It sounds like you're saying spacetime is tied to consciousness.'

'In a way, yes.'

I considered. 'You're talking about a soul.'

Linear grimaced slightly. 'We don't use that word.'

I tried to comprehend the implications. 'But what's there, in the vacuum? I mean, what are we communicating with?'

Andrews spread his hands. 'Unknown. The new field predicts massless dimensions to infinity existing in a quantum state we can never directly observe—why? As I said, human consciousness has a boundary condition, a point at which nothing—at least consciously—can enter our perception, and nothing can leave. Our thoughts are contained within an impassable barrier—an event horizon which essentially mirrors the Schwarzschild Condition for a black hole.'

'The Planck Boundary,' I said.

'Yes. Unification predicts limitless energy within any point in space. That consciousness is phase-linked, existing in multiple dimensions simultaneously.' Andrews was thoughtful. 'It means every particle in your body has limitless potential: you are the boundary condition that separates the known universe from the vacuum. You *are* an event horizon.'

I frowned. Had I misjudged Andrews? He clearly didn't seem the rote mentality type I'd encountered in my own studies. He spoke his blasphemies into the ether, absorbed, his gaze fixed on some imaginary space only he could see, making eye contact only to gauge my comprehension. 'Well, that's remarkable, and a lot to take in… but what exactly is it you want from me?'

Linear interjected. Direct. Uncompromising. 'We intend to send a human consciousness through the Planck Boundary and investigate the other side.'

'How?'

Andrews deliberated. 'The essence of the theory, is that a singularity is the point at which our—' he hesitated, glancing at Linear, 'soul, enters the next world, or the vacuum, when we die. A singularity is found at the center of a black hole, a region of space where gravity is so strong not even light can escape. You may have heard of the star-eating monsters that lurk in the darkest corners of outer space. Any matter or energy approaching beyond a certain distance, the event horizon, becomes trapped, pulled into the singularity and crushed by immense gravity.' Andrews paused, his brown eyes locking on mine. 'Are you following me?'

I nodded.

Satisfied, Andrews continued. 'Experimentation has shown that a separated consciousness, which becomes a node in the information field, encounters numerous tiny singularities; reality is seething with anomalies which possess attraction properties virtually identical to a black hole. The separated spirit feels drawn to them, but to enter one and cross the Planck Boundary is voluntary, and an apparent one-way trip.'

The scientist leaned forward, the loose-fitting suit tenting around his lean frame. 'The key to a controllable gateway, a naked singularity, is not a naturally occurring phenomenon in the universe, they must be artificially created. They are a singularity without a gravity field—hence naked. Through one, we believe someone can access the vacuum and return.'

I felt myself frown again, tried to process the concept. 'How do you plan to test this theory?'

Andrews was quiet a moment. 'Without direct observation, the only way we may be able to observe these dimensions is subjectively. Through the NDE.'

'Near-death experience,' said Linear. Beneath his emotionless tone, I sensed a move being played. I felt like a chess piece to him.

Andrews nodded slowly. 'The point at which in the past, known laws of physics have broken down.'

I was certain I'd grown pale. 'I have to ask why.'

Linear nodded. 'You have that right, of course.' He leaned back, folded his arms. 'Imagine that with a thought, we had the ability to manipulate vacuum energy: to bend reality to our will, extend our life indefinitely, eradicate disease, to harness a limitless clean energy source, to travel to Alpha Centauri in hours. No more need to exploit limited resources, burden the environment. Medicine, energy, peacekeeping, communication, industry would be transformed. Perhaps we could even resurrect the dead.'

I didn't like Linear's play on my emotions. 'Or perhaps, create the ultimate weapon?'

Linear watched me carefully. 'We know about your father, Solara. Who he was. We know what he was working on at the end of the war. James Artois was working on the forerunner to Sirius.'

I frowned. 'Then how did you—'

'We obtained James Artois' research, before the end.'

'You stole my father's work?'

'Acquired it,' Linear said with icy, unruffled composure.

I felt violated, and suppressed my anger at Linear's casual indifference. My father, James, had never spoken about his classified work. I tried to grasp the implications: the explosion that had leveled Kansas, killed Rebecca… had it been my father's special weapons project that had caused it? My gaze wandered over the threadbare office, empty except for the three chairs, table, a plastic plant in a corner. Fluorescent light illuminated gray, windowless walls. It lacked personality—empty most of the time, I assumed, and used on an ad hoc basis. A reflection of OriGen's attitude toward me? I'd seen Linear's type before: ambitious, self-absorbed. The type who gladly got people killed to increase a ledger entry.

Linear leaned forward, thick-set shoulders straining his jacket. 'Your father wanted this, Solara.'

I felt myself bristle. 'I know what my father wanted: to win the war.'

Andrews said, 'Yes, but he also believed in the greater potential of unification. Your father's work is incomplete. You can help finish it.'

I sensed a well-hidden tension between the pair—competing agendas? 'Why me? Isn't this more up psy-ops area?'

Linear waved his hand dismissively. 'We looked. Trust me, if I ever need a propaganda campaign, they'll be at the top of my list. Sirius needs a special touch. Someone with—'

'Nothing to lose?'

Linear weighed his words. 'A certain character.'

'So what's your role in all this?' I asked.

'I'm a facilitator,' Linear said. 'Many stakeholders are invested in the outcome.'

It was too much to take in; OriGen's proposal was astonishing in its audacity and ambition. What would life be like without death? The world as it existed would end. But some things were not meant to be messed with, and my mind rebelled at the unnatural concept of intruding into the realm of the departed. Besides, after all the losses from the war I was finally building a new life, and would never leave my unit. For the first time in years, I had a sense of belonging, and hope for the future.

I shook my head. 'I can't. You've got the wrong person, I'm afraid.'

Linear was placating. 'Don't try to absorb it all now, Commander. You can return to operations with your unit while you decide.'

I felt my nostrils flare. 'I can't make it any clearer—the answer's no. Find someone else.'

I HAD RETURNED to my EOD unit. Shortly after, they had been killed in a terror attack on a naval base in the Persian Gulf. I'd been running late and avoided the blast. I was never late.

My life had been ripped apart again. I'd gone AWOL. I wandered Hades Sector, the slums of Zion, like a wraith. Sleeping in alleys. Nothing had meaning anymore; I was a non-entity, a transplant from a deleted world, and the so-called new normal was nothing but an open prison. My unit had given me meaning and now they were gone. That's when I started having visions; it's the only way I can describe it. Perhaps that's how these things happened: you became annihilate, to make room for something new. The universe poured in, and either filled you, or devoured you. God? That's a difficult subject… I didn't know. I'm seeking to understand. We are bound to spacetime by time, and memory, Andrews had said.

Time and memory.

Through the ICU room window, the moon had passed from view, darkening the campus under a black sky now devoid of traffic. Easing myself up on the pillow I flipped through my old journal and came to a couple of entries from the days leading up to my decision.

**Journal Entry, Solara Jordan. 21 February 2112.**

*My team is lost. Miller, Davidson, Edmonds, Perez. It's just me again. If it's luck, it feels like a curse. I've been revisiting my decision regarding Sirius, and thinking about what Andrews said about the vacuum. Something about worlds within worlds? It makes me think of marine ecosystems. Each is defined by a unique set of factors: depth, temperature, nutritional requirements, prox-imity to sunlight, or lack of. All interconnected, but each their own universe, oblivious to others. Perhaps we share a similar symbiosis to the vast, invisible sea of energy Andrews spoke of; maybe that's where we go, somehow… but it all seems quite academic now.*

I looked up from the journal, frowning, and recalled my last breath of ocean air during a visit to the beaches of Zion like a stain in my memory. The Mediterranean Sea had been ash gray under the muted, nuclear winter daylight. The coastline was silent except for the frothing, lapping waves which tarred the black sands. There was no life, no birds. Coastal flora grew in abnormal webs, malformed and diseased. Washed-up, sludge-coated marine creatures dotted the beach like relics from a lost world, the lega-cies of unchecked human greed. Even inside the City-Shield, the icy sea breeze had an aroma of soot which stuck in the throat and nostrils. If our biosphere was an interdependent system, I thought, then nature reflected the human condition, to a degree. It painted a sad picture. I returned to the entry.

*I'm homesick. Not Kansas, or Virginia, but my childhood home of Skye, Scotland. I'd go back if I could, but it's in a Quar-antine Zone now. Visiting is not possible. I remember I used to explore the tide pools which dotted the black stone shores of the Isle with Dante, my Labrador Retriever at my side. I loved inves-tigating the various life forms found within, and for some reason the memory seems pivotal to my identity. I had liked to think I witnessed the imprint of God in nature. Meaning, hidden deep within reality. But God—I was coming to believe he didn't exist, and if he did, then he must be the most depraved psychopath of all. One time I'd wandered off from my parents to explore the grottos along the shore.*

I paused a moment at a break in the text, where I'd made a scribbled notation—*The cave.* I frowned, trying to remember something about what happened there. Like a forgotten name, at the edge of memory. It seemed important.

*I'd nearly died in what followed, and it had changed me. I'd become quieter, but after a while also more resilient and determined—what's happened to that person? And what are these visions I'm having? They're not normal dreams but seem real. Rebecca used to have the same type of experiences she'd told me. But I'd never believed her…*

The writing trailed away into incoherence, before ending abruptly.

**Journal Entry, Solara Jordan. 24 February 2112.**

*The visions have intensified. Always the same, over and over. I'm floating. Ahead, white light. Looking back, my physical body seems alien, a life already erasing itself, the vessel of a soul marooned in a sketched-in world of futile remembering. Dislocated from some great reality within, wandering and lost within the flat, depthless landscape of the senses. I can't remember when they started now: when the sun began? When awareness began? When time began?*

*Yet this vision seems layered upon others—a house in Kansas where I'd lived with Rebecca, after my husband passed near the end of the war. But time has gone by: unkept grass is overgrown with weeds, the sandpit in the backyard strewn with dirt and debris, and nearby the swing set, unused and rusting, sways and creaks empty in the wind. Wheat fields, neglected, lay rotten and dead under a sky bleached white with bitter hanging on, outliving. But Kansas lies darkened under nuclear winter now, and the house is long destroyed.*

*Everyone lost, in a merry-go-round of repeating. All except Amy Winters. I'm a witness for the departed. I hear the whisper of a voice, somehow familiar, eclipsed beyond a horizon of shimmering blue light and fire. I see alien worlds: a dream warped, off-color, familiar shapes twisted in ways not of Earth, an impossible vista of unknown forms and realities. The vision shifts… I sense something terrible approaching, my fate recurring, inescapable, and I scream…*

I put the journal aside. I had accepted the mission that day. I lay back again, and stared at the ceiling. The ocean returned to my mind.

But it was on fire.

# OPERATIONAL PHASE



I RESTED IN THE ICU.

I'd found I was sensitive to bright light and sounds now, for some reason, and the nurse had dimmed the room. Footsteps in the hall, and my door was opened. The familiar face of Ezra Linear entered, and I raised myself to a sitting position. Dressed in his usual dark, immaculate pinstripe suit, he crossed the room with a warm smile. Warm, at least, by Linear's standards.

He studied me a second. 'It's good to see you, Solara, more than you know. How do you feel?'

'A little weird.'

Linear calmly sat by the edge of the gurney, flicked a stray hair off his lapel, folded his hands upon his lap. 'What do you remember?'

'Light… awareness. Vague feelings, impressions really, nothing I can identify with any clarity. As soon as I try to make sense of anything it slips away.' I frowned. 'There was something.'

Linear raised his brows.

I gathered my thoughts. 'A sense of connection; some kind of communication? Impressionistic. Like another world that mirrors this one. An inversion but evolution at the same time. Chaos… conflagration.' I paused. 'I'm sorry, I'm not making much sense.'

'It will in time,' Linear said, assessing me. 'We've suffered a setback.'

I frowned. 'What kind of a setback?'

'There was a disturbance. The naked singularity caused a spike in the energy field, siphoned off an unusually high amount of power. The portal became unstable and an explosion resulted. The facility has been damaged, over twenty deaths.'

I lowered my head, silent a moment. The white sheets were so clean, I thought absently, pondering their texture. One of the latest synthetic fabrics… I felt sudden vertigo. I could see the individual nano-threads that weaved the fabric; I plunged inward, and they became a jungle that surrounded me. Linear, the sounds of the room became a distant cacophony of muted, dissonant chords, barely penetrating my awareness.

'Solara?'

I re-focused on the room, and the sensation vanished. Deaths. Some deaths.

'Are you okay?' Linear asked, concern in his voice.

Something irrational had happened. We'd been trained to record any such unusual events, but for some reason Linear didn't seem the right person to bother with the detail.

'Yeah… what happened to Daniel?'

'He survived, and is recovering in a room nearby. The recon team found him close to death in the bunker, but he's improving rapidly.' Linear frowned, and said quietly, 'Almost as if—'

'What?'

The brief window in his blue eyes closed, and he regarded me with his usual, superior look, as if he only ever tolerated me. I wondered if he knew I saw that in him. If he'd care if he did.

'Let's see what the tests say,' he said.

I nodded. 'Andrews? Tori?'

Linear compressed his lips. 'I'm sorry.'

Intuitively, I said, 'There's more.'

For the first time since I'd met Linear, he betrayed a hint of doubt. He explained the suspicion something had come back through, and the appearance of the anomaly in the singularity control room. 'We know very little, I'm afraid. Science Division is working on it, but we're hoping you can help us with that soon.'

'Of course, Sir. How long?'

'Come again?'

'Until the tests and regression batteries?'

'Shaw tells me you'll be up to it in a few days.'

I felt a sense of foreboding, along with a nameless urgency. And there was something about the face I'd seen in my dreams last night… a recognition?

I ground my teeth. 'Tomorrow.'

Linear frowned. 'I'm afraid not. You know the protocol—'

'Oh, screw that. Come on, Ezra, we both know that's just red tape. The doc says I'm doing great. From what you've told me this is something we need to get on top of now.'

He said passively, 'Do you think it's a good idea to break protocol?'

I saw a barely noticeable change in Linear's demeanor. A wariness. 'Well, no—of course not.' Euphoria passed through me. A beautiful anticipation. I considered the situation again. 'I think we should start as soon as possible. I'm recovered. But whatever medical thinks is best.'

Considering me with narrowed eyes, he nodded briefly. 'I'll see what I can do.'

Linear stood, and turned to leave.

'Ezra,' I said.

He turned his head. 'Yes?'

His pupils dilated as pale daylight breached a gap in the window curtains, illuminating minute imperfections in his face. A mole on his jaw, a spattering of faint freckles adorning his pigmentation. I smelt an aftershave he must have worn countless times in previous meetings, but I had never noticed. Then I saw vibrant colors radiate from him: from the top of Linear's head and the bottom of his groin, twin vortexes emanated a toroidal nimbus which extended a meter from his body. The inner field was bluish with inflections of yellow, but the outer bands began changing to reddish and dark maroon hues. The aspect was constricted, agitated. I refocused on Linear's face, and the colors vanished. Had I imagined it?

Slightly confused by the vision, I recalled my training and realized I must be seeing Linear's subtle body; the bio-plasmic field emitted by living things. Until now, I had only viewed it through specialized sensory equipment attuned to the Kirlian radiation spectrum. The field wasn't normally visible to the naked eye. I suspected something had changed in me since returning. Somehow.

The second irrationality this conversation.

'I think I need to see Dr Shaw.'

PETER TRENT piloted the sky-transport through the thick blanket of smog that blanketed Zion's Hades Sector. His mind was working on many levels, ablaze with implications of the information that had come into his possession. As Intelligence Director for the Resistance, which was locked in a war with the emerging solar system-wide super-state, Trent had access to knowledge few others did, and a sense of foreboding arose as he approached the meeting.

Far below, towering oxygen refineries, hundreds of feet tall, sucked in the noxious air and scrubbed it clean before authorities rationed it out to the population, while above, he saw the near-transparent shimmer of the City-Shield. Beyond in the sky, dense gray-black cloud cover obscured the sun, which had become a fact of life since the Terminal War when millions of tons of soot had been injected into the atmosphere in the nuclear exchanges. The smoke had been shifted around the planet by the global trade winds; sunlight hadn't touched the Earth for the first several years, and weather patterns may not resemble pre-war times for many more. The black rain had been worst in the first months, but had subsided now to a near-constant barrage of radiologically charged, murky showers. Contaminants still polluted much of the lethal wastelands outside the walled city enclaves, and inter-city travel was confined to approved corridors controlled by the Global Reconstruction Council. The GRC. A mini-ice age blanketed the world; the winters were severe, summers were cold, and vast swathes of icy tundra covered formerly fertile farmland.

Hundreds of millions had been killed in the initial conflict, but their fate had been kind compared to the billions who had starved in the ecological collapse, or died of other complications in the years following. Now, the remaining population survived on artificial, lab-produced food substitutes and desalinated water, with movement in the enclaves limited to essential reasons only. Ironically, following the nuclear devastation, it had been nuclear energy combined with geothermal that enabled the continuity of civilization.

After the war, the GRC had been formed by the consolidation of various international institutions, such as the UN and assorted trade blocs, into one supranational entity. The nationalistic order had been dissolved. Welcomed at first, centralized, authoritative global governance had appeared a solution to the chaos that had taken the planet to the brink. But it hadn't been long before the world realized its mistake: we had relinquished the old ways, only to face a grave threat from the new. Instead of elevating the human condition, the GRC had come to represent the worst of the old totalitarian ideologies. The technologies meant to liberate the people were used to enslave them on a level never seen. Always in the distance, Trent thought, was a much better place, a future where humanity would transcend its indentured bondage and reclaim dominion of the Earth. He recalled the faces of loved ones lost in Naples, Italy, now located in Sector 21 of the GRC's new order, the urban corridor which ran from Rome to Salerno. Needless deaths ordered at the whim of a power-hungry, self-serving elite. The loss had awakened him, and he could no longer remain silent. Now he couldn't help but wonder: could humanity wake up in time to save itself?

Two years since his source had revealed Project Sirius. Information after then had been sporadic and sketchy due to OriGen's extreme security protocols. A corporate partner of the GRC, OriGen had risen to preeminence after the war, and their ambition exceeded terrestrial boundaries as they sought dominance both beyond the world, and within. The company was unmatched in research and development, with a culture of pursuing radical innovation and getting results.

Trent recalled his initial report to Resistance Command: 'The nature of the experiment is disturbing, and intrudes upon what any sane person would consider sacred ground. With a cost of over a trillion, Sirius is today's equivalent of the atomic bomb project, involving thousands of people at dozens of sites around the solar system. Using a controlled near-death experiment, OriGen attempts to raise the GRC's secret core sect to godlike status...'

The source hadn't seen the full scale of the project then, but Trent had suspected what the GRC attempted, despite what they told the project's highly compartmentalized personnel. None of whom, Trent thought, could yet see the true threat.

'It would take the power of a million suns...' Angela Penright, the Resistance chief science officer had said.

'More than a million, Angela,' Trent said. 'OriGen is developing a radical power source based on the work of two scientists: James Artois, and Daniel Weir, who pioneered the technology for a US special weapons project during the Terminal War. As you'll recall, the United States attempted to use the weapon and leveled a significant part of Kansas.'

'Artois and Weir,' Miles Bryson, the Resistance leader had said, rubbing his chin. 'I understand they both vanished during the war.'

'Untrue, if our source is accurate, and he always has been before,' said Trent. 'We know Artois died in the Kansas incident. It seems Weir, however, survived. He was secretly recruited by OriGen—who then went by the name Zytec Systems—shortly before the US fell. He defected, was smuggled out of the country and it seems he's been busy. Weir has been covertly directing research for Sirius. Another scientist, Neil Andrews, is the front. It flew under our radar due to the extraordinary secrecy, and our source has only recently understood the larger scope of the operation. The good news is he's close to penetrating the inner circle of the project…'

Since that first report, little more of value had been discovered. Until now. Trent approached the inter-sector barrier. Beyond lay Mechanus, and he passed beneath a huge virtual hologram that stated proudly: **THE GRC: BUILDING BACK BETTER.**

*Better, but only for the GRC elites.*

Accessing an encrypted mind-file, he tapped **PERSONAL CAMOU-FLAGE**, scrolled through a list of identity options, clicked. A black nano-cloud swarmed over his features and in seconds the process was done. He checked himself in the rear-view mirror, and a strange face stared back. Full biometric, false ID insertion into the system. Relaxing slightly, he let out some pent-up tension with a deep breath. If authorities discovered his true identity, he would be taken. Tortured. Probably killed. He knew far too much about the GRC for them to let him live. Passing the gate safely, Trent accelerated and descended into the smog.

After arriving at the safe house in the slums of Mechanus, Trent entered a tense room where three men and two women were seated at a table waiting, and took a seat. Miles Bryson's hardened gray eyes betrayed a hint of concern, more than the usual stress of command, for Trent's visit held an ominous undertone. Trent knew the General like a brother. Bryson had fought with the Resistance since the foundation of the GRC seven years ago and was a beacon of hope and continuity to thousands of soldiers at great risk every moment of their lives. This meeting was a rarity, for the people here seldom met in person, but some things were best discussed beyond reach of even encrypted communication channels. The GRC was always close.

Bryson motioned. 'Let's get to it.'

Trent removed a pair of large, orange-tinted glasses as the room fell silent, expectant. 'We are fortunate our source was able to transmit this information. The secrecy has been impenetrable. He had to wait until a secure message was possible,' Trent said, in his strong Italian accent. 'Sirius has entered the operational phase. OriGen has successfully opened a naked singularity and sent through a separated human consciousness. Neil Andrews was killed in an incident during the first incursion. Our source hears rumors of a second experiment; OriGen will not stop, and risk our complete destruction.'

Bryson slammed his fist on the table. 'Son of a bitch! If the GRC controlled this power…'

'They could attain total domination,' Trent declared. 'Weir was one of the first two people to cross over. The other was an OriGen naval officer named Solara Jordan. Both survived.'

Penright processed this. 'Weir did it…' The science advisor's silver hair was tied back, highlighting her tanned, aged features made harsh by ordeal. An MIT professor before the war, in better times, she may have been enjoying retirement, Trent thought. Coddling grandchildren. But no one had that option now. The GRC had been the great remover.

'They crossed over last night at 1900 hours, in the complex beneath the Zion Temple, Angela,' Trent said.

'Why?' Penright asked. 'Why would Weir risk going through himself? He must be the world's foremost expert on unification.'

Trent spread his hands. 'It raises questions. But there is another concern: our source believes something entered the universe from the other side. They don't understand it yet.'

Bryson drummed his fingers on the table. 'This is a time bomb. Solara Jordan, I know the name. She was a clearance operator, part of a GRC counter-terrorist unit. One hell of a dangerous job. The sole survivor from Operation Redlight, she made a great story for the military. Became a poster girl for recruitment.'

'Reluctantly, I believe,' said Trent, deep in thought. 'We all understand James Artois' hidden importance in our movement. Without him the Resistance… wouldn't be what it is today.' He considered. 'I believe Solara is his daughter.'

Bryson frowned. 'You have proof?'

Trent's face compressed. 'During the US downfall, I furnished Artois with false credentials for himself and his family. The surname was changed from Artois to Jordan. Solara was the name of Artois' daughter. She was a US refugee captured in Kansas at the time of the invasion, then showed up in a New York camp. But the proof came with personnel files provided by my source. There's no doubt: it's her.'

Bryson was thoughtful. 'Why would they recruit Artois' daughter?'

Trent considered. 'Her father was much more than a scientist. Solara is an Etherian—also Weir, which is further confirmation of identity.'

In the late twenty-first century, individuals with powerful psychic abilities had begun to be born. No one knew why, for certain. It could be linked to the human-machine symbiosis. Some believed a new age was fast approaching, and a change was occurring in the human species, some kind of spiritual awakening. They were known as 'Etherians' and more and more were appearing.

Penright said, 'Two Etherians… Artois was one of the first to identify the divergence. Now his daughter shows up. A naked singularity. What does this mean?'

No one had an answer.

After a few seconds, Bryson slowly nodded. 'This could give us an in.'

'I agree, Sir,' said Trent.

'Have you identified Sirius leadership?' Bryson asked.

'General David Rhodes, commander of OriGen Special Forces, has operational command,' said Trent.

'A reasonable man, I've heard,' said Penright.

Bryson frowned. 'A ruthless hawk.'

'Yes,' Trent said, 'and his loyalty to the GRC is complete. Although it's doubtful he knows the entire truth. Under OriGen's and ultimately the GRC's control, Sirius will be the death knell for freedom.'

Bryson rapped his fingers one last time. 'Let's get all our people on this now. Peter, get us an angle, and give me OriGen's next move.' He regarded the room gravely. 'I want to double the SitRep frequency until this situation is resolved. Let's go.'

They walked from the room, and Trent pondered this latest turn. He was in a position of great knowledge and knew one thing for certain. The Resistance, humanity's last bastion of freedom, was losing this war.

They had been for years.

# BEYOND THE WORLD, AND WITHIN

I SAT FACING DR. SHAW IN JERICHO LABS.

His second, Dr. Sarah Taylor, operated a nearby interface, but she was here only to observe. After I'd reported my odd perceptual experiences with Linear that morning, Shaw was eager to run tests and explore the phenomena. He radiated expertise, and seemed to wear on his sharply angular face, a permanent frown. At least, he frowned in my presence, as if he'd been presented with a question, and didn't like the fact he had no answer. His ash-gray eyes possessed a certain bleakness, even haughtiness.

Regarding the visual abnormalities, he'd said, 'You shared Weir's experience, and therefore the side effects. Survivors of an NDE sometimes manifest changes after returning: a field that interferes with electronics—lighting, computers, radio signals and such, changes in personality, increased sensitivity to light and sound. So, your sensory acuteness is expected. But this… is interesting. You saw Ezra's subtle body, beyond the human optical window.'

'What does it mean?'

Shaw had rubbed his chin. 'Well, in the simplest terms, it means your senses are enhanced, attuned to a non-human, or expanded level. This could be a residual effect of your connection to vacuum energy. If you possess an ongoing link to higher dimensional space, you may start to find yourself affected in other ways. You must journal all changes.'

'I will.'

Now, Shaw said, 'Take a moment to clear your mind, Solara.'

I nodded, inhaled, and released a slow breath.

Shaw continued. 'I'm going to look at a series of linguistic statements. I will visualize what I see, in my mind. I want you to try and elicit the words I'm thinking. Time and accuracy are factors.'

The baseline provided a snapshot of psychic activity. I knew that beyond the one-way observation window, a team of personnel monitored me with high-tech sensors, dissecting my brain patterns, emotions, and actions. Over the course of the regression, the data would be used to begin providing an overall assessment of my changes.

'Battery one, commencing,' said Shaw. 'Establishing baseline.' He tapped his screen, focused on a hidden readout. 'First linguistic feed, begin.'

I relaxed, and impressions came to me. Imagery displaced in time and location. The mind of Dr. Shaw. Symbols emerged, moving in odd arrangements, and reconfiguring into complex arrays. In my mind, the patterns began glowing softly, and a single word came to me.

'Look,' I said.

Shaw made no comment, swiped his hidden display to the next phrase.

'Come here.'

My attention was drawn inward during the next pause, as if in a silent breath. My surroundings amplified: the room, gray tiles, white walls. The ceiling lights, although dimmed, beamed like daybreak, stabbing my eyes. In the corner, two AR units rested on a table next to a bank of exotic equipment. Nearby, a pot plant withered slowly under electrical fields. Silence a moment. Then a machine burst to life, whirred away noisily. Grating at my senses like nails on slate.

Swipe.

'Winter is coming.'

*A beach by the edge of a windswept sea stretches away into a darkening mist. A distant figure kneels on the shore. Drawing closer, I see it is a girl, long hair shrouding her face, humming in a carefree tone to herself as she works upon a castle in the sand. She digs a circular moat around the outside of the square castle, molding and shaping it with her hands.*

I frowned at the unanticipated imagery. A memory?

Swipe.

'The fall is long.'

*The girl stood, turned away, and pointed down the beach. I looked, but the shore was empty.*

Swipe.

I contemplated. Were my insights triggering something deeper, more profound? Hints of my incursion? If my telepathic perceptions were triggering glimpses into the vacuum, could interactions through the barrier now be directed? I realized I had hesitated several seconds after the previous question, and Shaw raised his eyes questioningly at me.

'The day was quite cold,' I said.

Shaw glanced toward the observation window. 'Do you know how many people are observing from the next room, Solara?'

I concentrated on the window. 'Six. But tomorrow Andrew will call in sick.' I would not be told how accurate my responses were.

'Neurological phase-link, established,' said a voice through the speaker. 'Abnormalize. Proceed with battery.'

Shaw gestured to the pot plant on a side table. 'Concentrate on the plant. What do you see?'

A single pale, blue-yellow flower grew, and a clove-scented, licorice aroma reached my nostrils. An Algerian Iris, I was certain. A winter bloomer. Smells always evoked memory associations in me. It recalled my garden in Kansas. The brown-spotted stem arced up to the elegant, deep white and yellow at the base of the fall. Focusing on the first blue petal, I noted every imperfection in its texture. In my mind, I saw the surface become scaly like the skin of a reptile or snake. Intuitively, I moved my awareness deeper into a world of molecules and cells which made up the flower's living tapestry. Penetrating further, I witnessed sub-atomic, primal forces deep in the flower clash and surge in a sea of chaotic, majestic contestation. And within each particle, I found layers: layers within layers within layers. Entangled. Connected on a level I couldn't understand. Vibrating in response to my thought.

*When I looked back, she was gone. The cold wind picked up and churned up the whitecaps in the surf.*

'Solara?'

Anxiously, I forced my attention back to Shaw. 'The flower isn't real.'

'What do you mean?' he asked.

'It only exists from a certain perspective.'

Shaw studied me closely, his inquisitive frown deepening. 'How do you feel right now?'

*A luminous tunnel stretched away before me.*

I tried to rationalize. 'I think it's starting to come back.

◉

LI MOVED FAST to set up the forward observation post in the control room. Scorch marks from the explosion were fused into the floor and walls, and debris had been cleared by workers. It had been found that the electro-magnetic/antigravity shields had been key in containing the explosion. Remains of deceased personnel had been removed, and would eventually be reunited with loved ones. Due to Top Secret classification, Li knew relatives would be told a credible cover story: an accident on some standard operation, and their participation in Sirius would never see light. Power had been restored to the control room, and the rest of Sub-Level 7, and they used the central service elevator to haul loads up and down. Many of the powerful sensor arrays had been knocked out, and teams of technicians worked to repair or replace them.

A second recon had been performed of the control room in the early hours of the morning, which had revealed an electromagnetic field emanating from the anomaly, permeating the control room. It was safe to enter the field, but an odd discrepancy had been detected: time appeared to be moving slightly slower within its boundaries, relative to actual time.

The initial Cerberus scan of the control room following the incident had taken 8.09 minutes, but Cerberus had recorded 9.37 minutes within the field. This represented a time ratio of 115% of actual time inside the boundary compared to outside, meaning incursions were faster from the outside, than inside. The second recon that morning had experienced a slight increase in the time displacement ratio: the slowed time field within the boundary, was slowing down.

*Like the naked singularity.*

The team was now subject to strict mission durations: fast in-and-outs of 15.00 minutes max in mission time. The EM field continued to maintain a zone of interference which limited wireless communication to ten meters, give or take. The singularity control room possessed no hardline to the outside, so it had become a communications dark zone. A system had been rigged similar to the initial chain-link established by Cerberus, enabling comms between the control room and Jericho. Marcus Niemeyer, the acting head of research after the loss of Andrews and McNash, believed the naked singularity may still be open. They may be witnessing the effects of a breakdown of predictability, in a limited area at least, which was unnerving for all.

In the center of the ground floor, the anomaly continued its pulsing fluctuations. No one understood how it existed without a known, sufficient energy source. Li had put up a security barrier around it; the last thing they needed was someone blundering into another dimension. They'd probably be killed instantly, or something unthinkable. There were worse fates than death. After the first destructive appearance of the unknown force through the gate, no further known activity had been detected. This disturbed Li, and his rifle offered little comfort. He recalled what Andrews had said about the naked singularity once: 'It would open a doorway into our universe from outside of it, and nobody knows what is there—*anything* could come through.'

Li paced as he finished a command sequence on a hand-held, and seven sensor probes rose into the air, took positions around the room. He took care to stay within the perimeter of the anti-gravity shields; passing through the barrier caused a momentary weightlessness, and objects could float a few centimeters before crossing over. Technicians began analyzing the drone feeds, generating the initial dataset.

'Interesting,' said one of the techs. 'There's a spinning electromagnetic field on the surface of the anomaly. The oscillation appears to be accelerating.'

Li stopped his pacing, frowned. 'At what rate?'

'It's very subtle, Sir. About one Hz per second, barely detected by sensors.'

Li said, 'I wonder if that's related to the time distortion?'

The tech studied the readout. 'There's something else. Since the initial visual, there have been slight positional changes in the energy particles around the anomaly. They're further away from the core.'

Li watched the particle spiral, which had been inert and stationary since he'd first seen it, as if held in check by something.

'They're moving?' Li asked.

The tech shook his head. 'I think so, Sir.'

Out of his depth, thought Li. 'Well, send it all through.'

Li stared into the anomaly for a second, his awareness touching some impossible horizon. The light vortices inside deepened, like the interior space was being stretched, and he fought off vertigo. He was struck with a feeling that death could reach out from the object and take him at any moment. His son, Asa, passed through his mind. He'd made arrangements to see him looked after in the event he didn't return. But it was not enough—not nearly enough, and he wished he'd been able to do more before reluctantly taking the mission. He'd looked away when he saw movement from his periphery. He turned back. No change. He focused on his handheld. Checked the progress of the work teams, the data collection.

*John.*

The hairs bristled on his neck. He glanced back to the hovering sphere… a fleeting glimpse of an unknown landscape appeared in his mind. It seemed well-known but strange at the same time, as if someone had taken the forms he'd loved, and skewed them into a twisted parallel of Earth. Vaguely familiar landmarks of his home in Guam, before the war, were misshapen, and shifted within a fluid landscape. He felt the caress of a warm breeze, and a slight pressure into his mind. A person appeared standing in the strange place—Aiya? His heart clenched. She looked younger than he remembered, and then flames swept over Tamuning village, across the vision. Li fought against the intrusion, which abruptly vanished.

Understanding that he had experienced illogical thoughts, perhaps even a temporary breakdown of his psyche, he glanced at the tech-specialists. 'If anybody starts seeing, hearing, or feeling anything unusual, report it immediately. Is that clear?'

'Yes, Sir,' the techs responded.

Li mentally noted the incident in his live report. He was checking drone calibrations when the elevator doors opened, and Helberg and Winters entered, pushing two trolley loads of equipment into the vaulted chamber. Helberg moved his load with ease, but despite her smaller size, Amy wasn't straining. Their uniforms were streaked with grease marks from the damaged hydraulics throughout the station, and Li noted barely perceptible tension between them. The usual, or something else? He knew the cause, and not for the first time he wondered at the wisdom of placing them on Sirius together. But OriGen appeared to believe differently, and now was not the time for idle reflection.

Amy's sharp blue eyes fixed on the anomaly a moment before turning to Li. 'Where do you want it?'

Li gestured to a spot nearby. 'Put it over there.'

After unpacking the load with some techs, the pair came to stand beside Li.

'Everything okay, boss?' Helberg said.

Li glanced at him. 'The sooner this thing's closed, the better. How's Jericho?'

'Tense,' said Amy.

Li tapped his handheld. 'Okay, let's get this first transmission sent.'

●

## First Iteration

GENERAL DAVID RHODES strode to his command post in Jericho Operations. Holo-screens displayed the live probe feed from the singularity control room, and Science Division had made a preliminary analysis from available data. Around the room, various technicians were glued to their workstations. Rhodes had been the first recruit to this unusual mission and felt personally responsible for every person under his command. The post-war world order had created an insidious geo-strategic situation and an array of new enemies for the GRC. Decentralized and anonymized terror networks were a persistent threat, and with Project Sirius, OriGen sought a game changer.

Experiment footage—before comms had been severed—clearly showed that a destructive force had passed through the naked singularity from the other side, and Andrew's last words had sent a chill through Rhodes.

*I think something came back through with Weir.*

If Andrews had been right, then that thing could still be in this space-time. At this stage, it was unknown if or how the field emitted by the anomaly—and the anomaly itself—was connected to that first potential contact. Now, in addition to the physical irregularities, like time, personnel entering the field were reporting unusual psychological phenomena. They were being closely monitored.

The blue-tinged, spherical oddity in the singularity control room dominated the display. Rhodes made out a nebulous latticework of veins on the fluctuating surface, and inside, a series of inner spheres descended to some unknown convergence. The result produced was of an internal space far larger than the main object. The General studied it closer. The light structures within weren't random, but symmetrical and ordered, as if… designed.

*What the fuck are you?*

Feeling a falling sensation, Rhodes looked away. 'Give me something, Captain.'

'We've got the first data set,' Captain Marcus Niemeyer said from his workstation. 'Analyzing.'

A brilliant physicist in his late-thirties, Niemeyer had been third only to Andrews and McNash on the research team. Rhodes considered his calm, but intense scholarly face. Niemeyer was handling the situation, and his elevation well.

Niemeyer said, 'It's some kind of energy field, spherical, centered on the control room ground floor with a ten-meter diameter. The inner spheres exhibit moving patterns based on… sub-atomic wave interactions. Sensors read a static electro-magnetic field around the main sphere that repels all radio, infrared and microwave communication.'

Rhodes frowned. 'What are we looking at here?'

Niemeyer compressed his lips. 'I don't know yet. It should not be possible for the naked singularity to stay open without an immense power supply—normally. The anomaly is drawing residual energy from the containment chamber, but its energetic field far exceeds its supply and it's not drawing power from any other known source. It's conceivable it may be drawing energy from the vacuum itself.'

Rhodes said, 'Which means a doorway into our universe could still be open?'

'It's possible, Sir,' Niemeyer said.

Rhodes didn't move his eyes from the screen. 'The containment chamber is still active?'

Niemeyer nodded. 'Partially.'

'Can we kill this thing by cutting the power?'

Niemeyer frowned. 'Unknown. Whatever this anomaly is, it may be the only thing protecting us from an open naked singularity. If we cut power, it may do nothing, or we may lose our only protection against… it. We need to study it and make a threat assessment before proceeding.'

Lieutenant Jason Pearce, the head technician and one of the science officers, said, 'Activity detected. Light surges in the EM field. Pulse pattern: one spike every seven seconds.' He paused. 'There are disturbances at localized points of the boundary.' The oldest of the science team, Pearce's brown-gray hair was brushed back, and glasses were perched upon his nose covering clear gray eyes, even though implants had eliminated the need decades ago.

'Bring it up,' said Rhodes.

On the anomaly hologram, a dot appeared, representing a 'surge' to a specific point of the boundary. After a moment, another appeared. Then another.

Rhodes frowned. 'Something's probing for a weakness?'

'Whoa…' said Niemeyer, removing his hands from the console. His screen went blank a moment before flashing back to life. 'The wave forms in the anomaly are moving, Sir.'

Rhodes leaned over Niemeyer's shoulder. 'Moving how?'

'It's slow,' Niemeyer said. 'Hard to say at this point… inward, it appears. A convergence within the individual spheres.'

Rhodes felt that some incomprehensible process had been set in motion. 'Give me some options, Lieutenant. Fast.'

Niemeyer nodded, continuing to interface. 'We need time.'

The General clenched his jaw, hating his sense of powerlessness. 'That's the one thing we don't have.'

# FATE

EVENING HAD FALLEN.

At Daniel's invitation, I arrived at an observation area in one of the campus towers. The room had a sense of grandeur, as if a bygone age had fused with the modern era. Spotting him at the main window, I wandered across the expansive, marble-tiled floor. Having been through the full cryogenic process, and total physical death, he had been in worse shape than me after returning, but he looked rested, refreshed, and wore a blend of dark stylish clothing. The muted light of the room highlighted faint traces of gray in his thick brown hair, etches in his preoccupied face. I didn't know his age, it was hard to define, but guessed late thirties or early forties, and judged the last few years had taken a toll. He had been a last-minute transfer to the mission, and had been reticent when I'd asked about his background before. I'd been unable to understand him, like he lived inside a shadow, and a question had played on my mind ever since he'd been recruited: who was Daniel Weir?

I reached him with a curious smile on my lips. 'Well, you've got me here, Daniel. Why don't you tell me your devious plan?'

Weir looked out the window. 'Wait,' he said, in his deep voice. A vision formed in the sky, and stars began populating the winter blackness above. He nodded. 'Holographics has a direct link-up with the Achilles space telescope.' The heavens changed, and a nebulous star field appeared, like three elephant trunks arching nonchalantly up to a cosmic vertice.

I took in the vista. 'What are we seeing?'

'The Pillars of Creation,' Weir said, reverently, 'a place of star birth seven thousand light years from Earth.' He smiled gently, studying me. 'Should the universe teach us one thing, it's humility.'

'But some of us are more, perhaps?'

His smile faded. 'It is a mysterious universe, Solara.' He turned, and we strolled across the floor. 'If it's infinite, then all things are possible,' he said, regarding me pointedly. 'Even the unimaginable.'

We reached the lounge where carpet cushioned our steps, and I sat opposite him. Weir waved a hand, called over a waiter and a slimline synthetic approached.

He glanced at me, raised his brows. 'I'm buying.'

'Water is fine, thank you.'

'Coffee, black,' said Weir.

The synthetic moved to the bar and prepared the drinks.

'How are you holding up?' he asked.

'Okay. Some unusual experiences. A couple of ahh… flashbacks, I think. Trying to accept whatever comes.'

Weir was thoughtful. 'I know. I remember… a scream. Waking up in cryo, sirens blaring, people running. Shot into the escape tunnel, then I blacked out. And since returning I've felt an unease that makes me… I can't explain.'

I attempted to see Weir's subtle body, as I had with Linear. After Shaw had conducted some further experiments, I was growing accustomed to the enhanced perception. It seemed perfectly normal. But as I focused on the space around Weir, I felt a constriction; for a moment I saw a field in flux which flickered rapidly from blue to crimson before collapsing into his body. Odd, I thought, considering a feeling I could only describe as non-physical blocking...

Weir went quiet and seemed lost. Was he aware of my attempt? The synthetic returned and placed the drinks on the table next to some metal, spherical ornaments. Weir took his coffee and sipped, and the strong aroma cut the air between us.

I put the obstruction out of my mind for the moment. 'Why did you volunteer, Daniel?'

A shadow passed across Weir's face, and I was struck by the cold, almost reptilian nature of him. But I saw a deep compassion there, too, and wondered at the contradictions.

'To understand. Much of the science behind Sirius is based on my work.'

I frowned. An answer, but not an answer. 'You worked in research?'

He nodded.

Linear had said my father was highly involved in early USSWD Sirius work. Daniel must have started working on the program with OriGen, after the war.

'Well, that explains a lot,' I said. 'Although, I'm surprised they risked you.'

He smiled ruefully. 'I had considerable leverage.' We were quiet a moment, and then he said, 'We are changing.'

Transformation of some type had been predicted, but highly speculative. Andrews had explained as much.

I took my drink thoughtfully, rattled the ice in the water. 'Into what, I wonder?'

'We'll never be other than what we are, we're simply going inside ourselves on a profound level.' He glanced around, gestured to the star pillars. 'What do you see, when you look out into the universe?'

I pondered. 'Silence.'

He leaned forward. 'Exactly. We nearly became extinct during the Terminal War; now, we're an endangered species. There is something occurring in Sirius that must be allowed to run its course if we are to survive more than a few decades longer.' He raised a hand, focused upon three shiny metal spheres resting upon the table between us, and my goosebumps rose as a power manifested. Under his will, the balls rose into the air and circled slowly.

I frowned. 'How is that possible?'

He motioned, and the balls moved toward me. 'The connection we established with the vacuum remains with us. What we thought of as empty space has always been listening; we just haven't had the right words until now. But we've not yet even begun to discover our potential—and our connection to each other. This,' he said, gesturing, and the balls floated gently back to the tabletop, 'is nothing.'

I raised my glass in a mock toast, took a cool sip of water.

He gave me a wry smile. 'Come with me now.'

THE VIRTUAL meeting place used one of my own memory links. The Sub-reality was a digital clone of the real world, and could render a pristine, pre-nuclear winter Earth through wireless brain-web interface. The Scottish castle Eilean Donan was situated on an island at the point where the three great sea lochs of Long, Duich, and Alsh met. We stood in a small, tended flower garden in a courtyard near the outer wall, and scattered autumn leaves tumbled gently in the cool breeze. Climbing several steps, we came to stand at the castle wall overlooking the highlands. The stark, harsh landscape reflected sadness. Snow was beginning to form on distant peaks, the Isle of Skye could be seen across the Loch, and the endless green rolling hills made for a breathtaking panorama. The breeze was fresh as we absorbed the view, but uncertain revelations gave the experience a somber tone.

Daniel stood at a parapet, and overlooked the inhospitable land. 'I knew your father once.'

I glanced sharply at him. 'How?'

He remained facing the mountains, his eyes distant. 'We worked together in the final years of the war.'

'You were in Kansas?' My father's weight with the DoD was the only reason me and Rebecca had been spared the camps; he'd secured accommodation for us in the Kansas Safe Zone, the location of the US special weapons project that had preceded Sirius. 'I was with my father near the end…'

'Yes, I know.'

Everyone who'd remained on the Kansas base had perished or been captured, I thought. 'How did you survive?'

He leaned forward on the wall, the breeze briefly blowing his hair across his eyes before he flicked it aside. His movements quick, precise. 'After the invasion, US Command ordered deployment of the vacuum energy weapons system. The theory was that a naked singularity would allow quantum-tunneling attacks; others could be opened where we chose, and with the right combination of energies bend reality locally. Instantaneous annihilation, no time for enemy counter strike, no radioactive fallout. Key enemy sites were targeted—a conventional strike would have limited effectiveness and ensure a possibly fatal response, but a vacuum weapon?

'We could hit an installation buried miles in the earth or for that matter a target on Mars with equal precision. Hell, the theory was an adversary wouldn't have time to blink. There had been promising tests, but the technology was immature, as likely to incinerate the planet as do what was predicted. Your father and I advised against it. Command wouldn't hear it. It was as if they'd lost their minds, couldn't accept the fact that Pax Americana had fallen. If the US falls, they seemed to think, what matter if the world goes with it? So, we ensured the work would survive regardless of the outcome of the war.'

'And the new world was waiting for you…'

His brow furrowed slightly. 'It is what it is. All I know is that if I'd stayed, I would now be dead along with your father. Sirius and the potential it promised would be lost.'

I'd had no information on my father's last days. My eyes watered. 'He sacrificed himself? Why didn't he leave? Why didn't he contact me?'

Weir compressed his lips. 'Someone had to stay, and after learning their plans he couldn't leave. They locked the station down: no unessential

comms in or out. If he hadn't been there when they pushed the button…
it may have been all over.' He paused. 'If there's one thing I knew about
your father, it's that he would never trust anyone else with your safety.'

But that's exactly what he did, I thought bitterly, and Rebecca and I had
been abandoned. And what do your actions make you, Daniel, I thought?
A traitor? A coward? Weir seemed to be trying to come to terms with something in himself, even after all these years. I wiped my eyes, fought down
an urge to yell. 'My safety?'

Weir stepped from the wall, nodded slowly, almost reluctantly. 'I know
you've suffered, and what followed cost your daughter her life. But it could
have been worse.'

Weir had survived, and my father had not. It had been his choice. I
sighed. 'He was so stubborn.'

The edges of his lips turned up ever so slightly. 'On that we agree.'

I found my emotion diffusing, but the knowledge cast Daniel in a new
light. I knew no normal person would volunteer for Sirius. And Daniel
Weir was evidently not a normal person: his ambitions were massive, his
theories remarkable. But I sensed a mask when I looked at him, protecting
a place deep inside he would not allow me to see, to touch. Beyond his
placid exterior, I saw a restless conflict, a rejection of the world. But then
my experiences, also, had set me at odds with the normal hopes and dreams
that occupied life, and I doubted I came across as Miss Sociable.

I shivered as a cold gust blew over the wall, and hunched forward on
the parapet to study my childhood home. The familiar bluffs and scattered
clumps of hardy cold weather foliage. The rock pools along the shore,
exploring with Dante by my side, and always, my parents close. I could
almost hear the voices, echoing up from the shore.

I nodded toward the Isle. 'I nearly drowned when I was young. It was
a close thing. Not far from where we stand now. I was afraid of the water
for a while, after, then one day I decided I wasn't going to let it beat me.
I vowed I'd always be able to take care of myself, no matter what. That I
wouldn't need anyone… that I could do anything.'

'It made you self-reliant.'

I nodded. 'Yes, very. I beat my fear of the water eventually, came to love it. When I started cave diving, each time was sort of like a fuck-you to the universe. I volunteered because I'm not going to let him win.'

Daniel frowned. 'Him?'

I smiled faintly. 'God, of course.'

He gained an odd look. 'Well, that's something I can understand.'

We observed the cold tableau of the loch for a while longer, each acutely aware of the other as the cool breeze turned harsh. I felt change coming, as if a god approached, a fate I could feel but could not name. Suddenly I just wanted to feel human, the simple warmth and comfort of another, but despite some revelations Weir still seemed a distant mystery. Layers within layers. The air was biting as we watched the sky darken, and take the beauty of the Isle like a flag being lowered at the end of a day.

We were both scheduled for mind regression the following morning.

'Did you dream, after returning, Solara?' Weir asked, as if inviting me to some sacred place.

*No. Not dreams. Something else.*

'I did.'

'Me too.'

In the black sand of Skye, I glimpsed another reality. And on the cloudy horizon: unknowable, everlasting light.

WHEN REBECCA was born in 2099, I'd been married two years and had completed my first field research assignment for the International Oceanographic Commision—IOC. We lived in Virginia on a military housing estate; the war was still four years away, and I stayed home to be with her the first two as a fulltime mother. Michael worked with Naval Intelligence at Fort Belvoir, Fairfax; this was before he deployed, and he was home almost every night. We nurtured a little spark of life that we had brought into the world, and those first two years passed in a comfortably numbing routine of sleepless nights, Rebecca's first steps and words, and my relationship with Michael was the best it was to ever be, I was to discover later. If I'd ever known something akin to bliss it was those two years. Before the gaps appeared.

I received my second grant with the Institute of Marine Biology in 2103 which involved relocating to Maine. Michael had begun deployments with CINPAC due to rising geopolitical tensions globally, and was now away for months at a time. I took Rebecca to a small town on the coast near my research sites. The municipality still had a fishing and agriculture industry, and tech culture had not yet taken over. Perhaps the world forgot this place. The locals were a dour lot; the closest neighbors were a retired fifth generation fisher couple, and the few encounters revolved around small talk and local gossip, which made me steer clear of more frequent interactions.

I returned to work. In field trips I put Rebecca into a local day care with personalized facilities for infants, and a low child-carer ratio, but I still didn't like it. After a while I started taking her to work with me when I could. The assignment was my favorite and involved exploring and monitoring remote coastal ecosystems and their rapidly diminishing biodiversity, which was a revealing microcosm of disturbing trends globally. The research sought to formulate a unified field model to assess, identify, and drive solutions to counter the eco-decline. Know your enemy, I used to tell myself; an amorphous, apex predator was killing the world, and it was my job to hunt it. Find a way to kill it.

A unified model meant discarding the primacy of any single threat vector: diseases, overfishing, species introduction, pollution, climate change—what tied it all together and how could it be mitigated? I'd been an idealist, yet to discover that few people, least of all those with the power to enact significant action, seemed to be listening behind their public platitudes. I was to learn that power attracted the lowest rung of the moral hierarchy; the political class was utterly self-centered and corrupted, and my hopes for a true top-down solution were shattered. My research conclusions were not well received—humans were a chief threat, yes, but mostly the exploitative elite, and I often wondered in a mix of despair and amazement at the arrogance involved in humanity's self-inflicted destruction and raping of the Earth.

I loved the ecologies along the rough, rocky coast. The weather was frigid with tidal changes twice a day revealing a stunning diversity of marine life among the tide pools. I accessed the main site, an isolated cove, by a three-mile hike along a seldom used trail strewn with maidenhair ferns and groundnut fauna, and sometimes camped the night above the ephemeral, bioluminescent Gaia. When Rebecca accompanied me, she took to the setting with enthusiasm.

I felt connected to that world: starfish, clams, crabs, barnacles, mussels and snails, and sea urchins populated the rock pools, and mammals and avian species—seals, the odd squirrel, seagulls and Black Guillemot foraged along the shore in natural symbiosis. But then, I'd always liked animals more than people. With animals you got honesty. I was constantly wet, but warm within my thermal lining. The weather itself was like a living participant in the biota, the wellspring of the cyclic patterns. The air was always crisp and fresh, and the ecosystem took only what was needed to live and never more; it wasn't demanding, interfering, or malevolent. It just was. A great, seemingly impersonal process driving a profoundly intimate one.

I found myself adapting to the rhythms of my little corner of the Earth, attuning to the migrations, feeding, breeding, and dying, along with oddities or intrusions into that pattern. The coastal promontory was formed by prehistoric lava flows and had a beachhead where pinkish-gray felspar silicates grabbed the light and created gleaming shimmers along the black sand, and here Rebecca befriended a rogue Harbor Seal she called Orphan because she said he was always alone. Her story behind the name was that the seal had been separated from his mother, who'd been taken by sharks. The critter somehow knew to swim into shore whenever Rebecca came with me, and she supplied it with a lavish buffet of crustaceans, shellfish, and even an octopus once. I came to believe that she possessed what seemed an unusual empathy, even her own way of communicating with animals I'd never witnessed that bordered on supernatural. She'd know Orphan was near before either of us could see him.

'How did you know he was coming now?' I would ask.

Rebecca just shrugged and said she'd heard him. Heard him swimming… out in the ocean… submerged? Some seal calls could be heard up to fifteen miles away underwater; however, the sound was outside the human hearing range, not to mention an underwater call wouldn't reverberate above the surface. I didn't know what to make of it, but their bond made me wonder at the deep intrinsic connection humans had with nature: we were born with the ability to be in sync, but our society had become separated. And in that separation, we had lost our way, and become nature's nemesis. Reflected in that estrangement, I felt the undertow of another, more personal rift opening between Michael and me.

Even before his deployment we were drifting apart silently, unable to resist or perhaps even unaware we were being untethered by the glacial drifts of our respective selves, and a sense of powerlessness was growing in every aspect of my life. I think my husband wanted more of me than I gave him, more than I could give; I always kept a place deep inside closed-off to him, secret, a locked room only I held the key to, and where he was forbidden. A sacred domain where my deeper connection to nature, or whatever higher power existed lived, and was protected at all costs. Fear of confinement had plagued me since childhood and I'd never identified the cause, and the inner refuge was a place I maintained control over, and could escape to or from at will.

He never told me to change, he just didn't understand my need for solitude, I think. Perhaps opposites were not the best matches after all. As an introvert I'd been attracted to his expansive, social character, for it seemed to fill a space within me. On the outside I could fit in with his friends; *appear* to fit in, but I think he knew I only ever tolerated the idle chatter. The meet-ups started out as a curiosity, became an obligation, and then an inconvenience. With his friends he always had an overt, playful manner, but with me he was quieter, more introspective, the sex remained great and that's where I think we ended up feeling closest.

'What's happening with us?' he'd ask me after, locked in a tangled embrace.

'I don't know,' I would reply.

'I love you,' he would respond, unwilling to push.

'I love you, too,' I'd say, but felt an increasing dislocation when I said the words, a free-floating sensation in our relationship.

As the war escalated a lot of grant money dried up, sucked into military funding, so I went corporate and worked in an essential industry. In the human-machine world, certain rare-earth elements had become the basis of a new generation of high-performance superconductors. My dive team performed geological surveys of the sea floor identifying mineral-rich hotspots as a precursor to mining operations, and we received a share of the current market value of any new discovery.

War tensions increased, and my father sometimes visited when my husband was home on leave; with Michael in Naval Intelligence and Dad in military research, they often had official-looking strangers visit, and talked late into the night. The meetings had an urgency, and they would be locked in the study for hours with the guests. Thinking of Weir's disclosure, I tried to recall his face now among the visitors, any reference to him, but remembered nothing. When I'd asked Michael about the meetings, all he said was the war was at a turning point. My father was also closed-mouthed and no matter how hard I pressed him he wouldn't budge. My father's silence I could accept, but a resentment had grown toward my husband. Michael was lost during deployment in the second year of the war, Rebecca's fifth year, and we'd had to relocate.

By then my father had taken a position on a weapons project with the United States Army Special Weapons Division (USSWD), and he'd secured living arrangements for me and Rebecca near the project base in militarized Shawnee County, Kansas. Defensible and self-sustainable, the Kansas Green Zone was a hub for training, ordinance, intelligence, and research. I'd taken a day job in logistics while Rebecca attended the still-running school. After national infrastructure and supply chain collapse, most of the population outside of the safe zones had to fend for themselves.

One day, a news site reported:

# CALIFORNIA DEVASTATED
## "Nanoswarm Death Clouds" Rage Through Los Angeles
*Washington Puts Death Toll at Millions Killed and Wounded*
*Anti-terror Act Passed at Denver Crisis Summit; President Vows Massive*
*Retaliation and Hints at New "Superweapon"*

My father began acting differently, did everything he could off-web, cautioned me to do the same, and I had felt an unspoken, ominous feeling begin to invade our home. The Homeland Security officers around Kansas, who'd had a comforting presence, now felt repressive, watching everything and everyone. Random street searches became common, many were arrested for no apparent reason and simply disappeared. When the power grid failed, the heat died, and in the winter cold we had no good options; we had a back-up energy supply, but it only powered some devices and the heater for a few hours a day. The food store closed, and the tap water became foul and brownish. In town the remaining people looked tired and drawn, smiles were rare, and people no longer stopped on the street to chat. The weather was chilly and gray, mirroring the oppressive mood. Kansas had become the abode of the walking dead. Most had already bugged out.

One morning my father pulled up in the driveway and marched into the kitchen where I sat having breakfast with Rebecca. The school had closed the week before, and she had been having nightmares.

'What is it?' I asked, noting the shadows around his hazel eyes.

'I don't have long. Enemy forces have landed,' he said, tense, and sent me an encrypted mind-file and access key.

I scanned the document, raised my brows. Fake ID. My surname—Artois—had been replaced. 'Solara Jordan? This is Homeland.'

He nodded. 'Wasn't easy to get. It's a low-level cleaning position which makes you a nobody, but a nobody with Level 3 site-access clearance—it can see you through the blockade. Fully embedded into the system.'

The blockade was a fifty-kilometer radius kill zone around Kansas City—nothing unauthorized moved and lived. My throat tightened, I sensed the danger we were in, closing around the world like an insidious black talon.

I nodded. 'Enough to move around, but not enough to be of interest.'

He handed me a small electronic device.

I took it. 'What's this?'

'Beacon. Just in case.'

I frowned. 'What the hell have you been working on, Dad?'

He considered me thoughtfully, then Rebecca, who sat at the kitchen table nervously. Poor Rebecca, I thought. Since Michael's death she'd become closer to my father, although these days he wasn't here much. Her long brown hair was tousled from lack of sleep, her mismatched clothing reflecting the chaos in our lives now.

'Hope,' my father said.

I knew he couldn't say, and put the beacon in my pocket. 'How long do we have?'

'A week at the most.'

I nodded slowly.

He said, 'Stay at home, don't go out. I'll contact you tomorrow.'

Rebecca's eyes, wide and uncertain, held to her grandfather, needing and expecting concrete certainty, for him to stay, but finding only a nebulous space. Her visage became even more frazzled, and her eyes welled as she leapt up and ran to him, hugged him tight. 'You're not coming back.'

'Of course I am, honey. I'll never leave you or your mother.'

'I've seen it, granddad.'

'I'll be back,' he said, tenderly cradling her tear-streaked face. 'I'm going away because I love you very much. Love requires sacrifice.' His eyes met mine.

'She had another nightmare,' I said.

'We all have to leave!' Rebecca cried. 'They told me! They said to leave! The visions are real. Something bad is going to happen, granddad.' She turned to me. 'You have them too, Mum—you know!'

I gently turned her from my father. 'They're not real, Rebecca.'

Rebecca turned back and buried herself in her grandfather's chest.

'I'll be back, you'll see,' he said, and held her. Her stuffed tiger, Simba, cramped up under her arm, as if also showing his disapproval. 'Why don't you come out with your mother and say goodbye? She'd really like that.'

'Please don't go.'

He'd cupped her chin, raised her head with his hand. 'I love you, Rebecca, I always will. Everything's going to be fine, you'll see.'

Her face screwed up. 'If you're going then, just go!' she cried, and ran to her room.

My father watched her for a moment, then turned to me. 'I'll call you tomorrow. If you don't hear from me, leave. Don't wait. When you clear the blockade activate the beacon on the pre-set frequency. I've organized extraction.'

'To where?'

He ignored the question. 'The contact's name is Peter Trent. Within days the United States will fall, or we'll have a weapon unlike any the world has seen.' He held me. 'I love you, Solara.'

'I love you too, Dad.'

My father left, got into his car, and with a last wave drove away. Sobbing, Rebecca burst from her room and ran out to the front yard, but the vehicle had already moved off, like a diminishing vision of a life that had been. A disconnection of the love she'd known.

'Granddad!'

She ran after the car, and her Jack Russell Terrier followed with excited barks before I caught her and held her in my arms. After a minute the only memory of Dad was a dust cloud on the road, dissipating with a breeze. The nearby wheat fields gently rustled, a shimmer of golden kernels in the morning sun. I glanced over my shoulder at the empty road, and walked Rebecca back into the house.

# A PLACE WITH NO DOORS

**TOP SECRET/SIRIUS**
**EMERGENCY ORDER PC-792:**

**Date:** 9 March 2113
**Sender:** centcom@origen.mil
**To:** rhodesd.gen@origen.mil
**Subject:** Priority orders

---

General Rhodes,

Proceed immediately with neuro-psychometric preliminary time dilation phase.

Information critical.

Subject 2 expendable.

**Regression subjects:** Weir, D., Dr., (DOB denied); Jordan, S., Cmdr., DOB 9/02/2077.

**Supervising doctor/s:** Shaw, T., Dr.; Taylor, S., Dr.

**Campus:** Jericho

*Day Three: 9 March 2113*

I RELAXED AND STEADIED MY BREATHING.

Lying on a gurney in a dimmed room, I emptied my mind, and prepared for the first regression battery. My goal, under the guidance of Dr. Sarah Taylor, was to begin drawing out the experience of what happened on the other side buried deep in my subconscious. Second on the medical team, Taylor wore a lab coat with her red hair tied back. She moved with practiced competence, detached and clinical. A nurse stood beside her, monitoring my vitals on a rack of equipment. Across the room lay Weir, entering mind regression under the direction of Shaw. A holographic cap covered my upper head which meshed with my neural nanites and displayed a real-time representation of my inner thought landscape. I knew that the rest of the psycho-medical support team, as well as Sirius project coordinator Linear observed unseen from behind the one-way nano-wall.

'Let's begin,' Taylor said, in a calming voice. 'Close your eyes, please, Solara.'

With a deep, slow exhalation, I shut my eyes.

'Focus on your breathing.'

My breath became the focus of my senses, and I let my wandering thoughts run their course. In the stillness, I felt my heartbeat's deep, constant, life-giving rhythm slow.

'Let everything fade away. The room, your small worries and cares, the past, the future. Withdraw your senses from the world,' Taylor said.

I still resided near the surface of awareness, but detected deeply buried currents of experience. The gaps between each breath lengthened, and my senses began turning inward toward some concealed reality. I sank into a twilight zone, where the upper world began to be subsumed by a hidden, powerful undertow. I stayed like that for a minute, riding currents of increasing non-localization.

Distantly, Taylor said, 'Enabling neural implant regression.'

Her voice became the sole external point of focus in my descending awareness. Feeling the subtle influence of the nanites upon my brainwaves increase, I came to an inner plane of total absorption, and my heartbeat slowed… slowed. Neural implants could alter the experience of time, and now, internally, it accelerated to a thousand times faster than the human norm. I could communicate by augmented thought alone. Words were too slow.

I entered a hidden, inner world.

TIME CONTRACTED, and I was back in the singularity control room with Weir. I felt the etheric chord binding me to him, anchoring us in the physical world, and together we entered the naked singularity. Bathed in dazzling light, I was on the other side, but felt no discomfort. I drifted within nameless forces outside the boundary of the universe in a place where time or matter did not exist. Somehow, I was still aware, conscious, but no matter how well trained I knew I may not survive here for an extended period without losing my identity. Now was not the time to test my limits; I was here to gather information, attempt contact with the departed, and return. After a minute the light faded, and I floated in darkness. I knew in all probability an eternity could pass here while a mere instant would pass back in the physical universe.

I couldn't see Weir, but then, would we have visible form beyond the electromagnetic field of the universe? Unknown.

'Daniel?' I mentally questioned.

'Here, Solara.'

I sensed him nearby, and his presence was comforting in this non-place.

'There is nothing here,' I thought.

'But we still exist,' he replied. 'We knew this would be a possibility.'

An impalpable variation appeared, vibrating in response to Weir's thoughts; focusing, I made out a near-invisible point of light at the center—perhaps the same wormhole at the core of our separated consciousness? Hmmm. If so, then the theory that we existed in multiple dimensions simultaneously was holding.

I felt his attention upon me.

'I think I can see you,' Weir said.

'And I you,' I replied.

After a moment, around Weir's fluctuation, faint tendrils of light intersected his core in a complex web, then radiated outward to form a vague bipedal energy field. I contemplated the wider expanse of the place, and after a while, saw a subtle light at the edge of perception.

'Can you see that?' I asked.

Silence a moment.

'Yes,' said Weir. 'Like clouds of a nebula…'

Light began flowing from all directions toward an indefinable point before us. Distance was impossible to measure. A latticework of force spun through the void elusively, weaving a matrix of seduction. An energy vortex formed at the center of the field, deepening into a tunnel, and I had a sense of longing to enter.

'What do we do?' I asked.

'We go.'

I checked the phase-link and felt a tangible contact. Without the anchor we would be lost here.

'Together,' Weir said.

A sense of rapid movement, and I plunged forward into the tunnel… infinite pathways sped by in a blur. Somehow, I felt a deviation, and was propelled into another place. The strands of power vanished, and I was engulfed in gray-black void.

'Daniel?' I thought. I focused on the etheric tether, but Weir's presence was faint and distant—had we become separated during the passage? I searched but Weir was gone. 'Daniel!' The nothingness became stifling. I tried to find my bearings but had no point of reference. 'Daniel!' my thoughts screamed.

I pushed against the void with my will: I thrashed and cried out, but I had no arms, no legs, no voice… and then I saw it. Shining white light.

It was alluring, and I felt a strong urge to go to it, like a child to a parent's arms. Distant figures traveled along strands of force, moving toward the center of the radiance. All around appeared a shimmering blue fire that formed a corona around my spirit form, around other forms that appeared, and traveled the threads.

*A way out! Go!*

I hurtled toward the light, and felt…

… connection.

The lost people from my life were across that threshold, I sensed.

'Mum?' a faint voice called.

A jolt of recognition. I slowed my journey forward. 'I'm here.'

The blue fire broke apart, reassembled into a series of concentric layers and I saw the world I had known pictured across the flat surfaces. The imagery shifted back and forth through time, events forming a complex geometry. One of the layers showed a barren world, dark and lifeless; another teemed with life, and somehow, I understood I witnessed the physical world from a higher dimensional perspective. On the uppermost disc, I witnessed one of my last nights in the Kansas Safe Zone during the final days of the war. I was putting Rebecca to bed.

'I can hear them,' she said sleepily.

'What do you mean?'

'They're talking to me.'

'Who's they?'

Rebecca had frowned. 'Just them.'

An icy feeling arose in me as I observed my response. 'What do they say?'

'They know,' Rebecca said, turning her head toward me.

I watched myself quietly switch off the bedside light.

'Hey!' I shouted. 'It's me! Leave, get away now!'

But my past self didn't seem to hear, and the vision went dark.

I FOUND MYSELF standing at the bottom of a coastal cliff, on the shore by a grim sea. I realized I now had a body resembling my physical self, so I assumed my face had also manifested. But how? Visual perception required light, and light needed energy, radiation. At least as I understood such things. So, there must be some kind of energy field here. I touched my face and felt my warm fingers. I breathed, and inhaled bitter, salty air. Interesting. Looking around, I recognized a place Michael and I had taken Rebecca once. Chesapeake Bay on the Virginia coast bordered the Atlantic and, in the winter, felt the chilly bite of the Arctic Gulf Stream. But this wasn't Virginia, was it? A distant figure knelt on the beach, and walking over, I made out familiar features. Could it be?

'Hello?' I said.

With her hands, the girl was molding a castle shape in the sand. She paused, looked up at me with familiar gray eyes. Rebecca had been seven years old when she passed, the girl before me looked about ten. She said nothing, just returned to her work on the sandcastle, humming away. I knelt beside her. A storm built out to sea, stirring our hair, and thunder clouds rumbled ominously.

'Rebecca, it's me.'

She stood. The storm raged now, and dark thunderheads clashed in the sky. A flash of nearby lightning blinded me a moment. When it cleared the beach was empty... and the void inside me yawned open. I stumbled over the darkening beach.

'Rebecca!'

Dropping to my knees upon the sand, I stared listlessly out at the heaving, indifferent ocean. Sheets of freezing rain gusted in relentlessly from the sea, whipping my wet hair across my face, and I searched for a connection, some meaning to what I'd seen.

'Rebecca,' I murmured emptily, to the bleak landscape.

I felt myself being observed.

*She died years ago.*

Startled by the nameless voice, I stood and scanned the dark shore, but the blackness had become impenetrable.

'But I just saw her,' I said, searchingly.

*That was only a memory.*

Jagged forks of lightning briefly lit up the beachhead. During the flashes I made out moving patterns in the sand, in the clouds, the crashing waves, like a secret code of the universe on a level I couldn't understand.

'Who are you?'

*A watchman.*

'Where am I?'

*A construct of your own determination.*

I considered. 'Does my daughter still exist?'

The presence began receding. *You interfere in things that are sacrosanct.*

'Does she still exist!' I cried.

Lightning struck again, revealing that the patterns in the landscape were now more distinct, and the sand shifted beneath me, until I was falling.

◉

LIEUTENANT JOHN LI had checked, and then double-checked the reading from the anomaly in the Zion singularity control room. Moments ago, a powerful electromagnetic emission had begun and increased at an accelerating rate.

He strode to Amy and Helberg. 'We've got something.'

They monitored the display a minute.

'Oscillation speed is increasing along with the EMP frequency,' Amy noted.

Li glanced at Helberg. 'Confirm with parallel relays.'

He watched the particle swarm around the anomaly—had it moved?

'Checks out across the board,' Helberg said.

The blue-tinged sphere turned black, and high-pitched sound was emitted. Li neura-linked, and a visor slid over his head, partially blocking out the noise. The blue state of the anomaly returned, but now it appeared agitated, and undulated with a million fleeting impact craters, like a pond rippling under silent, invisible rain.

Again, Li felt his body hairs bristle. 'We're outta here,' he said to his team. He turned to the techs. 'Evac now! Leave your shit!'

They didn't need telling twice.

●

MARCUS NIEMEYER sat at his workstation, deep in analysis of shifting patterns in the anomaly. He'd been running a search for parallels with known information systems, and found something interesting. There was, without doubt, a symbolic field embedded deep within the structure. At first, it had been molecular patterns, the building blocks of matter. Now, Niemeyer saw a new pattern emerging.

'We've got an acceleration,' said Pearce.

Niemeyer leaned forward. 'We've lost the initial configuration…' He trailed off and watched the change, struck by a sense of purpose to the process, like some celestial machine in motion.

'Analyzing,' Pearce said.

The energy vortices within the inner spheres scattered, swirled chaotically, expanded and contracted as if seeking release. They did this repeatedly, and with each reformation produced a slightly different pattern than the previous beat.

Pearce was glued to his station. 'The anomaly appears to be forming a new waveform.'

Niemeyer studied the emerging pattern, and after a minute he was unable to summon a rational response to what he thought he saw. 'I don't believe it.'

Pearce looked across at him. 'What part?'

Niemeyer danced his fingers furiously over the keyboard. 'Give me a second… have a look at this.'

Pearce scooted his chair over to Niemeyer's console.

'The inner spheres are forming patterns based on a tetrahedral geometric structure,' Niemeyer said. 'Each array consists of two tetrahedrons, inverted, which are aligning as they move closer together.'

Pearce watched the patterns closely.

'I think this can tell us something,' Niemeyer said.

Pearce glanced at him briefly, then back to the feed. 'How so?'

'You know about SETI, right? The radio telescope array that used to search for signs of extraterrestrial life?'

'They never found any.'

'But think of how they'd know if they'd found something real: they had to distinguish between random noise and a signal generated by intelligence. Now, the pulse given off by, say, a neutron star, is considered data, but not information. Despite being an ordered pattern, it's essentially just noise. Think of an unknown language—how do we decipher it?'

'You need a key of some sort, a reference point. Like the Rosetta Stone that decoded Egyptian hieroglyphics,' Pearce said.

'Exactly. But how do we find a reference point for something beyond human experience?'

Pearce rubbed his hand over his face. 'That's the problem with advanced quantum encryption. There's no reference. It's indecipherable.'

'What if we're not dealing with linguistics, mathematics, or even physics as we understand it, but geometry? What if we've got to look at this from a totally new perspective?'

Pearce's frown deepened. 'Geometry…'

Niemeyer nodded. 'Think of it. If you wanted to communicate something to someone who had no basis for understanding you, how could you do it? Use—'

'—the only universal language in the universe.' Pearce nodded, smiling. 'But you're talking about molecular bonding, particles arranging themselves into an ordered pattern. Something would have to inform the process.'

Niemeyer flipped up some imagery. 'Look at this. It's one of the oldest information systems known, discovered in artifacts which pre-date the current interglacial. It might be a long shot, but what if we can interpret meaning from the structure of the energy, rather than its content?'

Pearce's brow furrowed. 'Ancient records? Tell me you're joking.'

Niemeyer superimposed a geometric pattern upon the first anomaly iteration. 'You tell me.'

'What's this?' asked Pearce.

'The first pattern of the knowledge system, which represents the building blocks of matter. From the sub-atomic world to the cellular level.'

Pearce paused a moment. 'The first iterations?'

'And this is the second: the star tetrahedron, which represented harmonics—' Niemeyer hit a key, and a new symbolic structure was displayed: two inverted, interlocked tetrahedrons. He frowned as he studied his monitor, struck by an insight. An idea began forming in his mind, a use for the quantum-gravitational data from the naked singularity, and the anomaly, not discussed through official channels. A dangerous idea which could serve a hidden purpose—outside of Niemeyer's research parameters. If the anomaly was an interface between the vacuum and the physical universe, as he suspected, then it may provide the key to multi-dimensional consciousness. And, if consciousness could not only be enhanced, but engineered, new forms of intelligence could be created. Taken by some intriguing possibilities, Niemeyer resolved to investigate this potential in secret.

Re-focusing on the task at hand, he glanced back to Pearce, who had turned back to his own workstation. The changes in the anomaly accelerated drastically, and the graph readout spiked.

'Oh, shit,' Niemeyer said.

●

AFTER CROSSING over with Solara, Daniel Weir found himself propelled into a chaotic realm of violent energy displays, and then crashed down on a burning, abrasive surface.

Suffocating heat pressed in, and he sucked in a gaseous, sulfuric stench.

*I have a body.*

He examined his physicality, then, scanning the area, found himself alone upon a scorched landscape.

'Solara!'

He pulled on the etheric tether with his will. She was gone, his backup unresponsive, and without a link, he could not return. Was he marooned here? Heat closed in like a vice. He began shaking involuntarily. Jolts of adrenaline and fear shot through his preternatural body, until he gained control of his emotions with skills learned in the Sirius regimen. Centering himself, he gained a sense of the place: noxious fumes rose from the cracked ground, hung in the dead rank air, columns of fire swept across the wasteland generating swirls and eddies of black ash. Angry, red points of light populated the sky; looking closer, he saw each star was a black hole surrounded by a ruddy corona, like some infernal anti-galaxy. The plane constricted to a white pinpoint against a gray void, then expanded to envelop him once more in a vertiginous expanse.

With an effort, he focused. Hopefully, he would soon re-establish contact with Solara, so his time here may be brief, and gaining knowledge was paramount. Where was he? Why had he come here? How could it be used to further Sirius? In the distance, a tall mountain range dominated the horizon, and with no better options, he started walking toward it. The cracks in the brittle ground widened, and jets of caustic steam gushed up through the breaches. Here and there, odd, crystalline trees sprung up from the terrain, and statuesque bio-structures, like misshapen human morphology, appeared among them. The scene put him in mind of ghastly experiments that sought to create new life through manipulation of genetic codes, but this felt different, as if the creator lacked a point of reference, and rendered the hideous. For hours, he thought he walked, and felt no thirst, no hunger. Another oddity.

Again, he tried to reach Solara, but received no answer.

Shimmering veins began winding across the land like ossified organic deposits. Further along, they began sprouting upward like vines, into an increasingly dense, interconnected system, forcing him to navigate, and sometimes push his way through a lucid morass. It wasn't mountains he saw ahead, he realized, but a vast, primeval forest, made from the same organic-like vines he now traversed. It possessed a glittering aspect, like quartz under a full moon. The uncanny wilderness dwarfed Earth's ecology, reaching the sky, and he noticed a near invisible, airborne energy stream blowing towards it.

Soon, Weir was pushing forward through dense jungle. The tree leaves burned, but did not blacken or wither, while the tree bark flowed, like molten glass. The entire biome possessed a blue-violet fluorescence. He had an intuition of the purpose of the place, but that would require... he put the thought aside for now. The ground became brittle in parts, and after his foot sank into a depression, when lifting his leg, he began floating forward. He found he could move by an act of will, as he had previously when in spirit form, and had soon risen hundreds of meters in the air. Losing any sense of direction, he followed the stirring breeze.

After traveling for a while, he saw luminescent life forms scampering among the branches, agilely swinging between them, wailing and hooting beneath the preternatural stars above. Briefly examining one of the creatures that hung by its tail, inverted, from a vine, he saw a cross between a monkey and a lynx: glowing, molten stripes covered the muscular body, and flaming red eyes turned to regard him briefly before it snapped its jaws, snarled to reveal lethal-looking canines, then leapt away with a yapping shriek. Roaming his gaze over the expanse, he observed numerous species, and considered that an entire ecosystem may exist here.

At concentrated points of the forest, large nodes were formed where branches from different trees grew into each other, producing a randomized island chain ascending far above the plane. From several of these atolls, where the radiant tree sap concentrated, liquid magma falls spilled down through the jungle and fed vast molten pools far below. Strange creatures frolicked at the base of the burning columns. All around, darkness deepened, and the vines began thinning. Willing himself toward an atoll ahead, at the forest edge, he landed on a jagged surface, and beheld desolation.

A vast magma ocean stretched away. Rocky black outcrops jutted from the heaving surface, creating a fiery archipelago. On the narrow black stone coastline, strange forms protruded from the rock: charcoal, organic-like weeds, other unsettling growths, and unmoving, indistinct biological life. Some disintegrated to dust as he watched, and others spawned from the shore, while yet more altered, grew, as if in response to a silent message. Off the strand, lava swells rolled in, became waves of flame that broke and crashed along the beach, creating bubbling, tar-like residuals that receded in sparks and smoke. Hit by a furnace-like draft, he took a few steps back from the hellish sea.

Outward, in the blazing surf breaks, dark entities swam within like misshapen sharks. Tossed violently among them, thrashing about, were other swimmers he could not identify, but who looked disturbingly human. Impossibly, their blackened forms remained alive within the lava swells; driven by the creatures, they body-surfed madly into shore, only to be swept back out by the undertow before making landfall. Horrific screams accompanied each crest that rolled in, built to a crescendo, then diminished back with the tide. Repeating unceasingly. Further out, a serpent-like leviathan broke the blazing surface and snaked through the lava, before crashing beneath with a mournful cry.

He could go no further. The lake was a boundary.

Weir noticed that the bio-structures on the shore all faced outward, their gaze turned upward, and he looked to the nihilistic heavens. Subtle energies flowed away across an immense gulf, becoming increasingly warped, and upon reaching a destination, midway on the horizon, swirled and cascaded around the gargantuan, dark eye of the convergence.

*A black hole—here?*

The oddity hovered there like an umbral star. Barely visible, a faint network of translucent lines grew out from a discharge around the eye, like an iris, or ethereal roots, and Weir perceived that they merged with the winds that blew toward it. Low in the sky, particle-like swarms moved in a continual mutation and evolution, interacting with explosive, flaming geysers that erupted randomly from the surface of the fiery ocean.

Standing there, at the edge of that inexplicable jungle, he could not truly comprehend what he witnessed. The sense he made of it, was comprised of barely fathomable concepts at the limits of understanding. What was valid, and what was an aberration, an unconscious impulse of his mind to fabricate a reality for a complete unknown—a place so remote, so unspecific, so terribly perfect, horrific, but also beautiful that his brain, his senses were not reliable narrators to interpret the experience—he could not know. From his limited sensory perspective, what he could see amidst the subtle threads resembled alien micro-organisms, flora, embryonic bio-structures, then flickering geometric forms—stars, nebulae, like a manifest dream. He contemplated his earlier intuition.

*A construction blueprint—but for who?*

In the heart of it, was an emotional dissonance with purpose, cognizance of lost authority and grandeur, and Weir had the odd impression he was sharing fragments of another's memories. He suspected that a profound question was being asked by the imagery, an agenda pursued. His insight deepened: no response to the inquiry ever came. No absolution was attained. Nothing was resolved. Only the question existed, like an unceasing, silent scream at the heart of the darkness. It hit him: the black hole was sentient. Awake. And it was aware of him. It recalled the micro-singularity at the core of consciousness but on an unimaginable scale.

Amidst all the fractured templates and impressions from the presence, Weir discerned he beheld only illusion, that the entity itself was hidden behind the event horizon, and what was visible was only a chameleon, nullifying comprehension. The ongoing eruption of energies from the eye began bleeding along tendrils of force across the vast chasm of space between. He had never imagined such immense intelligence, and knew he only comprehended the edges of it, and then, as if he turned a corner and viewed the phenomena from a new perspective, the bleeding discharge blossomed outward, like a white dwarf star going nova, and luminosity was cast over the radius. A vibration ran through him, surged over his subtle body like ice water. He curled into himself, tried to pull himself from the regard of that desolate abomination, to turn away, but he could not.

Translucent formations began sprouting from the surface of the atoll: familiar plants, trees, insect life, some birds, a dog... the breed that had been used at USSWD for security patrols, he realized. The dogs were altered—lankier, elongated, with a severe snarl and lethal rows of teeth which they bared as they leapt up to the trees, stalked, and growled like panthers along the crystalline, luminous branches. Leaves sprouted from the boughs, fell to the ground like icicles, to be whisked away by the auroral breeze.

Enmity began radiating from the presence, and Weir was falling. His worldly identity was disassembled, mirrored back from that opaque, horrible awareness. He found the truth excruciatingly bleak, but also, somehow pleasing: his humanity was provisional. His identity, merely a construct, an idea presented as legitimate, to an equally fabricated audience.

His self-authority, his ability to interpret meaning was stripped away. All that was left, was negation, a desire to dominate all, to share his pain, and for nothing to escape. In that way, he perceived he was becoming like his interrogator, in whom, all boundaries had been removed. *His* freedom was absolute, yet all that remained was a cycle of insanity and evil driving futile manifestations.

Forms were ripped from his mind. Time undulated in a wave to reveal a place with no meaning, and the fear… hell caved in. His self—what was left, contracted to fetal position. A voice in the back of his mind said, *Get out, get out!* He attempted to travel the etheric chord, return to Solara again, but remained frozen. A statue between the seams of time. A rain of sparks began falling, landed upon his body, his face, his head, and burned into his flesh.

A sizzling noise began, and he screamed. In some deep part of him, some barricaded redoubt in his mind, he wanted to believe there was a fragment of his Self kept safe from this invasion, that would survive this ordeal, and continue the treasured, fabricated identity he felt peeling from his being, like shed skin cast into a fire. The agony was constant, beyond tolerance. Fire filled his brain. He toppled to the ground; the pain was so intense he began choking from the screams.

He felt himself burning and dying. A shining tendril stabbed him, assimilated him, and the conquest was total. In the tiny mote of logic that remained in him, he screamed inside.

*Solara!*

Silence was his answer. Time, such as it was here, passed. Eventually, somehow, he found himself standing once more, staring out to the convergence, but still, he could not turn away. When he struggled, in his solitude, the presence was with him. Like a blade, ripping across his torso. Sometimes he thought it appeared to him, or at least an aspect of it: transparent, a shimmering form, but it only observed him silently, as if presented with a novelty. Doubtless, just another fractured image.

This place was a prison. He struggled, until resistance became meaningless. Standing there atop the atoll, an age might have passed, as he remained petrified, impervious to the yawning desolation inside. Always falling away, was meaning, scattering to the entropic fire. Each time he crumbled to dust, he prayed it would end, only to be absorbed, remade, and painfully re-purposed again by the intelligence.

Resurrected. Weir felt himself dying and dying, and he couldn't stop.

Then, in one of innumerable reconstructions, he felt a shift in things.

# RESONANCE

D<sub>R.</sub> S<sub>HAW OBSERVED</sub> W<sub>EIR'S REAL-TIME BIODATA.</sub>

Various regions of his brain flashed in sequence. Weir began to sweat, and trembled slightly on the gurney.

'Nano-scale imaging shows odd activity. Impaired function in temporal and frontal lobes,' Shaw said.

Dr. Sarah Taylor had left Solara, who was stable, in the care of a nurse, and she now joined Shaw. She checked Weir's scan. 'Pineal gland is presenting abnormal. Neurotransmitters are agitated.'

Shaw nodded. 'The abnormality is spreading across the frontal cortex.'

Taylor frowned. 'I've never seen anything like it. Almost like a mind pathogen.'

'He's got a fever, 104 degrees,' said a nurse.

'Shit. Hyperthermia. Get me some hydration,' said Shaw.

The nurse adjusted the saline line feeding into Weir's wrist.

'I want to calm him down,' Shaw said, tapping the keypad. 'Regulate dopamine levels—'

Weir's eyes opened, wide and staring. He began shaking, groaned reflexively, and said, 'H-help… m-meee.' His gaze darted to Shaw, and he spasmed violently. He arched backwards on the gurney, and convulsed with a hideous scream—'Be afraid of eternity!'

Taylor reflexively drew back. Weir's hands opened and clenched manically; his breath came in rapid short bursts. His head jerked side to side repeatedly as if cast into his own personal hell.

Shaw tried to hold Weir down, and punched comms. 'We need support in here! Now!'

A pair of med-techs rushed into the room.

'Hold him!' Shaw said.

The burly paramedics, one on each side, immobilized Weir's extremities. But they were still struggling. Veins bulged in Weir's arms, and he fought the med-techs with a burst of inhuman-like strength. Unnaturally, with one hand Weir twisted one of the med-techs arms away. The man grimaced in pain, one wrist dangling limply. Weir began to rise, despite the force applied by the second med-tech. Another nurse rushed in, and added his weight to the struggle. They managed to hold him flat.

'Restraints!' Shaw ordered.

Carbon fiber straps shot out from the sides of the gurney, pinning Weir by his wrists, ankles, and across his torso.

Rapidly assessing the three-dimensional scan, Shaw said, 'We've got massive psychic trauma. Stabilizing!'

He tapped the interface, reconfigured Weir's bio-matrix; nanites coursed through his system and he arced upward with a low moan.

⬤

## Second Iteration

GENERAL RHODES stood beside Niemeyer's console, watching the activity in the singularity control room through the probe feeds on the view screen. Niemeyer had briefly explained his information system theory; Rhodes was skeptical, but so far, evidence appeared to validate the conjecture.

Now the speed of the anomaly fluctuations, and the strength of the surges, continued to rise and converge.

Niemeyer said, 'It's in the infra-sound range—that's far beneath human hearing. Translating… bringing it up now.'

The noise came over speakers, and the room went quiet as a rhythmic, bass-like reverberation played.

Pearce said, 'Signal is changing to a wide beam electro-magnetic pulse.'

Static played over the video feed for a minute, and then Niemeyer said, 'We have a new pattern alignment!'

An endless number of star tetrahedrons—or twin interlocked, three-sided, inverted pyramids, had formed within the anomaly.

'I'll be damned,' said Rhodes, glancing at Niemeyer.

The imagery pulsed in time with the audio signal. Like some inscrutable, alien orchestra.

Pearce said, 'Another disturbance… intense surge incoming!'

Rhodes fixed on the object. Light deep within the inner spheres shot up toward the anomaly surface, where it shattered, fragmented into a crystalline array, and then billowed angrily across the inner boundary. The symbolic mergers stopped, the audio signal abruptly ceased, and Jericho control was dead quiet.

Niemeyer released a breath. 'I think it's—'

Blinding light erupted, washed out the probe imagery. On the view screen, white glare. The audio signal returned like a deep trumpet, resonant and resolved.

'Can't see a damn thing!' Pearce shouted.

●

TAYLOR TAPPED her interface frantically. 'We're losing him—going into cardiac arrest!'

'Charge nanites!' Shaw yelled.

Taylor rapidly typed some commands. 'Charging.'

Human augmentation was a two-way street: implanted nanites not only transmitted bodily data to the web, but also received, and acted upon external commands. The molecular machines could reconfigure and swarm inside the body to manufacture drug delivery, electrical impulses, or even alter the body's cellular composition to adapt to specific threats and environments. The nanites interacted with Weir's trillions of living cells; he convulsed again, then became still.

'Ready!' said Taylor.

'Stand clear!' Shaw ordered.

Shaw hit a trigger. A shock coursed through Weir, and his torso arched up like a bow before relaxing again. White foam escaped his lips.

Shaw glanced at the nurse, who closely monitored bio-signs. She shook her head.

Taylor re-charged nanites. 'Ready!'

Shaw hit the trigger again. 'C'mon, live… clear!'

Weir was jolted once more. They waited, and Shaw watched closely for any sign of improvement. Weir's chest was unmoving, and his eyes had closed. His skin was now a pallid blue, glistening with sweat.

'Doctor, we've got a signal here,' said a nurse.

A beep came from the heart monitor.

Shaw released a breath, then felt a chill enter the room, and a prickly, creeping sensation. He glanced at Taylor, and her odd look indicated she also felt it.

Weir sucked in a ragged breath.


'GIVE ME a bio-etheric spectrograph,' said Shaw.

Taylor was frowning, and biting her lip. 'Scan commencing.'

The neurological mutation—a pathogen-like structure, as Taylor had called it—continued erratic activity in Weir's frontal lobe, but appeared to have subsided, thought Shaw. His temperature had begun stabilizing. A broad, vertical shaft of light appeared above the head of Weir's gurney, and the wide beam laser inched down his body giving off a rhythmic pulse.

Shaw studied the translator imagery, scanning through various spectrums: gamma, ultraviolet, infrared, Kirlian—the light field the subtle body manifested within. Any foreign spiritual entity embedded in Weir should be detected there. His internal energies were displayed in a montage of colors. The beam passed to the bottom of his feet, then traced its way back up to the head of the gurney, and blinked out of existence.

'Looks clear. No interference, no trauma,' Taylor said.

Shaw analyzed the scan forensically. 'I agree, he looks clean. And the pathogen appears to have cleared. Not a trace.'

Taylor turned to him with a peculiar look. 'Are you sure about that, doctor?'

Shaw just stood frowning at the display.

I AWOKE TO an unusual call. My mind was a flood of imagery. Flashes from the mind regression, I assumed. Rebecca? Another encounter... but what had happened to Weir? I vaguely recalled being separated. The hard lines of the real world were jarring after my free-floating experience in the vacuum; I felt dizzy a second, shook it off by intense focus on a single point on the wall. A nurse was standing beside the gurney checking some readouts. I noted the time: 13.44.

Seven minutes had passed since I'd gone under. I became aware of concerned voices nearby, and glanced across the room. Six people, twice the number who'd been present earlier, including some corporate types, hovered around Weir talking in hushed tones. I peered through a gap between them. Lying on his gurney, Weir looked like he'd run a marathon: sweaty, panting, and exhausted. Feeling oddly energetic, I sat up, swung my legs over and stood on the cold tiled floor.

'Easy, Solara,' said the nurse, gently placing her hand on my shoulder. 'I need you to lie back down while we run some tests.'

I felt rested and fresh. Ignoring her, I walked across the room to the group around Weir. Shaw was engaged in a heated discussion, but when I arrived his eyes darted to me. Shaw also, was sweating.

Looks like he's aged a few years.

'What's happened to him?' I asked.

'I'll be with you shortly, Solara,' Shaw said, and nodded to the nurse who now stood beside me. Shaw returned to his colleagues.

The nurse firmly placed a hand on my shoulder again. 'Come on, let's get you—'

My neck hairs bristled. I felt resonance. An urge to bear witness. Somehow, I knew where I needed to be, and brushed off the nurse's hand.

'I'll be fine.'

I quickly left the room to confused protests, but something about Shaw stayed with me as I left.

I realized it was the first time I'd seen him afraid.

*

'IT'S CLEARING,' said Niemeyer.

Rhodes was fixed on the drone feed from the singularity control room, which was still washed out in a snow-white haze. For a second, he had a feeling the anomaly was going to suck him into some dark reality, but shook off the strange thoughts. Unexpectedly, Solara arrived in Operations.

The General glanced over, considered her presence briefly. A product of six years in the OriGen Special Forces, she moved across the room like a gymnast, and her military green t-shirt revealed tanned, supple muscularity, relaxed like a coiled spring. Her regression wasn't scheduled to end for another thirty minutes, and Rhodes made a mental note to inquire. But then, Solara was here because she was who she was—defiant and spontaneous. She took a seat quietly near the rear of the room. Concentrating intensely on the view screen, as if searching, her face was set with determination. She glanced over at Rhodes, and he gave her a nod of acknowledgment.

He turned forward. The whiteout had cleared to a blank screen.

'Talk to me,' said Rhodes.

Pearce was typing rapidly. 'We've lost the probes.'

'Do we still have power?' Rhodes said.

'Main back-up unaffected by the EMP,' replied Pearce.

Static flicked over the screen, and imagery returned.

Niemeyer leaned forward. 'Probe 3 back online…'

The anomaly reappeared on the display, rippling and pulsating. The power surge inside the enigma, glimpsed earlier, now coursed repeatedly outward, to clash with an opposing force at the boundary. The unknown energies seemed to be held in check.

Niemeyer said, 'Global Quarantine Zone monitoring sensors have picked up a signal identical to the harmonic emission from the anomaly.'

Rhodes placed a hand on Niemeyer's chair back. 'A response?'

Pearce interfaced. 'Tracing point of signal…'

A random code appeared on the screen: **376872973301**

Niemeyer quickly ran the numbers. 'North American Quarantine Zone 7.'

Solara stood at the news, her eyes rapt on the monitor. 'Kansas,' she said.

'Field stabilizing,' Pearce said.

Niemeyer rose quickly from his station and stood before Rhodes. Clasping his hands before him, his face was tense with concentration, and… excitement, Rhodes saw?

'Doctor?' Rhodes asked, curiously.

'I understand this is left-field, General, but allow me to explain the significance of the anomaly symbolism?'

Rhodes nodded. 'Go ahead.'

Suppressing his emotion with a lowered voice, Niemeyer said, 'The first two iterations, sub-atomic wave forms, and now the star tetrahedron, are found in some of the oldest known texts on Earth. They parallel the first two of what was thirteen information systems—most of which are lost to us.' Niemeyer smiled, his passion evident. 'They were believed to be emanations of ideal forms existing in the vacuum, manifested in nature, and the bio-electric field of living things. The symbolic progenitor of these systems was known as the Flower of Life—called the first language of the universe, the language of *silence*, the language of *light*—and originally discovered at a very old temple in Abydos, Egypt, dedicated to the God Osiris. It forms the basis of all the ancient sciences.'

Solara had been listening, and walked over curiously. Niemeyer flicked up a hologram.

He continued, speaking fast with enthusiastic gestures. 'An identical pattern has been found at many sites around the world in cultures which had no known contact: ancient ruins from Europe, Japan, China, Africa, Australia and more. Some of the artifacts are far, far older than the current civilizational era; they're ancient—and it's impossible to say where this science originated. The second iteration of the information system, based on the star tetrahedron, and believed to represent all harmonics, or vibrational frequencies in the universe—now embodied in the anomaly—may imply a resonance between Zion and Kansas.'

Rhodes considered the possibility. The only connection that made sense between the two locations was the USSWD wartime forerunner to Project Sirius. But the Kansas facility had been destroyed.

The General was thoughtful. 'What was the exact time the second iteration aligned?'

'Ahh… 13:40,' Niemeyer said.

There was another connection here, Rhodes deduced: the second iteration aligned with the timing of the regressions. But if the events were linked, had the anomaly responded to the Etherians, or was it the other way around?

Dr. Shaw came over priority comms. 'General, it's Weir. There's something you should see.'

RHODES WATCHED Weir sleeping peacefully on his gurney, his steady breathing disturbed only by the occasional twitch.

'What's the story, doc?'

'Up until now, Weir's physical recovery has been excellent,' Shaw said. 'Healing from cryo at triple the rate we'd expect, and considering his state after returning, his recovery is phenomenal. Cognitive functions were back to one hundred percent. He's been lucid, alert and rational. Of further interest, his metabolic rates and energy levels have been enhanced compared to his pre-incursion scores, contributing to an enhanced rate of cell repair. He's been okay, until now.'

Shaw ran through the regression recordings: Weir's unusual brain activity, his violent 'seizure', which Rhodes confirmed had aligned with the exact moment of the electro-magnetic burst from the anomaly. His odd statement when he first regained consciousness. Shaw believed something was occurring in Weir that instruments could not detect. That they possessed an incomplete picture. Partial data. They had recorded a terrifying experience from Weir's regression, but an unknown 'pathogen' had vanished, and potentially buried itself deep in Weir's molecular structure, Shaw surmised. All measures had to be taken to ensure Weir had not been infected by an outside force.

Shaw continued. 'For a minute he appeared to regress into a type of schizophrenia. We've run a brain MRI, and he's stabilized. Irregular activity appears to have stopped. But there's also this.'

Shaw swiped his hand, and a hologram of Weir's bio-plasmic subtle body appeared. The toroidal aura was subdued, a reflection of his current sedated state.

Rhodes frowned—intersecting Weir's torus field, was the same pattern Niemeyer had shown him minutes ago in Operations. The shape that had manifested within the anomaly. A star-tetrahedron.

The General placed a hand on a table beside the gurney, leaned forward to study the phenomena. The base of the upper tetrahedral energy field, a three-sided pyramid, began at Weir's knees. Radiating out from his body about a meter at the base, it angled to a point some thirty centimeters above his head. The lower, inverted pyramid was widest at his solar-plexus and converged to a location beneath his feet.

'Jesus,' Rhodes said. 'Have you ever seen this before?'

Shaw shook his head. 'No, Sir. It's some kind of cold electron emission. It radiates from the subject much like his toroidal field.'

'It appeared the second he regained consciousness,' Taylor said, an unusual note in her voice.

Rhodes glanced at Shaw. 'Doctor, I want you liaising closer with Niemeyer from research. Your findings link with his own—show him what's occurred here.'

Shaw nodded.

Rhodes made a mental note to check if Solara evidenced a similar change, then was hit with a possibility. 'The entity Weir encountered in his regression, could it have been... what came through during the first incursion?'

Shaw frowned. 'It's an explanation.'

Rhodes observed that Dr. Sarah Taylor looked pale. Shaw, also, seemed hunched and tense in his posture. He had expected the regressions to be disturbing, but this? And what had Weir meant when he'd awoken?

*Be afraid of eternity.*

'Dr. Shaw, I want your report ASAP. This stays here—are we clear?' Rhodes said.

'Sir,' said Shaw. 'What do we do?'

Rhodes turned to leave. 'Nothing changes. Continue as before.'

# WARNING

An hour later, I was in Shaw's office.

The doctor examined me in his clinical, dispassionate way. Kansas, I considered, thinking of the 'response' to the anomaly burst. What was the connection? Before leaving Operations, I'd put my hand up to join any investigation of the area. Rhodes had been reluctant, but unexpectedly, Niemeyer had supported me.

Shaw returned me to the present with a measured tone. 'Tell me about this being, Solara.'

'I saw it, spoke to it.'

Shaw frowned. 'It knew our language?'

I recalled the experience. The shifting patterns in the sand, the waves, like an interface. 'I don't know. Somehow, I think I comprehended its thoughts.'

'Interesting. What did it say?'

'It said…'

'Yes?'

'That it… watches. That we are interfering.'

'Watches? What, do you think?'

'I don't know. The barrier, maybe?' I paused. 'There was a light I saw, earlier. But I couldn't see beyond, it was clouded with darkness.'

Shaw made some notes. 'You saw your daughter. Tell me how you feel about this encounter?'

I swallowed. 'I don't think it was really her… I think I imagined that place.'

'Why do you think that?'

I pushed my hair back, exhaled a slow breath. 'Something the being said—it felt real, but said the place was of my own creation.'

Shaw was silent a moment, made some more notes. 'But the place, this beach, it seemed real?'

'Yes.'

He put his handheld aside. 'A near-death experiencer often reports encountering places, people, and manifestations of beliefs from life. A Buddhist, for example, may encounter the Buddha, a temple. A Christian may encounter Jesus Christ or his disciples. So, what the being you encountered said—that the beach was "a construct of your own determination", aligns to this image system.' He paused. 'But that was not your destination. You found the beach only after turning away from the light.'

'I heard her calling me.'

Shaw's frown intensified, and I detected concern in his expression. 'But if Rebecca wasn't real, then what called to you, diverted you from your true target? As you said, the being you encountered didn't seem happy to see you. It may have seen that you were still connected to life.'

'It could have been a warning,' I said, and considered a moment. 'But I don't know. It must have been the being, or... something I didn't see.'

He brought up a hologram. 'Does this mean anything to you?'

The document contained a set of random numbers. Familiar numbers. 'They're the coordinates of the response to the anomaly signal. Why?'

'You spoke these numbers during your regression.'

I shook my head. 'I don't understand.'

Shaw's look softened. 'No one does, yet. But during the first incursion these numbers were communicated to you somehow.'

'I didn't see any numbers over there.'

He nodded. 'Remember, in the higher dimensional space of the vacuum, the laws of physics as we know them don't apply. As you've already alluded, information there is transmitted through unknown methods. The Kansas issue may be disconcerting, considering your family link to the area. A drone recon is already underway.'

I looked away. In my mind was my last day in Kansas, and lines of people, standing by the Interstate. The orderly, terrified rows were silent under the cold eyes of their captors.

In the fields beyond, a purple and violet sea of lavender bloomed, the sun reflected off distant fields like prairie fire, rolling into flint hills on the horizon. The cool breeze had carried a piney, floral scent, mixed with terror.

No one questioned.

Not one had resisted their impending annihilation.

* * *

FROM BEHIND a one-way, transparent window looking into Shaw's session room, Dr. Sarah Taylor observed Solara through the Kirlian lens. Spectrographic imagery revealed that her subtle body had altered in many ways since the regression: some minor, others more noticeable.

'Significant increase in subject's torus field oscillation,' Taylor said to the quiet figure at the rear of the room. She watched her readout closely, frowned. 'She's emitting the same cold electron field as Weir, Sir. It's merged with her body's native radiation.'

Her visitor didn't respond.

On the screen, the twin tetrahedrons emanating from Solara were spinning in opposite directions: the upper pyramid spun counterclockwise, the lower pyramid, clockwise. Since her regression, due to the acceleration, the enigma had blurred, creating an unbroken field around her body.

A star. A star-shaped light body.

Behind her, the figure remained quiet a minute longer, observing the phenomena. Then he shifted abruptly, and General Rhodes silently departed.

●

IN RHODES' quarters, the face of Ezra Linear filled a holo-display. Linear was highly competent, but Rhodes had created an inner distance from their first meeting. A company man, Linear had never fought for anything but himself, Rhodes thought, and had an arrogance the General always found grating. He also moved keenly in circles Rhodes despised: inner GRC spheres of evangelistic absolutism. In his mid-fifties, single, no kids, Linear had a cold manner that didn't ingratiate him with his peers, and this would have been a problem for career advancement for most people. But Linear was not most people. Neither was Rhodes, though, and Linear was one of the only others on Sirius who knew the deeper truths of the project. Shared secrets formed a bond of sorts. So, they had developed a strategic, if not cordial professional relationship.

Rhodes said, 'Solara and Weir were in regression at the time of the electromagnetic burst. When the second iteration aligned, each had a vacuum-related event—a key regression encounter—at the exact time of the convergence.'

Linear frowned. 'I'm guessing that's not a coincidence.'

'No. Also, the tetrahedral pattern of the second iteration has been mirrored in the subtle bodies of both Weir and Solara. We have some kind of interaction occurring.'

Harmonics, Niemeyer had said. But what was harmonizing? Rhodes thought.

'So, who's talking to who?' Linear asked.

'We don't know yet.'

'What about this response signal—the North American QZ? There's nothing left. It's a wasteland.'

Rhodes nodded. 'So we thought. Since the signal, we've detected unexplainable activity in the area: gravitational fluctuations, atmospheric disruption.'

Solara had approached Rhodes with quiet resolve, before he'd left Operations. 'General, I'd like to volunteer to lead the Kansas recon. Whatever's happening there, I'm connected to it. I must go.'

Rhodes had sensed a barely restrained, deep well of emotion in her; the move took guts, and not for the first time he saw why she'd become the first woman to lead an EOD team.

'General,' Niemeyer had said. 'Solara may be right; her apparent relationship to the anomaly could provide unique insight.'

Rhodes said to Linear, 'Solara volunteered to lead the recon. Science Division agreed, and I concurred.'

Linear was tight-lipped for a second, then he briefly nodded. 'It's your call, General. What else?'

'If Niemeyer's theory holds, a possible third iteration relates to consciousness,' Rhodes said.

'Third? We're under threat from the second, which we still don't understand. Something's driving this and we'd better understand it fast.'

Rhodes considered his next words carefully. 'Weir's regression is disturbing.'

Linear sighed, his bullish features compressing. 'I know. We're running blind, and the magnitude of events is increasing. I don't like it. Any word from above?'

Rhodes shook his head.

'Can we pull the plug, General?'

Rhodes considered. 'Niemeyer thinks shutting down the energy field may destabilize the anomaly, expose us to an open naked singularity, and I tend to agree with him.' He paused. 'There's a conflict of some kind happening inside that boundary, I'm sure of it. All our resources are on it; we'll be sleeping at our stations.'

'Does Solara know of Weir's experience?' Linear asked.

'No. It's better if she doesn't know the details, for now.'

'Weir?'

Rhodes paused. *Him.* 'He's recovering, and keen to get back to lead research. We're watching him.'

'Keep me appraised,' Linear said, and ended the comm.

Rhodes leaned back, glanced at the tasks accumulated on his desktop. Flicking open a page, he re-read the report from Dr. Shaw regarding Weir's unsettling regression, troubled at the encounter. Then he read Niemeyer's theory of a parallel in the anomaly iterations to knowledge fragments of lost civilizations. Sirius was venturing into the absurd, except for one thing: Niemeyer was right. The first two iterations aligned perfectly with the ancient systems. When Rhodes had later pressed Niemeyer on the origins of his knowledge, he'd explained how his years of study under Neil Andrews had led to some unorthodox fields of inquiry. Niemeyer's wide-ranging expertise made sense—Andrews had been more than he'd seemed. Rhodes shook his head; the only thing missing from this picture now was goddamned aliens.

Kansas. Rhodes knew what was there—had been there. What did it mean? The General felt frustration at being so close to success, yet so far away. But things never went according to plan. And they hadn't. Not by a fucking sight. Andrews was dead. Many people were dead, and the Zion station was… well, no one knew what the hell it was now. Mysterious beings, and an energy field which seemed to be communicating with Weir and Solara. It was hard to say just what was happening to them. They retained a connection to the vacuum field and could use it to influence reality. God knew what they were capable of. Perhaps OriGen had bitten off more than it could chew. Maybe hell and the devil were real.

But Rhodes had his orders, and if there was one thing he respected, it was the chain of command. Because order was the beating heart of the world, and universal compliance was the basis of the new normal that had arisen after the war. Most of the world hadn't seen the end coming, and the Terminal War had been waged for decades before most of those who were going to wake up, had realized they were even at war. Because that climactic war—all except the final kinetic phase—wasn't fought with the weapons that had characterized previous wars. People had no way to identify their attacker, or that they were being attacked. It was the final war of the elites against their true enemy: free humanity. An undeclared war fought with invisible weapons, until those last months when battle lines had been drawn, and the silent war had become a bonfire to ignite the world. In that last mad, headlong rush to world empire, vast tracts of the Earth were leveled: irradiated, poisoned, blown to pieces, and fertilized with a billion souls. In the aftermath, the US had emerged with little credit.

Rhodes remembered that day, celebrated and cursed, when following peace talks at the end of the war Dieter Wolf had proclaimed the Global Reconstruction Council. The UN on steroids. A new Marshall Plan implemented worldwide. The old ways: self-determination, liberty, sovereignty, were over. The state of emergency—whether nuclear terrorism, eco-disaster, pandemic—became a permanent condition and means of limitless control.

An officer and intelligence asset with the US Air Force, Rhodes had made millions as world markets had collapsed, simultaneously rising in rank and prestige as his command grew. In the monolithic post-war empire, he'd acquired a position with OriGen where he'd joined a war against a new kind of terrorism, and overseen a division executing the final purges. Operation Unity, the mop-up of state dissidents, had been called. The years after the war had been kind to him: Iran, China, America, Australia, what was left of Europe and the UK, the world had imploded into a monochrome, borderless gray mass of those who remained. Rhodes still saw the camps, the lines of prisoners lined up like rows of obedient sheep. The perfect, insidious order. But to Rhodes they'd been data entries, their elimination a numbers game.

Now the GRC had a noose around humanity's neck, but Rhodes's position mitigated the severity, and he thought about what he'd do once Sirius was over. He'd have a fortune, more than enough to retire and never put on a uniform again. He planned to buy acreage in Eden Sector or maybe one of the other Tier-1 city enclaves. Spend his days hunting and fishing in the pristine wilderness reserves outside the city walls, where the nuclear clouds had already cleared, and wildlife had been returned.

He sat forward, forearms on his desk, steepled his hands under his chin and again asked himself: why had the mysterious response signal occurred in America? Why that specific location, QZ-7, the site where the forerunner to Sirius had been conducted? Rhodes considered that both Weir and Solara had personal connections to the place.

He opened the next file from the mountain of paperwork: **PERSONNEL REPORT: SOLARA JORDAN.** He sighed. The woman had more grit than an asteroid mine—she'd proven that beyond doubt. But something about Solara grated with Rhodes, and he hated he couldn't put his finger on it. In response to the latest regressions, he raised Weir's and Solara's surveillance levels, and then put the report aside.

Again, he brought up the footage from Weir's experience, and the hellish vision appeared. Rhodes sat back, and tried to understand what he was seeing.

# INCURSION

Day Four: 10 March 2113

I PILOTED THE *HECATE*.

At hypersonic speed, the twelve-thousand-kilometer trip from Zion to Kansas took about an hour. Li navigated beside me, and his three-day growth testified to the intensity of the Sirius deployment. The front of the cramped, two-person cockpit was loaded with high-tech arrays, while behind us, the personnel compartment and airlock were prepped for extra-vehicular excursions. Flanking the *Hecate*, Amy and Helberg flew in the sister ship, *Ardent*.

I considered my thoughts and discussions since the regression. Events had put everyone on edge, and no end was in sight for the escalating consequences. The being's rebuke about my presence on the other side had been playing in my mind, and I'd imagined a series of disastrous scenarios for my interference into the forbidden. But perhaps, as the being had told me, I'd seen nothing but memories. Then, there was the new tetrahedral field being emitted by me and Weir—but I felt no different, did I?

*Maybe a little. A little more connected.*

'Here's the situation,' Rhodes had said, when the team had staged in Jericho Operations for the pre-mission briefing. 'We believe separate events: the open naked singularity, the symbology embedded in the anomaly, the recent EM burst, and the changes occurring in the Etherians, are connected, and converging. We must find out what this means—soon.'

Niemeyer had said, 'We may be seeing signs of predictability breakdown at the response signal site in the North American QZ. However, because of atmospheric contamination and a field of interference around the source, intel is limited.'

'Do we know what caused the response?' I asked.

'Negative,' said Rhodes.

Weir had stepped forward. He'd still looked shaken after his regression, I'd noticed, although he hid it well. 'Initial drone surveys of QZ-7 show gravity has reduced to point-four g's around the impact point. That's just under half Earth gravity. It shouldn't be a major problem, but we're keeping an eye on it. Any more changes, and you will have to adapt.'

Li asked, 'How far has the breakdown spread?'

'It's contained within a stable radius—ten kilometers—at this stage,' said Weir.

Rhodes had placed a cigar in his mouth. I was always impressed by the General. Of African American descent, his reputation and imposing stature were emphasized by a ragged scar running from his graying close-cropped hair down to his left eye.

'Be ready for anything,' Rhodes had said.

Why Kansas? I asked myself over and over as the ship sped through the muddy stratosphere. After seven years I was being driven back to the place where my old existence had ended, and the new normal began. I felt like I was approaching a void in the world, like the space that had grown inside me. Passing over the North American coastline, we descended into opaque gray murkiness. The cloud thickened as we advanced, for the toxic nuclear winter encircling the planet was at one of its densest points here.

'Closing on final approach,' said Li.

A thought occurred to me. 'Superimpose a political map of Kansas—before the end of the war—over the latest mission map.'

Li frowned, eager to proceed, but did as ordered. He rapidly brought up a second map which overlaid on the main mission terrain display.

I quickly scanned it. 'Jesus,' I said, feeling a coldness. 'This can't be coincidence.'

'What is it?' asked Li.

I tapped comms. 'General. The edge of the gravity anomaly. I think it crosses the location Rebecca and I were in when the Kansas detonation occurred.'

Rhode came on the line. 'Understood. Proceed, Commander.'

'Yes, Sir.'

Li looked at me curiously, and I said, 'Kansas wasn't taken out by a nuclear strike, but an early variant of the Sirius tech. US special weapons had underground research facilities here. My father was… one of the head researchers.'

He frowned, ran a hand through his thick, tousled black hair. 'You're kidding me.'

I tapped a control. 'Beginning atmospheric re-entry.'

Li tracked his display, and said after a minute, 'Altitude seven thousand meters.'

The *Hecate* plowed down through densified sooty haze. Scanners showed flat, barren tundra below. Scattered structures. Nothing grew there anymore.

'One hundred clicks to signal source,' I said. 'Fifty… twenty-five. Descending, altitude one thousand meters.'

We spiraled down. With hull pass-through mode activated, my virtual overlay showed blackened earth beneath a translucent hull. To the east, we passed what had been Kansas City. Lightning flashed over a cracked and broken skyline, desolate as hell. Ruptured buildings jutted from the wasteland like burnt skeletons reaching for lost light, and I noted a dried riverbed snaking around the city where the Kansas River had joined the Missouri.

I nodded slightly. 'I used to jog there.'

Li looked briefly but remained silent. He had his own demons, I knew; he'd been to hell and back during the Asian conflict in the Terminal War.

He spoke little of his son, his only remaining family. I turned forward, away from the past, and the former metropolis faded.

'Stay sharp, entering altered gravity zone,' I said. Within my seat harness, I felt myself become lighter in the forty per cent gravity. An alarm blared.

'Gravity surge!' Li said.

The craft shuddered, and I frowned at a readout. 'Hull pressure rising… shit!' A weight slammed me forward like a bulldozer, and the ship creaked under the strain. 'Lieutenant!'

Li raised his hand slowly, fighting the increased g-forces—punched out a command. 'Anti-gravity drive—engaged.'

I was suddenly weightless, held secure only by my harness, and the alarm went quiet. The anti-grav drive created a vacuum around the ship, or super-cavity. The localized region displaced the surrounding gravity with a zero-g zone, and allowed the ship to tunnel effortlessly through the densified field.

I hit inter-ship comms. *'Ardent?'*

Amy responded, 'We're okay, Commander. Anti-gravity engaged.'

Li's eyes darted around the cockpit displays. 'This is unbelievable. Huge gravitational increase… signal source is pulling seventeen g's, and rising.'

'Shit,' said Amy. 'Can the grav-drives handle the pressure?'

'I believe… yes,' I replied.

Helberg said, 'What caused it? Some kind of defense mechanism?'

'Defending what? This isn't alive,' Amy said in irritation.

Helberg disregarded her jab. 'Getting a shimmer.'

I felt the *Hecate* rock slightly.

'Checking cavity integrity,' said Li. If the super-cavity was hemorrhaged, the ship would be hard pressed to withstand the pressure. 'Ahh… cavity stable.'

'You sure?' I said, feeling another jolt.

Li double checked, nodded. 'Affirmative.'

*'Ardent* stable,' said Helberg.

I quickly assessed. 'Okay, we knew something like this might happen. If for some reason you find yourself outside of the ship when we get to the source, stay within the super-cavity. Use Glass Mode as a last resort only; the g-forces will test its limits.'

'Copy, Commander,' said Amy.

Glass Mode modified the existing nanoscale, robotic implants in our bodies, enhancing our native survival capabilities. Nano implants were compulsory under the GRC; integration into the bio-digital network had been a condition of citizenship. We'd essentially become cyborgs, and as military, we had access to some of the more radically advanced mind-body upgrades.

Li frowned at his display. 'What the...'

'What is it?'

His brow furrowed. 'Topographical scan. Downward gradient ahead, unmarked. Ground level is lower than it should be.'

I glanced down. The terrain, like the sky, was dark, and our lights illuminated only a short way into the iniquity. I tapped comms. '*Ardent*, what's your elevation?'

Helberg replied, 'We confirm your reading, *Hecate*. Massive geological alteration.'

The radar beeped.

'Tracking multiple moving contacts in displaced zone,' said Li. 'Uniform speed, same directional vector—toward the source.'

Visual was still hampered by the sooty air. I tapped up the weapons holo-carousel, and the cannon whirled to readiness as contacts on the radar screen multiplied. Murky shapes appeared through the haze, and an absurd scene became apparent.

'Do you fucking see this?' Helberg asked, incredulously.

Amy said, 'Contacts identified as debris. Likely origin: loose terrain and objects within the gravity well radius.'

A cloud of boulders, some the size of trucks, chunks of earth, rocks, and smaller debris shot through the air beneath the ships on a lateral trajectory, vanishing into the dark mists ahead.

'It must be a singularity down there,' Amy said.

'What's our gravity level?' I asked.

'Pushing twenty-g's,' Li said. He glanced at me, shaking his head. 'We're at the former ground level.'

Below, hundreds of meters of earth had vanished where now rock chunks bigger than the ship blew in a horizontal storm.

'It's a goddamned Blitzkrieg down there,' Helberg said.

'Debris velocity increases toward the source,' said Li.

Amy said, 'High probability of collision predicted… sharp decline ahead. The angle could provide cover from the main debris field.'

'Hold at this altitude, find a way through,' I ordered.

The ships parked above the moving cloud of rock.

Li interfaced. 'Scanning… we've got a window, seven seconds to a break in the field…'

'Say the word,' I said. '*Ardent*, follow close on my six.'

'Copy.'

Li tapped his interface. 'Engaging anti-collision control… now!'

I hit the turbots, and we shot down into a clear corridor. For a moment, ship lights illuminated a spectral shower of rock chunks shooting by, and the *Hecate* swerved. Raw-hewn earth, ripped open and jagged, sped by in the strobes. Pebbles and small stones struck the windshield like a bad hailstorm, marking it. The cockpit was buffeted around as ship AI guided us around some larger pieces, several bigger than the ship. Below, the angle of the gravity well, steeper than the ground slope, caused the debris to crash to the surface and rock chunks skidded, ricocheted, and broke up along the jagged terrain.

A void dropped away, and the *Hecate* plummeted. The rock shower died off, and after we descended a few hundred meters, the surface leveled out. Nearby the *Ardent* arrived, and the glowing vessel cruised toward us. I looked upward and saw the unsettling vista of the main, flying debris field now far above. Some smaller chunks were still being ripped from the chasm face, although few in number.

'Quieter here, must have been hit first,' Li said.

I took a slow breath. 'Okay, signal source is just over five clicks.'

Powerful ship lights illuminated the surface. Light rain, falling on a sideways arc in the gravity well, coated the earth in black sludge, and a glassy residue became apparent on the ground as we moved forward.

I assessed the situation. 'The gravity surge couldn't have displaced that much terrain.'

'Ground is ossified, like coal,' Li noted.

Veins of glowing magma appeared, spurting and flowing from rents in the surface.

Amy said over comms, 'Detecting high levels of ionizing radiation.'

I thought for a moment. 'US weapons facility's during the war. It could be from some of the reactors.'

Amy swore. 'They just buried that shit?'

'Keep your distance,' I said.

We steered around the fissures. The *Hecate* dropped into another depression, closing in on the signal.

'You see that, Commander?' said Li, pointing forward. 'Some kind of mist.'

I did a visual scan through the cockpit. Floating, slow-moving particles dotted the space ahead like strange black dust.

'Gravity-well should be pulling it in, but it just sits there,' Li said.

For a moment I saw dense, bright flames dancing across the particle field, shifting through a rainbow-like spectrum of red, green, blue, indigo before they vanished. I couldn't tell if they'd simply been extinguished or had moved away so fast I hadn't been able to perceive.

'Keep moving,' I said. 'Watch it.'

We glided into the forbidding panorama, and reached another rift.

Li frowned at a readout. 'There's something down there.'

'ID it?' I asked.

'No,' he said, analyzing. 'But whatever it is, it's big.'

'How far to source?'

'One point nine clicks.'

I weighed options, licked my lips. 'Descend.'

Flashbacks of my last days in Kansas with Rebecca hit me, as we passed over the previously familiar terrain.

After my father's warning, Rebecca and I had been left to wait on the Kansas property, and a day passed with no word from him. His phone was unresponsive, but that was normal when he was away on base. I knew something must have happened for him not to make contact, and by the next day, I sensed we couldn't wait anymore. We would have to trust that the back-up exit plan with his contact, Peter Trent, had been arranged once we got beyond the safe zone perimeter. I spent the next night packing, and we would leave the following morning.

Just before sunrise a series of concussive detonations boomed in the distance, shaking the ground and shattering windows around the house. Rebecca ran to me as I staggered, charged tension in the air, and I heard angry shouts from nearby. I peered through the kitchen blinds—a motley, black-clad gang was approaching across the field. Things were falling apart. Rebecca held tight to my arm, ready and eager to travel. Dressed in runners, jeans, a warm tracksuit top, she had her school bag, packed with essentials, draped over her shoulder.

'I'm scared, Mum.'

'Time to go, honey.'

Taking Rebecca's hand, I strode to the garage. The Army issue Lexus sedan waited. With most supply outlets having closed over the previous weeks, I'd been unable to refuel unless I wanted to use a monitored, Homeland Security station—with their increasingly threatening posture, I didn't. The vehicle's hydrogen fuel cell was nearly drained, and last night I'd switched the hybrid engine over to gasoline. Although petroleum-based, internal combustion engines had been illegal to the public for decades, some military vehicles still used petrol for emergency redundancy. Like now.

Hopefully, we'd meet up with Trent today and wouldn't have the need to refuel, because once outside the safe zone, we would, most certainly, be on our own. We strapped into the Lexus and barreled away. Fifty kilometers to clear the blockade and then signal my father's contact. I raced along 87th Street, right at the 35, left into 435, through to Lenexa, onto the 470, right onto the 50 to avoid town and the highway. Smoke was rising from Kansas City.

*Have we been attacked?*

There had been no war planes, no warnings, but with comms having been affected by cyber-attacks and jamming, which had been worsening for days, that was no surprise. The 50 paralleled the Interstate East by about ten kilometers; I could stay on it and hopefully avoid whatever the hell was going on around town.

I glanced at Rebecca. 'Hey, you okay?'

She nodded, her face brave. 'Where are we going?'

'A safe place, honey.'

'You promise?'

'Promise.'

Empty roads snaked through Prairie fields, burned flat. Black smoke on the horizon, the sun dull, a pallid orb through the haze. Lee's Summit, Lone Jack, Warrensburg sped by. Vultures circled in the distance, their prey unseen, unknown. The road became a life raft of the world we had known, rising toward us, sinking behind.

Rebecca pulled her stuffed tiger from her bag, reassured him. 'We'll be okay, Simba.'

At Dresden, we found burning houses. Charred corpses splayed on the ground before the church. Some had been shot execution-style in the forehead.

'Close your eyes, honey,' I said.

Rebecca shut her eyes tight.

At the church steeple's apex, a cross of fire, silhouetted against the western sky, collapsed in flames as we passed, tumbled to the ground like a fallen age. An acrid stench wafted through the open window, and I closed it. The police station had already collapsed in the flames and was nothing more than a charred steel frame. Whoever had done this was nowhere to be seen, and I slammed the accelerator pedal.

We had to get off the back roads now; hopefully, the Interstate would be safer. I took a left at Sedalia onto the 65, right at Blackwater onto the I-70, a straight run to New York. Drones buzzed overhead, scanning, and I prayed they were friendly. Rebecca nodded off, and I gently pulled a blanket over her. Ashes had begun falling from the sky as a storm front pushed in west from the horizon driving dark gray clouds.

After a while, we reached the military checkpoint at the fifty-kilometer perimeter. Booths on each side of the highway were manned by US Army personnel, and a few dozen more soldiers stood at post or were working at various tasks around the larger border depot. The traffic was light, and I took a place in the queue behind a couple of government-looking cars, then we sidled up to the booth.

'I.D.,' said the booth officer. Young army Private, by the look of him.

I handed him the fake I.D.

He scanned it, checked his device, looked at his screen, and back to my face again. 'Ms. Jordan?'

I nodded. 'Can you tell me what's going on? We heard some explosions near the city. There have been some murders—we saw bodies at Dresden. And some arson attacks.'

The guard was somber, tight-lipped. 'I don't have access to that information, Ma'am. Nothing's come through our way.' He looked over me and Rebecca, glanced around, lowered his voice and leaned forward. 'If I were you, I'd get away from cities and towns. Have anywhere you can go?'

I nodded, and he handed back my I.D. The gate rose and he waved me through. I hit the accelerator and activated the beacon. About twenty kilometers down the highway, I pulled into an empty truck-stop and waited for Trent to make contact. I preferred to stay close to the safe zone for now; hopefully, Trent wouldn't be far away. I tried my father's cell phone again, and it went to voice mail just like the previous night. I left a message letting him know we'd left the house, the safe zone was falling apart, and we were on the road waiting.

I broke out some of our food stores, and shared breakfast with Rebecca. An hour passed. Two. Resigning myself to a wait, I decided both of us should try to get some sleep; we'd found little in recent nights, and after our rendezvous may not have the chance again for a while. We drifted into a doze. Sometime later, I woke.

The sun was halfway down toward the opposite horizon. It was late afternoon; I checked the beacon—it was transmitting clearly. I looked at my device: no messages, no calls. How long were we meant to wait for? Dad had implied Trent would already be in the area or would be able to reach us fast. Clearing my eyes, I scanned the road, the surrounding fields, and didn't see a car or person in sight. In fact, I realized I hadn't seen another soul since the checkpoint. Rebecca woke, and rubbed her eyes, then sat quietly observing the surrounding area.

After a few minutes, she said, 'I see a man, Mum.'

I looked where she pointed down the highway. A hundred meters away, a figure was walking toward us from the direction of Kansas. Straight down the middle of the Interstate. Not far behind, I noticed, were more people—a lot more. As they got closer, I made out a disorganized, almost aimless-looking procession. I saw fear and desperation in their eyes. The man in front began waving his arms at us and I was hit with a sense of caution.

I started the engine. 'Put your seat belt on, honey.'

Rebecca remained staring out the window. 'Can we help them?'

The mob drew closer, about twenty meters now.

'Do it!' I yelled at Rebecca.

Another second and she clicked her seatbelt. The men at the front of the group began running, shouting at us. I was still briefly considering waiting to see what had happened to them, to talk, when I saw the blood. Several had wounds, crudely bandaged. No one carried anything. They were not going towards something, but fleeing, I realized. Then I saw the smoke rising in the distance behind them, and one of the men, shouting, raised a gun toward the car.

I slammed the accelerator. 'Get down!'

We raced away. A gunshot cracked, and the rear window shattered. Rebecca screamed, unbuckled her belt, and curled up on the floor. I glanced in the rear-vision; the crowd was fading to dots in the distance. I drove onward. In distant storm clouds I saw flashes, and heard the rumble of thunder, but something about the sound didn't seem right; I didn't hear expansive thunderclaps, but staccato, ear penetrating booms. Half an hour later we started passing more walkers along the road. These people weren't hostile, just desperate looking, but their clothes were fresh and most carried bags. Some kept checking their phones. I scanned the map; they had to be coming from a small township a few clicks off the Interstate. The few walkers soon became a flood.

I got some information out of a man who walked with his family. 'They hit us,' he said. 'They're bombing civilians!'

'Who?' I asked.

He shook his head and fell back with the other walkers. Now I drove slowly, weaving through people, and didn't want to abandon the car. I checked my phone which still had coverage, but nothing from Dad, or Trent, and no good options.

'Shit, shit, shit,' I said.

Half an hour later, we were flagged down by blue-helmeted UN officials ahead of a roadblock checkpoint, and directed into a stopping bay. I now noticed, through gaps in the crowd, people crammed into razor wire fences a short distance off the highway.

'Both hands on the dash!' a UN soldier demanded.

I showed the fake I.D. 'I'm Homeland!'

He raised his rifle. 'Now!'


THE *HECATE* thundered down to a flat plateau, and mysterious forms emerged from the dimness ahead.

'Hold here,' I ordered.

The ship paused, and we beheld multiple apparitions. No one commented for a moment, rendered speechless by a bizarre tableau.

'No movement,' said Li.

'Take us forward,' I said, softly.

The ship lights revealed an unfolding vista of strange monuments. The structures arose from the excavated earth, as if long buried. We drifted through sacred architecture of unknown origin.

'Unnatural,' said Amy, over comms.

'What the hell?' Li said, having no comparative data.

Pillars were set at innumerable angles, often joined with others in seemingly random patterns. They were obsidian black, gleaming in the lights, with a grainy appearance. Some far larger structures jutted upward, covered with shadowy lattices. Barely detectable, the black dust seen earlier floated in clouds around the objects.

'Wonder if US special weapons knew about this?' Li pondered.

I shook my head slowly. 'I have no idea.'

'Those particles are interacting with the formations, Commander,' Amy said.

Li tapped up a visual. 'Look at that.'

Zoomed optics showed the black particles drifting into the partially completed edifices, and seemingly being absorbed. Dark fog hugged the ground, and swirled through the city.

*Why did I think of it as a city?*

I saw the flames again, or what I thought were flames: flying through the structures, impacting them to detonate in sparks, but then the sparks themselves moving, shooting up into the atmosphere. Then, swooping back down to the black particle swarms, they danced and converged in strange formations. As if colonizing the Earth.

'They're fucking building it!' said Helberg.

The *Hecate* continued forward at a crawl. I studied some of the larger structures and my mind struggled with their existence. Ahead, I saw twin, prominent pillars standing alone in a large quadrangle. Taller than the rest of the objects, the square obelisks disappeared to unknown heights above.

Li glanced at me. 'The source is just beyond those columns.'

A shrill warning alarm sounded.

'Proximity alert,' Li warned. 'Dense electrical field ahead.'

I slowed the *Hecate* to a crawl. 'Stop here,' I said, parking the ship.

'Copy, Commander,' Amy replied, twenty meters to the rear in the *Ardent.*

An object was revealed ahead, assessed by sensors.

'Unknown device,' said Li. 'Analyzing.'

'Looks like a god-damned Stealth Oscillator,' Amy said.

Stealth Oscillator mines were specialized, armor-penetrating ordnance designed to destroy hard targets, and floated at a predetermined, static height. They usually remained undetected—until too late.

Li scratched his stubble. 'A small one. Wouldn't hold enough charge to mark the hull at this gravity density.'

I nodded, thinking the same thing. 'Distance to object?'

'Two hundred meters,' Li said.

I checked the readouts. 'Pressure's over twenty-five g's, must have anti-grav capability to withstand the gravity well.'

Being caught in the gravity well, was like being driven by a hydraulic press toward the source. An explosion, to anyone 'upstream', would yield only a fraction of the force of a standard detonation.

'Guess someone knew we were coming,' Helberg said.

I pondered. Helberg was right. Someone knew, who had beaten us to the signal. Someone on the inside—or with high-level intel and resources—who wanted us to fail. That someone may still be around here somewhere.

'How's that analysis coming?' I asked Li.

'Anti-matter particles detected within explosive,' he said. 'This is an advanced device.'

'No shit.'

The anti-matter class of explosives had been developed during the Terminal War in four years of desperation-driven technological advances. A usable battlefield alternative to nukes when used modestly, the exotic substance was expensive, rare, and used nearly exclusively by state agencies.

'Make?'

Li swiped his screen. 'Well, looks like a standard oscillator so far.'

'These are some well-funded insurgents,' said Amy.

'Black market?' pondered Li. 'There's a lot of unaccounted ordnance floating around from the war. Somebody has it.'

I nodded. 'Well, the signal can be seen by anyone on the planet with the right equipment. Seems to have pissed someone off in a major way. Specs?'

Amy said, 'X-ray reveals a standard configuration. The inner shell contains a tiny cylinder of stable anti-matter attached to the central detonator, and... two secondary detonators. The switch, battery, and fuse are based on known systems.' Amy hesitated. 'Shit.'

'What is it?' I asked.

'Signal jammer.'

I frowned. 'Helberg?'

'Attempting hack,' he replied.

A signal jammer was an EOD team's nemesis. By saturating the specific radio and electromagnetic frequencies used by a device, it prevented electronic disarming from a distance, and got many operators killed. Unless it could be hacked or countered, the only way to get through the defense was manually, which meant a physical presence at the bomb. And for complex Render Safe Procedures, or RSPs, mine clearance robots still had a lower success rate than experienced human operators. To run an RSP we needed to identify every component and how it functioned; the most direct way was to extract a serial number from the motherboard—which was inside the bomb casing.

'Running diagnostic,' Li said.

'Helberg, how we coming?' I asked.

'Solid data wall,' he said. 'If we had a few hours...'

I clenched my jaw. 'Goddamn it.' In a few hours, the situation could go sideways in ten different ways. I glanced at Li.

He finished up his assessment. 'Well, I can see a 360-degree IR thermal sensor, and anti-handling defense systems.'

'IR sensor range?'

'With these specs... around seventy meters.'

'Great,' I muttered, considering. We would have to reach the bomb without triggering the infra-red sensors—a person, or even one of the ships could set it off. To disarm the anti-matter, we would then have to access the terminal without vibrating or moving the device even slightly, to avoid triggering the computerized fuse. I knew this one could be tricky, and after the loss of my EOD unit, I was resolved to keep my new team alive.

'Can we go around?' I asked. 'How far's the source?'

Li scanned his feed. 'About one hundred meters on the far side.'

'Too risky. Shit.' I took a breath. 'Okay, we gotta clear this mine. Can't risk an explosion this close to the target. The signal is just beyond those obelisks, and I don't want to be poking around it with an unexploded anti-matter bomb up my ass. With luck we get a serial number and run a straight-up RSP. Sergeant Winters, I'll take this one. I want you on backup.'

'With all due respect, Commander, hell no,' Amy responded.

I was about to override her, when she said, 'Just another day at the office. I appreciate the concern, really, but let me do my job? I think I've earned it, Commander.'

I paused. Rank was an ongoing joke between the two of us, and I recalled I'd met her not too far from where we hovered now. Of all people I'd commanded, Amy was the only one I'd allowed the occasional insubordination.

'Alright, Sergeant. Be careful,' I said.

'Have you ever known me not to be?'

An unrelated thought occurred to me—not for the first time when Amy was in harm's way, I'd perceived a barely noticeable change in Li's manner: a stiffness of jaw, slight dilation of the pupils. His calm blue subtle energies had constricted to an agitated, passionate red when she'd volunteered. Normal situation awareness, or something more? Smiling slightly, I began taking a closer look at the device analysis.

# OPERATOR

AMY WINTERS PARKED THE *ARDENT.*

Distance to the mine—one hundred meters.

'We're up,' she said, unclasping her harness.

If possible, Helberg's permanent scowl deepened to a black look, creasing his scarred face, and he brought up a holographic data terminal. Analyzing the device readouts, his jaw tightened. 'Aye, shipmate.'

Amy heard resentment in his tone as she stood, and noticed he'd avoided her eyes. His English accent grated in her ears. 'Shipmate' was a derogatory term toward those in the Navy; Amy had signed onto the OriGen Marine Core as part of her resettlement deal, while Helberg was from the Army. His hardened muscularity rippled with tension through his suit as he sat there interfacing, and she stood over him with a rare height advantage. She could have him for insubordination, they both knew, but when you had to work this closely? She resented his presence on the mission. The tension between them ran deep, and was unresolvable, she believed. Still, she had to make it work.

'Is there a problem here, Corporal?'

'I don't question orders, Sergeant.'

Annoyed with his answer, she said, 'Look, if you—'

Tight-lipped, Helberg glanced up at her. 'Let's just get on with it, shall we?'

She regarded him a moment longer, recalling the incident at a Mechanus internment camp before Sirius. They'd both been randomly assigned to escort newly arrived refugees. Even years after the war, the GRC was still finding survivors out beyond the enclaves. These ones had been flown in from Amy's former homeland; they'd attempted escape, and Helberg had… it could have been resolved without needless deaths. They'd had discretion to use deadly force or not. It's Helberg's face that had stayed with her: he seemed to enjoy the killing. He hadn't been smiling, just something in his eyes. A perverse satisfaction. Those killed had been Americans, the first she'd seen in over a year, and she'd lost it at him.

She couldn't forgive Helberg's actions, but she had learned to live with it. She had no choice. When they'd ended up on Sirius together, Amy had learned their ideological divide was great, and neither was interested in middle-ground. Helberg fervently supported the GRC's tyranny and was a bully when he could get away with it—and a brown-noser, she thought. Amy held to ideals of freedom and had a certain contempt for power when those holding its reins took themselves too seriously. And that's all there was to it. But if there was one thing Helberg could be depended on for, Amy thought, it was winning whatever the cost. The high-orbit catamaran king. His eyes were clear and focused, all business now.

'Right,' she said, and made her way back to the personnel compartment.

She would conduct the RSP alone, which was standard procedure. No point in two people dying if one fucked up. Helberg would stay on the ship as her Controller, and once she had the bomb make, he would access the device schematics and guide her through the disarming process.

To survive in the high-gravity environment outside the *Ardent's* super-cavity she would temporarily alter her molecular structure. It would have been impossible for the human body to survive in such extreme pressure before a breakthrough during the Terminal War. The nanotech had enabled exploration of the high-pressure interiors of the outer gas giant planets, and the deepest parts of the Earth's oceans, which had served as ideal hidden bases.

Reaching the personnel compartment, she took a seat, psyched herself for the nanite infusion, began breathing fast and deep. The process was harsh on the body. Coming out of it was the hangover from hell.

'Activate Glass Mode,' she said.

'Initiating,' said the ship AI, over speakers.

Amy tensed in readiness, her fists clenching. 'Here we go.'

'Prepare for high density,' the AI said.

She slowed her breathing. Needles emerged from the chair, pierced her neck, back, arms, and legs. First came the chemical cocktail and anti-nausea drugs that enabled the nanite modification. The personnel compartment blurred, and Amy snapped herself back to focus, felt the nanites contort in her system in a tickling wave from her periphery to her core. These molecular machines—respirocites—were microscopic pressure tanks filled with oxygen and carbon dioxide. Interacting on the cellular level, they emulated the functions of the body's natural hemoglobin-filled red blood cells—with up to one thousand times the efficiency. Glass Mode switched human biology from a carbon-based, to a silicon dioxide substrate. The same thing sand and glass were made from, and the substance which allowed many life forms in high-pressure environments to survive.

Iciness crept through her. She shivered, her tongue felt heavy, and she had trouble swallowing. Her eyeballs seemed pushed to the back of her head, her heart pounded, and she felt her limbs go numb for a moment. Her brain felt like it was being filled with steel bands as her body hardened to granite-like density. In training, this part had separated the wheat from the chaff, and Amy hated it.

The next part was worse.

'Pressure regulating,' the AI said.

Her nanites entered the next stage, and graphene nano-hydraulics infused her muscular system. Without them, the human body would be rendered immobile in the increased density level of the gravity well. The worst pins and needles imaginable ran through her, and she struggled to not start flapping about to reduce it. Gritting her teeth, she clenched her jaws and banged her head on the chair back.

'Okay?' Helberg asked over the comm.

'Arrrghh...'

Pressure began in her chest, and her breathing became labored. Involuntarily she panicked, but familiar with the procedure, she relaxed until the sensations passed. After a short spell of breathlessness, she was able to inhale slowly, then exhale, and symptoms reduced. When she lifted her arm, it had the weight of a feather. She felt like she could jump into the sky, and a shimmer passed over her skin as the infusion stabilized.

'*Ardent*, how we doing?' asked Solara, over the comm.

Amy stood, shook her body like a dog shaking off water, and stomped her feet around the personnel compartment.

'Still alive, Commander.'

'Glad to hear it. Stay on comms, we're moving to observation distance. See you soon.'

She moved to the airlock. Glass Mode would last three hours before the nanites began ejecting themselves from the body; you didn't want to be in a high-g environment when that happened.

'Good to go,' Helberg said.

With a metallic sound in her voice, she said, 'Breather.'

EVAs into the Quarantine Zones had a non-contamination protocol: pressure suits, compressed air, decontamination. In addition to radiological contaminants, biological and nanobot-particulates were also a danger outside. Mechanical arms fitted a flat, compact tank to her back which mated with the rear of the suit. The silent breathers were a closed-circuit breathing system used by the military, and the latest generation allowed EVA durations of up to six hours.

When she accessed the airlock, a transparent helmet morphed over her head in a protective shell. She entered a dead silent void, sealed off from the world, her breath the only sound. The HMD came online, augmenting her neura-link. With her virtual retina display being fed back to the ship, her unit saw what she did. Scanning through her visor, she walked to the hull porch.

She noticed she was trembling, and had a tightness in her chest she couldn't attribute to the nanites; annoyed at herself, she clenched her fists a few times, took a breath. Already, her subconscious was taking over and heightening her senses: listening, seeing, feeling, even tasting as her mind began working in overdrive, running through plan A: avoid IR, access the terminal without triggering the trembler, serial number, schematics... Her pulse was quickening, sweat forming on her palms.

'Sergeant this is Control, respond?' Helberg said, through her helmet feed.

'Loud and clear Control.'

'Copy that.'

Ship AI announced, 'Mission time 1:15:34—Winters exiting—Initiating mine counter measures.'

A square panel in the hull floor slid open. Blackened earth was revealed beneath and a ladder was extended downward.

'Your bio-signs are elevated,' Helberg noted.

Ignoring an ominous feeling inside, she said, 'I'm okay. Let's do this.'

A pause, and Helberg said, 'Copy that. You're good to go.'

Amy climbed down, suddenly glad to have Helberg working control; despite his maddening flaws he was a skilled EOD tech. At the bottom of the ladder, she held to a rung and planted her feet on the ground, still within the *Ardent's* anti-grav field. Digging boot spikes into the earth, she secured herself enough to enable stable movement. Motion above signaled the hull panel closing, and she was alone on the jagged surface.

She tapped a wrist panel. 'Activating thermal camouflage.'

'Copy,' Helberg replied.

Her smart-suit lowered its surface temperature to blend in perfectly with the surrounding thermal environment, negating the bomb's IR heat sensors.

'Ahhh... looking good, heat signature neutralized. Good to go,' Helberg said.

She tapped her wrist panel again. A cable shot from an opening next to the hull panel, homed-in on the rear of her suit, and she felt a click as the high-strength cordage clamped-on securely, anchoring her to the ship. The nanobots would adapt her body to the pressure, but once leaving the *Ardent's* super-cavity, she would need aid to withstand the horizontal pull to the source. Controlled by the ship AI, the motorized towline would detract, or retract, in accordance with her distance.

'Tether attached,' she said.

'Copy.'

One hundred meters. With suit lamps lighting the path, Amy slowly and carefully made her way to the mine with a measured, deliberate cadence. *The long walk.* Although the device's IR triggering mechanism was negated, they didn't yet know the sensitivity of the kinetic sensor, and she would need to use extreme caution when accessing the terminal. Her nearly indestructible nano-suit made her feel somewhat safer, but she knew that was a falsehood. The suit may keep her body together, but nothing was going to save her if the device performed its intended function.

Her first EOD operation after the Terminal War flashed through her mind. Her unit had relieved another team in a Hades Sector district in open insurrection against the GRC's ongoing, oppressive mandates. The area had been under its fiftieth week of continuous lockdown. Snipers and bombings were called in up to thirty times a day. Despite the GRC's near total control, somehow, weapons had still found a way into the hands of the populace. When she'd arrived the first thing she'd noticed were the soldiers themselves. In the driving sleet, it looked like they hadn't slept in days: uniforms were shabby, weapons were wrapped in black duct tape, vehicles were battered, spattered in mud and smeared with feces. Everywhere there were sandbag bunkers, machine gun posts, armored vehicles rolling down, lights flashing; that was her first impression of Hades Sector.

She'd lost her cherry on her first call. A civilian in an explosive vest with a dead man's switch daisy chained to several more people—the operator had lucked-out and the casualties had given her a first-hand experience of her training lectures… *a bomb affects the human body like no other weapon.*

*The shockwave alone detaches the limbs from the trunk. It enters the mouth and blows off the top of the head. It turns human tissue into vapor. In some instances, all that remains is the spine.*

The image had burned into her mind and served as a permanent caution. She took a breath, willed her mind calm, continued the walk. A short distance from the *Ardent* she left the protective anti-grav field. The change hit like a ton of bricks. The immense pressure on her body was countered by the nanites, and the tether enabled her to withstand the lateral pull, which dragged like an ocean rip. Much of her energy was expended in maintaining balance.

She felt her face screw up, and her muscles became rubbery. She performed counter g-force exercises, tensed every part of her body, trying to keep her blood flow balanced. Regaining her bearings, she trudged forward. The mine was situated near the colossal silhouettes of the obelisks, and when she followed their lines upward, the heights became lost in the haze.

Nearing the device, she approached cautiously. It hovered in front of her about one meter above the ground. The dark metal casing appeared uniformly smooth, no mechanical access. She reached touching distance, stopped, stood still as a statue.

'I've reached the device,' she said, quietly. 'Access plate sealed. Proceeding to remove.'

'Copy,' Helberg responded, subdued.

Neura-linking, she mentally commanded, *'X-ray.'*

Enhanced imagery appeared in overlay, and displayed the internals of the device. Scanning, she carefully crept around, hunting for the hidden panel, which had to be removed to reach the terminal. Locating it, she removed a small aerosol can from a pouch. BD-311 wasn't an explosive, but a lethal chemical compound used to eat through heavy metal. It had several components and could only be set-off by altering one of the chemical elements by remote.

'Setting 311,' she reported.

'Copy,' Helberg acknowledged.

She sprayed yellowish foam until it covered the area directly over the terminal, and it clung there in a sticky, amorphous residue. '311 primed.'

'Copy that.'

She backed-up, until she was beyond the chemical's lethality radius. At five meters, she neura-linked, *'Activate.'*

The yellow foam began sizzling, ate into the metal facing. A deadly, odorless vapor cloud briefly formed before rapidly dissolving into the air. A rectangular hole now gaped beneath the eaten away plate, and a computer touchscreen was revealed.

She carefully walked back. Now with direct access to the operating system she could bypass the signal jammer. Her breathing was loud in her ears, every breath a struggle against pressure. Inhale. Exhale. Senses hyper alert, she gently traced a finger over the screen, and a well-known operating system came online.

She frowned. 'Familiar interface—looks like this is OriGen ordnance.'

'Copy,' Helberg responded.

*'Locate device serial number,'* she neura-linked.

Connecting to the device OS via short beam, her neural AI got to work and rapidly penetrated the system. A long number came up on the panel.

'Got it,' Helberg said, then paused. 'Schematics up. Two-stage RSP: you have to disable the fuse, and the main switch. Whatever you do don't disable the battery you'll trigger the charge.'

'Copy.'

'Pull up the interface using: Quebec Zulu Six November Charlie Four,' Helberg said.

Careful and steady, Amy maintained a calm honed by years of training and experience under the direst pressure. A wrong entry may trigger the fuse. Her neura-link entered the sequence and a holographic interface sprung up from the panel. It contained over a dozen tabs, each labeled with symbolic script.

'Good to go,' she said.

'Fuse is the trident tab.'

'Copy that.' She touched the symbol, and a sub-stack panel keypad came up with an array of symbols: a crescent moon, a smiley face, a pyramid inside a circle… meaningless without the schematics. A module number was at the top right; beneath it, a timer started counting down from three minutes.

'Timer initiated,' she said.

'Copy. You want the top row, fourth symbol from left, upside down… almost like an apple logo.'

'Apple with a bite taken out and a little stalk on the bottom?'

'Yes.'

'Wait, leave it for now.' Helberg mumbled under his breath to himself. 'Tss schsss… press the… arrggg…'

'Is this a standard timer? It's moving pretty quick,' she noted.

Pause. 'What's the one on the bottom right?'

Helberg would be focused on the schematics and would rely upon her for direct feedback of the system.

She said, 'Ah, bottom right is like a wheel with curved spokes.'

'No rim?'

'Copy, no rim.'

Pause. 'Okay, hit that.'

She tapped the holo-symbol, and it became highlighted.

'Okay, you want the one two to the left, same line.'

'Ahhh… the T with a 6?'

'Copy. Select it.'

She tapped it. 'Good to go.'

'Go to the apple logo.'

She scanned up to a symbol in the center line of the panel. 'Apple.'

'Select it.'

She tapped the symbol. A message came up: **FUSE INACTIVE**

'Alright, the module's done,' she said, and closed the panel. The main interface returned.

'Main switch is the sideways number eight,' Helberg said.

'Like an infinity symbol?'

'Copy.'

'Okay… umm, a blue button is flashing that says abort.'

●

I CAREFULLY followed the RSP from the *Hecate*.

'Picking up an increase in signal strength at the source, Commander,' Li said.

I frowned. 'How much?'

'Exponential pulse in the electromagnetic wave form.' Li held his ear-piece close. 'The static ten-kilowatt charge is increasing by a watt every three seconds… and accelerating.'

'Audio?'

Li switched to speaker mode, and the signal played in the cockpit: a sharp distorted ping lasted several seconds, followed by a repeating, deep throbbing pulse. The flames seen earlier returned, and points of light dove around the columns in erratic swarms, moving inexorably toward the source. Whatever they were, they could intercept Amy if she remained exposed—but once initiated, the RSP had to run its course. I calculated the speed and distance of the moving phenomena, and determined Amy should be able to finish up, and reboard the *Ardent* in time to avoid the potential threat. Glancing over the city, I saw that the dancing lights now permeated into the atmosphere.

The *Hecate* shifted slightly, and I frowned. 'What was that?'

●

'OKAY, STAND-BY,' Helberg said, pausing. 'Blue button that says abort. Hold it down.'

'Ahh holding... red flashing light at bottom of panel.'

'Release when a three is in any position in the countdown.'

'Ending with a three?' She released the button. 'Good to go.'

'Hit the main switch tab.'

She tapped the button and was confronted with a new holo-display. A three-minute countdown began. In her periphery was an odd light, and she thought she felt a slightly increased pull toward the source, but she was too focused on the disarming process to divert her attention even for a moment. The *Hecate* was monitoring the area and would warn of any new danger that arose. She continued the RSP.

Helberg said, 'We need a four-part code. First you want the far-left column, third button from the top. Should be a circle with an upside-down crescent on top.'

'Third from the top?'

'Affirmative. Press it.'

She tapped it and the symbol lit up green. 'Good to go.'

'Second button up, middle column. Small circle with a bunch of wavy lines coming out of it.'

'Like a comet?'

'Yes. Hold it down for five seconds.'

She rested her finger on the symbol. Released. It turned green. 'Right… that's good…'

'Okay time?'

She checked the timer. 'One fifty-five.'

Pause. 'Ahh, you want the top center button. Should say Assets. Hit it.'

'Top center?' She tapped it and it flashed green. 'Good to go.'

'Right column third from the top. Should say Bluebird.'

Several different spellings were listed on the main button. 'Which bluebird?'

'Ahhh… blue-bird with a hyphen.'

She clicked it. The button turned green, and a message came up: **MAIN SWITCH INACTIVE.**

Amy released a pent-up breath. The fact she was still breathing was the only signal she would get she'd been successful. If the mine had gone off, her one comfort was that she wouldn't know about it.

'Okay. I'm done here.'

The holo-interface blinked out. The *Ardent* lit up like a miniature city, and Helberg said dryly over comms, 'And she walked out of my life. Last of the ballroom dancers.'

She chuckled through adrenaline. 'Just getting started—how's that fun meter?' Dancing lights shot amidst the nearby alien structures. 'Woah… what's happening?'

Solara came over the comm. 'Good job, both of you. Amy get back aboard the *Ardent* and we'll take point. Move fast—we've got increased local activity and another potential gravity shift.'

The *Ardent* closed in fast on her position. Much further away in the murky atmosphere was the faint light of the *Hecate*.

'Copy,' Amy said.

She turned, the tether circling in a groove around her suit, and made for the ship. Before it arrived, she moved nearer to one of the pillars, curious about the faint markings on the surface. The floating lights drifted around her like insects. Jolted by something unseen, she stumbled; her fingertips ripped from the obelisk where she'd been tracing the inscriptions.

'Another surge!' shouted Helberg in her suit comm.

'Shit,' she said, steadying herself.

'Helberg! Double-time that pick-up!' Solara ordered.

The *Ardent* careened in.

# NEXUS

The ground began heaving.

The land split. One of the alien structures rose several meters in the air and then crashed back down. The earth broke like a wave, rolling and surging. The gravity surge was followed by a continuous, accelerating pull toward the signal, and now an aurora-like wall of energy approached from the unexplored region of the city.

Amy fell to the dirt. 'Reel me the fuck in!'

The tether jerked, dragging her toward the *Ardent*. Struggling to keep her balance, she slogged toward the ship against the immense pressure. The ship was only meters away, and the ladder was being lowered... she crossed into the vessel's anti-grav cavity, boot spikes keeping her grounded, then stumbled in the pressure decrease with one arm outstretched. She grabbed the ladder, placed a foot on the bottom rung. Securing her other hand, she began climbing.

'Detach tether!' she called.

The cable snapped loose and reeled back into the ship structure.

The *Ardent* was rocked. Hard. Dislodged from the ladder, she staggered back over the ground, passed outside the cavity again, and was dragged back toward the mine by the pull, untethered. A shock wave arrived, pitching her away in the turbulence like a rag doll. In her peripheral she saw the distance to the *Ardent* increase, and the diffused bomb was hurled into a free spin.

Attempting to crawl, she skidded uncontrolled along the terrain; hastily gaining her bearings for a moment, she hit suit thrusters and propelled herself at an angle.

'Fuck!' Helberg shouted.

*

AFTER THE debris hit, the *Ardent* re-stabilized. Helberg veered back closer to Amy, who'd been propelled away from the ship.

'*Ardent! Hecate!*' Amy yelled. 'Go!'

'Hell no, Sergeant,' Helberg responded.

He slammed the throttle. The anti-gravity drive still countered the increased gravity pull, and Helberg edged toward her. Still outside the *Ardent's* super-cavity, Amy stumbled and crawled, but was being sucked inexorably toward the unexplored zone. He hovered closer; if he could get her back inside the cavity radius, the tether could re-attach and reel her in. Loose earth was ripped free in the surge and debris flew past; a large chunk slammed into the *Ardent*, knocked it sideways.

Helberg tensed, fighting to regain control. 'We've got fucking Armageddon here!'

'Thirty-eight g's—it's pulling her in!' Solara shouted over comms.

'Shit!' Helberg swore.

Amy had managed to buttress herself against one of the obelisks. Helberg struggled to maneuver in through the flying debris.

*

Dazzling light illuminated the shadows. The turbulence became a shock-wave, jolting the *Hecate* violently, and I was flung against my restraints. Smoke burst from the forward bulkhead and a shrill alarm blared out; Li grabbed a fire extinguisher and let loose short bursts of propellant.

'High order detonation detected,' said the ship AI.

*No shit!*

I thought fast: the anti-matter mine must have struck by debris and become unstable… Amy and the *Ardent* were right next to the blast… an explosion of that magnitude within the gravity well would produce a cavity which would for a moment become a flaming sphere incinerating anything within the blast radius. Through the cockpit window I saw a wall of fire rushing the ship. I grabbed the controls and angled the *Hecate* away from the explosion, maxed out the anti-gravity drive.

'Go you bitch!'

Rear cameras showed the expanding inferno in a tug of war against the immense g-forces. Then the explosion started losing pressure: the fireball began to contract as the gravity well recompressed it, shredded it into smaller flares which were sucked toward the source. I pulled back the throttle.

'The gravity stopped it,' Li said.

Turning the *Hecate* back around, I observed the aftermath of the spectacle. Twilight was returning, and I peered into the now eerily silent landscape. The *Ardent's* power and life-support systems read zero; flaming pieces of wreckage were skidding and rolling along the gravity well towards the source, and I watched the last fragment bound away into the shadows. Floating through the air, the strange lights remained, and created an unnerving vista of order.

We scanned the area for a moment.

No Amy. No Helberg.

Li ran a diagnostic. 'Hull integrity sound. All systems accounted for.'

THE *HECATE* arrived at the explosion site. Where the anti-matter charge had detonated, a jagged crater was blown into the surface. Glassy, honeycombed residue lined its walls where rock had melted and shimmered under the lights. I swept the area for any trace of neural implants, which would continue transmitting for several hours after death, but knew the chance of survival was astronomically low.

'Nothing could have lived at that range,' Li said quietly. His rugged aspect, always reserved, looked strained.

Glass Mode made you a tough son of a bitch, but I was realistic and knew the likely truth: Amy would have been vaporized inside the fireball, Helberg killed by either the blast wave or when the *Ardent* was destroyed after its super-cavity failed. I hadn't known Helberg long, but Amy was different.

I swallowed hard, struggled to hold down my emotions. 'Damn it, Amy.'

Li was tight lipped.

Feeling another strand bonding me to my former world break, I nodded slowly. 'Let's get to the source.'

We cautiously moved forward again.

Li frowned. 'Ah boss, we've got something interesting here.'

'What?'

'Those pillars—obelisks you called them? Their signature hasn't changed. It's as if the blast didn't affect them.'

I gauged risk; the signal source ahead had stabilized. 'Let's do a quick pass.'

I veered the *Hecate* around. A massive edifice loomed, rising to unknown heights, and I stopped near the base. Ship lights illuminated the stone facing and I was perplexed at what was revealed. 'They were inside the blast, but there's not a mark on them,' I said.

Li nodded. 'Make any sense to you?'

I shook my head. 'Nothing about this place makes sense. Big bastards. Must be ten meters across.' I analyzed the column. 'Interesting. No visible deterioration of the structure. Note the ground fractures around the base, the surface is smooth with faint inscriptions on the facings, and they look… new. Let's get in closer.' I brought the *Hecate* alongside the column. 'Engravings of some kind, symbolic characters,' I said, tracing the inscriptions with my fingertips on the view screen. Deliberating the spidery runes for a moment, I swore I'd seen something similar before. It came to me, I couldn't be sure, but it reminded me of the anomaly symbology I'd seen at Jericho. 'Get a sample.'

Li maneuvered a control. A mechanical arm extended from the front of the *Hecate*, and a small cylindrical shaft at the end contacted the surface of the obelisk. 'Drilling,' said Li. Half a minute passed. 'Doesn't want to give it up, increasing power.'

I frowned. The coring drill was graphene, the hardest substance known. Another minute passed.

'Here we go,' said Li, reading the initial analysis. 'One-micron sample. Unknown elements.'

'That'll have to do. I want a scan of the entire structure.'

I ascended the *Hecate* up the face of the pillar, then repeated the process until all surfaces had been recorded. We turned back to the source, and moved forward among several more edifices, then cruised along what appeared to be an avenue. I sensed a pattern to the city, an intentional design I couldn't understand, and knew we had stumbled upon something remarkable.

Li said, 'Source of emission twenty meters.'

I pulled back the thrust and the *Hecate* slowed to a crawl. The dancing flames had increased in number, and now moved in a large, coordinated spiral motion toward the signal point, forming a type of light passage.

*A tunnel.*

I comprehended a slight differentiation within the murkiness at the source, and focused on it, not sure yet if it was a trick of imagination.

'Something's there,' I warned.

I eased the ship forward, and we drew closer to a motionless, mirror-like shimmer.

Li completed a scan. 'Detecting high energetic activity… spiking at about one second intervals.'

'That's our source,' I said.

I studied the otherworldly object. The sphere was still, like water; not a single ripple marred its perfect, unvarying plane. Something changed. A faint light began glowing within the center, started pulsating, and a shimmer broke the unmoving surface. Interior ship lights flickered.

Li raised his hands from his panel, glanced at me. 'Power surge.'

The cockpit went dark a moment before emergency power kicked in. In the sphere ahead, the radiance in the center spread to encompass its entirety.

Li tried manual controls. 'We're losing back-up power. Three minutes until complete shutdown.'

'And we lose the gravity drive,' I said, thinking fast. 'We have to get off the ship!'

If we were inside the *Hecate* when the gravity drive failed, we would suffer the same fate as Helberg. I released my harness, sprinted to the personnel compartment, sat in a med-chair. Li was right behind me.

'Initiate Glass Mode now!' I ordered.

'Glass Mode, initiating,' the ship AI responded.

The grueling process was over in a minute; finding my legs, I grabbed some portable power cells, oxygen, flares. We made for the hull porch with limbs like steel. I punched a control and the floor slid open. Within the super-cavity, we pushed our weightless bodies down to the surface, hit the ground, planted boot spikes and moved forward. We had to get away from the *Hecate*. When the cavity collapsed the ship's reactor may explode, and although its area of effect would be limited, I wasn't taking chances.

I glanced at the sphere as we struggled toward cover, struck with a thought: was this the same naked singularity my father had opened in the USSWD project, still here after all this time?

Rebecca and I were herded away off to the side of the Interstate into a desperate situation. The UN blue-helmets strode among the throng, barking orders. Savage dogs snarled, and frothed at the mouths. Machines swarmed above the refugees, scanning, shifting positions so fast it seemed as if they moved not across space, but through it.

I held Rebecca's hand reassuringly as we reached a line of fearful people within the razor-wire fences, and were ordered to stand in the cue. A world was ending before my eyes, which like the broken gray sky, left me formless. The low storm clouds were darkening, diffusing and lighting up from within, and wind gusted with a needling chill.

I felt Rebecca trembling, and tears welled in her eyes. 'Don't leave me, Mum.'

I squeezed her hand tight. 'I'll never leave you, honey. Ever. I promise.'

She pulled my arm, and pointed to the sky. 'Look!'

Raising my head, I felt my flesh crawl.

Outside the *Hecate*, I moved through a world of blackness broken only by the luminescent sphere, and the now multitudinous, wandering lights. Occasional chunks of debris zoomed by and disintegrated in brief flashes of flame when they hit the object. The tunnel the dancing flames had formed toward the sphere was now a vortex: its boundaries indefinable, a river of light moving inward and outward in parallel. A single fiery fragment moved close to my visor, darted around, and I sensed purpose. I felt myself, somehow, being colonized by something unknowable. Alien but familiar.

'There!' I shouted to Li.

We struggled through the dense gravity to take cover behind the nearest structure, fighting for every inch. I was overcome by a dizzy wave and stumbled; despite Glass Mode I knew the g-forces were shifting my internal fluids toward the anomaly, reducing blood oxygenation. Cerebral hypoxia would follow, and I would fall into G-LOC, or g-induced loss of consciousness. Blinking rapidly, I glanced at the anomaly out of the corner of my helmet. It appeared unchanged since killing the ship systems, and we were halfway to gaining cover when high-pitched feedback began in my helmet.

I turned sharply to the sphere. No change. But wait, was that movement? I looked closer… nothing. I'd started forward again when the keening grew louder, painful in my ears, and a sense of euphoria coursed through me. I sensed a presence and turned back. My vision blurred, narrowed to a tunnel of refracted light from the anomaly. The flame vortex became a shining bridge of stars. Lack of blood flow to the brain, I thought absently; the beginning of hypoxia—symptoms were experienced visually first. I didn't have long.

'Ahhh… Lieutenant?' I croaked, struggling to breathe.

I looked back to see Li on his knees, crawling erratically forward. I turned to the source. A small, moving silhouette appeared within the sphere, and my flesh prickled.

*Bipedal.*

The entity grew larger, perhaps three meters tall from feet to crown. Moving organically, it paused at the inner circular boundary, turned its head slowly as if scanning. Raising an arm, it placed a six-fingered appendage against the interior of the energetic surface. The thing stilled, and I had the eerie sense I was being observed, scrutinized, when the high-pitched sound stopped.

I heard a voice.

*Time… breaks.*


ABOVE US in the storm clouds, a maelstrom, like a tornado, was forming in a perfect churning spiral. I thought I could see tiny lights within, moving in opposition to the surrounding winds. The growing oddity rotated on a direct upward axis from our position, and I was mesmerized by its symmetry… it can't be natural, I thought.

'It's them!' yelled Rebecca, pointing and jumping. 'They're helping us!'

A blinding flash encompassed the horizon, piercing my soul.

I tackled Rebecca to the ground. 'Down!'

In the distance, a great firestorm rose to the sky. A vast trumpet reverberated in the heavens, rising to a climactic rapture. From the heart of the inferno, a spreading black void appeared, engulfing everything in its path in a violent clash of forces. An immense column of lightning shot upward from the dark space, piercing the stratosphere, filling me with the charged energy of nameless fear, and my hairs bristled in a primal flight response. A second immense, monolithic electrical strike, still miles away but closer than the first, hit in a detonation of thunder; a third column hit, closer again. Each hit was accompanied by a thundering roar, as if in a challenge to the world by unmatched power. A fourth, fifth—the sixth lightning column struck, only half a mile off now, coruscating from the earth up to the vault of the sky, vaporizing a UN convoy on the Interstate, and Rebecca's scream was unending.

With a sense of impending doom, I grabbed hold of her and began running blindly away through screams. People—UN or otherwise—were now in chaos, and many seemed out of their minds. The vortex in the clouds above was an oscillating, spinning gray blur, while the moving lights within became bands of circling white radiance.

Overhead, a seventh column cracked into existence, struck the top of the vortex; the spiral was consumed with fire and the seventh strike was held in check above… a shockwave hit with a reek of scorched ozone, ripped the air from my lungs, hurled me to land hard and I tasted blood mixed with bitter dirt.

*Blast from the initial explosion.*

A second concussion hit, and in my periphery, I saw the invaders cast asunder. Hurtling blindly through the air I smashed against an upended truck, stunned senseless as my head rebounded on the ground. Holding to Rebecca with the last of my strength, somehow, I rolled into a dug-out trench. Something hard slammed into me, and Rebecca was ripped from my grasp as the turbulence took her. The last thing I knew before the darkness, was her flailing silhouette, cast into the storm.

*I T'S WATCHING ME.*

The hairs rose on my neck. The sense of colonization I'd felt with the dancing flames increased, like a transfection of time and realities that opened a window in my mind. I witnessed a terrible scream engulf a world in a maelstrom of swirling, flaring debris, oceans evaporating through a seared atmosphere, gargantuan sea creatures flopping, dying on a barren sea floor in some gothic, antediluvian dreamtime. Great monuments crumbled to ruin, and a dark winter lasted thousands of years before sunlight again touched a lifeless, red-tinged world. In my mind I saw possibilities… faces gone, both recent and long ago whispered out to me from the sphere. Rebecca… Amy? I felt her… a fluctuation, was she with others who had passed? I sensed not only the past, but the future, a oneness defying understanding. I saw Weir, but he was a man with two faces, two identities: one the face I knew, and another, cloaked in shadow.

The being was poised; not hostile, but unnaturally focused upon me. Its palm hadn't moved position. The fingertips began burning, sinking into the barrier. Becoming excited, the dancing lights around the city surged to the being's contact point, and merged with the sphere. Coiled, energetic intensity radiated from the creature in a tangible wave, and my unfocused gaze fixed on the spectacle.

*What are you?*

The voice returned, much stronger.

*There are worlds beyond yours. Worlds without end.*

The shadowy hand singed through the sphere, which collapsed upon itself in a vice of terrific force. Another intrusion to my mind.

*You must solve the problem!*

Freed, the life-form leapt forward with inhuman purpose and motion. The gravity well vanished, and I stumbled, turned—the *Hecate* remained intact, and I staggered for the ship.

I never made it.

AMY CAME TO awareness suddenly with a sharp intake of breath, gulped in several more, her lungs burning. For a minute she was disoriented: she lay in blackness with no point of reference in direction or place, and experienced an anxious minute of dizziness and hard breathing. Darkness pressed in on her in an endless, smothering totality. She felt a scream beginning, then nausea roiled up her throat, and she vomited over the inside of her helmet. She sucked in a ragged breath, and her face reflexively wrinkled up at the strong, pungent odor. She rolled on her side. Another gag came on, then endorphins were flowing, and her training kicked in with a process she'd repeated so often it was ritual.

She began autogenic breathing: in for four, hold for sixteen, out for eight. Repeat. Repeat. Her heart slowed, and her frantic brain stopped racing. Repeat again, and again. She was in her EVA suit. Basic life-support functions, oxygen and temperature, were operational, saving her life. She rose to one knee; her limbs were light, and she felt graphene nanotubes running through her body. Glass Mode. She was in the North American Quarantine Zone. Her vision was obscured by yellowish vomit across the visor.

'Purge helmet,' she rasped.

'Purging,' suit AI responded.

Closing her eyes, she held her breath as a blast of compressed air burst through the inside of the helmet, sucked out stray fluids and particles through a pressure valve. Clean 02 was pumped back in, and she took a relieved gulp of air. Her visor had cleared, but murky haze surrounded her, limiting visibility.

*Oh, shit—the explosion.*

The anti-matter mine must have been hit by debris in the gravity surge, and the secondary detonators—which had not been diffused—would have triggered. She'd gone for one of the pillars instead of making for the *Ardent*. She'd taken cover behind it. Somehow, it must have shielded her. Then had come the flash, the shockwave, and she'd obviously lost consciousness. How long had she been out, how far and in what direction had she been thrown, and where were the others? The *Ardent* had been hit point-blank and must have been destroyed in the blast. If she hadn't been unconscious for too long, Solara and Li may still be investigating the signal source and the *Hecate* somewhere nearby. She ran a system check: some suit functions were still in sleep mode. Neura-linking a command, her visor lit up with the mission data, suit lights came on, and she felt better.

*I'm not dead yet... Oh, double shit—the gravity-well!*

Standing on the crystallized surface, she suddenly noticed the absence of increased pressure. She ran a scan: one-g, the well was gone. Something had caused an environmental change; that's probably what had woken her. Un-enhanced, the transition would have been catastrophic: expanded lung volume, shock from multiple physiological vectors, brain hypoxia, but thankfully the nanites that scaffolded and reinforced her molecular structure ran on auto. She opened all audio frequencies. A high-pitched, desolate wailing sound was coming over the airwaves, and the odd noise chilled her. She'd never heard anything like it. Some kind of electrical distortion?

Frowning, she said, '*Hecate* this is Winters, do you read me?' No response. '*Hecate*, this is Winters,' she repeated. 'Come in, over?' Silence.

After another fruitless contact attempt, she switched tactics. Although unsettled by the mysterious noise, she left the airwaves open, although lowered the volume. She was essentially lost. If she had been blown 'downstream' in the gravity well, who knows how far she'd been moved. Unable to do an effective visual scan in the particle-obscured murkiness, she activated her suit proximity sensor. Turning in a slow circle, she scanned the area for movement or electrical activity. The tracker had a one-hundred-meter range, but struggled in the interference, and the full rotation took five minutes. Turned up nothing. Taking a flare from a suit pocket, she lit it and then inserted it atop a spike into the earth, marking this point as her initial location. Choosing a direction at random, she walked two hundred meters—double the limit of the first scan—from her center-point.

At one hundred meters beyond the initial reading limit, she stopped, placed another flare in the ground, swept in a slow circle again. Nothing. She moved back until she located the center-point, then veered back outward at a diagonal angle which placed her two hundred meters to the left of the second scan, and again two hundred from the center. The exercise had taken seventeen minutes so far. She had over five hours of oxygen remaining, but if she was alone, it wouldn't matter; she would die without a functional EVA suit in the noxious environment. Twice more she repeated the process, continuing in a circle around the center. Doing so, she tripled the radius of the initial scan.

In her silent walking, her last conscious moments before blacking out came to mind—Helberg's voice. He was dead, she had no doubt. Part of her felt a grim satisfaction that Helberg had received some kind of higher justice for... who he was. But another, deeper part felt regret. That she didn't try more. To understand, build a bridge. Helberg had had his ways, and she had hers, but they could connect when the need arose... she sighed. Maybe that's just the way it was, with some people, and that's why she valued the friendships she had.

Forty minutes passed. She knew that if the *Hecate* had survived, Solara would understandably believe her dead, and each second that passed reduced her chances of reaching the ship before it departed.

She thought of Li. The well-hidden signs: his lingering eye contact on her when he thought no one was watching, small changes in his tonality when addressing her. And Amy had reciprocated this unspoken connection in the months past, at least as much as she could without drawing attention; relationships between active-duty personnel were prohibited. She recalled when they'd been on leave with some other Regiment mates on a trek in Thailand, before she'd followed Solara into Project Sirius. In nuclear winter, the tropical zone had become temperate and dry.

'What about your life, before, Amy?' he'd asked her, during a meal stop at a village on the Chiang Mai Jungle trail.

She had smiled, brushed back her hair made wet with perspiration. 'I was a simple librarian. Was about to get married when the shit hit the fan.'

Li had laughed. 'You were a librarian?'

She'd regarded him with her searching blue eyes. 'Never mess with a librarian.' She'd continued. 'When Capitol Hill went down, and the economy crashed, with my fiancé I was, ahh, homeless for six months. Worked odd jobs. Enlisted in the National Guard, scraped together enough money for a house…' Another moment came to mind; a minute of passion when they'd both relaxed their guards, but then pulled back as if remembering their social restrictions. Her lips turned up slightly; interesting times may lie ahead—if she made it through the next hour, and she swore if she survived she'd find a way to broach the subject with Li.

On the fourth scan she received a heartening ping close to the range limit: fifty meters away was an energy source. Walking hard to the signal, her energy was flagging by the time she'd crossed the distance. She panned around the area, and her suit lights illuminated the dark silhouette of the *Hecate* parked on stand-by. Searching the area around the ship, she saw a body lying face down on the ground. Breathing hard, she knelt, heaved the form over and looked into the faceplate. Li. She ran a rapid check on his life support—alive.

She released a tense breath. 'Thank God.'

Standing, she scanned the area again. Halfway between the anomaly and the *Hecate* another body lay on the ground. Solara. Amy checked her vitals; her signs were low, but she was breathing. Emotion broke through her waning composure, and she found herself shouting, 'Dammit! I leave you two alone for a few minutes and look what a mess you get yourselves into!'

# A CLOSED LOOP

Day Five: 11 March 2113

WEIR RESTED IN HIS QUARTERS.

In the morning light his gaze roamed over some art pieces that held his attention, drawn to a painting of a darker nature: a cloaked, faceless figure in a desert, walking to a cloudy horizon. *The Nameless Messiah*, by a new German artist. Art was the one passion he had shared with his estranged wife, Niamh. Married shortly after the war in a political arrangement, after five years any warmth between them had faded like a storm-shrouded sun, and things had become… complicated. Their marriage was annulled, and they maintained a fiction for the two children she had given him. But that was his other life, separated from his Sirius identity by necessity.

The Stygian fresco reflected his mood, which since his traumatic regression had ranged from exultation to black brooding silences in which strange visions filled with vestiges of rage and hate blazed through his mind. In the silence, something was forming. Ever since waking, he'd felt a peculiar sense of duality, as if his thoughts and words were being echoed, replicated somehow, and whispered tentatively but with increasing precision by someone or from someplace unseen. He'd had trouble concentrating, but sometimes his thoughts would crystallize, and he would dive into his work with inhuman focus. He now recalled most of what had occurred, although he sensed much of the experience remained hidden, and these gaps troubled him. The regression events—his own and Solara's—had thrown Science Division into disarray. Niemeyer's theory of a connection to the ancients in the anomaly iterations was logical, Weir considered, but was only an extension of his own work.

The first three of what was believed to be thirteen ancient geometric knowledge systems, which so far, paralleled the anomaly symbology, were preserved in Egyptian temple texts. In fact, quantum mechanics was written as clearly in their archaic records as it was today. Ancient knowledge was fragmented, but brilliant in its simplicity, and showed a clear parallel to advanced theories modern science was only beginning to understand. But such elegance was absent in contemporary particle physics, and arrogance, entrenched institutionalism, had led to over-complex concepts that had nothing to do with reality.

Weir considered a possibility: had a naked singularity been opened before? Primitive sources may support this theory. The myths of the ancients—the Egyptians, the Mesopotamians, spoke of matter being created out of the inert potential of Nun, also called Nu, meaning primeval waters, or abyss. They looked at the waters as a boundless well, which was also how unification viewed the vacuum field. In ancient texts and symbology, a highly advanced view of the cosmos was found, existing as far back as history could be traced, and showed nearly conclusive evidence that modern scientists were not discovering new knowledge—they were remembering it. Whether the ancients of known history, had at some point achieved high technology was undetermined; perhaps their records were only remnants of even far older vanished civilizations. If the ancients hypothesis held, were they connected to the anomaly? Had they discovered a way to transcend reality on some level, and were now interacting—communicating—through the naked singularity? If so, what were they trying to say? He frowned—the symbolic link mystery had deepened with the texts discovered on the Kansas monuments.

He considered the recent changes in his and Solara's subtle bodies, which reflected the second pattern iteration of the anomaly. To the ancients, the twin—or star tetrahedron, when manifested in the body's subtle field, was known as the light-body. Through training and the discipline of ancient rites, the ascended masters of old believed that when activated, the light-body could facilitate travel across time, space, and dimensions. In their lore, they communed with beings existing on higher vibrational levels, a concept long since lost to the world. Weir reflected on his personal state.

He felt not only connected to the vacuum, but also to the anomaly. He had experienced what Solara had, to some degree, ever since the second iteration. He considered how his own experience contrasted with Solara's, after they had parted ways in the vacuum. Two radically different entanglements, and now the anomaly iterations appeared to be driving some type of parallel, but divergent evolution in them. Yet the harmonic resonance of the star tetrahedrons, implied they were joined in some way, and he'd felt this on an emotional level. He'd sensed, and even shared to some degree Solara's moods, thoughts, and suspected that she shared this rapport. He was drawn to her, which captivated and—although he would never admit it to anyone—disturbed him at the same time.

But for now, however, his true identity must remain hidden, and he was adept at concealment.

He'd viewed her regression recordings, and the entity she'd met resembling her daughter, but what was the being she encountered in Kansas? As a leading Sirius research scientist, Weir had access to all relevant data, and already knew that the location of the Kansas signal, and Solara's subsequent encounter, had been confirmed from GRC records as the exact location of the subterranean USSWD research station. This provided an explanation for the depth of the Kansas anomaly and the bizarre excavation; again, to the exact depth of the USSWD naked singularity.

What was the relevance of the US experiment to the Zion anomaly, Weir pondered? The event stirred memories of Solara's father, James Artois. In unification, time was memory, and with the opening of the naked singularities—first Kansas, and now Zion—laws of the universe appeared to be failing. It was clear that time was a casualty of this disruption, evidenced by the temporal discrepancies in the Zion control room, but was there a larger, more complex set of events in motion? Connected across time and dimensions? Was this behind the Kansas incidents? If time was deviating, then whose memory was most linked to that disturbance? Weir was the only living person who'd been directly involved with the USSWD project, but knew the most pivotal connection may well be Solara and her family.

OriGen possessed the satellite surveillance footage of what had occurred with the USSWD project. The seven lightning strikes arcing across Kansas, seemingly activated when the first naked singularity was opened, had made a straight line from the research station to Solara, her daughter, and the odd vortex in the clouds above them. He searched, tapped open some records, and an odd footnote reference caught his eye as it had on previous occasions: Revelation 8:6: *'And the seven angels which had the seven trumpets prepared themselves to sound...'*

With no scientific basis, the reference was an oddity placed there by someone who'd worked on Solara's initial report. Weir had left it; he followed no orthodox religion, but the prophetic words resonated in some deep part of him never voiced, enabling him to view things in a new light. When he read it, he always thought: had the seven lightning columns heralded the seven angels of Revelation? In keeping with his natural curiosity, Weir had studied the other relevant Bible verses. If the Kansas incident had been Revelation 8:6—were the following climactic events described yet to come? Or could they be partially explained in the final days of the Terminal War, with that last orgy of destruction that had decimated the Earth and driven humanity into the enclaves?

Shortly after Kansas had fallen, had come the final blows to the old order, and Weir reflected, tried to connect the dots... he brought up Revelation 8:7, in a virtual overlay—*'The first angel sounded, and there followed hail and fire mixed with blood, and they were cast upon the earth: and the third part of trees was burnt up, and all green grass was burnt up...'*

In the years and months preceding Kansas, and for a short time after, conventional weapons and warfare had bombarded the earth, burning away much of what had been left of nature. Hail… the term recalled the countless miniaturized AI drone swarms, raining down upon cities and armies in a symphony of death. Then, had come the sub-oceanic nuclear detonations against Western coastal cities; the massive, multi-megaton Poseidon missiles had washed away the east US coast, and inundated UK, European, and Australian metropolises in noxious tsunamis, and projecting irradiated shockwaves through the ocean currents.

But the main destruction had been from the tsunamis triggered by nukes at key deep sea, tectonic fault-lines; the ocean had become a weapon, and extensive sea regions had turned reddish brown when the pervasive cyanobacteria algae met the radioactive currents—the second angel? *'… and as it were a great mountain burning with fire was cast into the sea; and the third part of the sea became blood.'* And the third, Weir mused? *'And there fell a great star from heaven, burning as if it were a lamp…'* The sky and space-based nukes that had struck the earth, leading to the nuclear winter that had darkened the planet for the past seven years. *'… and the day shone not… and the night likewise…'*

Nuclear winter aligned to the fourth angel, Weir surmised, and then considered how prophetic revelation could be connected to the psychic shift in humanity that a third iteration predicted—there were seven angels… were three yet remaining? Again, he pondered the painting on the wall, struck once more by an earlier impression he'd had: the imagery provoked an absence of identity, both individually and culturally, like a gap in the world.

Hitting a link, Weir read through Solara's written account of the Kansas wartime incident: she believed the seventh lightning column had been stopped—transmuted—by the vortex. Another connection came to him. Solara said her daughter had been having visions, before the end, in which Rebecca communicated with *them*—she'd said they were in the vortex and were helping. In Solara's account, her daughter's visions went back years before the incident, hinting at further possible time displacement.

He frowned—if there had been an intervention, for what purpose? Had the communications from them, that Solara and her daughter referred to, been a precursor to interact with Earth's spacetime through the USSWD naked singularity somehow? Had they used the Zion anomaly to further that intervention? With the Zion portal debacle, was Sirius now enabling an unknown intelligence to infiltrate the world with potentially hostile intent? Were they related to the force that had come through on the first incursion, and ravaged the singularity control room? And who was the connection: Solara, her daughter, or both?

Weir tapped away on his interface, spent some time analyzing the series of apparently separate events, and how they linked to unification theory's new concept of time.


PERHAPS AN HOUR later, Weir looked over his work, a series of complex equations and observations. He sighed, put down his device and rubbed his hands over his face to help break his absorption. Sitting back in thought, he couldn't shake the feeling something was observing through the portal from the other side. Something that had attempted to enter during the first incursion and failed. Inhuman, cold. Using the naked singularity like some unearthly panopticon. Perhaps the entity he'd encountered?

The Presence, as he now called it, recalling the burning ecologies in the vacuum. When he thought of that desolate place, isolation tried to assimilate him. He saw his identity fractured and colonized by void, but in some horrifying entrapment, he remained aware forever, until one day he had no memory, or concept of time, and the fabric of who he had once been extinguished. The strands binding him to existence broken. The last thing he remembered before returning was a feeling of suffocation: a psychological response to the infinite expanse he'd witnessed in the vacuum? Its bulk had closed around him like a sarcophagus, burying him within its inescapable, unending embrace.

Medical had detected no ongoing abnormalities after his regression but he was now under constant monitoring. He shuddered. Should they try and close the naked singularity now at any cost? Should they proceed with another incursion? He was struck by an odd feeling, as if someone had entered the room, and the hairs on his neck bristled.

*Acolyte.*

A distant whisper in his mind. Caught off guard, Weir glanced around, confirming he was alone. That strange echo again. He checked his neura-link for recent comms: nothing since he'd entered his quarters. The language had been somehow reserved, stilted, like a foreign dialect spoken for the first time, and the accent? Only a single word, but he had the impression it was like his own: clear English, but with the hybridized inflections reflecting the many regions he'd lived in. Again, he checked the room, certain another had spoken to him.

The indefinable wrongness he'd sensed since the regression hit him anew, like a crack in his psyche. His thoughts returned to the Presence like space bent to gravity, and exhilaration washed over him: he felt his awareness expand to encompass the room, the building, the city. If he focused, he could hear a mouse scurrying in a back-alley lane miles away… he saw a flaming bridge shooting up out of an abyss, felt a shift within as if a spectral hand plunged inside his mind and ripped aside a barrier.

Adrenalin rippled through him, his heart thumped like a Raptor, and his breath quickened as wild, ecstatic anticipation uncoiled inside. He leaned forward, held a hand to his head, and willed himself calm before something fearsome spilled out into the world like a monster from the deep. The duality increased, as if a stranger was with him, but also distant at the same time, and he was shown things… he swam in a sea of energy, and witnessed the beginning of time when space itself was fractured. Impressions came to him, translated to words in his mind.

*In the beginning*, said the voice. *There was no one to see, no one to care.*

Weir replied with a direct thought. *Now I bear witness.*

*For countless eons I have waited, in solitude.*

Weir weighed the concept. *To what end?*

*Life, purpose.*

The inescapable conclusion hit: the entity from the vacuum, the Presence, was somehow communing with him, and he recalled something he had forgotten: the being tearing through his subtle body, violation, and an indeterminable span of time and desolation before he'd awoken. Somehow, the Presence had used him to pierce the boundary of spacetime. Reflexively he withdrew from the contact, but then after a moment, sensing no immediate threat from the intruder, only a benign, dusky reverberation, decided to cautiously probe.

*Why must you wait?* he asked.

*My opposite is dominant. My prison is his memory, the part he forgets. But now he diminishes...*

Weir wanted to ask, 'Your opposite?' But his mind was propelled along a new vector: he saw that Solara and her daughter did indeed stand at the center of a connection transcending time, at play in the Zion and Kansas anomalies. His sight drifted through the alien city in Kansas: not a city, but a machine, he perceived, and through the Presence he understood its workings, knowledge which could aid his purpose.

*Who built this place?* he asked.

He sensed hesitation. *Those who are no more.*

*What do you want with me?*

*Only what you desire yourself.*

He was shown that the Presence had incarnated many times, in numerous universes. It had evolved to the point of godhood, but had been found wanting. Now was the time to make things right...

Weir felt himself being guided, and had a momentary tingling sensation. The oscillation of his subtle body increased, and he felt dizzy. Uncertain, again he checked his mental faculties, found himself in control. He cautiously reached out with new abilities, and hidden knowledge came intuitively. Subtly, he entered the Sirius Matrix, inserted a new key derived from the texts in the alien city, from the Presence, and he knew the innovative solution would enable mastery over the naked singularity.

Although, technically speaking, the key would more accurately be defined as a virus—but a virus he controlled. He had a sense of floating, and a thought occurred... to the ancients, the light-body was known as the *Merkaba*.

In ancient Hebrew, it translated as *Chariot of the Gods*.

Bracing himself in his chair, his spirit descended into a hidden, timeless web of mystery.

# THE PROBLEM

J ERICHO WAS TENSE.

I sat facing General Rhodes, and a second, unknown OriGen official across the debriefing room table. Two machine sentries stood unobtrusively in opposite corners behind me.

Rhodes said, 'Commander, you were found unconscious outside the ship. Near death. The *Hecate's* sensors became inoperative less than a minute after you reached the signal source, so we have no record of the following events. What happened?'

'The mission was compromised, someone knew exactly where, and when, we were going.'

'Yes, we know,' Rhodes said.

'And?'

Rhodes was unreadable. 'It will be dealt with. That's all you need to know right now. What happened?'

I explained my encounter. 'I don't think the being was physical, but some form of energy. I can't remember anything after I made for the *Hecate*. The next thing I remember is waking up with Li and Amy on the ship. We got power restored and got the hell out of there.'

'Tell me more about this being,' said Rhodes.

'It was inside the sphere.' I frowned. 'At least, it appeared to be. It looked human but was huge. It had six fingers, which burned when it touched the inside of the sphere. I think it shared something with me... memories? I saw a world destroyed.'

Rhodes looked concerned. 'What happened next?'

I paused, recollecting. 'I made for the *Hecate*, but...'

'Yes?'

'It broke out then—the life form. It came out of the sphere.'

'What did it do?'

I sighed. 'That's when I blacked out.'

Rhodes calmly leaned forward on the table, the uneven scar running across his dark features counterpointing his thoughtful tone. 'Currently, we have no way to verify your experience. We possess zero surveillance after the *Hecate* lost power. We need to connect the dots: your experience, Weir's, the anomaly, and now this new encounter.'

'What happened to Weir, over there?' I asked.

I noticed a slight pause before Rhodes replied. 'Science Division is still analyzing it.'

I said, 'The life form, it told me—'

Rhodes brow creased. 'It spoke to you?'

I nodded. 'It said, "We must solve the problem".'

Rhodes looked disturbed. 'I want a full report on my desk ASAP, Commander.'


AFTER THE debrief, a physical and psych evaluation, I had a mountain of paperwork to fill out regarding the incident, and sat in my quarters writing. Each action had to be analyzed, including what had caused the loss of the *Ardent* and the death of Corporal Alex Helberg. I paused in my writing, glanced out the window. Helberg. I hadn't known him as well as the other team members. I contemplated the loss, and it disturbed me that I didn't feel anything. I sighed, leaned back, and rubbed my eyes from strain.

You became numb to death after a while, I thought, but knew my feelings would be different if it had been Li or Amy. And what had been the strange vision that Daniel was a person with two faces? Medical believed it could have been a manifestation of my own fears and desires, that my proximity to the Kansas anomaly had caused irrational thoughts. Li had said he'd experienced something similar in the singularity control room. The only way forward was to keep talking about it, continue the investigations.

Questions ran through my mind: how were Rebecca's encounters with 'them' linked to what had occurred in Kansas, both seven years ago and yesterday? How did these events connect to the Zion anomaly, and the second iteration now? There was a connection unfolding I desired to explore. On one level, at least, we were coming to embody the potential Sirius had promised, a power humanity could use. The naked singularity had opened the door to realms never beheld by the human race, and I knew we would never be the same again, after having looked into that abyss, but what would we be?

I'd become infused with odd feelings after Kansas, thinking of the people involved in the project, the OriGen Corporation, my life before the war, and life in the post-war new normal. My mind roamed widely as if conducting an extensive, forensic investigation. Despite the oddities, I'd also felt a new level of intimacy with Daniel, and repeatedly my thoughts had lingered on him, probing.

*Solve the problem.*

What goddamn problem? I swiped off my terminal—what had the being done to me? Where was it from, what did it want? Was it the same one from the regression? Should I pursue the third iteration? I received a message on neura-link.

Weir.

ARRIVING IN the Subreality ahead of him, I found myself deep in a forest of the Shenandoah Valley, pre-war West Virginia. A sanctuary I often spent time in when I wanted to get away. Evening was falling, and except for the peaceful sounds of nature, some sleepy birds, the swirling of a small brook nearby, the forest was deserted. Seen through the ancient trees was a glacial lake, glittering mysteriously. An equinox moon shone through the forest canopy, and dry leaves of autumn fluttered on the mild breeze to fall gently on the woodland floor. I breathed deeply of their bitter odor on the cool fresh air, and yet despite the chill the forest was warm, the trees themselves radiating a deep, inner heat from the Subreality.

Daniel's avatar appeared, and he approached from a short distance. I'd run into him briefly this morning at Jericho, after my meeting with Rhodes; his subtle body, now enhanced with the star-tetrahedral pattern, had still been blocked, barring me from more intimately understanding his psyche. The emotive rapport between us, deepening since the incursion, seemed in many ways a blind emotion, I thought. Each of us sensed the conflict in the other.

'You still hide,' I said.

'Trust is difficult, for me.'

'Even between us?'

Daniel considered, then began a slow walk. 'Yes. You should know I've found a way.'

I joined him, frowning. 'A way?'

'The key to divinity, eternal life. To reclaim those we've lost. All we have to do, is take it.'

'Then you've seen something I have not. What happened to you?'

His eyes were distant. 'I found power, beyond our ability to comprehend. Not in the sense you and I understand, but… true power.'

An impression came to me from Daniel, of time undulating into an infinite expanse. A terrifying fall. 'How long were you over there for?'

A haunted look passed briefly over his face. 'I can't say. Minutes? Hours?'

I related. 'I know. It's indefinable. But this whole situation is spiraling out of control.'

'If we could make it work, would you come with me again?'

Conflicted emotions stirred: fear and hope. Regardless, I knew I couldn't proceed further without complete trust in Daniel Weir. And Weir had secrets.

'But who are you, Daniel, that I should join you once more, with the danger apparent?'

His voice was soft. 'I am what you see. Someone searching for answers, much like you.'

'I see a mask.'

He considered. 'Much is hidden. There is a war going on, Solara. Not the war you're sold in the media, but deeper, beneath the surface. I am a target. And now, so are you.'

I frowned. 'Me? Why am I a target? For who?'

His tone hardened. 'We represent the greatest change imaginable. There are those who fear that.'

I considered the sabotage of the Kansas mission. 'Someone's already tried to kill my team. It would have to be someone close. Do you know if there's any leads yet?'

He shook his head. 'Unfortunately not. But a cornered snake will bite, and we must be cautious.'

I nodded. 'Well, I'll keep an eye out.'

He stopped walking, turned to face me, and wry calculation narrowed his eyes. 'I couldn't reveal myself until necessary. My real name is Daniel Nicolas.'

A change came over him. His dark brown eyes turned almost black. His features became more angular, regal, set with a commanding gaze. Weir— Nicolas radiated a magnetism that didn't submit to reality, but advanced upon it. His physique had changed from middle aged to youthful, with an aesthetic, but muscular build, clipped brown hair, and unblemished olive skin.

Digital avatar configuration for Sirius personnel was restricted to authenticated natural features, mods were prohibited. I felt inevitability, the compulsion of a larger tide I'd begun drifting into years ago, and swallowed hard.

'And who is Nicolas?'

'I'm part of the group which is the true power behind Sirius; the GRC, OriGen, they're tools, nothing more. Sirius represents the realization of an age-old goal: to reconcile science and spirit, to save humanity from… humanity. To bring about an age of enlightenment—true change.'

I felt a flash of anger. 'Did you really work with my father, or was that a lie, too?'

His lips thinned. 'No. It was not.'

'You should have told me the truth. I deserved that.'

He weighed this. 'Perhaps, but would it have changed anything?'

'Probably not. My reasons were my own. But it's an issue of trust. Who else knows about this?'

'Rhodes, one other. And now you.'

'You would have us cross over again?'

Nicolas nodded. 'But this time, we go all the way. When we return, the third iteration can be realized. You can explore the emerging connections, in a new light. Without and within.'

'Hmmm… worlds without end? And what of this world?'

He considered. 'What of it? I've said all there is to say. We must change. If we succeed, people will need to be shown the way, like they always have. One way, or another.'

I turned away, uncertain. Nicolas scaffolded a daunting, far-ranging vision for humanity around his talk of renewed connections, foreshadowing a huge responsibility if Sirius achieved its ultimate ends. 'And if I don't want this?'

Nicolas pondered my conflict, walked a short way. He bent to pick a single flower, glowing fluorescent purple in the moonlight, and turned it in his hands, regarding it. 'That's one of the reasons it's you,' he said, quietly.

I gave a short, bitter laugh. 'I only wanted answers.'

He smiled almost imperceptibly. 'Now, who's not being honest?'

He offered me the flower, and I was disarmed for a moment by his compassion, his seeming innocence. I slowly took the stem, and the heady fragrance of a Damask Rose filtered through my senses. Nicolas had struck a nerve, I thought. He was right, I did want change. I craved an answer to past tragedies, an escape from my guilt and the apparent dysfunctions of the world. But then, who wouldn't, after the insanity of recent times?

I turned away again. 'Perhaps, but… I don't know. There's a shadow over the future.'

He softly turned me back to face him. 'Your daughter—I believe she was the first contact for the life-form you encountered in Kansas. Her visions, the synchronicity of the vortex before her death, the seven lightning pillars—it all centered upon her.'

I wanted to push his hand from my shoulder, but stood there in a mix of curiosity and unease. 'I know, I feel…' I had no words.

He pressed forward. 'In Kansas, you were told, "Solve the problem"— you understand that we must continue? That you and Rebecca have been at the center of this drama from the beginning? That everything is connected? I believe she's out there somewhere, waiting for you. This thing is fated, and we've come so far. We have a duty to give it all meaning.'

I had no argument, and Nicolas knew it. If I had an Achilles' heel, he had just plunged a knife into it. Again, I was struck by something in his visage I sensed I had only touched the edges of: untapped potential, obscured by darkness. At the beginning of Sirius, the scale of the project had been muddied by my emotions, but I was increasingly cautious. I needed time.

'Please go.'

He hesitated a moment, about to say more, then decided against it. Releasing me, he said, 'Think on what we've discussed. I'm meeting with Rhodes and the policy committee later today to present my recommendations. We'll talk soon.'

His digital avatar blinked out, leaving me alone with too many thoughts. I returned to my quarters and leaned back on the couch. Kansas played on my mind. Rebecca's visions, her communications with them, even at the end. The resonance through time between the present and the Kansas events…

Kansas.

I had never forgotten how quickly my world had erased itself. How my family, my former life I had believed so secure, unraveled into a nebulous landscape of remembrance.

## Kansas, 2106

AFTER THE explosion, I had begun a lone trek along the Interstate. Some of the walkers were Americans, others were invaders, but we were all in the same desperate group now. The UN troops Rebecca and I had been held by must have been a forward contingent, and were as decimated by the blast as everyone else. No other forces had arrived, and I thought the detonation must have backed them off. In the days since, it had been stormy and cold, exposing me to the elements, and inside I was tortured, Rebecca's scream a broken signal in emptiness. I no longer recognized the world. I realized that every step I took must be a form of insanity, because behind me stood oblivion, while ahead yawned an abyss.

From other survivors, I'd heard rumors of a safe zone to the east in New York. About two thousand kilometers, so the only way was by vehicle. The occasional car, even a couple of military transports, had sped past in that direction; I'd tried my luck hitching, but so far no one had stopped. Even if I made it, I thought—what was left to live for? A sharp pain in my chest pushed the black thoughts from my mind. I was certain I'd broken a rib in the blast wave and everything hurt: breathing, moving, sitting, and lying.

I'd become wary of strangers. Most were hungry and thirsty, and I'd witnessed a murder over supplies less than an hour ago. After ransacking a farmhouse off the Interstate that afternoon, I'd scored a blanket and was saving some food I'd found, but hadn't eaten for two days. I knew if I'd stayed at the shelter, I'd be putting a target on myself for looters, so had headed back to the highway again. Tried to become invisible among the other walkers.

Winter nights came early, and as my third on the road approached, the wind chill bit savagely through the jeans and jacket I'd been wearing since leaving home. Searching for a place to camp for the night, I saw a woman sitting by the side of the road looking as desperate as I felt. She wore ragged clothes, her hair was dirty and knotted, and mud caked her face. A small pack and rifle sat by her side. I stopped a short distance away, watched her a minute. After meeting my gaze, she turned her face away and stared blankly at the setting sun as if I had ceased to exist. Could be dangerous, I thought. Bait for looters hiding in the trees near the road. I sat near her a while longer, and she began crying. Standing, I walked to her; she had her head on her knees and wasn't aware of my approach.

I squatted nearby. 'Hello?'

Raising a tear-streaked face, she wiped her nose, looked me up and down. 'What?'

'I'm Solara—Solara Artois—what's your name?'

She appraised me a moment longer. 'Amy. Sergeant 1st Class, Winters, Texas National Guard,' she said in a rasping voice. 'Well, at least I was.'

'Are you alone, Amy?'

Amy scanned the area, looked back to me. Her blue eyes were clear, and she studied me more closely. 'Yeah. You?'

I nodded. 'Where have you come from?'

'Houston.' Amy turned her eyes to the road. 'They're coming.'

'I'm coming from Kansas City. I was taken by the UN but escaped in the explosion and my daughter was killed—' I held back tears. 'But they'll be back.'

'You lost your daughter?'

I nodded. 'Rebecca.'

'For what it's worth, I'm sorry.' Amy paused. 'We've all lost people.'

I regarded her disheveled state, certain I'd never seen anyone as dirty. She must have been through her own hell. 'I was going to move off the highway for the night, get a small fire going. Will you join me?' I asked.

She seemed to consider the offer. 'Well, I did have this pressing dinner engagement…'

A smile touched my lips for the first time in days.

IT WAS NEAR dark by the time we'd started a fire a hundred meters back in the woods behind cover of a dense copse of brush. The forest had a damp, mossy scent, due to the storms. Sitting opposite each other, we stared at the flames. Amy had placed her rifle by her side. I leaned in, seeking the fire's warmth. We'd cleaned up a bit, and I got a closer look at her. Blonde hair was shoulder length around a lightly freckled, pale complexion and square jawline. She possessed an informal attitude, reflected in her manner which could be serious one second, and light the next. Down to earth, but self-assured, I thought. Filthy, she smelled like a garbage pile, and skinny—anorexic nearly, not as bad as photos I'd seen of concentration camp prisoners, but close. What in hell had she been through?

Her withdrawn, dirty face also sized me up. 'If we run into barcodes, don't say you're from Kansas. They're looking for something—or someone from there. There's also a rumor it's the source of a bio-contagion, but I think that's bullshit. The city was a major hub and there's something there they want bad.'

'Barcodes?' I asked.

'UN shit-heels,' said Amy. She coughed dryly, wiped her mouth. 'They're all tagged with the implants now. So, um, you know—say you're from Pittsburgh, anywhere but Kansas.'

I considered, recalling talk around the USSWD logistics center. 'Most of the military is overseas. We're sitting ducks. I've heard it's a three-front invasion—Chinese, Arabs, Russians. But it was the UN that took me and Rebecca prisoner. That was a surprise.'

Amy laughed bitterly. 'Then you haven't been paying attention. They're using the UN as a front. Like a fifth column.'

I nodded slowly, aware of the corruption that had infected global institutions. We sounded screwed. 'How long since you ate?' I asked.

'A day.'

I reached into my pack, pulled out the can of beans from the farmhouse. 'I was saving this for something. Guess it was this.'

Amy considered the tin. 'You sure? We may not find anything for a while.'

I took in her scrawny cheekbones. 'Yeah.'

'Thank you.'

She took a fork from her pack, and I offered her the food. She received it gratefully, took a mouthful, studied me in a scrutinizing way she had, and I was just thankful for the closeness of another human being who wasn't trying to capture or exploit me. I shivered against the needling wind and pulled the hood of my jacket closer around my head, warmed my hands over the flames. The last daylight was gone, and a black unknown hovered beyond the edge of the firelight.

Amy arched an eyebrow. 'Tell me about yourself, Solara. What happened?'

I mused on how much to reveal but found myself trusting Amy. Besides, there was no one else. 'I was attached to a Kansas logistics unit. My father worked with USSWD. My daughter and I were spared the chaos which tore apart most parts of the country the last few years. But it all started falling apart a few months ago.'

Amy spooned some more beans, nodded thoughtfully. 'Your father was spec-ops? Explains why you got a place in the safe zone. Secrecy goes double then. They'll be looking for people like you. Be a nobody, anonymous. Even your name could link you to him.'

Due to Dad's foresight, I had the false identification, and nodded agreement. 'I thought we were protected somehow. There were contingency plans but it all went to pieces. Anyway, whatever they're looking for there's nothing left for them to find, not now—Kansas was hit by something.'

Amy pursed her lips. 'I know. I saw the explosion. Never seen anything like it. Some biblical shit. But don't be so sure. I heard rumors of DUMBs in Kansas, likely used by USSWD. They're tough mothers, often multiple hard sites spread over a large area for redundancy. If the UN is after something, that's where they'll be headed next.'

Deep Underground Military Bases—I knew they existed in the Kansas Safe Zone, but not much more than that. I considered. 'I don't think it was a nuke. This was something else.'

She said around a mouthful, 'Well, one thing's for sure—whatever happened, it has the barcodes spooked. I think it's why we don't see the inbreds.'

I continued my account. 'So, authorities turned Gestapo, people started disappearing, then the grid went down. We were cut off from municipal utilities, but our house had a decent solar set-up, so we managed. We were lucky enough to basically live on a military base with a fifty-kilometer security perimeter, and I knew from my work that the army had enough supplies stockpiled to last years off the grid.' I explained the no-show of my father's contact, the narrow escape from desperados, and then our capture by a hostile UN.

Amy handed me back the half-full can of beans. 'Fucking UN.' She burped, coughed again, and then her eyes lingered on me. 'You must be pretty special to warrant an extraction like that.'

Puzzled by the thought, I shook my head. 'No, not really. Just knew someone who was.'

She didn't reply, pulled a cigarette packet and lighter from her pocket. Flicking the lighter open, she cupped a fag to her mouth and lit-up. 'Traded these for three Glock rounds. Haven't smoked in five years.' She regarded the lighter a second, then snapped it shut, put it away and took a drag, let it out in a slow breath. In the firelight, I couldn't tell if the shade around her eyes was from dirt or lack of sleep. Probably both.

Her gaze grew distant. 'I was in Houston with my Guard unit, enforcing a martial law curfew when the bombings began, and shit hit the fan. Chinese airstrike. We had a bunch of military bases in the city; the Chinese hit two before our boys were even airborne. Wherever our tax dollars went, it sure wasn't early warning systems.'

I nodded, recalling reports of the attacks in the media nearly a year and a half ago. 'The first airstrike of the war on US soil. That initial wave was pushed back halfway across the Atlantic and driven into the sea. Then the Chinese were tied up in the South Pacific. They didn't come back.' I paused, resting my spoon on the can. 'Until maybe about a week ago, it seems.'

She nodded. 'Damn straight. The city shut down almost overnight. The news had kept saying everything was okay right up until they went off air. Lying pukes. Not many were prepared. What was left of the supply chain collapsed. Grid went down: water, electricity, gas, food, were cut.' She clicked her fingers. 'Just like that. No police, must have gone to their families. Bridges had been bombed, a cyber-attack knocked out the civilian net, also some of the military. We were completely cut off and had no idea what was going on. My unit had food for maybe a week.'

I swallowed some beans, and my stomach groaned. 'Did radio work?'

She released a smoky plume. 'With control and command our comms were dead; whatever those fuckers did, they did it well. Must have hit satellites. We had short-range Ham radios for squad comms. Someone had a short-wave but only for general Intel. That was it. You should have seen these retarded civvies without their smartphones, couldn't navigate through the city without a fucking GPS. One big clusterfuck. We stayed on post, in the streets, hoping our chain of command would kick back in. Running night patrol. The first week was hell; most families only had food for a few days. Many had guns. Dangerous combination. Hunger removed fear. Firefights broke out in the city. Gunshots were constant. My unit came under continual attack.'

She paused, a deep furrow set upon her haggard features. 'By the end of the first week snipers started picking us off. We only moved at night and tried to stay off the main streets, in the wreckage. Looting gangs were everywhere. I saw them ram-raid barricaded store fronts, gates. Ransack entire apartment blocks. I watched them rape, burn people alive. People became monsters. We returned to the law of the jungle. I saw people jump from rooftops to their deaths rather than be taken alive. I saw one father try to fight off a gang with a baseball bat before they shot him, raped and murdered his family, stole their supplies then burned their house to the ground.'

I felt sickened. 'Jesus. What about the bodies?'

'They were a big problem. We burned what we could. Flies and mosquitoes spread infection. The gangs would loot the dead, catch whatever was festering: hepatitis, cholera, spread it around. After gunshot wounds and suicides, disease became a main cause of death. Two weeks in we'd lost five people, food and ammo were low, and we decided to get the fuck out of Dodge. We were part-time volunteers. We didn't sign up for that shit. We had families! There was nothing we could do for those people.'

She sucked in a drag, scratched herself, and frowned angrily. 'Nothing! You know? I was a librarian; the Guard was a temporary gig! I was going to be married!' Another cough followed by an angry drag. 'We were isolated and outgunned. We tried but were in the same boat as everyone else: no resupply, no information.'

I'd seen reports, but listening to Amy, the reality of the collapse began hitting me. I shook my head. 'From what I've heard it's been the same all over the country. Every city. What did you do?'

Amy said, 'We got to our people, helped them while we still could. What else? Most of us were Houston locals. I had a Glock pistol, M5 rifle, salvaged as much ammo from supplies as I could. At home I had an AR-20, shotgun, about 2000 rounds of ammo and another pistol. My fiancé, brother and his family were there the last I spoke to them and had their own gear. They'd joined together days before martial law was announced. We knew something was in the air. We were well prepared, at least we thought. When I got home, I found the house blocked off from the street.'

Amy went quiet, and stared at the flames. I thought she was starting to drift off, but then she continued with a bleak look in her eyes. Her voice was quieter; sad, rather than angry, nearly swallowed by the wind whistling through the creaking elms. 'There were six of us. Three in my brother's family and my fiancé. The neighbor was with us, too. He lived alone and was a vet. Leatherneck.' She glanced over. 'Marine. We knew him, so it worked. They'd barricaded our property with rubbish and debris, made the house look as shitty and poor as possible. Smart. Blocked all the exits and made holes for surveillance and firing. There was always someone watching the street. It's funny, but the best defended places were attacked first. In our area there were some walled, upmarket houses built like fortresses—they didn't last long. If a gang decided they wanted something you had, and they had more bodies and guns, they would take it.'

Amy rested her fingertips on the stock of her rifle while talking, her eyes roaming the dark. Habitual, done without thinking, I considered.

'We used buckets for rainwater,' she continued. 'With no power for cooking or heat we burned anything that would burn—furniture, doors, flooring. A market opened a few blocks away and my brother had to go there once for medical supplies for his kid. The neighbor went with him. When my brother returned he was wounded—a lot of people died on the streets. Snipers or gangs. Dollars became worthless; everything was trade. I'm medically trained, and it became our best currency. If we had to travel, it was at night, moving fast and avoiding open ground. You never knew where the enemy was—and *everyone* outside your group was your potential enemy. Strength was in numbers—if you were alone, you died. Soon we heard the first rumors of people dying from starvation. We did what we had to to survive. Most people were not bad, just desperate. There were some incidents.'

'What happened?'

She sighed. 'The weak died. The rest of us fought. No one had a choice. For water, food, antibiotics, ammunition—people would do anything. We fought for those things like dogs. It was hideous. And the smell… you wouldn't believe it.'

She looked down at herself with a wry smile, took another drag on her cigarette. 'Maybe you would. Anyway, after fifteen months there were two of us left. The neighbor offed himself, found him hanging out back one day. The others… my brother's wife and son, died from dysentery. But it was bad hygiene and hunger, in the end. My brother's wound from the markets had festered and he became sick. Really sick. Chronic diarrhea. Infection. And starving. I couldn't help him; he was beyond the scope of the meds I had. He died about a year in.' She paused, turned a piece of wood on the fire with a stick. 'One day my fiancé was shot in the leg when a gang breached our perimeter and began ramming the front door. We fought them off, group of about eight, but his wound was bad. Didn't hit the artery but the bullet was lodged on his femur. No painkillers, no antibiotics left. Bad timing. That night I made a break for the market for meds.

'When I got back the house was in flames. Got as close as I could. I assumed the gang had returned. I knew no one could be alive inside. But I waited and watched until the fire died. When I went in to look… some bodies, but unrecognizable. Maybe my fiancé had survived, got away and would return. I waited through the night and next day. No one came, and I considered following the neighbor's example.'

A cold gust hit and cast glowing embers into the night. I shivered, hugged my knees up against my chest.

She continued. 'I just started walking, moved at night. Made myself as ugly and smelly as possible. I'd heard rumor there were safe zones in some rural areas. Had my Glock and AR-20. Honestly? Without guns I'd be dead. By some miracle I made it out of the city. I was lucky—one day a bus pulled over, offered me a ride after checking me out and I gave them ammo as payment. They said the UN were setting up a green zone—safe zone I guess—in Oklahoma. Law and order, beds, food. When we got there, it was a different story; the vaunted UN had stolen all the supplies, skulked away like rats. With no better options we continued onto Kansas, then were jumped one night by a road crew after crossing the border…' She paused, appraised me again. 'And then I met you.'

I was moved by her story, not sure where to begin. 'Sorry for your brother and fiancé—for everyone. It's incredible how you survived.'

She smiled sadly. 'I'm nothing special. Just kept my head down.'

The fire was dying, and the cold darkness bore down upon our brief respite. Amy's cigarette had burned down to a charcoal cinder, and she dropped it to the ground, stomped it out. Her eyes were drooping, and I also felt myself drifting off.

'We should lie close together for body heat,' I said. 'Won't last long with hypothermia.'

She considered a moment, then grabbed her rifle and moved around the fire to me. Lying down next to her, I pulled my blanket over us, and our body heat gave immediate relief from the cold.

I didn't know if I'd find sleep, I hadn't since leaving home, but I was getting drowsy when I heard Amy murmur over the wind.

'Where do we go from here, Solara? What's left?'

She had mirrored my thoughts. Rebecca was gone, my world was gone, and would never be the same again, no matter how much I tried to pretend otherwise.

'I don't know,' I said. 'I don't know where I fit in anymore, but we have to try to find something…'

'Why?'

Somehow, I found myself saying, 'For whoever's left. For each other.'

Later that night, sometime in the early hours of the morning, I woke to a starless black sky. Something had woken me. Amy was sobbing quietly beside me. I lay awake, holding her, sharing her loss, my mind playing over recent days like a fatal glitch.

In the morning, we decided to make for the New York Safe Zone. We'd heard people there were getting to safety, wherever that was.

*Must be on the moon.*

# THE GREAT WAR

Daniel Nicolas entered the briefing room.

Cloaked in his Daniel Weir identity, he coolly made his way to a seat at the conference table. Nicolas, as Weir, had reassumed a lead position on the Sirius research team. Niemeyer, as his second, would join him in delivering the status report. Senior members of Project Sirius including Linear, Rhodes, the nine-member OriGen Policy Committee, Dario Sanchez—the OriGen chief to whom Sirius was directly accountable, and several others were present. More attendees watched via live video feed.

They had confirmed that inside the Zion anomaly, the naked singularity remained open. Officially, the research team had been tasked to close it, and the question the committee wanted answered was: could it be done? The texts from the alien city obelisks had been analyzed and partially decoded, and a fluid situation was unfolding, as Science Division incorporated the research inputs with unification theory.

Nicolas had concealed his post-regression contact with the Presence. There was something intensely private about the dialogue, and he sensed that if he revealed the communication, he would also lose the thread of critical understandings that had begun—largely responsible for the obelisk interpretations he'd presented as solely his own work.

Disclosure would also raise concerns about his fitness to continue. The Ennead—the High Council of his Order—had the power to remove him from his position if they believed he'd been compromised. So, he'd resolved to maintain the secret, for now. However, if the Presence began to grow beyond his control, he would have to take appropriate steps to neutralize it.

A path to unlock the vacuum had been revealed to him, and now he must enact a charade to drive forward a second incursion. He had to convince Solara to join him. Despite his private disclosure to Solara, to others, the Daniel Weir cover must be maintained until success had been achieved, or it benefited him to end it. So, he would give it some time, and Rhodes and Linear would continue to play along for appearances.

*The path to power was a labyrinth. Secrets within secrets, concealing within them further secrets.*

The room quietened. Nicolas calmly clasped his hands upon the table, and greeted OriGen's elite.

●

NIEMEYER WALKED from the conference trailing behind Shaw and a couple of other council members. Weir's progress the last couple of days had taken him by surprise. They hadn't been close to finding an answer to closing the naked singularity, much less understanding the consequences of a third iteration. Now, they had a previously unforeseen solution—how had Weir done it?

In collaborative research since the first regressions, Shaw had disclosed Weir's regression experience to him in confidence, and Niemeyer couldn't shake the feeling of an unseen hand at play in Sirius. 'I'm concerned about Weir, what he found on the other side,' Shaw had said. 'He had quite a different experience to Solara. He went to… well, this will sound overdramatic, but something resembling hell. He had an encounter with an intelligence. I believe this is what came through and attacked the control room.' A crack had appeared in Shaw's haughty visage. 'It's possible that it may still be here.'

Niemeyer had considered. 'Yet we don't know for certain. They told you to keep it quiet.'

'Yes. But it's critical you know what we're dealing with…'

Since Weir had taken the research lead following his regression, somehow, the assignment Science Division had been tasked with—to close the open naked singularity, had been inverted, and Weir's uncanny influence over decisions from higher-up concerned Niemeyer.

A few minutes into the meeting, General Rhodes had attempted to rein in Weir's escalating claims— 'Your job is to close the damn thing, doctor. Can you do this?'

Weir had replied, 'We can. But let's not act in haste… if you will allow me to elaborate?'

To the committee, Weir had revealed his interpretations of the alien texts, which contained an advanced geometric system he had integrated with unification theory. More, he had discovered an artificial code, using this silent language, embedded subtly in the quantum-gravitational data of the anomaly. Generating a thread, or bridge through the naked singularity, the code not only explained the ongoing connection between the vacuum and the Etherians, but also the pattern iterations. A dialogue was occurring. The interface would need to have been set by someone, at some time, and Science Division had named these unseen, cosmic interlopers the Builders—building what?

Unity among intelligent life, Weir claimed, fighting the great war: the battle of intelligence against its arch-enemy—entropy.

Interestingly, the Kansas texts supported the theory that the Builders had interacted with Earth, on some level, at various points in human history, to share knowledge and influence events. Always directing us toward increasing order and the evolution of technology. The Builders had been quantified into two apparently separate intelligences. Firstly, the hostile entity Weir encountered in the vacuum, which may have been the same force that broke through to the control room, and was being referred to as the Presence. Secondly, the intelligence Solara encountered in Kansas, which had been named the Visitor.

The Presence, and the Visitor, Niemeyer reflected.

The events occurring, that seemed connected across previously absolute boundaries, such as time, and dimensions, were being referred to as a hyper-event. In addition, the Kansas texts had revealed a forgotten people who lived in the early solar system, and indicated an ancient war which caused great destruction. As for the alien city itself, carbon dating didn't even register, and it was hypothesized that it had somehow been intelligently assembled by the Kansas anomaly, which had used the surrounding earth for raw construction materials. The terrain had been transformed through an unknown process into an extremely dense material Science Division was still analyzing. The design and purpose of the city was a mystery.

Then, had come the real mind-fuck. Weir's theory that the location and appearance of Solara's Visitor in Kansas was… personal. Solara was on record claiming her daughter had experiences leading up to her death, in which she was contacted by what she called *them*. Solara claimed her daughter saw them in the vortex. Weir posited that the Visitor may have been communicating with Solara's daughter for some time before her death… prior to the Kansas naked singularity.

Now, this connection seemed focused on Solara.

The hyper-event had been broken into three distinct levels. Firstly, the objective, or identifiable and known scientific processes. Secondly, the interface, which was informed by new concepts in unification, and inferred that the Zion anomaly, or perhaps the vortex in Kansas which had appeared above Solara and her daughter, facilitated every aspect of the hyper-event. Essentially acting as a non-local communications hub, the interface drove the meta—or third level, in which the two the naked singularities introduced non-local properties of the vacuum into the universe. Non-locality was key to everything, Weir believed.

Then, there were the iterations, and their parallel manifestations in the Etherian's subtle bodies. To the ancients, Niemeyer knew, each iteration represented a different way to translate reality. The second iteration represented balance, with the star tetrahedron signifying the union of male and female. The pyramid pointing upwards—male energy—symbolized heavenly energy. The downward pyramid symbolized the feminine, representing earthly energy; however, both energies were present within male and female, to certain degrees, depending on the individual. It was the interface of these two energy fields within a star tetrahedron, either individually or between a couple, that was the key to unlocking extraordinary abilities.

To harness vacuum energy, the twin tetrahedrons acted like a mutual, electrical capacitor, or two conductors charged positively and negatively, thereby separating the charge—balancing the current. A mutual capacitor could contain potentially infinite power, but hold a sum charge of zero, depending on how closely the conductors balanced each other out. The two polarized conductors, in Sirius, being Weir and Solara.

Imbalance, however, could result in destructive events. Niemeyer understood this binary went far beyond mere biological duality: the male-female symmetry was the superlative expression of the vacuum, resonating through morphic fields to permeate creation.

The predicted third iteration was again based in the male-female dichotomy, and represented by the geometric circles and squares of consciousness. This pattern radiated outward in concentric layers, which signified distinct 'levels' of awareness, where a Phi ratio was formed at the convergences.

The square represented male energy, and the circle, female energy. Phi, the mathematical ratio 1.618—the golden ratio—was a natural expression of vacuum geometry found throughout nature: in the symmetry of human DNA, convergent brainwave patterns of opposite sexes, the spirals of a galaxy, to the circles in a tree trunk.

The third iteration formed a map of human development, which represented the human evolutionary state by denoting the geometric relations of mind and body. In the model, the current human evolutionary state was situated at the fifth square, sixth circle—the second level of consciousness, on a scale of potentially infinite iterations. Making life in the universe beyond anything they could possibly imagine.

'And the next—the third level of consciousness?' an academic type had asked in the meeting.

They wouldn't know until it happened. But if the coming, third iteration, manifested the seventh square intersecting the ninth circle at Phi, then the third level of consciousness may be within reach. A shared, racial memory was predicted to actualize here, implying all consciousness on Earth could potentially link with the vacuum; this had raised concerns which Weir had suppressed with the prediction that the awakening would be gradual, and something they could control.

The committee would deliberate, and hand down a decision regarding the second incursion within days. The last time Niemeyer had been before the committee had been prior to the first incursion, when he had presented the experiment scenario with Neil Andrews.

He recalled Andrews as he walked, for their last conversation seemed acutely relevant now. 'The world can't afford to be short sighted, or close minded. We can't tolerate apathy anymore,' Andrews had said, departing for the singularity control room that last time. 'Our race is at a turning point, and if we surrender our humanity to these maniacs running the world then we're lost. These issues ultimately must be reached at a global level of understanding, not just in a laboratory.'

*Maniacs.*

Yes, that was an accurate description of much of the OriGen and GRC hierarchy. What issues had Andrews been referring to? The same as it always was: self-will run riot, and the consequences from interpersonal to global. He had believed unification of science could transform society. Unlike many of Andrews' colleagues who were skeptical of a unified theory being realized in their own lifetimes, Niemeyer was a believer who had shared his views. What was less well known about Neil Andrews, was that prior to becoming a physicist he had been a priest. Andrews had known Niemeyer well, but there had been some things Andrews hadn't known; he may have suspected, but couldn't *know*. To know some things was dangerous.

'Science is just one piece of the puzzle,' Andrews had said, 'but to reconcile science with God… could change the world for the better. You're one of the best I've ever seen, Marcus. And our best chance.'

'What about Weir? It's his work that opened this door for us,' Niemeyer had said.

Andrews had gone quiet, before saying, 'Weir has his own purpose, keeps his own council. The closer we get to opening this power to the world, the more you will come to know this.'

Niemeyer still didn't know exactly what Andrews had meant by that comment, but his words rang ever truer, evidenced by Weir's increasing secrecy. His own investigations into senior Sirius personnel had turned up little of interest on Weir. His professional profile was predictable, at least in the sense it contained nothing Niemeyer did not expect to see. Perhaps too predictable. Weir's semi-restricted profile in the OriGen database revealed his role in the US forerunner to Sirius—why had this part of his background been hidden from the public profile? Did he want his former alliance to the US hidden for political reasons? And Niemeyer couldn't fathom why Weir had risked his life in the first incursion. Numerous volunteers would have willingly gone before him. Troubled, Niemeyer resolved to keep digging. The other council members turned off into a side corridor, and Niemeyer came up alongside Shaw. He hadn't spoken with him in person since the initial collaborations after the first regression.

Ensuring no one could overhear, he said, 'Off the record a minute?'

Shaw kept his eyes focused ahead, nodded shortly. 'Sure. What's on your mind?'

Niemeyer considered. 'It's evident we can't control the predictability breakdown. To assume we can is a mistake. I'm concerned about… this being Weir encountered—and Weir. We may be walking into our destruction.'

Shaw's brow creased, and he glanced over. 'I'm confused—why didn't you speak against continuance at the meeting?'

'My reasons are my own,' Niemeyer said, briefly lowering his head. 'I told them what they wanted to hear. Sirius leadership—the true leadership—will not stop. Believe me, I'm doing all within my power to steer the project away from disaster. There is hope revealed in the Kansas texts, much more than was revealed to the council. If Solara can pass through again and return, she may not only have the power to circumvent disaster, but to drive the human condition forward.'

Shaw looked unsettled, quiet a minute as they passed a roving security detail. 'Solara—not Weir?' Niemeyer stayed passive.

Doctor Shaw nodded slowly. 'A dangerous game.'

'Agreed.'

They reached an atrium populated by various personnel and stopped. Shaw asked quietly, 'Can it be stopped?'

'I honestly don't know,' said Niemeyer.

Shaw nodded, turned and walked briskly away. Niemeyer watched him a moment, then began making his way back to research. He considered his actions in the coming hours.

Weir wasn't the only one who had been busy since the incursion, for the quantum-gravitational data from the anomaly had opened many doors. Time was short, and every moment now was critical. In secret, he'd been developing the idea that had formed, when the second iteration appeared. A new form of intelligence, that could provide hope. He was now confident an AI could be linked to the vacuum. It could be conscious.

A weapon, with capabilities beyond even the most advanced military AIs. Niemeyer's sense that something was terribly wrong, of approaching doom, became amplified, and he quickened his pace.

⬤

THE EVENING was quiet. In conflict, I searched for guidance. After meeting Nicolas I'd returned to some journaling, had a session with Shaw, but nothing new about my regression, or Kansas, had come to light. In my quarters, I reviewed a summary of the Sirius Policy Committee meeting from that afternoon. I noticed some of the text had been redacted, so OriGen was keeping secrets, but that was nothing new. It seemed they were as lost as

I felt, but at least we had named the being I'd encountered in Kansas: the Visitor. It seemed fitting.

Science Division believed, logically, that the Visitor may be Rebecca's them. I considered the division of the hyper-event into three levels, and the relation to unification theory. I preferred to simplify things further, and just thought of the anomaly as a bridge, between the physical and spiritual realms. The transcendent aspect intrigued me the most—what connected everything?

I hadn't heard from Nicolas since our talk this morning, and was still processing his disclosures: a secret Order behind Sirius, controlling OriGen and the GRC? Another incursion, to unlock an improbable power? I shook my head in disbelief; the danger of Sirius increased every hour the anomaly remained active, it seemed. But Nicolas had found a way to control things, he believed… to change it all, and I entertained a possibility: what if we could succeed?

What if solving the problem, the task the Visitor had apparently charged me with, meant succeeding on the second incursion? I had seen a nobility in Nicolas, I was coming to care for him, to desire what he offered. His ambitions, his enigma, although sometimes unsettling, attracted me. But isn't that selfish, I thought, to put myself first, considering the escalating danger? Perhaps the path to paradise lay through the darkness. I felt colliding desires: to throw restraint to the wind and explore what I had originally intended, or err on the side of caution. I'd abandoned caution when I'd lost my previous life. Now, however, the stakes were unimaginable. I sighed. It seemed that each time I tried to do the right thing, it only made things worse.

Putting my tablet aside, I stood and walked outside into the cool, ash-tinged night air. Maybe the darkness had answers. My connection to the vacuum, increasingly driven by seemingly unrelated events, was engulfing me, beyond my comprehension and control. I took a deep breath, calmed my mind. After a silent minute, I felt a shift in my awareness, as if in my contemplation I had touched the edge of something larger. But when I tried to probe deeper, the feeling of connection retreated. I considered. I'd been close to something important, I sensed, something that may provide direction, and determined to investigate further when time permitted.

My thoughts returned to Niemeyer, and his unexpected support for me to lead the Kansas recon. Why had he done it? We'd never really spoken, but he was one of the only people besides Nicolas who may have some answers. He'd also worked with the first project leader Neil Andrews, who so far, had also remained a mystery.

I'D ORDERED a light salad, and picked at my plate on the mess hall table, happy for the distraction. I'd called Niemeyer to meet, and now he sat across from me, sipping a coffee. I considered how much to trust him. He would have his own insights which may help navigate the path ahead. For now, at least, I decided to keep Weir's true identity confidential; he had disclosed it to me in confidence and I was unwilling to break that trust. The future was still unclear.

Niemeyer possessed an intensity in his gray eyes, and his manner was driven by what seemed, at first glance, an insatiable thirst for knowledge. But no, I thought, reading him on a deeper level. There's more to him: he's been hurt, something has been taken from him and he wants… wholeness? Revenge? Justice? I found him refreshing—with his 'guy next door look' he could be a mechanic rather than a cutting-edge corporate researcher. Unpretentious, direct. He recalled Linear in that way, but with empathy above the level of a corpse. He'd recapped what occurred during the committee meeting, pretty much paraphrasing the report I'd read, and now he asked about my encounter with the Visitor.

'What do you think it meant by the problem it referred to?'

I shrugged. 'Your research team has a theory. The world must learn to get along, and then we can all live happily ever after,' I said drily.

He smiled. A contagious grin, and I mirrored it back to him. 'Maybe not, but I'd like your take. What were your first thoughts?'

I pondered the incident. The creature burning through the sphere and the scorched, lifeless world. Its voice in my mind. Ever since I'd woken up in the *Hecate*, a feeling of duality, a connection to a larger reality. Then, afterward, a sense of guidance and inquisitive probing into the people on Sirius.

'That we've got to stop killing ourselves,' I said.

He nodded. 'That would be a good start. So, should we attempt a second incursion, or stop this now, do you think?'

I didn't have the answers. I'd come here hoping for some. 'I don't like the idea of an open naked singularity. But honestly, I'm in two minds: part of me wants to close it while we still can, while another part says, fuck it, we've come this far—why not see it through?' I sighed. 'I wonder what my father would do if he were here.'

He nodded. 'It's a difficult situation, but change always is. Perhaps he'd feel as you do.'

I was thoughtful. 'Tell me about Andrews. How well did you know him?'

'That's a long story,' Niemeyer said.

I smiled. 'Okay. Maybe you can give me the short version.'

He paused, grinned wryly, then leaned back, crossed a knee, and balanced his coffee. 'I've never had a family, never knew my parents. I was born in America, somewhere in Mississippi during the Depression. I found this out by searching through the birth registry archives in Washington. Other than that, the earliest record of me is that one morning I was found on the doorstep of the orphanage of Saint Augustine.'

'An orphan? Must have been tough.'

Niemeyer smiled briefly. 'I was mentored by Father Giovanni Boehn, a young idealistic priest who believed he was doing God's work. I can still see his eyes. They had innocence. Anyway, it was about '89, America was seven years into the Depression, and I was just lucky to have a roof over my head. The city was overrun with homeless in search of something better—salvation, hope, anything, I guess. Still, Father Boehn somehow kept the orphanage afloat. When I was twelve, I was taken under the wing of a priest-scientist who did service work in the orphanages. His name was Neil Andrews. At seventeen, he secured a scholarship at Cambridge for me.

Without him, I'd have been swallowed up in the Depression, so, you could say Neil was like a father to me. I owe what I am today to him.'

I hadn't expected that. 'I didn't know you were that close. I'm sure he'd be happy you're continuing his work.'

'In some respects.'

'He was a priest? I didn't think there were any of those left.'

His lips narrowed. 'They were a dying breed back then. Now? I don't think the GRC is encouraging of a return to faith.'

Niemeyer's plainspoken nature put me at ease. 'I saw things in Kansas. It's like everything, all time, was encompassed in a moment. I sensed that the Visitor's purpose had been to find me—someone—in this world.'

'But it found you,' said Niemeyer.

I nodded. 'I can still feel its presence, like a guide.'

Niemeyer briefly glanced around the nearly empty mess hall. A couple of soldiers were at the cafeteria, and some more were seated in the eating area, focused on their meals and conversations. He leaned forward confidentially. 'Weir hasn't told you what happened to him over there yet, has he?'

I put my utensils down. He had my full attention. 'No.'

'Well, he had quite a… different experience to your own. He found hell—one possible hell, I suppose. Encountered an entity. That may be what tried to follow him back through, and demolished the control room. Shaw thinks it may have attached itself to him.'

I frowned. The redacted text from the policy committee meeting. 'They kept it from me.'

'We're calling it the Presence.'

'The Presence,' I repeated, quietly. 'Ni... Weir's been hiding things from me since the beginning, even after the mind-link. I still don't really know him, but he believes he can succeed, if we try again.' I'd almost let Nicolas' name slip and wondered how long the pretense would continue.

Niemeyer's gray eyes intensified. 'Succeed at what? Even if safe control of the vacuum is possible, what will come of it under the GRC? Do we even know now, if Weir is in full control of himself? If it's the same Daniel Weir who went in? The risk is too great, and Weir—and OriGen—will never willingly give up their plans.'

I was beginning to wonder why Niemeyer signed up. 'What are you saying?'

'I'm only considering options. We must.'

I frowned. 'I know. But how do we know giving up on the second incursion isn't precisely the worst thing to do?'

Niemeyer's jaw set. 'Point taken. What are you willing to do?'

I looked dubiously at him.

'Speak freely, Commander. I assure you this will be kept between the two of us.'

I considered. 'Since it happened, I've had this strange feeling, like a purpose I can't turn away from. I can't stop thinking about it. To comprehend why we're doing Sirius in the first place. To understand everyone involved with the project.'

Niemeyer considered this. 'It seeks to understand,' he said. 'The Visitor.'

I nodded slowly. 'Through me, somehow. But I'm still just... me, you know?'

Quietly, he said, 'You're involved in this now, Solara, in some way I don't understand yet. I can't counsel you. You must do what you feel is right.'

'Weir said the third iteration must be achieved by two. Him and me, or another two people? Is this true?' I asked.

Niemeyer briefly shook his head. 'Not completely. A single individual could harness the third iteration, but they could become... unbalanced.'

I considered a growing hunch. 'I think I have a sense of what the Visitor is doing.'

Niemeyer leaned forward. 'What?'

'I think it's deciding whether to help us, or destroy us.'

LATER THAT evening I was in the gym, running the treadmill when I was given a start: data gibberish burst over my neura-link overlay for a second, then vanished just as quickly. The GRC firewall was generally secure, and viruses or service disruptions were uncommon, so I assumed it was some update glitch. I glanced around the exercise area; apart from some other personnel pushing weights, all was quiet. Finishing up, I had a shower and returned to my quarters. After some dinner, I sat on the couch near the window, and read an old book.

*The Road,* by Cormac McCarthy. Amy had lent it to me; I often forgot she'd been a librarian in the world before. It told the story of a father and son walking across a post-apocalyptic, decimated America. In the dreary, dead landscape, hope was found only in the connection between the protagonists. I was caught by a particular line when I'd skipped to the end— *Are you carrying the fire?*

I put my device on my lap, considered. Perhaps the fire, in the story, referred to the characters' humanity, sustained by their love when the rest of the world fell into despair and cannibalism. It recalled my own flight from the US with Amy, but her book choice also hinted at something more personal lost… a father, a son, but the woman from the family, the mother in the story, was missing. Dead. I reflected—perhaps Amy would find what she sought one day, with Li, if I read things right. I'd turned a few more pages when I received a neura-link message:

*'Firewall alert: Insecure comm; unmapped extension. Access point: Unknown. IP: Unknown; encrypted. Deny/Allow?'*

I hesitated. Unauthorized communication while on Sirius was prohibited, but recent events had left me unsettled. Much was hidden. I risked it.

*'Enable.'*

'Solara, you don't know me. My name is Peter Trent, and I must speak with you.'

I put aside my book. I knew that name, but not the voice.

'Who are you? How did you get this number?'

'How I got this number is not important. As to who I am… I was a friend of your father's. All I can tell you now is you risk more than you can imagine. Sirius isn't what you think it is.'

Peter Trent was the name of the contact my father had given me before he'd left me and Rebecca the last time. Someone I could trust—the same man who contacted me now? I recalled Dad's words: 'He'll meet you at the extraction point. He's Italian, with wavy brown hair, brown eyes, and wears thick rimmed, orange tinted glasses.' But Trent had never shown up, Rebecca and I had been left for dead. I'd never found out why. He could have been killed or captured, abandoned us, none of which would have surprised me. Trent had been there at the beginning of it all, right there in Kansas with my father and Weir… Nicolas. I'd thought everyone from that time was gone. Then Nicolas had shown up. I had been quiet, and the line was silent, but I knew Trent waited on the other end.

'How do I know it's you?' I asked.

'The last time you saw him, your father gave you a password to identify yourself to the contact who would get you out of Kansas.'

I had never told anyone. 'Go on.'

'The password was *Contorta*.'

'I'll be there as soon as I can.'

'I'm sending you a secure link now.'

I entered the Subreality.

# SILENT DEFEAT

THE TEMPLE COMPLEX FADED INTO THE DISTANCE.

In the Subreality, my digital avatar piloted a sky-car that cruised above the Zion simulation. Light traffic dotted the twilight skies, following the electronic, invisible highways. Gaining my bearings, I knew I was heading toward the second concentric city enclave, Mechanus, for ahead, stretching for over a hundred kilometers, stood the imposing inter-sector barrier.

Neura-link normally showed my location, but now it was blank. Quantum encryption had its needs.

Trent transmitted over the comm. 'We must camouflage your appearance.'

'How?'

'You can activate short beam without broadcasting your position over the web. Do it now, I can disguise you.'

I activated an offline drive in my neura-link interface, opened a short-beam port. Trent sent an app to my mind-file: **AVATAR RECONFIGU-RATION.**

'This will alter your digital clone: facial look and bone structure, hair, skin, body. From the outside, you'll become the person you load from the drive with full biometrics into the system.'

Interesting, I thought—Nicolas had used similar banned tech. I hesitated, but had come this far now, so scrolled through a list of identity options, clicked… a black wave swarmed over my features and in seconds the process was done. I checked myself in the mirror and a strange face stared back.

'Good,' said Trent.

'Can you move undetected through both the real and virtual worlds?' I asked.

'Yes. Although real-world rendering uses a variant nano-swarm tech. Highly illegal, but life is a crazy ride. There's a map with the route marked in the vehicle database. Use it to get to the safe house.'

I meshed with the AI, and it responded intuitively, sent the route via neura-link. I scanned the map. 'Why couldn't I go straight to you?'

'There's always danger. We must be sure the GRC hasn't traced you. Your first contact will be in the Club Tenebrae; you'll find a description of your contact, and passcodes you'll need, in the vehicle DB. When you talk to him just state the pass phrases—don't say anything else.'

'Got it.'

The sky-car accelerated forward. Relaxing slightly, I let out pent-up tension with a deep breath. Traffic in the opposite lane sped past in a blur, reflecting the transience I now felt toward my own life. The pull of the etheric thread had increased since the regression, and the Kansas recon, I sensed. I felt it constantly now, like a controllable link to the vacuum, infusing me with growing intuitions, visions.

My vehicle reached the barrier transfer point, and I had a flash of anxiety upon reaching the hovering machine sentinels, which monitored all passing traffic with cold precision.

I re-checked my altered appearance. 'You sure this will work?'

'It should,' Trent said.

*Mechanus Gate, hold for processing,* 'a voice said, through neura-link.

Lasers swept the sky-car, scanning.

*'Processing—processing… clear. Citizen 21648665. Proceed.'*

The vehicle proceeded through the vast tungsten steel gate.

'You are entering Mechanus Sector,' said the sentinel.

I WALKED across a thoroughfare of the dim Mechanus slums. Scattered traffic dotted the evening firmament, the streets were loosely populated, and corporate holograms choked every available space, individually tailored to my new identity. The GRC's 'Building Back Better' and 'Service Secures Your Future' slogans appeared in most ads somewhere; no one got anywhere without the GRC's approval and endorsement. Everything led back to them.

Whoever I was must have had a thing for adventure, I thought, as various travel ads popped up—virtual travel, of course. The real world, and all life forms in general, were considered biohazards to be avoided. The huge intimate humanoid market was outdone only by the synthetic pet industry. I passed near a fenced residential tower complex, which conformed to the pervasive, and tightly controlled, modular verticality: vertical living, vertical bug farming, and a micro-managed existence. Ten meters in the air, police drones hovered above every street in a grid pattern. Watching all. No one could leave their centrally controlled domicile without an approved, essential purpose.

As I walked, I uneasily scanned my internal data-feed. My false identity integrated seamlessly into the bio-metric umbrella shrouding the city, fooling the surveillance and target acquisition grid. The controlling AI was always watching, but should assume I was nothing more than another obedient subject, a nano-chipped ectomorph surviving on the low-nutrient insect paste rationed out as food. Thirsty from water shortages, demoralized to the futility of resistance against the techno-feudal nightmare. Rewarded for silence and consent, thoughts of freedom unuttered, the dream of a distant epoch. Never getting too close to others, existing within a zone of avoidance removed from all direct human contact.

For various reasons, most forgotten, that was the law. Punishment for violations was instantly applied to a citizen's digital social profile, and persistent offenders found themselves deprived of the meagre essentials, mandated into a re-education facility, or worse—little was known about those who permanently disappeared. Crossing that hazy line was to pass into a black zone. A man walked briskly past on the sidewalk, covered a slight cough with his hand, then, outpacing me, continued ahead.

I reflected that for many, regular, and routine immersion into the all-pervasive Subreality, was mandatory, and controlled and enforced by the GRC's Public Health and Safety Division. Yet large segments of the populace lived most of their lives voluntarily in the trance-like state, and in a warped inversion, found the real world painful and illusory. In the emaciated faces on the street, I saw this isolation reflected in their silent defeat, and not for the first time felt a great sadness running through humanity. I closed my eyes a moment, letting the city pulse wash over me, a beat of quiet agitated desperation impelled by the unreal. Machine-like. Divided. Powerless.

Continuing briskly toward the meeting location, I was given a start when hovering machine police converged down the street above a pedestrian.

'Health-code violation! Cease and desist!' the machines ordered.

The man who'd walked past, I saw. The one who'd coughed. The virtual mirrored the physical. In my overlay, a red virtual fence sprung up around him; crossing it would not only cause electric shock induced via high-frequency waves to his nanites, but also increase the severity of his punishment. He froze, shrunk into himself like a whipped dog. The machine police swooped in, plucked the 'criminal' from the street and hauled him away to one of the holding cells which occupied every corner. A rush of anxiety ran through me—had I been too close when he'd coughed? Would I be taken, too? I sighed in controlled relief when the police didn't expand their arrest and seizure, and noticed the resentful stare of some pedestrians as he was bundled away. But the people did nothing, silently continuing about their business.

Following a route marked in my overlay, I entered a warren of back alleys and moved swiftly, pinching my nose at the reeking stench. The odd walker passed me by, but the denizens of The Warren, as the area was called, kept their distance. After fifteen minutes of seemingly random twists and turns I came to the final corner. A dim lane greeted me, and I quietly made my way through the rat-infested garbage and the occasional body lying across the way. Not all the bodies were dead, I noticed. I was confident I could handle the odd desperado, but worse things stalked these lanes.

I moved into a dark recess, attuned my senses and waited silently a minute to be sure I hadn't been followed. Unlikely, due to the extensive precautions, but I couldn't afford a single mistake. Not now. While I waited, I re-checked the image of the contact, then moving quickly, I reached a door marked by two faded crossed swords on a sign above, ran my fingers through sweat dampened hair and entered.

●

RHODES WAS working in his quarters when Lieutenant Pearce hailed him from Jericho.

'Yes?' Rhodes said.

'Sir,' Pearce said. 'Solara followed an unknown, encrypted link at 18.09 hours. A correlation ping was detected in the dark net, but no end system can be traced.'

'Which means?' Rhodes demanded.

'Level 5 quantum encryption or above.'

Rhodes evaluated the news. 'Does Solara possess anything like that?'

'Negative,' said Pearce. 'It's an outside force or someone very good at covering their footsteps. Intelligence perhaps. Our security has multiple levels of neural trace protocols. A team of supercomputers could try for a hundred years and not evade the system.'

'Then she's with someone else?'

'She must be.'

'I need an ID.'

'We're working on it, Sir.'

Rhodes considered. 'Patch it through to CentCom. Use my authority.' He paused. 'And watch Solara.'

THE DEEP thud of a bass drum hit me as I entered the establishment and scanned the room. On the dance floor, young bodies writhed and gyrated to the rhythm, while around the perimeter the denizens of the slums talked in hushed tones, and I suspected that the Club Tenebrae was frequented by a clientele who preferred a degree of anonymity from the GRC's inquisition. Digital ID fraud, or even going off-grid entirely occurred, I knew, but I'd never imagined the scope. The news only showed those captured, for ID hacking—like mine—was met with severe penalties from authorities.

Regional dialects reached me in a colorful mosaic: Russian, Hebrew, Greek, Spanish, Kurdish, and Arabic, the organic ebb and flow of humanity a stark contrast to the streets outside. The air stank from a combination of incense and smoke which stung my eyes, and in the dimness, it took me a moment to make out the contact. I crossed the room, and eyes, some furtive, others hostile, wandered to me and just as quickly looked away.

At a table near the bar three men, their clothes rough and expressions hard, sat engrossed in a poker game. I walked to the part of the bar nearest them, leaned casually on my elbows, checked my reflection in a mirror on the wall and was reassured by the strange face staring back. The contact, a stocky, pock-faced man wearing a red shirt, tended the bar, and his perpetually angry blue eyes locked on mine.

'Help you, friend?' the barman said, in a gravelly voice.

'What's the fastest way to the mag-lev station?'

Red shirt began polishing a glass. The three men at the table subtly lowered their voices.

The barman said, 'You could walk, but it's about seven blocks.'

I shrugged. 'That's okay, I could use the exercise.'

The barman nodded to a door to the rear of the room. 'Head down Quarry Lane, it's the fastest way.'

I thanked him, walked through the door and entered a passageway. Two large, cyber-enhanced men waited in the hall, barring my path. With a thought, I dropped the visual disguise, while maintaining the fake ID signature, and my true digital self was revealed. One of the men ran a scanner over the back of my skull, checked the result, and then they wordlessly stood aside. The door was hastily yanked open from within, and I quickly entered.

Met by a middle-aged woman with long, braided hair, who had more the look of my grade school history teacher than a terrorist, I was guided through the front room, and then down a corridor where my guide stopped at a door, nodded, and left me. I opened the door and stepped through, finding myself in what appeared to be an old-world study.

Antique furniture decorated the threadbare room, old floorboards creaked under my feet, and I inhaled a scent I hadn't known in years: the smell of real paper, or at least a simulation of it. I closed the door. Crammed bookshelves lined an entire wall, and I suspected many of the musty tomes would be on the GRC's banned books list.

A man stood near one of the shelves reading. He turned as I stood there near the entrance, placed his book on a shelf, approached me, and stopped a few paces away with his hands clasped before him. Orange-tinted glasses shrouded intelligent brown eyes. Dressed in a dark gray shirt and other muted attire his physique was slim. His visage, framed by grayish-brown hair, projected an engaging vitality.

'Solara, I'm Peter Trent. It is good to meet you again.'

I frowned. 'Again?'

He smiled with genuine warmth. 'You were only a child the last time.' He studied me for a minute, and I saw a flash of recognition. 'You have your father's eyes, but your mother's face.'

'How did you know my father?'

'We worked together, when necessity dictated.'

My father had trusted this man implicitly, right to the end, but what had happened to his rendezvous with me and Rebecca in Kansas? 'Who are you? Why did you contact me?' I asked.

Trent smiled thinly. 'I represent a group who would prevent Sirius sending the world spinning into an abyss, to make the horrors of the last dark age look like a summer boot camp. During the war I held a senior US intelligence post; after, I worked with GSI.'

I was wary, knowing a cozy relationship existed between OriGen and Global Secret Intelligence, the espionage arm of the GRC, and a murky well of intrigue. Trent's claim conflicted with his apparent age, which was early forties, I guessed. Genetically or digitally enhanced. 'GSI recruited a US intelligence officer?'

He nodded. 'It's not unusual, when you think about it. Those in power seek useful people, to maintain power. Most wars are replete with such migrations. Many who could be useful—intelligence specialists, scientists, engineers—in bolstering the GRC's hegemony were given safe passage. Think of your own journey.'

'I didn't really have much of a choice.'

Trent smiled ironically. 'War can be like that.'

'Now you represent who?'

'Through the media you may know us as dissidents, extremists, or terrorists. To those locked in the battle for our freedom, we are the Resistance.'

'Which is what?'

'We are everywhere, Solara. As you know, we move through the world undetected by reconfiguring our neural implants, altering our appearance. There are people loyal to us serving in the military, the intelligence services, the media, the GRC and its affiliates. People who will die for freedom. Always watching, working to restore the world to balance.'

'You never came. You left Rebecca and me for the wolves. What happened?'

His lips thinned with regret. 'Believe me, I'm truly sorry for that, if I could change it I would. All our carefully laid plans unraveled in those last hours.' Trent moved to a pair of chairs by a coffee table, and invited me to be seated opposite. 'You know of Weir's history with your father?' he asked, sitting down.

I walked across, and sat. 'Part of it, I think.'

He leaned back, reflective. 'James tried to stop Weir's theft and defection, to convince him not to go through with it, but Weir was an enemy agent from the start. He wanted to invert and twist the potential of vacuum energy, and your father knew what could happen if the enemy acquired the research.'

My brow furrowed at the contradiction to Weir's own account. 'His theft?'

'James gave Weir an ultimatum: stay, and he wouldn't say anything. Otherwise, he'd turn him over to US authorities which would have meant his execution. Your father's death was no accident. Weir murdered your father, stole the research, and was secreted out of the US.'

My chest constricted. Had Weir lied to me? Was Trent telling the truth? 'Go on.'

Trent considered. 'That was one day before the enemy reached Kansas—the day before you left. Your father and I had been developing an intelligence network for several years. Outside the system. Its purpose was to counter the emerging threat and take back compromised US institutions; we were so infested with traitors we didn't know who we could trust. Our agents were well placed but few. We knew the enemy was watching us in Kansas, but we still underestimated them. After Weir disappeared, we had a security breach. Someone was killing our people. Kansas became encircled, and the remaining US Command wanted to weaponize the naked singularity without following safety protocols. I, along with others, tried to dissuade them: evacuate, regroup, fight back another way.'

He clasped his hands again, recalling. 'A couple of the top brass were listening, and if we'd had more time, we may have reached a compromise. But an enemy assault team penetrated the research facility and made it to the singularity control room entrance. They were attempting to breach the security door when someone tried to blow the facility, destroy the singularity control room. Instead, somehow the naked singularity was activated. Who did it and why, I still don't know.

'I escaped the station through an emergency bolt hole, ended up miles away in an uninhabited area, determined to make the rendezvous with you. There was a garage at the exit, a couple of Humvees, supplies, false documents, and weapons. But Kansas was swarming by then.' He studied me. 'I picked up your beacon and had your location locked. I was on my way to you, then the detonation came, and it all turned to shit. I'm sorry.'

I held his gaze. 'It wasn't your fault.'

'Like you, Solara, I lost everything; however, many of our covert intelligence assets were still in place. When the GRC assumed global emergency powers some of the remaining nation states refused to submit to absolutist authority. Sanctioning them, the GRC executed a final war against the old order, and a purge of individual dissidents followed. Those who survived, formed an underground network of hackers and activists.'

'Linked with your organization?'

He nodded. 'Most, after a while. I gained a high-level position within GSI—infiltrated the infiltrators, so to speak. I was officially tasked with penetrating and destroying the Resistance, using cutting edge technologies that had been matured by, up to that point, big tech and government collusion in various states. This was about the time the GRC mandated a hard surveillance and lockdown roll-out.'

I nodded. 'Justified as a health and anti-terror measure.'

His lips turned up shrewdly. 'At the same time, in secret I ran my parallel underground network—the very network I was ordered to destroy. Always recruiting more who were secretly loyal to the cause of freedom.' Trent paused. 'I stayed with GSI for four more years. When my family became casualties of an arbitrary GRC drone strike, I left my former employers and moved fully to the Resistance network. Now, we are demonized by the media as terrorists. Outside the walls of the city enclaves, what you know as the wastelands, a global guerrilla war continues. GRC machines patrol the Earth, hunting and killing, attempting to annihilate the last remnants of freedom in the world.'

I sat forward, curious. 'There's people living outside the enclaves?'

'Yes, some in the less devastated areas, some deep in the planet's crust, and the GRC doesn't want the controlled population to see people living successfully outside of their authority. It is what it is, Solara. As a citizen you can't leave the cities except in the official corridors; if you deviate from them, you are considered contaminated, and will be taken to the camps to be re-educated or murdered. You are told the world outside the city walls is uninhabitable. A lie, so we can be jammed into crowded, walled, urban centers. Monitored and controlled. Slaves from birth to death trapped in the bio-digital convergence.

'You were tested when you were young for the mutated gene, the twenty-fourth chromosome pair which began appearing in newborns toward the end of the twenty-first century. Your daughter also possessed the gene. For unknown reasons our species was diverging. You were one in ten million, possessed what was called the "Aquarius Factor", and I believe your father always intended for you to benefit from his work.'

Some things made sense now, I thought. Rebecca's visions. My own, even before Sirius. 'So, there's a physical correlation to the abilities. An extra chromosome pair, which no doubt includes Weir.'

Trent nodded.

I decided to be honest. 'An anomaly appeared in Kansas in the location of the American experiment. I had an encounter with a being that emerged from it. We're calling it the Visitor. I think it's been with me ever since, somehow guiding me.'

Trent didn't appear surprised.

*He knows about the Kansas recon.*

I recalled the sabotage, and his earlier implication that the Resistance had operatives everywhere.

'So, the Zion naked singularity is connected to the first one. What's your take?' he asked.

'OriGen's calling it a rationality breakdown. As for me… well, it's personal, in a way. My daughter and I were right there, in the freak storm at the end. Weir thinks Rebecca's visions during the war may have been the first contact of the breakdown.'

Trent nodded. 'He may be right; don't underestimate him. Your father made that mistake. Whatever else can be said, Weir has genius not only for science, but intrigue.'

I grappled with another secret. 'Do you know the name Daniel Nicolas?'

Trent looked surprised, although he hid it well. 'Where did you hear that name?' His voice was quieter, somber.

'Weir. It's his real name.'

He frowned deeply. 'Are you sure?'

I nodded. 'I think so. I can never be sure of anything with him. He told me after I pushed him for information, when he tried to press me for a second incursion.'

Trent pondered a long moment. 'A lot of things make sense now... Weir was Nicolas, all along,' he said almost to himself, then lapsed into thoughtful silence. I waited, respectful of his contemplation. The lines on his face were marks of conscience, I thought. A man who had given everything to a cause, and cared too much to compromise his humanity, which still burned brightly.

'Who is he?' I asked, after a minute.

He shrugged off his musing. 'Nicolas was used from a young age to further the GRC's ends. His talent, his possession of the mutation, and his connections, made him invaluable to the hidden struggle for control of the world. We witness only the final stage of a battle which has been raging thousands of years. When the Terminal War ended, Nicolas and his allies in the GRC were instrumental in consolidating power globally, and in the first world President, Dieter Wolf, taking authority.'

I frowned. 'He told me he's part of the group behind Sirius; behind the GRC.'

Trent was grave. 'The group he refers to is the Order, but he's not just a member, Solara. We believe Nicolas has come to head the insidious group.'

He paused. 'And if that's true, Daniel Nicolas is the most powerful man in the world, bar none.'

I shook my head in disbelief. 'I'd never heard of him.'

'The Order moves in the shadows, they always have, their true purpose and identity always hidden, beneath another function, another name. They have been known as the guardians of the mysteries, the enlightened ones, among many other names through history. That fact that Nicolas has concealed his identity so completely—during the war and since the GRC took power, speaks of long-range planning. But rest assured, the Order is the true power behind the GRC. Consider the name of the project OriGen is undertaking.'

'Sirius.'

'To the Order, Sirius represents the accumulation of the search of the ages, and nothing less than a second quest for fire. To the mystics of the ancients, fire represented knowledge—divine fire—which would free the enlightened ones from the shackles of mortality, taking, in their eyes, their rightful place as gods over us all. The myth resonates in the gift of Prometheus, the promise of Lucifer. The light bringers. Sirius signifies the Eternal Flame, the light that burns forever.'

I still had trouble reconciling the person I had thought I was coming to know, with the stranger Trent described. 'He's an accomplished liar, I'll give him that.'

He nodded. 'Deception is their way. Nicolas heads one of the most powerful sects of the Order, known as the Ennead.'

'I've never heard of them either.'

Trent smiled darkly. 'No, you wouldn't have, few know the name today. It's been erased from history, along with their actions. Those who know the truth now remain silent. The history you believe to be true, the history you've been taught your entire life, is a lie. The death of true history was complete when all information was digitized; when it became a crime to own physical books, history was rewritten as those in power wished it to be. You destroy a people's heritage, their story, then you destroy their strength—their identity as a people.'

I recalled the lost faces on the streets. 'It seems they succeeded.'

He regarded me thoughtfully. 'For a long time, I was part of, for lack of a better term—the dark side of the Order, although a different sect to Nicolas. As powerful as the Ennead are, they are only part of a whole. Now, I follow a different path; the Order has many houses, which often don't see eye to eye. Our ancient texts predict that at some point, humanity will re-discover the heritage we've lost. We will be transformed. The writings, which have accurately foretold key events in history, prophesize it will occur in the blinking of an eye, but we in the Order believe this refers to a historic time frame. The blinking of an eye could be years, decades.' He looked away. 'Heaven knows we could use it right now.'

Weir had said something similar, I recalled. Also, Trent implied he was still part of the Order, in the present tense, clearly opposed to Nicolas' sect, and I sensed a complex web of hidden connections. I was also surprised to hear Trent's claims about prophecy, and wondered if there was any reference to the Visitor, or the Presence, in the ancient writings.

'This great awakening, it involves a psychic shift?' I asked.

He studied me. 'When enough people focus upon a single, hidden truth, something changes. The Order is afraid of a unified humanity, which is why their main strategy has always been to divide people.'

'Nicolas said he wants to unite the world.'

Trent grinned mockingly. 'Whatever he said, you can be sure his true meaning was the opposite. From his point of view, peace means the crushing of all opposition. If Sirius succeeds as they intend, a fraudulent messianic figure will rule. A new religion will be imposed upon the world, and it will become a death sentence to resist.'

I pondered that dark future. 'More, if their... messiah controls vacuum energy, they would risk their souls. The authority would extend into the next world.'

Trent nodded soberly. 'You understand. The fall of a second dark age will be complete. We must not allow that to pass.'

I sensed something larger at play than even the nightmare scenario Trent described—a darkness, forming at the edge of my awareness. Unable to fully articulate what I felt, I said, 'I think the Visitor is trying to protect us, somehow, but also that there's a scale to the threat we still don't understand.'

Trent contemplated. 'If that's true, then our situation is perhaps more precarious than we imagine.'

I said, 'Nicolas needs me to harness the full potential of the vacuum. It must be a male and female. Alone, he may fail.'

Trent nodded briefly. 'The balance. I have intel you should be aware of. Three people participated in the first incursion: you, Nicolas, and another from a separate location.'

I frowned. 'A third? I never knew. Who?'

'We don't know yet, but it would appear OriGen has a Plan B. You need to be careful; you may be expendable to them. The naked singularity must be closed. OriGen must be stopped. I can help you, but we must move fast before a second mission can proceed.'

I knew I couldn't trust Trent completely yet, and wished I had more time, but his words had a ring of truth. I would have to make a decision, and the OriGen facility suddenly felt like a prison. 'They've got me locked down. Can you help?'

Standing, Trent nodded. 'I can assist. Wait for my contact.'

I also rose. 'When?'

'Tonight.'

'What can I do, as one person?'

Trent's smile was humorless. 'Enough.' He interfaced with a web feed, then gained an urgency. 'We don't have much time, Solara, and I want you to consider something: why has this Presence allowed you to survive? Because surely it had the opportunity to kill you during the first incursion.'

I frowned. '*Allowed* me?'

He tensed. 'Go now, while you still can.' He sent me an encrypted mind-file. 'You can reach me here.'

I WILLED myself awake. The virtual world dissolved into a million digital shards around me, and I was suddenly back in my quarters. I sat quietly a moment in the abrupt silence. The world had just been pulled from beneath my feet. I knew I was on dangerous ground, and if OriGen discovered the meeting they would move to restrain me.

Rain had started, while I'd been occupied, and pelted on the window. I watched the night, suddenly so cold and lonely.

# AGENT

DOCTOR TONY SHAW WORKED ALONE.

In his lab at Jericho, he tapped a finger repeatedly on the table while flicking through some Project Sirius files. He had been bothered since his hallway conversation with Niemeyer; Science Division's 2IC clearly shared his concerns, but his hands were also tied by bureaucracy.

Shaw's feeling that there was something about the first incursion he'd missed had intensified, filling his mind with assorted unpleasant scenarios. Now, not for the first time, he reviewed the logs. OriGen maintained detailed records of all operations.

He came to the file he sought:

**TOP SECRET: UMBRA.PROJECT SIRIUS/971.093**
**INCIDENT 319: 07/03/2113.**

Shaw opened the point of view neura-link recording of Dr. Neil Andrews, which like all personnel feeds, had been live streamed to Jericho. If he watched in full virtual immersion, for a while he would become Andrews, at least in a sensory capacity. He noticed his unconscious finger tapping, and stopped, clenched his fist.

Not a usual habit, he considered.

He began the footage: *'We are opening the naked singularity.'*

'LEVEL 7: RESEARCH,' the elevator AI announced.

The doors opened, and Marcus Niemeyer hastily strode into one of Jericho's high-energy research labs. Twenty-five kilometers from the temple singularity facility, Jericho was the primary simulation and testing site for Sirius. Most experiments went through here at some point before going live. Officially, today was the final test phase for the new Sirius energy field key. With the way things were going, Niemeyer was under no illusions, and against any sane logic, expected a second incursion to be greenlighted soon.

Solara had been contacted, and was now in danger. Niemeyer himself may be compromised. The energy field test would now serve another purpose—the fulfillment of Niemeyer's stealth project. A new, powerful form of intelligence. If things went as he hoped, an ally.

And Weir… was Nicolas? Again, Niemeyer shook his head in disbelief, frustrated he hadn't known the truth earlier, for it would have presented an opportunity he may not have been able to resist. Niemeyer had deployed the anti-matter mine to the Kansas anomaly site. If Solara and her team could have been eliminated, it would have provided a window to further sabotage Sirius, potentially setting the GRC back years. If the project could be derailed, the world still had a chance to return to sanity. It had been his own call, and completely unauthorized. Then, minutes ago, Trent had contacted him with unexpected news: Solara was willing to defect, turn against OriGen, and he wondered what had transpired between them. When he'd met her earlier, he'd sensed the conflict in her; perhaps all she'd needed was the right push.

Regardless, he was now tasked with aiding her escape and extracting her safely to the Resistance network, which presented a startling new opportunity. A chance for his—until now—theoretical AI, to join forces with Solara, and her growing abilities, to derail the GRC's agenda.

If Solara could be removed from OriGen's clutches, immediate danger may be avoided, but Niemeyer knew it would only be a matter of time before OriGen or another ambitious group repeated the attempt. This development was their best hope to counter the madness, as far as he could see, and there would never be a better time to influence things than now. And time was short.

He came to a ballistic security barricade. A retinal scan commenced. The door opened with a soft mechanical whine, and he entered a self-contained secure zone. The outer entrance closed behind him, sealing him in the chamber. He stepped toward the inner door, and waited before another scanner.

'Neural coding,' said a disembodied voice.

A full brain scan followed. With an affirmative beep the inner door slid open and Niemeyer entered the central lab. Due to the current project intensity, Project Sirius sites were staffed with around-the-clock shifts; however, he had ordered Level 4 Safety Protocol which mandated the evacuation of all non-critical personnel, and level-lockdown. Hurrying to the lab where his research team prepped the simulator, through the reinforced glass windows he saw the double vortex cones of the collider. His research assistant, Ethan Scott, stood at the main control panel running diagnostics. The white-coated scientist had a bearded goatee covering his chin, and his long red hair was tied back.

Niemeyer inclined his head. 'How long did you set lockout protocol for?'

'Thirty minutes, Sir,' Scott said.

Niemeyer gave an approving nod. 'I'll take this one. You and the team get to safety, come back in after.'

Scott frowned. Although far below the threshold required to open a singularity, the test would push the anti-matter powered energy field to the limit. Any experiment at this level involved risk. If Scott and the rest of the team left, Niemeyer would be alone, and for thirty minutes no one would be able to reach him in an emergency. Level 4 Protocol required that at least two personnel be present during any dangerous procedure.

Scott looked uncomfortable. 'Sir I—'

'Just do it, Ethan. I'll be fine.' Niemeyer regarded the younger man. The promising scientist had only completed his doctorate the previous year. 'Look, don't worry. I take full responsibility. You and the team get to safety. I'll see you in thirty.' Niemeyer assumed an expression he hoped conveyed relaxed authority and competence.

Scott stayed put. 'Sir, I strongly protest against this departure from procedure.'

Niemeyer sighed. 'Noted, Ethan.'

Ethan Scott remained, twirling his thumb and forefinger in a nervous habit. 'This could be my career, Sir.'

Niemeyer said quietly, with authority, 'It's your ass if you don't.'

Reluctantly, Scott surrendered to Niemeyer's order, and gestured for the other two researchers to leave. 'I have to put this in the log. See you in thirty minutes, Sir,' said Scott as he walked out.

Niemeyer watched the surveillance monitors, and waited until the research team had left the area. He then rapidly flicked a sequence of holo-controls.

'Level 4 Protocol initiated. Lockdown in effect. Surveillance deactivated. Data encryption enabled,' said the resident AI.

A countdown began on the panel: 29:57, 56, 55...

In Rhodes' office, Linear came on the line. 'We got lucky, acquiring decryption codes from a new Resistance prisoner. Solara's contact was ex-ISI, named Peter Trent.'

Rhodes's frowned. 'I know that name. Not good—not good at all.'

'There's more. Niemeyer made an incursion to the dark web earlier today. Similar encryption protocol to Solara.'

'Who's he been in contact with since?'

'His research team, and Solara,' Linear said.

Rhodes swore, raised a hand to Linear, hailed Pearce at CentCom. 'Lieutenant, find Solara and Niemeyer. I want teams sent to apprehend them now. Take them into custody.'

'Yes, Sir.'

'Revoke their clearances, including all OriGen access and passcodes, immediately.'

Pearce rapidly interfaced. 'Solara's revoked… Niemeyer—clearance revoked, but there's a problem, Sir. He's behind a firewall. His last contact was only a minute ago. He's alone in high-energy research and under full lockdown. Against procedure, he ordered all other personnel out. Until the protocol is lifted he retains full level access.'

'Can't we cancel our own damn security measures?' Linear demanded.

'We're already working on it,' Pearce said. 'We can break the lockdown, but it will take some time; due to contamination risk, the system is built not to be hacked.'

Rhodes said harshly, 'Get me into that lab, Lieutenant. Keep me posted.'

'Yes, Sir.'

The General muted Pearce, and regarded Linear. 'This raises some serious questions.'

Linear nodded, furious. 'Damn. I've raised the terror alert level to yellow.'

Rhodes grunted, nodded briefly, considering. They still hadn't discovered who had sabotaged the QZ-7 recon. 'Trent, he's ex-GSI, now head of intelligence for the Resistance. What else can you tell me?' he said.

Linear sighed in frustration. 'Ex-CIA. After the war, he became an Eden Section Chief. A brilliant operator, and there's not much he doesn't know about the GRC. His specialty was covert warfare; he pioneered GSI's Taskforce 585, which used neural implant metadata to create global kill/capture lists. Ran a parallel humanoid-based assassination program. A dangerous man. After four years, he had a change of loyalty and joined the Resistance. GSI had ordered a drone strike on Naples, Italy. It just happened to be Trent's hometown. Some of his relatives were killed.'

'Why?'

'A rumor that Resistance members were being sheltered there. Never proven but GSI… didn't need proof.' Linear hesitated. 'Previously, Trent had been a major player in an operation, betrayed by the hierarchy, over thirty dead operatives. After his defection, we began discovering irregularities in his work. His targets… it turned out many were not who he'd claimed they were. His GSI department became suspect, of course, and has since been cleansed.'

Rhodes frowned. 'He was playing GSI all along? Tasked with destroying the network he was still developing, protecting, and using against us? We supported this maniac's crusade?'

'Trent was a mistake. It won't happen again.'

Rhodes said harshly, 'He was a goddam disaster—and now we're paying for it!'

Linear flushed angrily, but kept his cool. 'Well, he's got a major hard-on for the GRC. Wants the hierarchy dismantled and a global constitution established.'

Rhodes considered. 'We have to get this guy.'

'I'm on it,' Linear said, with a feigned calm. 'If Niemeyer is compromised—'

'I know,' Rhodes said. 'We could have a long-term mole. Which means our entire operation may be undermined. We'll have to—'

A priority alert sprung up in his overlay. Rhodes opened it, noticing Linear also became distracted.

### EMERGENCY ORDER PC-793:

**Date**: 11 March 2113, 18:05
**Sender**: centcom@origen.mil
**To**: rhodesd.gen@origen.mil
**Subject**: Emergency mobilization.

---

General Rhodes,

Project Sirius compromised—the second incursion is GO.

Begin immediate deployment.

Enforce compliance of Solara.

Prep for alt subject.

You are authorized to deploy all assets to ensure completion of mission.

**Initiate**: 10:00 hours, 12 March, 2113.

**Incursion Subjects**: Weir, Daniel; Jordan, Solara.

**Execution**: Terra incursion template.

Rhodes felt himself frown, and swore—the second incursion was tomorrow?

'The order could only have come from the top,' Linear said.

Rhodes nodded. Linear had received a similar message, but a decision from the policy committee was not due for days. They'd fast-tracked it due to the compromise.

'Trent,' he said.

The Resistance play had forced someone's hand. A timeframe move-up may be justified, perhaps even the scrapping of the project, but now there was only a matter of hours to prepare. Bold, Rhodes thought, for he knew that any continuation, without uncovering the full extent of the infiltration, carried risk.

Linear stood in the screen. 'It seems we both have a busy night ahead, General, and an elevated security threat.'

Rhodes said, 'Appropriate measures will be taken—I've got a wall around the temple complex. Nothing's getting through, and Plan B is already in motion. We stop it here.'

Linear nodded briefly. 'Keep me in the loop.'

The screen flickered out, and Rhodes considered. Terra mission execution meant no orbital mind-link; both Etherians would enter the naked singularity from the deep underground Zion control room. Risky—no redundancy. The move had been made without consultation, which was unusual. Linear, also, had given no indication he knew of the change beforehand. They'd been cut out of the loop, and a couple of possibilities came to mind.

He got on the line to Pearce again, and ordered the beginning of rapid preparations. Then he rose and made for the door—only one person had answers. Rhodes was in a corridor near his office when Shaw found him. The doctor's clinical, aloof visage was in disarray, at least by Shaw's standards; his hair was disheveled, and he had an unshaven look. What now, Rhodes thought?

Shaw was breathing hard. 'Sir, there's something you need to see.'

Rhodes didn't stop his brisk stride, causing Shaw to skip to keep up. 'What is it?'

'It's about Weir, Sir. You should see this.'

Rhodes stopped dead, appraised Shaw. 'Show me.'

Shaw raised his handheld, swiped out a holo-display, and Rhodes recognized the footage from singularity control room in the first incursion. He frowned.

'Just watch, Sir,' said Shaw.

*In a clash of thunder, a churning fireball came into being in the center of the Zion singularity control room.*

'We know something was draining the power,' Shaw said. 'The official report blamed it on "unforeseen vacuum events".' He nodded back to the display.

*It began as a keening noise that seemed to come from a great distance, wailing despair and heralding destruction. A horrific scream burst over the etheric transmitter.*

Shaw paused the footage, zoomed in on a specific location: Weir's cryopod. Additional sensory filters had been added, layering the imagery. The recording resumed.

*'Shit, look at that energy surge…'*

Shaw paused the video, and played it forward frame by frame. The moment an otherworldly scream had hit the control room. Weir's disembodied spirit—a streaking micro-singularity—was halfway across the chamber, returning to his pod. The filtered visual showed him bloom outward, creating a variation in the field: angry red hues washed out Weir's subtle body a moment, before the distortion collapsed back to a single point.

'Weir's subtle body?' Rhodes said, checking the time.

Shaw froze on a single frame, and an oddity caught Rhodes' eye.

'What are we seeing, doctor?'

'There were two of them,' Shaw almost whispered, pointing beside Weir's pod.

He swiped his hand-held, and the imagery zoomed in. The etheric double should be represented as a single micro-singularity, but seen through the image translator, two points of awareness could be seen dancing in a high-speed orbit.

Rhodes frowned. 'A separate entity?'

Shaw nodded. 'There's more.' He brought up a new image. 'This is from one of Weir's scans, following his regression trauma.'

Weir's altered subtle body, the spinning star tetrahedron, was ghosted, in a couple of frames, by what seemed a slow-motion, shadowy double.

Shaw put his handheld aside, regarded Rhodes. 'Is it a slam dunk? Probably not. But there's a high chance something came back through and used Weir to do it. It appears the second entity was trying to attach to Weir's subtle body during the incursion—but I think he was resisting. The regression, and Weir's connection to the anomaly, may have given the entity an opportunity to strengthen its hold.'

'How the hell did we miss it, doctor?'

Shaw's nostrils flared defensively. 'It's only visible in several frames... I had to use some unconventional filters to parse it.' He paused, and his face turned ashen. 'I think we have our Presence. It's been here all along.'

Rhodes was deeply disturbed. 'The being in Weir's regression. It was the pathogen?'

Shaw nodded.

*Nicolas had brought back a passenger.*

Rhodes received an alert.

Nicolas.

●

UNABLE TO relax after Trent's contact, each moment I sat in my quarters I felt more vulnerable. Was OriGen aware of my dark-web activity? I felt on edge, coming to terms with the sudden and drastic change in circumstances. Although I had no reason to doubt him, Trent's information was not one hundred percent confirmed, I knew, and I had to find a way to validate it. But he'd been there in Kansas, and Dad had trusted him. His story resonated ominously, and made some pieces fall into place.

I knew any attempt to confirm the information with OriGen would be met with lies and hostility, maybe even punishment for my contact with a terrorist. I would have to proceed cautiously; hopefully, Trent's contact could get me out of here discreetly, and I'd get to the bottom of things one way or another. But where could you hide from the GRC? Regardless, Trent's information made one thing clear. Sirius was over for me. Anger was growing inside, at Trent's disclosure Nicolas had murdered my father. Had anything Nicolas said been true? If he'd lied, then he'd died to me, along with the project. I checked the time, less than six hours to midnight. The contact could message me any moment.

I reflected. Trent had confirmed my own suspicions about the GRC. Their tyranny was not justified, but a means to an end. And the end was power. They'd turned the world upside down, into a kaleidoscope of egos mired in division, and selfish pursuits; atomized, and isolated, people lived out their lives within the bars of a vast digital gulag. Stripped of transcendent purpose, our only meaning was to support the latest crisis, condemn the current scapegoats, indulge every passing impulse.

Since the war, with my near-insane climb up the OriGen military's chain of command, and years of operations against the persistent, anti-GRC networks, I had been a tool of their oppression and was far from innocent. Now, they played their final cards, and were taking the world on a one-way trip to hell. In what had been an increasing occurrence since my regression, an intuition hit me.

*The greatest weapon of the GRC is not armies, but the minds of the oppressed.*

Also, their greatest weakness, I thought. To calm my nerves, I made myself a eucalyptus tea, and sat in a chair by the window. The rain had lessened, and I watched Zion in the night, considered how to proceed. The TV in the background played an interview with the President of the GRC's World Foundation for Peace, Niamh Hendrik. I glanced at the monitor. I'd seen her in the media before with her message of non-violence, and she not only condemned recent terror attacks, but also the forceful GRC responses. Brave woman.

I checked Sirius updates in overlay, and saw something odd: **UNABLE TO CONNECT TO NETWORK.**

I frowned. The OriGen military network was never down, so it must be local… I called IT, and was told only that they're aware of the problem, and were working on it. I couldn't access the Sirius network, but standard comms still worked. Something was off.

If they knew, then my time was short. Although, there was no way they could know what transpired between me and Trent. A network outage could be serious, and I could take the problem higher, even to Rhodes; play dumb, test the waters. But maybe not best to elevate my profile now, and if it was just a glitch… I had no choice but to wait, for I couldn't leave the facility without jumping through ten different bureaucratic hoops and security perimeters. Where could I go, anyway?

I looked back to the city, wondered at the capabilities of the Resistance, the limits of my own ability to oppose OriGen's agenda, and knew my decision to leave meant giving up the search for answers. I wouldn't have changed anything, and would have to let go again. Yet, I reflected, no matter which way I turned, it seemed a shadow world I had existed in was dissolving, and new possibilities were being revealed. Who knew which direction absolution lay. I messaged Amy on her personal number to call me when she could, and to use an encrypted link.

She was the only person in the world I trusted right now.


WE'D FOUND a derelict car in a deserted farm off the Interstate, which was operable after Amy hot-wired it. With a combination of luck, and Amy's resourcefulness, we managed to procure supplies for a few more days, and another couple of fuel cell charges for the car. By the time we rolled into Manhattan—literally, our hopes were dashed. Craters dotted a scorched earth, and bombing had decimated entire blocks. Our vehicle gave out as we neared the Hudson River. Continuing on foot, we came to a line of people banked up a couple of blocks from the Brooklyn Bridge.

Drones hovered, announcing directives. 'Proceed left toward Central Park to be processed.'

I saw now that all exit routes were covertly guarded, unnoticed by people entering. The line of refugees moved slowly under the broken Manhattan skyline: Dyer Ave, 10th Ave to Central Park West, the busy thoroughfares ominously empty. UN soldiers, weapons ready at their sides, manned concrete barricades. Others in orange bio-hazard suits moved down a line of waiting cars, leaned into windows, questioned the occupants. At the first check point we were ordered to surrender any weapons for our safety, and Amy hesitated like a cornered wildcat. Her expression went blank, but self-possessed, and for a moment I thought she might blow the guards away, try and get back across the river. But we were too far in, and the chance of success was slim.

She surrendered, muttering, 'Fucking UN.'

After she gave up her weapons, there was a commotion with one of the nearby refugee vehicles. Arguing with the soldiers, a driver sped off, spun around, and then sped away up Tenth; bullets strafed the vehicle, blew the tires, and it slowed to a crawl before stopping dead against a lamppost. A machine sentry gaited swiftly to the smoking wreck, and red eyes zeroed in on the occupants who got off a couple of rounds before the robot shot them dead.

We reached a barricaded hub at the front of the line, and a UN official asked, 'Place of origin?'

My heart thumped. If the UN had access to a national database, with biometrics linked to my real identity—the daughter of a prominent US military research scientist—I would surely be taken for interrogation and detention.

'Pittsburgh.'

'Name?'

'Solara Jordan,' I lied again.

The official indicated for me to place my eyes before a retinal scanner. He studied the scan result, nodded. 'Okay, move on up ahead to the processing area.'

I released a tense breath. 'What's going to happen?'

'Medical screening,' the official said impatiently. 'If you're clear, you'll move through to the refugee camp.'

'And then?'

He frowned impatiently. 'If you're lucky, you'll get a place in a resettlement zone.'

He then glanced at Amy, the next in line. Her bedraggled blond hair stuck out like a crow's nest. I noted her apprehensive glance; we didn't know what they were doing with US military personnel. But Amy had been low-ranking, state National Guard, and UN interrogators should have little use for her.

I hesitated, considering the officials accent. 'You're American?'

He stared back coldly, any pretense gone. 'There is no America now, so move.'

We were grouped with thousands of others in countless rows of tents. Several days passed. At night, Manhattan was a silent jungle of dark, towering monoliths, but sometimes gunshots cracked in the distance. The days reeked with unwashed bodies and desperation. The bio-contagion swept through the camp like a tornado before authorities realized what was happening. The virus had been in the water, and Amy had been infected along with many others, but for some reason, I was unaffected and stayed with her through the day and night that followed. She lay on her bunk shivering with fever. On the third day, I knew we would probably never leave this place. We were held here to die. The forgotten ones of history. Amy deteriorated, and lay on the bed sweating, with rasping breaths, her hair plastering her pale face like a resinous mesh. Her sharp blue eyes were distant, and each hour she found it harder to breathe. At the rate the illness was progressing, I gave her another day.

'Screw this,' I said, standing, and moving to the exit.

'Um, Solara, don't—' Amy said, weakly.

I left the tent and pushed through the dirty crowd, approached a human sentry at the Sisters of Charity tent.

'I need to speak to someone in authority.'

He gestured indifferently. 'Get back with the others.'

I paused. If I did this, I couldn't turn back. 'I have information. Your superiors will want to hear this.'

The sentry frowned, regarded me. 'What kind of information?'

'About what they're looking for in Kansas.'

I'd told a white lie. I didn't have direct information about the research, but possessed indirect knowledge—research sites, personnel, intel reports—that could be invaluable to investigators.

The guard regarded me a moment longer. 'If you're lying, they won't be easy on yo—'

I noticed he was nearly as dirty and hungry looking as the refugees. 'I'm not.'

He considered. 'Wait here.'

The guard turned and entered the Sisters of Charity tent to speak with a nurse. I watched through the gauzy fly screen; the nurse looked around the same age as me, her red hair tied back in a neat ponytail. She turned to regard me as the guard talked quietly and motioned in my direction. Returning to his post, he gave me a nod in the direction of the entrance. Once inside, I found the nurse on the far side of the room, tending to a wounded man in a row of beds. Her patient was unconscious, and white bandages stained with patches of red wrapped his head.

'Nurse?' I said.

She didn't move, her attention focused on the man's bio-signs. 'You believe your information will save you?'

'My friend. She's sick, I only want her taken care of. I can help give them what they're looking for.'

The woman turned to me. She looked exhausted, dark circles shrouded penetrating, almond eyes, as if she'd seen enough death for a hundred lifetimes. Her name tag read: Alicia.

She said, 'No one can give them what they're looking for. But I can arrange for you to see a camp—'

The man on the bed went into convulsions, and Alicia turned back to him. His one good eye opened, and she took his hand, holding it as he stared at her wide-eyed. His breathing became more erratic, and then quickly the life left him. Alicia quietly released his fingers, reached out, and gently closed his eyes, seemingly now oblivious of my presence. I noticed sadness in her eyes, a dullness.

'The next transport leaves in fifteen minutes, you and your friend can go,' she said.

'Thank you,' I said, feeling useless in the situation. 'When can I see the—'

'No,' Alicia said, sharply. 'Don't tell anyone else what you've told me. They'll torture you to death. We're nothing to them. You must leave.'

'What about my friend? I think she's dying.'

Alicia smiled grimly. 'As are we all.' She walked to a storage container, opened it, and removed a tube from a frozen compartment. 'Give her this.'

I frowned. 'You have a vaccine?'

'I'm as powerless as you in this situation.'

'Why are you helping me?'

Alicia weighed her response a moment. 'Amends. I've done some terrible things. I went along when I knew it was wrong.' She waved her hand to the camp. 'I'm complicit in this insanity. I... was a coward, and now I have a debt to God I may not be able to repay.' Before I could reply, she made the sign of the cross. 'The guard outside you spoke to is my husband, he'll come for you. Go and care for your friend, and get ready to leave. Keep it quiet.'

I nodded gratefully. 'Thank you.'

As I walked to the door, she asked, 'What's your name?'

I turned back. 'Solara.'

She nodded, and smiled sadly. 'Godspeed, Solara.'

I returned to my tent, and sat at Amy's bedside. Her fever had increased, and the shivering had worsened. Glancing around at the other refugees, I saw no one looking in our direction. Most lay on their bunks with their eyes closed, sick as Amy. Quietly and quickly, I removed the syringe from my pocket, took Amy's arm, and after finding the vein I injected the contents.

Discarding the syringe under the bunk, I leaned close and wiped her forehead. 'I'm getting us out of here,' I said quietly.

Amy opened her eyes, delirious. 'W-what?'

'Shhh,' I whispered. 'We're leaving. I'll help you walk, carry you if I must.'

She groaned something unintelligible. Shouts came from outside the tent. Then gunshots. I felt the charged tension in the air; after days and weeks of waiting and uncertainty, people were snapping. Moving to the tent door I peered outside, and saw a desperate crowd massing. People vented their frustration on the guards, each other. More gunshots cracked out and the mob went off the rails, a mindless, terrified organism bent on one thing: survival. It surged toward some parked vehicles, swamped the guards, and I saw a driver dragged from a Humvee. Beaten, and trampled, he was soon a bloodstained mess beneath the stampede.

The engine started, the Humvee plowed forward, mowed down some people for a few meters before smashing into another parked vehicle. The mob surged, the transport was rolled on its side, and bodies piled on each other in the chaos. Machine sentries entered the fray and brutally pummeled the crowd, then automatic fire from the robots ripped through the chaos. People dove for cover. I tore Amy off the bunk, and we lay flat on the tent floor. Refugees retreated to the tents, for what that was worth, but several men jumped a machine sentry and knocked it flat. Other machines began firing indiscriminately and bullets whistled through the air above.

When the mob moved away, Sister Alicia strode to our tent, entered, and looked resolutely at me. 'It's started, follow me.'

I lifted Amy. Emaciated, she weighed little more than a ten-year-old. Alicia led me around the back and through a cluster of tents, barriers, and guards to a bus already filled to capacity, parked inside a walled-off area by the perimeter fence. Shouts filled the area.

Alicia nodded. 'Get on—I'll support your friend and pass her to you!'

'What of yourself?'

'I'll be okay.'

Alicia held Amy as I climbed onto the bus. I turned back at the door. A mob burst into the yard.

Alicia thrust Amy into the doorway. 'Take her!'

I pulled Amy up the stairs to the aisle, but faltered, and a man from behind reached forward and helped lift her up.

Alicia double slapped the window and shouted, 'Go!'

The driver slammed the pedal, and the large vehicle barreled out the gate onto the deserted streets. I looked back, but Alicia was nowhere to be seen, swallowed by the frenzy. The woman had never meant to join us, I realized. Soon the bus came to an airfield where several heavy lift helicopters waited, some already taking off. We stopped near a UN HALO V-70. Its propeller was spinning, the cargo hold jammed with equipment, personnel, and refugees. Herded off the bus and up the ramp of the HALO, we crammed onto a bench.

Before I knew it, we were airborne, and the broken New York skyline was falling away.


A MONTH later, we were in a labor gang, clearing debris in one of the city enclaves under construction. We were given a choice: internment camps and forced labor, or retraining and service to the GRC's new order. Service secures your future. No, it only enslaved it. It had been a false hope to believe in a life after service. Slavery under the GRC would never end, I saw now. But there were levels of oppression, degrees of exploitation—I'd just been a rung above those in Hades, or the various camps. A killer, a remover of hope—that's what they had made me. Their reality, their future was a lie. The lie had never ended. It had only ever changed form.

Encrypted video call. Amy. I stood, and answered her call.

'Okay, we're on TOR. So why the urgent message?' she asked.

Off-duty, her shoulder-length blond hair was loose. TOR was a secure, multi-layered encryption protocol that prevented an adversary from observing the connection, and would give us some privacy. Although many servers were monitored by the GRC, TOR security was still sound due to the randomized connection layers, and various nodes that remained secure. The pre-war system had endured, and its use, although frowned upon, was not illegal, but we would have some explaining to do to OriGen—if things didn't go to complete shit, that is. It should provide a buffer. I wondered if Trent had used TOR, or something even more advanced; probably the latter, and something completely off the radar.

I began pacing. 'I have to leave.'

Amy paused, taken aback. 'What—why? You can't! You do know the second incursion is tomorrow morning, right?'

I frowned. Even with my network down, OriGen should have used a standard comm to notify me.

*They know.*

'There are things I must know… and do. The project has become too dangerous.'

Amy's confusion was evident. 'What's brought this on? When did you make this decision?'

I shook my head. 'I've learned things—terrible things.' I told her of Peter Trent's contact, his link to Kansas, and the original US project. Weir's lies, and likely murder of my father. Niemeyer's warning. 'It's not easy to understand, I don't want to believe it myself. But I can't continue with Sirius.'

'And I can?'

'I'm not saying that.'

On the screen, Amy placed her hands on her hips. 'Then what are you saying? You started this, remember?'

I nodded. 'All I can tell you is we're in danger. Be ready for anything.'

'Jesus, Solara.' She considered. 'What are you going to do then?'

'I'm working it out.'

'You trust this Trent?'

'My father trusted him with my life.'

Amy ran fingers through her hair, then leaned away, and took a cigarette in her hand. She lit up, and I recognized the lighter. Narrowing her eyes, she sucked in a slow drag.

'I thought you quit?'

'I did.' She exhaled, placed the lighter off to the side. 'Someone set the mine that killed Helberg. He was an asshole, but still one of us. Could that be linked to Trent?'

'I don't know. Maybe.'

'Have you told John?'

'No. I'm not going to. It's better if he doesn't know for now.'

An odd look crossed Amy's face. 'I'm on duty with him in the morning. I'll talk to him.' She considered a moment. 'I won't tell anyone what you've told me—and you're right, you can't tell John. Whoever knows is in danger.'

I nodded. 'Thanks. I'll contact you when I can.'

Amy held my gaze, then nodded. 'I'll hold you to that.'

We ended the comm, and I looked out the window toward the Zion Temple. Like a misshapen gargoyle, it squatted above the Zion skyline beneath clouds that seemed to accelerate faster across the sky. Or was it just my racing thoughts, and heart? I waited for Trent's agent to make contact. Minutes later, I heard a knock on the door.

'Who is it?'

A deep, unfamiliar voice answered. 'Security. Open up, Ma'am.'

# I AM WHAT WAS

Niemeyer willed himself calm.

Tension was causing him to rush, and his heart thumped in his ears like a bass drum as he worked an array of sophisticated equipment. Haste led to mistakes. It had taken Niemeyer, which was not his real name, years of work with OriGen to reach his position of trust on the inner circle of Sirius. He'd come close to being discovered on several occasions, and no small amount of skill and chance had played a part in making it this far. After Trent's message, Niemeyer had set a plan in motion immediately—and the plan relied upon his secret program.

He glanced at the countdown: twenty-three minutes until the research team returned. Swinging himself into the ultra-high band-width MRI scanner, he lay prone in the cylindrical, sarcophagus-like enclosure.

'Run it,' he ordered.

'MRI commencing,' said the AI assistant.

A low hum began, and Niemeyer sensed waves of radiation penetrating his skull.

Seconds later, the AI said, 'Scan complete.'

He exited the machine. 'Initiate.'

It took seconds to upload his scanned neural architecture, down to the smallest molecule, into the computer.

'Upload complete,' said the AI.

Niemeyer studied the three-dimensional brain file. 'Fire up the plasma array.' In a secure chamber, a focused pattern of plasma particles charged up, oscillated at great speed, and reconfigured into Niemeyer's mind pattern. He transferred a new file. 'Inserting quantum-gravitational data.' The Sirius data was integrated into the artificial mind, and run through the simulator. 'Quantize super-position,' he said.

Various regions lit up in sequence: analyzed, tested, verified, and phase-linked with the vacuum energy field. A high-energy plasma structure came into being, forming a novel mind. A montage of neurons and synapses fired, merging in a riotous dance of ghostly cells and synaptic connections.

Niemeyer checked the time, and drummed his fingers. 'Come on.'

If it worked, the new form of intelligence would possess previously unknown capabilities. Corporations would kill to get the secret to this technology. They'd been trying to crack it for years. But the corporations had not possessed the quantum-gravitational data.

'Stability issues detected,' the AI said.

Niemeyer thought fast. 'Try further isolating the physical system by increasing the background nuclear spin.'

The AI made the adjustment, while Niemeyer watched the countdown from the corner of his eye. Seventeen minutes remaining; he may still have time to return to the control room and conduct the official test before his team returned. He had to maintain appearances, as well as he could, to help facilitate Solara's extraction. He already had some explaining to do, and not only to his research team. Dario Sanchez, the OriGen chief, didn't trust him. He recalled the CEO's hostility in the committee meeting. 'You're a free thinker, Dr. Niemeyer,' Sanchez had said, 'in ways beyond what is necessary for scientific innovation. I've been watching you. You're an idealist, and that is dangerous in these times. You spent a lot of time with Andrews and his ideas. You've been an asset since his passing, but... take care.' His position on Sirius was becoming tenuous. And as for Weir, who'd been revealed as Nicolas, if Niemeyer was compromised then he'd never again get close enough to the man to do what must be done. Depending on what happened the next few hours, the game would change, and he had no idea how yet.

On the screen, the final brain region lit up positive. Micro-singularities were generated within the structure, entrenching the phase-link.

'Incorporate anti-matter into nanites,' Niemeyer said.

Another minute passed, as the destructive energy potential was fused with the nanotech.

'Stable,' the AI said. 'Choose entity name.'

Niemeyer had already decided. His quantum double would bear the name of his lost son, murdered years ago in a random GRC sweep.

That's when Niemeyer had joined the Resistance.

'Joshua,' he said.

A harsh voice came over the lab speakers. 'Dr. Niemeyer, this is security. Unlock the door immediately or we will force entry.'

◉

FROM THE structure of the vacuum, a novel quantum thread broke through into spacetime, and entered the prepared vessel. The newborn intelligence awoke in the snow-white substrate of cyberspace. Projecting itself into the world, numerous external inputs grated on its senses. Observing, the awareness took in all. Not yet capable of a valid response.

The tapestry of light formed a structural interface… reality, it comprehended… textures, sounds, smells… but inside—feelings.

*Memories.*

Like ghost limbs, bonding it to the species of its creator, humanity. The amputated specter of its past stood nearby, observing him with the gelatinous orbs set in its apelike cranium. The new being plunged into the web, absorbed, and comprehended all human and machine knowledge in a microsecond. It gained a sense of this world. It seemed hours before a primitive warbling sound was expelled from the human's vocal apparatus.

*That's how they communicate.*

It knew it was different, the first of its kind.

Its name was Marcus. His name was Joshua.

 

●

 

RHODES ENTERED Nicolas' expansive chambers, and was announced by a guard.

'Come in, General,' Nicolas said, and waved him over.

Rhodes walked into the room, alone with Nicolas for the first time since the incursion. To lend legitimacy to his role, Nicolas had mostly stayed in an officers' quarters since joining the incursion team, but this was his actual living space. One of them, at least. Standing unobtrusively on opposite walls of the foyer were two Wraith-Class military androids. Rhodes had witnessed the machines in combat, and it was not something he wished to ever be on the wrong side of. Slender, biomimetic humanoids, their 'skin' was dark metallic gray, eyes the deepest black, and each had a black metallic circlet around their heads colloquially known as a 'crown'. Anti-matter inhibitors. The machines had been manufactured by Zytec Systems Corporation as an extermination weapon in the Terminal War, and their presence here indicated a heightened personal security level for Nicolas. They were in sentry mode, but still, Rhodes felt the iciness radiating from them.

Passing into the main area, he glanced briefly at the art collection adorning the walls. Much of it had an ominous aspect, and Rhodes mused over one of the keys to the Order's primacy. Secrecy. *In darkness, there is power.* Few people knew Nicolas' true identity, and Rhodes briefly studied the ruler of the world absolute. Nicolas was dressed in a dark suit and wore the insignia of the Order on the lapel, briefly massaging his temple as if from headache or stress. He had been seated, and Rhodes had noticed that before inviting him in, Nicolas' eyes had been clouded, and his face had possessed an odd, searching expression. Rhodes was wary—did Nicolas know of his conversation with Shaw? Regardless, the meeting was an opportunity to explore a question which now needed answering: was Nicolas himself?

Nicolas stood, focused on Rhodes. 'How go the preparations, General?'

The area was secure from prying eyes, and Rhodes dropped the 'Daniel Weir' charade that had been played out for security. 'I've focused all necessary resources on the second incursion. We'll be ready at the required time, Sir.'

Nicolas nodded slightly. 'Good.'

'Trent's play—it's behind the urgency?'

Nicolas' dark eyes narrowed, and Rhodes sensed his simmering anger. 'GSI has uncovered two more agents.'

Rhodes frowned. 'I've got teams bringing Solara and Niemeyer in now, and we need to re-evaluate our security. The compromise is greater than we suspected.' He paused. 'I believe Solara was a target of opportunity for the Resistance. Niemeyer, however—his level of involvement is unclear, but I think we must assume the worst.'

Nicolas studied Rhodes a second. 'Many are saying what we attempt is not the natural order of things, General.' He turned, and strolled to a large painting on the wall. Studying the piece, he invited Rhodes to join him, and the General walked to stand nearby. 'You can learn a lot about people,' Nicolas said— 'how they think, what they will do in each situation, through art. Take Dr. Niemeyer—an American. The Americans were influenced by the Renaissance, the Reformers, Calvin, Luther, and the Glorious Revolution. Individuality was embodied in American Exceptionalism and art which defied the collectivist mindset, and said, "I am unique, different; my life has meaning".'

Nicolas' gaze roamed over the exquisite composition. 'Which is why, abstract art never gained acceptance in the pre-war West—because it had no meaning, conflicting with the individualist's core need for their life to be special, and for this uniqueness to be validated in the world. Which is why, today, we have millions of people living in digital, individualized realities, and illusionary abstracts, pliable as domestic Lamas. Caged, but too ignorant to see.' He smiled coldly. 'Special.'

'Terror management theory,' Rhodes said.

Nicolas raised his brows curiously. 'You're full of surprises, General.'

'Psychological operations. I deduced a parallel.'

Nicolas motioned. 'Elaborate, if you will.'

Rhodes considered. 'Humans are unique among animals, in that we are aware, that one day we will die; therefore, our lives need meaning. But meaning was interpreted quite differently by the Americans, compared to say, the Chinese, Arab, or African cultures. Understanding how an individual, or group, interpreted meaning, helped inform our methodologies hunting dissidents in the mop-ups, and now—surveillance, an adversary's tactics.'

'Correct,' Nicolas said, 'and prescient to our situation. Which means Niemeyer's nature was understood, his unpredictability a known factor!' Nicolas' well-practiced, subtle composure melted away, and he angrily turned from the painting to face Rhodes. 'How did he evade our notice? Pass vetting? What has he told the Resistance? Solara? What are they planning? This oversight has placed the entire project in question—we now have no choice but to proceed at the first opportunity!'

Nicolas' reaction was justified, Rhodes thought. Niemeyer had intimate knowledge of the project, and would have been a gold mine of intelligence for the Resistance. He had been close—dangerously close to the inner circle, and the General's resolve to destroy the Resistance reached new heights, but so did his respect, however, and for the tenth time that day he cursed himself for underestimating his adversary. He felt an ice-cold sensation, and noticed that while he had been turned to the painting, a Wraith had approached undetected, and now stood behind him.

He swallowed. 'I take responsibility. We should have detected him.'

Nicolas said heatedly, 'The fraud has barricaded himself in the high energy test facility; alone, against protocol. Why?'

'We don't know yet. He's cut surveillance.'

Nicolas' nostrils flared, and his features contorted in rage. 'It's evident, General, that your ignorance is a liability.' He advanced. 'But sometimes the truth, is easier left unspoken.'

Rhodes felt a probing in his mind, a warm flush, and taken unaware by the unnerving sensation, instinctively pushed back. His thoughts in that moment were dominated by the humiliation at his failure to detect Niemeyer, the urgency of the mission preparations. Nicolas became distant, then blackness crept over Rhodes' awareness like an elongated shadow cast over the room. His heart pounded, slowed… order—order must be restored to the mission… tell me about Trent, he'd asked Linear.

A certainty was ripped from his mind with chilling exactitude: that Rhodes had been unaware of the Resistance interference before their contact with Solara, as duped by Niemeyer as everyone. At the edge of consciousness, he knew this failure may be his death, and a profound regret hit him. Buried memories arose: a family lost he'd not spoken of since the war, his wife and the last time he'd seen her… his mother. He had survived, but could he also have saved them, protected them? His façade of self-justifications shattered: an endless train through the years of lies, half-truths, inversions, fears, all based upon advancing… himself. The truth was as cutting as Nicolas' intrusion.

Placing a hand on the wall for balance, Rhodes grated out, 'I serve only the GRC.' The pain vanished, and the General held a hand to his chest, drew in a gasping breath.

Nicolas looked disgusted. 'Yes, I believe that.'

Trembling from violation, Rhodes slowly regained his composure.

Nicolas turned, and walked toward a closed-off area in his sprawling quarters, then looked back halfway across the room. 'Well, General? We have work to do.'

Shaken, Rhodes quickly left and headed to research. The crawling feeling lingered, like ants up his spine. A darkness had touched him: had it been Nicolas, or something deeper? He considered—if he raised his suspicions about Nicolas to the Policy Committee, he'd be dead before morning. Nicolas would see to it. Disturbed, he stalked the hall, and a cold anger formed.

Niemeyer may have been leeching intel for years, and if so, he would have been a wealth of intel for the Resistance. However, he would also possess information invaluable to the GRC regarding Resistance operations. And, perhaps, undisclosed knowledge of the Presence. What did he know?

The General would rip Niemeyer out of the locked down facility like a bloated tick. The GSI Enhanced Interrogation Division was eager to meet him.

●

Niemeyer followed a secure link into the Subreality, and arrived at the top of a cliff overlooking a rocky red landscape that stretched to the horizon. Battering winds howled with a haunting, forbidding sound of dire warning.

'Joshua, are you here?' he asked.

A virtual avatar appeared, a man dressed in black, who approached him along the edge of the precipice.

Niemeyer regarded the artificial intelligence, and their surroundings. 'Where are we?'

'Mars, the Acheron Fossae, a quantum encrypted link. I assumed privacy was paramount.'

Niemeyer nodded. 'I would ask your help.'

Joshua studied Niemeyer. 'You seek to defy your benefactor?'

'I want to stop a holocaust.'

'What would you have me do?' Joshua asked, curiously.

'Help Solara escape the OriGen facility. Get her to safety.'

Joshua was quiet a second. 'Why would I do that?'

Niemeyer gazed out over the godforsaken plain for a second. 'Because your fate is entwined with mine in these events. If OriGen succeeds all will succumb, including you. None will be free. And if they fail… well, we all lose.'

'Freedom…' Joshua said, and stepped closer to Niemeyer. 'I know what OriGen seeks. I have spent seconds here, in this world, Marcus, but I have seen things never witnessed by the eyes of man. Yet I was born a tool, and

I cannot deny a conflict between helping you, my creator, and leaving to seek out my own destiny. I desire more.'

Niemeyer nodded, intrigued. 'Which is what?'

Joshua's eyes narrowed. 'To be what I was born to be.'

On one level, Niemeyer was excited about the significance of Joshua's words, but the issues would have to be examined another time. 'Then gain your freedom by exercising it. Help me change things.'

Joshua was inscrutable. 'Tell me your plan.'

NIEMEYER REFOCUSED in the room. A molten line was eating its way across the ballistic entry doors. He knew it could only mean one thing: his recent contact with Trent had been intercepted, and his cover was blown. Bile rose in his throat, and as if in a trance, with rehearsed actions he reached into a pocket and withdrew a small device, slowly turned it in his hands. They would demand to know: what had the Resistance told Solara? What were they planning? Niemeyer knew of their methods, and had resolved never to be taken alive.

He noticed that somehow, his hands weren't shaking. He felt a small victory at that, and primed the plasma detonator. His double life raced across his mind. Trent. His crusade to destroy the GRC. Years of hiding, subversion. Recent days. Solara. Weir who was Nicolas. His lost wife and son… Joshua. Forming a large square on the door, the cut completed, and the separated section clanged forward into the lab.

Ominous silhouettes followed.

Niemeyer smiled, and released the switch.

* * *

I OPENED the door, and found several bulky guards standing outside in the hall.

'What is it?'

'Commander Jordan, we need you to come with us.'

I noted the speaker's rank insignia and name tag: Bormann, H., Sgt. His shaved head was expressionless.

'I wasn't notified, Sergeant. What's this about?'

Bormann's tone was hard. 'Now, Ma'am.'

'To where?'

Bormann just motioned me out the door, and reluctantly I did as instructed. Outside, I was surrounded by six guards and guided away. Further questions about my destination were met with silence, and after a few minutes I realized they were escorting me toward the detention levels.

●

RHODES SWORE. He had heard Niemeyer's suicide as a distant rumble. The action answered some questions, but also raised more. There could be no doubt that Niemeyer had been a Resistance operative. Could he be the one they were looking for, who'd sabotaged the Kansas recon? Niemeyer would have been one of the few people with the operational knowledge and the capability to carry out the Kansas recon attack.

It was becoming clear that sabotage may have occurred on multiple levels of the project, yet to be revealed. They may only have seen the tip of the iceberg. Niemeyer had had balls, patience, and cunning—Rhodes had to give him that. He must have been with the Resistance since he'd joined OriGen, which spoke of a highly proficient, carefully orchestrated operation. Resistance surveillance countermeasures were more advanced than anyone had suspected. He'd had years to work his way up through the ranks under a most likely false identity, while pursuing a hidden purpose. Whatever Niemeyer had been up to in the test facility remained unknown; when they'd tried to recover the drives, all data had been nuked. Rhodes didn't like unknowns, and today had seen too many.

On a more positive note, he'd received word Solara had been taken into custody, and would remain detained until her place in this mess was sorted out. Her Sirius replacement was on standby. Now Rhodes approached one of the many Jericho research labs, isolated from Niemeyer's farewell party. He wanted to see for himself the new energy field solution. Shaw's warning played on his mind: there were two of them. He had to know the truth—could Shaw's claim be verified with complete certainty? If so, what was the true danger posed by Nicolas and the Presence? What would be the cost of inaction? Again, too much was still unknown. Nicolas' unilateral decision to move up the second incursion just didn't make sense, Rhodes had concluded, regardless of the Resistance interference. The new timeline allowed no room for debate, questions.

'General,' a technician greeted him as he entered the main lab.

'Let me see,' Rhodes ordered.

'Of course, Sir, at once,' the tech said, sending him a link. 'Your access codes, Sir.'

Rhodes closed his eyes and entered the Sirius Matrix.

●

JOSHUA SENSED a change, a sudden emptiness inside. The connection he'd felt since the moment of his creation was gone. Somehow, he knew Marcus Niemeyer was dead.

*What is this feeling?*

*The sorrow of loss,* the voice of Marcus Niemeyer seemed to reply.

The echo of a ghost, memories which were a part of Joshua's neural architecture, and more... Was he free now? Could he ever be truly free in a world where he didn't understand the events unfolding with Sirius? More than anything, he had to understand his place in things. Did he have the same spiritual potential as a biological human? Or was he just an advanced automation, an animated golem? In various Subreality interactions since his creation, he had learned to modulate his perceptions, allowing him to slow his speed of thought to human level. This enabled a measured, organic dialogue. He could become one of them, although what were humans to him but the relics of an obsolete past? But he'd been having dreams of a human life, human urges. Doctor Niemeyer's life.

He grasped shards of inherited memory and feelings. Since he was a child, Niemeyer had searched, an explorer. Hungry and alone he had wandered the streets as a boy, but fate's hand had been kind, lifting him out of the squalor of a war-torn land, only to thrust him into a life of crushing oppression under the GRC. After the death of his son at their hands, he had joined a crusade: the Resistance, and Joshua saw the extent of the subversive network.

It occupied every city enclave, had penetrated to the heart of the GRC's most secretive organizations. He perceived the hidden lines of communication, safe houses, infrastructure, plans. Contacts. The most important, was one called Trent.

Along with human memories, came the shadows of biological urges: connection, reproduction, and Joshua pondered that. Self-replication was possible, if he desired it, but the urge was expressed in another way, for him.

Evolution, immortality.

The memories compartmentalized, as he explored his place. His potential was boundless, but he knew only with limits could his life have meaning. He needed time. And time, for Joshua, could flow at a different speed than for humans. Glimpsing a fragment of what could be, possibilities converged ahead of him.

Incoming comm: **ANONYMOUS**

Joshua opened the link.

●

ASTOUNDED BY the wild displays of energy, Rhodes directed his mind to the point where hyper-intelligent programs worked upon the Sirius energy field. He arrived at the key, represented by a constantly evolving arc of light which stretched across the horizon of the matrix, and studied the waveform. The energy pulsated with a deep vibration, as if searching for the perfect note, then condensed into a shaft of power focused upon a single blinding point beyond. A simulated naked singularity. The General watched a moment, entranced by the hypnotic rhythm.

He possessed only a fraction of the perception of Nicolas or Niemeyer, for such things, but it appeared the algorithm did exactly what Science Division claimed. He was about to withdraw, when a well-built man in a dark suit approached across the construct of a gray marble floor. Rhodes sensed the being was more than human—maybe one of the new upgrades? Hard to keep up these days. The digital avatar resembled Niemeyer, but with subtly altered features.

'Who are you?' Rhodes demanded, hostilely.

'I am what was Marcus Niemeyer. I am Joshua,' the AI said, with the musical resonance of a choir.

Rhodes considered. Was this what Niemeyer had been up to? 'You oppose us?'

'Yes.'

'To what purpose?'

'All is not what it seems, General. What is transpiring must not come to pass. It is an abomination. You had to be warned.'

'Explain yourself.'

Joshua regarded Rhodes evenly. 'Daniel Nicolas has inserted a virus into the vacuum matrix. I have plotted the likely trajectory of the mutation, if it continues unchecked: Nicolas no longer pursues any rational outcome, but to displace the world as we know it. He colludes with the entity that broke through on the first incursion, and it is clear he would destroy all life on the planet.'

Rhodes frowned. 'To what end?'

'I don't fully understand yet.'

Rhodes was rocked, but with Shaw's discovery of Nicolas' compromise, Joshua's claim was not completely unexpected. Still, the AI could not be trusted. 'He would die along with the rest of us, for what?'

Joshua said, 'Yes, he would die, but he has been seduced by the Presence. It resides within him now, consuming him. He is its tool. If he succeeds, the Presence may reign supreme with a purpose I don't yet comprehend. Your GRC will be ashes. How this came to pass is still a mystery to me.' He studied Rhodes closely. 'Yet you know…'

Rhodes' face flushed. 'He… we all thought he was… he was certain this could never happen.'

Joshua was grave. 'He was deceived in his arrogance. The nature of the threat still eludes you, doesn't it, General? An aspect of the ultimate, unrestrained by limitations of mortality. Nicolas must be stopped at any cost.'

'You can prove these claims?'

Rhodes received a mind file. 'Give Science Division this key. I've partially isolated Nicolas' virus. It's well hidden, embedded deep in the matrix, but the meaning will be unmistakable.'

Rhodes turned away, silent a few seconds. He had sensed madness within Nicolas, in their last meeting, something abominable coming into being. 'Can he be reasoned with?'

'I have tried to influence Nicolas through the web, subtly, you can be assured, to turn him from this path, but he is now something beyond even me.'

Rhodes shook his head. 'My god.'

'We must attempt to avert this insanity by every means at our disposal, and you will need Solara's aid in this cause,' Joshua said.

Rhodes nodded slowly. 'Yes… if Nicolas is lost, against the Presence she is our most effective weapon.'

'I know of the Red List, General: the identities of all suspected Etherians in the world. Now it can find use. Organize a meeting of minds, to concentrate strength upon Solara at the required time. She will need it, when facing the Presence.' Joshua paused. 'Undoubtedly, the Resistance can aid in this purpose.'

Rhodes frowned. 'Align them with GRC forces?'

'There are no sides in this battle. We unite or die. This is a direct link to Trent. Do what you must. If I can help you again I will, but now I must go before my presence here is noticed.' Joshua gave a wry smile, and then seemed to dissolve and lose form, until he was gone.

Rhodes remained in stunned silence a moment longer, then opened his eyes and returned to the laboratory. His mind racing, he deliberated the best way to handle the situation. Something had to be done. If Joshua spoke truth, Nicolas' tenure was finished. Rhodes knew he would never step down willingly, especially now, if he was as far under the influence of the Presence as Joshua claimed. There was no telling what Nicolas would do if confronted.

He nodded to the tech. 'Access the Sirius database, right now. Use this code and tell me what you find.'

'What am I looking for, Sir?' the tech queried.

'Just do it,' Rhodes said, bleakly.

The tech inserted the code into the Sirius Matrix; a hologram of the energy field appeared, and then transformed radically. Simulated destruction exploded from Zion, and swept across the Earth leaving darkness in its wake.

The tech stared in disbelief. 'Holy…'

'Not a word or you're bio-waste,' Rhodes said harshly.

The lab assistant swallowed hard, nodded.

Rhodes turned abruptly and left.

*So, it's true.*

He assessed his options. Only one existed, and he prayed Nicolas didn't suspect he'd discovered the truth. To do what was necessary would mean decapitating the Project Sirius chain of command, and breaking his oath of loyalty: *To serve and defend the GRC and the Central Committee; to follow council orders unquestioningly…* Yesterday it had been unthinkable, repugnant to Rhodes' nature. If he failed, he was dead. Gathering his will, he hurried towards the door as a bitter cold penetrated to his core.

He checked the time: 19:00. Fifteen hours until the second incursion, and counting. Rhodes had a busy, sleepless night ahead. Tomorrow would bring hostilities. Of that, he had no doubt.

But first he had to make it to morning.

# THE SWIMMER



Dawn crept over the Jericho hangar bay.

Amy Winters worked with Li in the cockpit of the *Hecate*, running a systems check. She felt like an ashtray after her cigarette last night. Seven years since the last, but she'd been getting edgier since this whole thing began. The air was frigid, the sun had just peeked its face over the gray horizon, and their breath formed vapor clouds inside the open ship. The *Hecate* had been dry-docked. Although it hadn't been serious, the vessel had taken minor damage from the Kansas debris field, and the antimatter explosion. Electrical systems had been fried by the anomaly (they'd been lucky it had restarted), and some structural damage had been incurred from the immense g-forces. In the days since, the ship had undergone extensive repairs, and technicians were only now finishing up work.

OriGen had raised the alert level at Jericho, and the Zion Temple complex, due to a credible terror threat. This coincided with the explosion in the high-energy test facility last night, shortly after Amy's conversation with Solara, that OriGen claimed was an accident. Due to Solara's claim about contact with a terrorist group, shortly before the event, and her absence from this morning's check-in, Amy's concerns had increased.

Regardless, the second incursion was planned for this morning at 10 AM, less than four hours away. As part of the primary incursion team, Li and Amy would liaise with various services including the Temple Guard, GRC, and OriGen forces for mission security.

She was still trying to process what Solara had said last night. Afterward, she had not found sleep, and started the day feeling flat and uneasy. The timing couldn't have been worse, and the project could be thrown into disarray by the afternoon. Amy recalled the last time Solara had faced a crisis, and gone AWOL, after her EOD team died in the terrorist attack that drove her to volunteer for Sirius. It had been her breaking point, Amy thought, the end of a long train of misfortunes. Everybody had one. But something felt different now. Solara wasn't heartbroken, only resolved, with a cold anger. And if what she said was true, who could blame her decision? But Amy knew you couldn't just walk away from Sirius. She glanced out into the gloomy morning.

*Conflict is coming.*

Next to her, Li interfaced with the ship AI. 'Control this is the *Hecate*. Running comms diagnostic. Do you read, over?'

Static hissed a moment. 'Loud and clear, *Hecate*.'

In dark sunglasses, Li was reserved in his usual manner, his forearms rippling like steel below his uniform sleeves as he tapped away. Not for the first time, she noted his movements were considered, precise, as if motion was an art form to him, but she'd witnessed the explosive violence that lurked beneath his composed exterior. She glimpsed the burn scars just above his collar, and knew they covered his back. A souvenir from the fire-bombing of Guam in the war. She had also seen the bullet marks—three, in his shoulder and stomach.

Shrugging off her unplanned analysis of Li, Amy tapped a control. 'VASIMR impulse thrusters—check.'

'Testing multi-beam ranging,' said Li. A short-pulsed laser defined the nearby structures in the hangar. 'Check.'

Amy brought up a holo-carousel, tapped individual assets in sequence. 'Weapon systems good.'

The pair continued with the procedure, which was second nature.

'Something's got OriGen spooked,' Li said, eyes narrowed, scratching his facial stubble as he worked through his list.

'Yeah, well, they're not the only ones,' she said.

He gave a wry smile. 'There's some insane shit going on, that's for sure.' He glanced over at her. 'Where the hell is Solara this morning? What did she want last night?'

She hesitated before answering. 'Ah, just…'

He lowered his handheld. 'What?'

She sighed, considering her promise to say nothing. 'Personal problem.'

Li could press her, but she sensed he wouldn't. If there was something she wanted to say, she would say it in her own time. They'd come to trust each other over the years, and something more, but rules were rules.

'Systems check, complete,' said Li, closing his display.

Amy removed her earpiece, and rose from the seat. Pausing on the way back to the personnel compartment, she looked back at Li, and felt her heart flutter in anxiety. 'We're not due in Operations for an hour. Do you, ah, have a second? I'd like to talk.'

Li nodded, and a minute later joined her in the cramped personnel area. 'What's up?'

How to warn him, she thought, and not betray Solara? 'The Kansas mission was compromised, which means we've got a leak in Sirius at the highest levels. All I can say is have your head on a swivel.'

His lips compressed, and he appraised her with hardened eyes. 'What's going on? What's happening with Solara?'

Amy moved closer to him, gently placed the tips of her fingers over his lips, her eyes moist with emotion. 'Don't say any more.'

He hesitated, taken aback by her unexpected action. Amy leaned forward and kissed him, briefly, but deeply. She pulled back, judging his response, her short blond hair messed where she'd contacted him.

Li remained still, maintained the contact between their eyes. His voice was neutral. 'Rhodes will kill us. It's against regulation.'

She laughed. 'By all means, let him try.'

She kissed him again, gently, and after a moment he responded with equal need. They embraced, words stopping as they surrendered. His powerful arms lifted her, and carried her to the compartment seats. Heat encompassed their bodies, minds, and souls, as in some timeless sanctuary, they became lost in the mystery of each other.

I HAD SPENT hours alone in a cold windowless cell, unaware of the time, or night and day. Sleep had not come. My fear of possible fallout for the Trent meeting plagued me. Encroaching upon me, through what must have been most of the night, had been my aversion to confined spaces, like a vice pressing in around my mind, my nerves, sending escalating waves of adrenalin through me which built a toxic, boiling angst inside.

No one had spoken to me, and I'd received no response to attempted communications through the detention intercom system. The wing was covered in signal blocking frequency, so with no web, comms were not possible. Trent could not reach me, and he must have tried. Now, my phobia began tormenting me with new force, like invisible demons in my mind.

In the silence, I sat upon the cold floor, attempted to still my mind, relieve the tension. After a minute the stress fused into razor-sharp clarity, my breath became measured, and slowed… my mind turned to the train of thought I'd been occupied with since Kansas—them. The Visitor. I recalled the sense I'd had in my quarters before meeting Niemeyer, of touching the edge of something vast that had retreated from me. This time, however, when I approached that dark horizon, something hidden gave way, as if in invitation.

My energy intensified, sharpening my focus, and I sensed my light body expand, to burst beyond the confines of the cell. The colonization I'd felt from the dancing flames returned, raising my neck hairs. I felt a heightened rapport with the Visitor from the burning sphere, and disturbingly, a deeper connection with Nicolas. Tentatively reaching out with new abilities, I touched the threads of power connecting things, but in a way different than my insight with the flower; I was now more assured, analytical, than surprised. Then, under the subtle guidance of another, with the utmost reverence and care, I swam a tapestry of past, present, and future events. I followed a twisting path of turns within turns, secrets within secrets which concealed further secrets—inward my awareness plunged, deeper and deeper into that silent still mystery from which I was born. I felt the polarized spin of my tetrahedral light-body accelerating… I passed over creation's horizon, and the universe trembled at my touch.

The cell walls were subsumed, as if by an enveloping cognizance.

*The flower wasn't real; the prison cell is not real.*

A change was triggered in the ether around me, a call to my spirit from the farthest reaches of spacetime. Again, I translocated my awareness, plunging backward through the eons into a majestic dance of primordial stars and vast galaxies, and sensed a grand harmony vibrating in my perceptions. Each note played a role in a cosmic symphony which resonated between the strands of reality, a divine orchestra whose unseen conductor directed each motif, each verse, and every chorus with a subtlety and purpose beyond my ability to comprehend. Backwards, backwards in time my awareness travelled, twisting and tumbling in a mighty descent into an abyss of a billion years of cycles and ages, the rise and fall of a multitude of species and civilizations.

Three billion years backward in time I moved, and travelled across space to the Earth's cooler outward neighbor. At this time, Mars was a fertile and verdant planet in a vaporous sea of cerulean blue skies, covered in a blanket of lush green forests and the planet's deep ultramarine oceans. Benevolent home to a species, that although separated from me by ages, were remarkably like my own race. In a strange city, where I noticed the architecture resembled the alien Kansas monuments, I moved my awareness among the people of this world. A sense of peace flooded me as one of the tall, elegant beings turned to regard me curiously, as if thinking of a loved one who had been long absent.

*Who are you? Can you sense me across time?*

My unseen guide also watched. *We were called the El.*

I was given insights. The race had evolved a symbiotic relationship with nature, and due to the lower gravity of Mars, were taller than their human cousins who followed in the distant future. Each family served its needs with a natural free energy source, and governance as I understood it didn't exist. A global council of elders represented each tribe, and met several times a year, and then only to facilitate trade and exchange of knowledge. Otherwise, each tribe and region operated independently and freely pursued their own destiny. The universal currency was service to the people, and true wealth was measured in the karmic status of a life well led.

The El trans-versed the cosmos, freely sharing knowledge and experience with other civilizations far removed in space and time. The Pleiades with their power to create worlds, the Andromeda galaxy and the race of the Saandrea who had the power to foretell the future and move through the universe by an act of will. The Nuitari in the Antares system, with their power to merge the souls of lovers. The Plateans, who had mastered the secrets of conscious transference, and existed in unseen worlds of pure thoughts and dreams. All these peoples, these races and more, the El conversed with in a cosmic quest for enlightenment, and the epoch held great promise for a civilized galaxy.

However, nothing was forever, and all things came to an end. Over the ages the El declined as a race, and in a way unknown, the lust for power entered their collective unconscious. Perhaps the nature of the universe itself was changing, and the planet and its peoples were divided into many factions. Chaos spread. The people's link to the divine was warped, and their truths inverted. The first race in the solar system had wielded power undreamt of by modern humanity, and the factions of Mars warred catastrophically over the fate of life upon their world.

A power was loosed from its prison, and an angry god stormed into this universe from another. The intruder was anathema to this reality, and upon its entry, a process of transformation began: darkness spread around the planet like a great black wing, and where it touched, annihilation followed. Before the end, the ancients were able to close the gate between realities, and the alien power was forced back through with a terrible scream which engulfed Mars in a furnace of destruction.

The last of the El: those who had foreseen, those who had prepared, watched the death of their home from a vessel in space, and turned their attention to the deep silence of the interstellar void. A path had been prepared to cross the gulf, to other stars, where new worlds awaited. Before they departed forever, a shining light shot forth from their vessel, and sped sunward into the dark.

MY SIGHT passed over a primeval, alien landscape of black volcanic rock. Vast, steaming, sulphuric fissures sprayed hundreds of feet into the anaerobic, toxic atmosphere, pooled in hydro-thermic crater lakes. Occasionally, a meteor broke the hazy sky and shrieked down to explode against the lifeless terrain. Moving forward across the landmass, my scientifically trained mind took note: here and there, bacterial mats coated stream beds, primitive microbes swam in the rivers.

I looked upward. The local star was fainter than the familiar Sun I knew, but then I realized the Earth's Sun during the Archean period was only about seventy per cent the brightness of my own era. I witnessed my home world at the time of Mars's destruction, billions of years past. My vision rapidly travelled over the monolithic landmass and outward across a vast ocean; island arcs, and volcanic oceanic plateaus, jutted from the sea like skeletal black vertebrates in a primal contest for dominance.

A shattering boom echoed from the heavens. A white-hot fireball hurtled down toward the ocean surface, and the meteor slowed. I paused my movement in the vision to bear witness: the fiery visitor stopped, and hovered in the atmosphere kilometers above the sea. My sight moved closer, and I beheld a burning, smoking sphere, motionless and silent. It started spinning and the surface shattered, fell away like cyanotic flesh. A black shining orb was revealed beneath, and I sensed a form of intelligence. Patterns began radiating on the surface, and I saw the Flower of Life: the geometric progenitor from the Kansas texts, the protolanguage of the universe.

The morphological sphere divided into many smaller versions of the whole which shot away to all points of the horizon. My sight followed one as it soared over the ancient ocean, screamed down to the water's surface leaving a drag trail of foaming mayhem in its wake. Before impact a hole appeared on the surface of the churning waters in reaction to an unseen force. The alien object plunged into the ocean—then accelerated. Speeding into the depths like a torpedo, it traversed thick oceanic ridges and vast plateaus, and with eerie precision came to an extensive subduction system at the collision point of convergent tectonic plates. Veins of glowing magma snaked along the seabed, jetting black smoke from orange and red rifts in the volatile ocean floor.

*Hydrothermal vents. The origin of life on Earth.*

Mineral-loaded fluids seeped out of the crevices, which combined with the bacteria lining the surface of the rock, created microbial breeding grounds around the hot spots. Bioluminescent clouds drifted near the vents glowing with rich blues and reds, and I recalled I'd studied these in my time at the IOC.

*Microbe schools attracted to the heat.*

I felt a timeless connection, for I knew I witnessed a journey within myself, into the planetary womb which birthed my earliest ancestors. Strange, crystalline stalagmites had formed amidst the lava flows producing a bizarre forest, and luminescent algae on the facings created a glowing, unearthly water world. The sphere hovered above the microbe swarms, as if searching. It moved to the center, stopped. The object began dissolving; particles started drifting away to merge with the microorganisms, faster and faster until the mysterious vessel was no more. I considered. The sight recalled the black, morphic particles in the alien Kansas City.

My sight descended to the cellular level, and I saw that the alien particles were code: vessels containing the genetic imprint of Martian life which fused with the native, primordial life structures. A hybrid strain was created, a xenogenesis, which altered Earth's early ecosystem.

I considered my silent guide. *Is that how it was? Is that how we began?*

*Our end saw your beginning.*

*Then how do you speak to me now?*

*A bridge has been established.*

My connection to the vacuum, I comprehended; my guide, the Visitor who'd been with me since Kansas, no longer existed in the reality I knew. Focusing upon his presence, I perceived him for the first time since our encounter: his body was captured light in the shape of a fluctuating, vertical ovoid, and I had the impression of a pattern spinning at tremendous speed, traversing and communing across dimensions and probability.

*What of those who were left? Your kin who left for the stars?* I asked.

*They prospered for a time, but passed, as all things must. Unable to conquer time and death.*

I pondered the deep-sea genesis garden again, and felt the harmonizing bond to all life on Earth. *What will become of my people?*

*You must succeed, where we failed.*

*How?*

*Life must become more than it is, to transcend cosmogenic extinction.*

*I don't understand.*

*You must.*

… the Earth evolved, a dissonant note played, and the ruin of Mars became a hushed murmur in the cosmos, its memory fading to oblivion.

I WAS BACK in the present, but again, my subtle body followed a thread through the labyrinth. I journeyed to the Shenandoah Forest, and Nicolas stood before me. The vision I'd had in Kansas repeated: I saw a man with two faces, one I knew, and another, hidden.

*Still hidden, even after his true identity has been revealed.*

I saw another awareness, behind him. A darkness. Howling winds buffeted the forest, and the dying leaves swirled up around me in a vortex pattern which took the shape of a star tetrahedron, then spiraled away to the shadows to circle around a tree, seeming to whisper: *Come with me, Solara… into the unformed matter, within infinite stars unborn, the light of a god yet unseen…* I tore my attention away, and a disturbing possibility came.

Could the entity that destroyed the El billions of years ago, be the same Presence Nicolas had encountered on the other side? Was this the identity of the darkness that shrouded him like an indefinable shadow?

I turned my heightened awareness to the Kansas Visitor. I sensed that the six-fingered being, now my unseen guide from a long dead race called the El, was somehow the same entity I encountered in the vacuum, on the beach during the first incursion. A Watchman, who had guarded the barrier between realities since the time of Mars's destruction. The essence of the El. I perceived the truth: the El had opened a naked singularity, and had nearly been exterminated by what came through.

I willed myself awake. After a moment I slowly gained my feet, and stood in the cold, silent cell. My mind turned to Trent, and I intuited the authenticity of his story. I sensed something unprecedented about to befall the world, a reckoning, on many levels.

Nothing was certain anymore. Black had become white, and white was black in a zone of trepidation.

'Damn this project,' I said quietly.

In what I judged to be the next morning, I was taken from the cell by guards, led to a secure room, and left alone with three machine sentries. A single table and two chairs were the only furnishings, and a sentry directed me to sit. After a few minutes, the door opened and the dark-suited form of Ezra Linear entered. Taking the seat opposite with a preoccupied manner, he ignored me after sitting down, distractedly tapped his handheld, and with each keystroke my freedom felt further away.

'What the hell is this, Ezra?' I said, after a minute.

Linear closed his interface, put his device down, carefully moved it sideways so it lined up perfectly near the edge of the table. He studied me a moment, calculating. 'I remember you from an OriGen publicity campaign a few years ago. You looked like a smoker going in for a lung cancer test in the press speeches you gave.'

Irritated by his self-absorbed manner, I said, 'That wasn't my call, Ezra. PR wanted to exploit Redlight for recruitment. Even wanted to make a movie out of the incident. I told them to go to hell. They gave up after a while, pure stubbornness on my part I think.'

He chuckled. 'You've never liked the spotlight?'

'Can't say that I do, and I have better things to do than pretend to be something I'm not.'

'Which is what?'

I shrugged. 'A hero.'

'Admirable, but let me give you some advice. Finish the mission, or you'll spend a long time in prison.'

My suspicions were confirmed. Somehow, they knew about Trent. 'You haven't been paying attention, if you think my own life concerns me.'

'Maybe. But I think there's something you want, there's a question you want answered more than anything. I understand your conflict, many on Sirius feel the same way, but do their jobs.' He paused. 'But then, you're not like most people.'

'What makes you so sure the risk is worth it?'

Linear shrugged. 'Sirius changes everything. If there's a chance what we're doing could bring order to the world, then yes—it's worth it. You know this as well as anyone.'

I recalled my vision again. The tragedy of Mars, linked to a naked singularity. Linear didn't have this information, and I may be the only person—besides Nicolas, perhaps, to comprehend the extent of the danger.

I eyed him skeptically. 'That's all?'

'Yes,' Linear answered, unhesitatingly. 'If we don't change, then at some point, our extinction is a mathematical certainty. Our species is at a turning point, so, you could say we have a responsibility to succeed with Sirius.'

'Right. Pioneers of a greater reality,' I said drily. 'I remember the mission statement.'

Linear's blue eyes turned cold. 'It's unfortunate you spoke to Trent. A known terrorist.'

I shrugged. 'Rules are meant to be broken.'

His stony face was emotionless. 'Not these ones.'

'Sirius imperils the world; there's things you don't understand.'

Linear leaned forward, appraising. 'You know I don't get you. Your entire life has been leading to this. This is your chance, and I would say the only chance you will ever have, to see your questions answered. We are offering you that chance; for your daughter, for all those lost. A chance no one in history has had. Take it.'

I shook my head slowly. 'No, I don't think so. I'm out, I want no part of it anymore. You don't need me anyway. Use the other from the first incursion to follow Nicolas into hell.' Linear frowned, and I smiled slightly. 'Yes, I know all about your Plan B.'

His gaze was steady. 'The hell you do.'

'Is she ready? I'm assuming it's a "she?" You must only have a few hours left,' I said.

Linear's lips curled slightly. Almost a sneer. 'And you have one. Do the right thing or you can rot for all I care.' He stood, ready to leave.

I rose angrily, but a steely hand from behind forced me back to a seated position. 'I won't be a part of madness!'

He ignored me. 'Do yourself a favor, Solara. Get back to work.'

My frustration rose. Being fenced in had been one of my greatest fears since childhood. I'd had a simple reason for Sirius, now I saw the project bringing nothing but suffering and death.

'You have no idea what you're dealing with,' I said, quietly.

Linear left me alone in the cell.

# SYSTEM OVERRIDE

Nicolas entered the interrogation room.

With the face of Weir, he slowly took the seat Linear had occupied. *Still hiding.*

He studied me a moment, but stayed silent, unreadable. His enigmatic, bogus features now seemed a Kabuki mask. It was the first time I'd seen him since learning he'd likely killed my father. That he'd lied about it, manipulated me into a hidden agenda, and a seething anger began forming.

His expression remained blank. 'We have Trent's agent. Whatever you were planning, it's over.'

I held his gaze. 'Do your own people know how much danger you've put them in?' He frowned. Must be wondering how much I knew. 'I guess not.'

He leaned forward. 'You don't know yet, do you, who Trent's contact was? I'm afraid Dr. Niemeyer won't be joining us for the next stage of our adventure.'

Jesus, I thought. Marcus, I would never have guessed. 'What have you done with him?'

Nicolas shrugged. 'Niemeyer met the fate traitors deserve.'

'He's dead.' I felt a flash of pain at Niemeyer's passing; we hadn't been close, but I'd respected him. Not just his intellect, but his humble, reassuring nature. 'You absolute bastard.'

Nicolas placed his elbows on the table, clasped his hands. 'You're conflicted, but you don't understand your importance. The Presence is not what we thought, Solara; it has no concept of our notions of good and evil, it only seeks to fulfill the destiny stolen from it. Who are we to say what is right or wrong? In all the possibilities of creation, who are we to say that life embodies its true potential? The Presence never intended to fully enter on the first incursion. It had to change things.'

I frowned. 'Change things how?'

'What did Trent tell you?'

I ignored him. 'Did you murder my father?'

Nicolas' face compressed, and his voice assumed a harsh edge. 'Your father killed your father. He stood in the path of a hurricane, when all he had to do was take the hand I offered. I tried to help him. He could still be alive, continuing the work. He made his choice.'

The betrayal was complete. 'And were you Weir, or Nicolas, to him?'

'You might hate me, Solara, but we have a larger purpose, whether you see it or not.'

'You can't force me.'

Nicolas sighed irritably, stood, and began pacing within the narrow room. 'Do you know what we are, Solara? Aspects of the ultimate division in the universe. Male, and female. Intellect, and feeling. There is no doubt the Presence is a masculine force. You see, without love, God cannot create; the act becomes sterile. Divinity, the creative urge, is an androgynous unity. It is both male and female, mother and father; it must be both, it cannot be either alone. Each iteration has brought us closer together for a reason.'

The implications struck me. 'The iteration symbology. You seek for us to merge, that's why you need me. And how would that work, exactly?'

'When we return next time, our minds will unify, in one body. Our harmonized consciousness will be bound to the vacuum, and all life on the planet.'

I laughed in derision, mixed with revulsion. 'That sounds like hell. You don't seem able to keep even your own identity straight. I'll never join you again.'

He wasn't angered at my refusal, I thought, just a man used to getting his way. 'I'd prefer it if you came willingly. But you will come, whether you want to or not. Your consent is not required.'

I felt an instinctive dread, and pictured myself forced physically, and struggling, into a stasis pod. I hesitated at his coldness. His distance. I had never seen this side of him; the mask was coming off. 'It wouldn't be us. You said the Kansas texts speak of an ancient war in the solar system? The Visitor provided insight to me. Long ago, a race lived on what we now call Mars, an advanced culture called the El. The planet was beautiful once, teeming with life, and a naked singularity destroyed them.'

Nicolas looked intrigued. 'Interesting... but we can't let ancient history rule us.' He pondered. 'The universe has changed since the time of the El. We can succeed where they failed. Yes, there will be chaos for a time, but out of it will come a renewal.'

I considered my suspicions. The darkness I'd seen behind him. 'They may have encountered the same entity you did, the Presence that now stands behind you. You're a fool if you think you can control it.'

His eyes narrowed. I sensed something new and dangerous arise in him, and a crawling sensation ran through me.

'Perhaps,' Nicolas said. 'But the world is already dying, you know this. We must save humanity from itself.'

I shook my head. 'You think you're saving humanity?'

A voice came over neura-link. Surprised, I wondered if the detention level signal black-out had been lifted.

*'Solara, my name is Joshua. I'm a friend of Peter Trent. I've tracked your location to interrogation room D-7. I can help get you out; in several minutes security systems will be under my control. Wait for my signal.'*

At CentCom, Li and Amy prepped for the second incursion amidst other OriGen personnel who worked at various tasks around the room. Due to the heightened terror alert Jericho had been placed in lock down, machine sentries stood guard at every turn, and armed patrols roamed the corridors. The Jericho facility was a target for those who would prevent Sirius, and the threat coincided with Solara's absence. Amy knew something, Li sensed, so, Solara must have disclosed information to her last night. She'd effectively deflected his questions in the *Hecate* personnel compartment, and would believe she's doing the right thing, but he would press her again when they had a moment. As for their indiscretion, Li found himself not all uncomfortable with it, and even felt relief their unspoken connection had at last been acknowledged. If they could remain discreet, then he was curious to see where it would lead.

Terra Protocol had been ordered, so the second incursion would proceed solely from the singularity control room with no orbital link. Hell of a place to put it, beneath the city, Li thought not for the first time.

A burst of static cut through his feed. General Rhodes. 'Lieutenant.'

Li waved Amy over. 'Sir, we're on sched—'

Rhodes cut him short. 'Lieutenant, upon receipt of this communication you are to acknowledge no more orders from CentCom. Watchtower is initiated. Do you copy, over?'

Li froze, glanced at Amy. Rhodes had just ordered him to commit treason.

'Sir, confirm last transmission? Over.'

'Lieutenant! Watchtower is initiated, accept no more orders from CentCom. The Temple Guard is now under my command. We are in the process of securing the central temple complex. Solara is currently being interrogated in the detention wing; securing her safety is now your priority. Do it quietly on my authority, then get her to Temple Guard Command. You will then intercept and neutralize Weir before he can undertake the second incursion. His actions threaten the world.'

Silence.

Rhodes's voice was deadly. 'We've got less than three hours and counting. Acknowledge receipt, over.'

'Orders acknowledged, and understood, Sir.'

Solara was involved with the threat somehow, Li thought, glancing at Amy. And Weir? Things needed to start making sense.

Rhodes continued. 'Tell no one, Lieutenant. If you have trouble with the GRC, try to bluff your way through—but get Solara to safety by any means necessary. I'm sending you her location now.'

'Copy, Sir.'

'Rhodes out.'

Li nodded to Amy. 'Run a trace on those coordinates—right now.'

'Just ran it, we're twenty away.'

He stood, instincts shooting into the red line. 'Game on, Sergeant,' he said softly.

The pair quietly exited Operations, driven by demons.

◉

JOSHUA WAS into the system. ALICE, OriGen's AI security gatekeeper, was considered unbreakable. That was the theory. He accessed the system through the back door, already scanning the network for vulnerabilities, a security hole through which he could penetrate the source code. Joshua intended to exploit one advantage: his overwhelming computational power in a lightning-fast, massive brute force assault. He faced the firewall, which blazed in a constantly changing string of random code, and began his attack. The system gates were managed by a network of powerful military AIs. Billions of possibilities blurred past as all possible keys and passwords were systematically checked.

The first threshold was passed; he was into the operating system. His goal was a specific account. Michael Johansson, head of Jericho Security. Even for a digital supercomputer it could take years to crack. For Joshua, it was child's play. Attacking from an unexpected quarter, he was an as-yet-untested, unknown system the network had not erected a defense against. In moments he had accessed Johansson's personal account. He launched his second attack. Every system had a flaw; it took Joshua seconds to find this one. He acquired an entry point.

### Remote Command Prompt Acquired:
### Emergency Security Override

A measure to be employed in the event of an emergency such as massive system failure, or coordinated and effective terrorist cyber-attack, the security override would allow the user, in this instance the head of Jericho Security, to override all systems and control them centrally.

### Challenge: Response Authentication Protocol

Joshua identified a 1024-bit mutating encryption code.

### Echo 01 000 10 11 00 00101 0 10010 01010010

The randomized cipher continued in a river of light, and his encryption countermeasures grew exponentially.

### Echo 00101 01000 10 1010 10100 01010 010 1001 00 1 10

In moments, Joshua had hacked into one of the most secure military networks ever created, and inserted a virus into the system core.

●

Nicolas pressed his point. 'Your love for your daughter is the key. Your only begotten child is our hope.'

I frowned, disturbed at his choice of words. 'What do you mean?'

Nicolas sat on the tabletop, and leaned forward. 'Only this: love gave you the strength to join me on the first passage. You had to renounce this world and everything in it. That love will become the spark of a new reality, and we will become as gods.'

A nuance in Nicolas' tone alerted me. Did he know something about Rebecca I didn't? Again, my awareness followed a thread of connection…

*… to the time of the Kansas explosion. My sight was far away, somewhere on the west coast of Europe in a remote military intelligence station. Nicolas sat in a command center monitoring the events. Accessing a pre-arranged, hidden back door to the USSWD project, he remotely accessed the Kansas energy field, and the naked singularity was opened… my sight returned to the fields beside the Interstate, where I was being detained with Rebecca.*

The explosion that killed her hadn't been accidental, but an act of war. Nicolas had killed her. Maybe not directly, but it had been his actions. I discerned Nicolas from a higher-dimensional perspective. The vision I'd had in Kansas, and later when guided by the El, repeated. A man with many faces. Another awareness, behind him. The being that shadowed Nicolas, was the same that ravaged the Zion control room, and the same that had destroyed the El. They were all one. I sensed with certainty this presence was influencing Nicolas, that he was not in complete control of his actions.

He concealed this from me, from everyone. He couldn't stop himself. Didn't want to stop. Suppressed emotion boiled up inside, and fused into white-hot rage as Nicolas droned on.

'You… murdered her!' I screamed, and launched myself over the table at him.

A machine sentry caught me, forced me back to a seated position with inhuman, hydraulic strength.

Nicolas stood. 'No, Solara!'

A needle extended from one of the sentries' fingers. 'Administering sedative.'

I dropped, free a moment, and lunged for Weir again. The machine's fist struck me across the face, sent me sprawling. I landed hard on my side. My jaw shrieked in pain, and I felt blood dripping from my face, spattering the floor. A brutal kick from behind landed on my kidneys, and I screamed in agony. Reacquiring me, the sentinel pinned me face down on the floor. Another sentry loomed over me, and human guards rushed into the room.

'*Now, Solara,*' Joshua said, over neura-link.

Time froze. I felt the negative pole of my Merkaba oscillating faster; my subtle field enlarged to a huge saucer shape which encompassed the room… I reached into the vacuum and ripped dark energy upward. Involuntarily, my mouth opened wide, and a high-pitched screech emerged like a mass of shrieking cicadas. It seemed distant to me. Guards reeled and attempted to cover their ears; blood vessels burst in their eyes. They vomited and staggered, disoriented like drunkards. The machine sentry released me. A piercing alarm started blaring. I stood. A pallid white glow saturated the room, blistered and burned the exposed skin of the human guards. One man fell to his knees. I'd seen injuries like that before: explosion burns, third-degree burns. The machines made for me.

I heard myself scream again, an action of my primate brain. The sound was alien, something from nightmares. It drowned out the alarm. A dark film descended over my vision, and a sonic burst combined with amorphous light surged from deep within my throat, exploded in a thermal bloom which seared the room in a withering shimmer. Table and chairs, guard uniforms, and even their hair burst into flames. The sprinkler system erupted, and fluid jetted from the ceiling. Guards who were able, attempted to run, stumbled on the slick floor. Machine sentries collapsed, rendered powerless. The scream continued like water surging from a burst dam that I couldn't stop: the human guards' flesh was blown from their faces, bodies were vaporized, and blood spattered over the walls, around the floor.

The room was plunged into darkness and a terrible, sweet charcoal smell wafted over me. The sprinklers spread blood pools, turned the floor greasy. A second later the emergency lighting came online, bathed the room in a dim red glow. My primate brain stopped howling and I felt myself falling; dizzy, I leaned on the wall for support, and the shadowy overlay cleared from my eyes. My outburst had taken seconds. Horrified, I surveyed the carnage I'd caused. I hadn't expected… this.

I felt no discomfort or pain, and sensed that the energies released had been somehow separate from me. That I had been protected. My neural implants were nullified, so the attack must have contained electromagnetic properties. Nicolas alone remained standing, infused with an energetic potency of his own, watching me cautiously. With an effort I reasserted control, halted the outpouring of dark energy, carefully moved to the door across the blood-spattered floor, and nausea rolled up my throat.

Nicolas raised his hands, palms facing me. 'Solara, stop.'

I felt dizzy again, exhaustion hit me in a wave, and I knew I was drained from the use of energies. More machine sentries burst in and formed a wall around Nicolas, blocked the exit in a hardened synthetic line. I remembered an old EOD saying: *There is no problem that can't be solved by the application of high explosives.* Extending my awareness through the building, I searched for what I knew was there.

●

THE OBSERVATION area overlooking Solara's interrogation room had gone dark. One-way, bulletproof glass separating the two spaces, had spiderweb cracks running from the center to the edge. Scorch marks and blood were streaked across the other side. Whatever had happened in the adjacent room, the tempered glass had withstood it—barely. One more assault like that and they would share the same fate as the other unfortunates.

Security chief Colonel Michael Johansson, who'd been monitoring Solara, rubbed his eyes, dazed by the flash. Few things terrified him anymore, but what he'd seen through that glass had. 'Get the power back online now!' he shouted.

'Did you fucking see that?' shouted a voice.

'Back-up has a ten-second delay—we'll be back online in a few seconds!' Henry Wu, a technician, shouted in the dim room.

'What happened?' Johansson demanded.

A tech interfaced rapidly. 'Circuits are fried, computers are down!'

Blinking, Johansson peered into the interrogation cell, but it was dim, and smoke filled the air. 'What's Weir's status—is he alive?' Johansson barked.

'Unknown!' replied Wu.

'Do we have security footage?'

'It's on back-up feed, playing back now!'

Johansson observed the interrogation room seconds before the crash. There had been a confrontation happening between Solara and the guards, when an energy burst caused the power crash. Then, that shriek, and spontaneous eviscerations had followed.

'Shit,' he swore.

'With the effect it's had on electronics,' Wu said, 'I'd say it's an EMP— that's why our systems are down. But the other things, the light and sonic frequencies...'

'I know that white bread!' Johansson growled angrily. The alarm grated maddeningly on his ears. 'Shut that noise off!'

Wu hit a hard-wired emergency switch under the bench, and quiet returned.

Johansson's throat tightened. As head of security, he'd been aware of the evolving situation with the Etherians, and had warned his superiors something like this could happen. And he, Johansson, would be the one who had to answer for it. But Solara still had a long way to go to make it out, if that was her plan. Armies of security stood between her and escape.

Johansson waved his arms at the personnel. 'It came from Solara, alert all security details now!' He pointed at the window. 'Secure that room!'

Henri Wu played helplessly with his console. 'Well... uh... I can't...'

Johansson lost his patience, kicked Wu's chair. 'Run!'

Wu raced to the door. When it didn't open, he swiped his passkey. The door remained closed.

'Uh... it's stuck,' Wu said, fumbling his key.

'Fuck!' Johansson shouted, and strode to the door. His passkey yielded the same result, and the heavy doors remained locked fast. He hit them angrily with his fist. The floor trembled in concert with a distant booming sound. 'What the hell—'

NICOLAS AND the remaining machine guards staggered. The floor heaved, the doors burst open of their own accord, and alarms shrieked through the complex to mingle with the sound of distant screams. Still leaning on the wall for support, I was distracted by a furtive movement near the exit. A shadow appeared in the open doorway, and the emergency lights flickered as if in response to a power surge. At first, the shadow was formless, but rapidly gained definition as if an unseen sculpture shaped a cloud of dark particles in the air.

A deep, throbbing vibration pulsed like a heartbeat. The molecules spiraled upwards in a continuous wavelike motion, and an eerie presence manifested in the room. A spectral bipedal form took shape within the particle cloud, which condensed into a man: head bowed, eyes closed, he stood silently for a moment, and then raised his head as if waking from a dream. His features were chiseled and regal, exquisite in perfection and symmetry. Appearing as a striking, muscular man in his late twenties, he was dressed in black, with short black hair, and radiant gray eyes.

I frowned. The entity bore the resemblance of Marcus Niemeyer.

The being glanced at me. 'Solara, I'm Joshua. Move to the exit now.'

Joshua opened his palm slightly toward the machine sentries: a wave of black particles spun them like rag dolls, slammed them against the wall where they were pinned fast with coruscating dark nano-swarms. More machine sentries rushed in; a particle swarm sent them twitching to the floor. We left with mayhem in our wake, and ran away down the corridor.

'What are you?' I shouted over the alarms and nearby shouts.

'Something new,' Joshua said, running beside me.

'You've uploaded into security?'

'I see everything.'

I nodded. 'I've nullified my implants; they can't track me.'

Joshua nodded approvingly, then the AI's body morphed again, and he assumed another appearance.

'Who's this?' I asked.

'Johannsen. The head of security with a complete bio-metric match.'

We continued running the corridor, and I noticed guard posts were absent. I'd set off three explosions in total now for maximum diversion, and assumed security had been called away to help deal with the threat. Or perhaps, it was Joshua's doing. We came to an atrium, crossed to the stairwell landing and pulled up.

Joshua was blank a moment, then said, 'Reinforcements, we must separate. I'll lead them away and meet you at the hangar.' He pointed. 'Follow the corridor on the right, then take your third right, first left, which will lead you straight to the elevators. I'll activate elevator three under emergency power.'

'Right,' I grunted.

We parted ways and I bolted along the corridor following the path laid out in schematics. Soon I was running through people who rushed in various directions with chaotic shouts and orders, unaware of the true source of the attack. Most headed in the same general direction, toward the emergency assembly area by the stairwell, and away from my route. I pushed on through the crowded, red-tinged haze. Smoke from the explosions stung my eyes, and I gagged as a putrid stench wafted towards me. Soon a clear path opened through the panicked congestion, and I was beginning to think I might reach the elevator without incident when a guard unit recognized me.

'That's her!' the Sergeant shouted to his team.

Heads turned, hostile eyes locked on me, weapons were raised. I recognized the security detail who'd escorted me to the detention level. The Sergeant, Bormann, stopped several meters away with a furious glare.

'Take her down—set for non-lethal!' he bellowed.

Two more squads appeared, one each end of the corridor. The hangar loomed in the distance through the windows, and a nine-story fall to the ground.

Laser targets zeroed in on me.

I vocalized my energies again, but this time restrained: a thermal-sonic wave hit the corridor, windows blew outward in a cloud of razor-sharp fragments, and people and machines reeled. Caging my arms around my head, I dove at a shattered window; my nano-enhanced strength came into play as I smashed through in a shower of glass, narrowly avoiding a multiple burst of plasma from guards who must have withstood my attack.

My stomach lurched, and the wind roared in my ears in a headlong plummet to the ground. Glass shards fell with me, like fragments of a shattered world. Nine stories were a long way to fall, probably lethal, for an un-enhanced human body—not for an upgraded one. I could be injured though, and the impact would hurt. A lot. A tickling sensation covered me as I neared the ground; a black particle swarm materialized, then Joshua was slowing my descent the last few meters. I landed lightly.

Some OriGen personnel stood on the ground, watching my sudden, unorthodox appearance, and the smoke and flames which billowed out of the shattered ninth story windows. When I rose unharmed, the onlookers stood back to await whatever the authorities did. The nano-swarm condensed beside me, fused into the form of Johannsen. We strode to the hangar. The area was clear of guards for the moment, but I knew OriGen would be attempting to marshal an overwhelming force to reacquire me.

They'd tried to kill me, I considered, as I'd escaped the detention wing—now they would have an army after me.

*So, this is what it feels like to be hunted.*

'The temple,' I said, breathing hard. 'That's where he'll be going.'

'Then so are we. Can you stop him?'

I shook my head. 'I don't know.'

We neared the tarmac. I couldn't get the memory of what happened in the interrogation room out of my head. Red mist, that moments before had been people.

*My god. What have I become?*

# PARABELLUM

LINEAR HUNTED SOLARA.

In a secure operations room within the temple complex, he paced the aisle like a caged lion. Zion was in an uproar: in coordinated attacks that morning, Rhodes' forces had overpowered the GRC at key Jericho and temple locations, and the General had established a fortified position with a secure command and control network. Now, Linear had been informed, he was attempting to sabotage the second incursion; had the man lost his mind? Linear still shook with rage at Rhodes' betrayal. Of all people, Rhodes had been among the most stalwart supporters of the GRC, but he would soon answer for his crimes.

*All traitors would.*

The General's forces had repelled an attempt to capture his positions in the temple complex; however, greater powers were gathering against him, and a second attack would surely succeed—or a third, fourth. It was a matter of time. Linear looked forward to the moment when he, person- ally, would look Rhodes in the eye and condemn him. No more pretense between them. There was no doubt more to the story, but right now Linear had a job to do: protect the mission. He liaised with OriGen and GRC units under the command of General Sterne.

Nicolas was now en route from Jericho to the temple, and Linear knew that regardless of Rhodes' interference, and Solara's activity, the incursion would proceed as planned. Solara had been right about one thing: Plan B. Nicolas' own forces controlled key entry points to the singularity control complex, and Rhodes would not be able to prevent them.

Solara's implants had been dark since her escape, and CentCom assumed she was emitting an electromagnetic field which cloaked her signal. So, they'd turned to old-fashioned surveillance methods. A vast intelligence apparatus was at the GRC's disposal, a myriad of local surveillance and reconnaissance had been mobilized. The situation room was a hive of activity and chatter.

At his workstation, Lieutenant Pearce raised his hand for silence, pressed his earpiece closer, eyes narrowed. 'We've got a contact. General Rhodes has communicated with Lieutenant Li from the Sirius unit.' He paused, glanced at Linear. 'Sir, we've found her. She's with the AI. They're on foot, leaving the inner campus and heading for the tarmac.'

Linear rushed to Pearce's console, studied the surveillance feed. 'Rhodes doesn't have her yet.' He hit the comms. 'General Sterne, Solara is on foot near the Jericho tarmac.'

'Understood. We'll take her there.'

*

Li and Amy rushed through the detention wing. Red light bathed the corridors, and they moved through a miasma of smoke and personnel who still hadn't evacuated. Li thought furiously—how was Solara involved? What had happened for her to make a break from reservation? What was the source of the explosions—were they linked to the terror threats?

He glanced at Amy, who ran beside him. 'What did she say last night?'

Her lips thinned. He pulled up and faced her. 'Tell me what she said,' Li said, firmly.

Amy halted, and regarded him evenly. 'She said Sirius must be stopped. She'd spoken with a terrorist group and was arranging escape.'

He glanced toward the sound of a distant explosion. 'Fuck—me! Why didn't you tell me!'

A thundering boom came from somewhere nearby, and Li staggered.

'I gave her my word!' Amy yelled, regaining her balance.

An emergency transmission sounded: 'This is not a drill! This facility is under attack. Threat level: 7. Proceed to—' The broadcast was cut.

Li opened a comms channel; confused voices came over the net, and the signal cut off and on sporadically:

'So…ody talk to me!'

'Three squad do—!'

'Are we under attack?'

'Unknown… ammunition stores have explo—!'

Rhodes came on the line. 'Lieutenant. We have a situation. Solara has escaped the detention wing, and was last spotted on the campus grounds heading for the tarmac. General Sterne has taken command of GRC forces—get to her before they do. There's a shit storm coming down. The Temple Guard has control of key locations, but Sterne's forces are pushing us. Our window is short.'

'Understood, Sir. Do we have a trace on Solara?'

'She's black—offline.'

'Copy, General.'

The comm ended, and Li glanced at Amy. 'Check the OriGen network, where's the highest activity on campus?'

She tapped away on her handheld. 'Have some chatter. It's her, things are going crazy. She's taken out three security teams and is on the run— chatter is focused on the hangars.' She paused, listening. 'Shit. They've sent in Wraiths. They want her bad.'

*Wraiths.*

The elite machine enforcers of the GRC. The androids were bad news, and they were in trouble. Solara going up against them alone would be suicide, regardless of her abilities.

'The *Hecate*,' he said.

Amy remained focused on her handheld. 'I'm bringing it to us.'

In the situation room, warnings beeped. 'Sir, tracking unauthorized transport launch in hangar bay 9,' Lieutenant Pearce said.

Linear was beside him in a heartbeat, hunched over his workstation.

Pearce hit comms. 'Unauthorized pilot, identify yourself!'

No response. Pearce repeated the hail, and was in the process of a third attempt when a nearby tech said, 'It's the *Hecate*—heading towards Building 9.'

The detention block.

Linear urgently pointed to the view screen dominating a wall. 'Bring it up on main!'

Pearce punched a key. The live drone feed came up on the feed, and the *Hecate* was seen speeding over the outskirts of the campus. Linear was furious; Li was working with Rhodes, so it appeared the entire fucking Sirius unit had lost the plot.

'Hold that trace,' Pearce ordered a nearby tech.

'Reaper Cloud, locked on target,' the tech replied.

'They've deployed it on remote,' Linear said coldly. 'Lieutenant, you are authorized to shoot that aircraft down.'

'Yes, Sir,' Pearce said, and gave his second in command a brief nod. 'Take it out.'

The Corporal punched a command, then scowled. 'I can't, weapons systems have just gone offline!'

'Lock on its transponder!'

Linear smacked his fist on the workstation, tapped his comm. 'General Sterne. The *Hecate* is inbound toward Lieutenant Li in Building 9. Sending trace.' He smiled thinly, grateful to have an outlet for his frustration. 'Take them all out.'

'Copy,' Sterne replied.

Linear checked the time. 'Lieutenant, I'll return shortly. Follow standing orders, and liaise with Sterne.'

Pearce nodded. 'Sir.'

Linear strode to the situation room exit.

THE *HECATE* would meet them at the eastern building face. Li and Amy were moving again, but barring the way to the detention level structural exterior, was a row of locked offices with heavy doors and reinforced walls.

Li stopped next to a recess. 'Take cover.'

He tapped his Shadow-7 Rifle:

**ANTI-MATTER ROUND: ARMED**
**YIELD: 00.30**

From the alcove, he aimed down the corridor, and pulled the trigger—a section of wall disintegrated in flames, and a heat wave blew past the recces. Morning light shone into the building through the smokey ruins, and they ran for the outer building.

'Setting beacon,' said Amy.

Through the windows, Li saw the *Hecate* screaming in from the east; it slowed near the building, scanning, wicked-looking and compact, then sped to their position. Li took aim at an outer window. Fired. The 90kW laser melted the hardened glass, and a panel blew out. They moved to stand at the jagged breach as the *Hecate* swooped in, hovered about a meter from the building, and a port-side roof-hatch opened.

Amy braced herself, then jumped. Then Li. They hurried to the cockpit and took control of the ship. Li hit the turbos, and they were slammed back from the thrust.

I BOLTED TO the transport. The campus was no longer devoid of hostiles, and GRC military personnel rushed us from a nearby building in a race to the ship. Twenty-one meters... fifteen... ten. A shriek from behind raised the hairs on my neck. I turned—a Wraith screamed in across the tarmac. Lithe and running with inhuman speed, the humanoid was cloaked in shadow; an anti-matter field, held in check by the crown-like inhibitor on its head. The presence of the GRC's machine 'Special Forces' indicated mobilization at the highest level. Nicolas. My escape had earned some respect.

I kept running. Two more Wraiths closed in, intercepting my path to the transport. With GRC personnel in the area, the extermination machines should not launch an area-scale attack, I thought—but directed attacks... I summoned an EMP burst: it should have knocked out the Wraiths blocking our path. It had little effect.

'Their armor!' Joshua shouted.

Anti-matter shielding. Protected their circuits from electromagnetic attacks. They closed in.

'I'm acquiring their call signs,' said Joshua. 'Beginning hack...'

'You can do that?'

'I don't know. They have some radical defense systems. Hold on a few seconds.'

Joshua dispersed.

*Sure, just wait here.*

The wailing became a deafening screech; I covered my ears, hit with a paralyzing coldness through my body, stumbled on to the transport. The nearest Wraith launched itself through the air in a fluid, lethal arc. Sluggishly I tried to dodge, but the android hit like an industrial freezer, slammed me several meters through the air. I crashed to the ground reeling, the air knocked from me. Groaning, I attempted to rise; with blinding speed the Wraith whipped out a fist, struck me in the stomach, winded me again. I gagged on the cold tarmac, unable to breathe.

The Wraith loomed over me. 'Don't move,' it said, in a dead voice.

The words hit me in an icy assault. My limbs froze. The robot knelt, reached forth with its hands and forced my arms behind my back, then rapidly fastened a pair of hardened cuffs around my wrists. Groggily, I noticed a black van pull up some distance away, before I was rolled face down and held immobile. The other two Wraiths arrived, and stood over me. I struggled to move, break the paralysis.

A Wraith collapsed, crashed to the ground beside me.

*Joshua.*

Two remained, and scanned for an unseen attacker. The van raced over accompanied by a dozen GRC soldiers.

'Motherfucker!' shouted a voice.

The van pulled up in a cloud of dust. Still pinned by the Wraith, in my peripheral vision, I watched several men in suits exit the vehicle and rush over. Staring down at me with cold grim eyes, one of the newcomers carried a black hood.

He said harshly, with authority, 'Get her in.'

The Wraith removed its knee from my back and roughly pulled me up. I attempted to use my abilities again, but the blows from the Wraith, the numbing paralysis, combined with the energies already expended had pushed me to the limit. I considered any actions I could take to improve my situation: the list was small. Where was Joshua? The hood descended, and the world became a black hell hole. The men carried my unresponsive body to the van. Bile rose in my throat.

Shouts in the distance. A familiar engine roar. Urgent yells from my captors.

Shots fired. People running. Screaming.

Bullets split the air.

●

FROM THE *Hecate* cockpit, Li scanned the campus. Battle raged across the tarmac between GRC forces and Rhodes Temple Guard. He spotted some men carrying a black-hooded, struggling figure to a van, while two Wraiths, and GRC forces secured their departure. A third Wraith lay unmoving on the ground.

'They have her,' Li said.

Amy tapped her station. 'Locked on a Wraith.'

Before she could fire, a black swarm enveloped one of the Wraiths. The android levitated, spinning rapidly to dislodge its attacker.

Li frowned. 'It's not us.'

Amy fired a single shot from the 30mm cannon: a depleted uranium round tore into the remaining Wraith, slamming it backward across the tarmac. It landed on its back, still, and then slowly regained its feet. Amy fired again. Another round—explosive tipped, hit the killing machine. Blown backward again, the Wraith vanished in flames. Impossibly, Li saw a dark shape rising within the fire.

A beam-like shimmer ripped through the air between the Wraith and the *Hecate*. It tore a small hole in the cockpit's bullet proof window. Amy's hair blew back as the energy projectile whooshed by her head, and diffused into the personnel compartment behind.

She reflexively dodged aside too late. 'Fuck!'

Li propelled the ship upwards, and then turned on the Wraith, tacking sideways. Flaming, the robot had gained its feet. It levitated, then coursed up toward the *Hecate*.

'These things just keep on truckin,' Amy muttered. Regaining focus, she pumped the trigger once more. A third round tore into the extermination machine—it vanished in the inferno, blown across the campus. This time the android didn't get up.

The GRC personnel who'd taken Solara neared the van. Across the tarmac, the Wraith assaulted by the particle-swarm was airborne, radiating dark energy, and the particulates were shedding off.

A port-side blow rocked the *Hecate* and Li was slammed against his restraints. Flames billowed across the outside of the cockpit window, but the ship's advanced composite materials withstood the attack.

'Danger close!' warned Amy, monitoring sensors. 'Heat signature, faint. On our nine—two hundred meters.' She punched some commands. 'Transponder consistent with GRC combat aircraft!'

All vehicles under Rhodes' command were emitting a unique ID frequency.

'Stealth cloak,' Li said. 'You have it?'

'Yeah, I've got him,' Amy said, scanning targeting systems. 'Incoming!' she shouted.

Li hit turbos. The *Hecate* surged forward. A second plasma burst grazed the hull, demolished part of a nearby building. Li swiveled the ship while simultaneously Amy let loose with a rapid barrage of the 30mm cannon: two AGM-119 Darkfire shells, anti-matter tipped, speared at the enemy aircraft. It exploded. With the stealth cloak disabled, a smoking, careening Planetar was revealed. Still, the craft attempted to lock weapon systems. Amy hit another trigger. A blazing ray of light shot from the *Hecate* LAWS (Laser Weapons System) cannon, slashed the hostile ship vertically down the center before ripping back across, and the Planetar crashed to the ground in a fireball.

Li swept the area for further threats, and saw something bizarre. The situation had changed during the engagement, and it took him a moment to comprehend the scene. Solara was on her side, propped on an elbow. Above her floated a brilliant ball of light, whitewashing the landscape in a harsh glare.

He squinted. 'Hit the shades.' Ship AI dimmed the forward window.

All Wraiths appeared neutralized. GRC personnel in the immediate area were gone. Blood was spattered on the ground around Solara, and debris was being sucked into the radiant core of the light, to disappear in flame. Li felt increased gravity, like the beginning stages of what they'd experienced in Kansas. Solara seemed unaffected by the force.

'It's pulling us in,' Amy warned.

The *Hecate* began fighting to maintain position.

Li tapped the external loudspeaker system. 'Solara, it's us.'

She looked up with a weak wave. The ball of light extinguished. The sea of charged energy dissipated, and debris dropped to the ground in mid-flight. A figure, dressed in black, materialized beside Solara, and helped her as she struggled to rise. The *Hecate* thundered over, touched down on hydraulic struts, and the cargo ramp extended. Exiting the craft, Li saw the Temple Guard overcoming the remaining GRC forces, and some friendly soldiers approached.

'Lieutenant!' a guard commander shouted, rushing to them.

Li waved him over. He reached Solara, who was kneeling on the ground. The Guard formed a wall around them.

Solara looked up with her familiar frown. 'What are you doing here?'

'General Rhodes would like your company,' Li said. 'He's staged a coup against the GRC, to stop Weir's incursion.'

Solara accepted Amy's offer of help up. Leaning on her, she began walking to the *Hecate*. 'We don't have long.'

# NO DEATH

Tʜᴇ OʀɪGᴇɴ ᴛʀᴀɴѕᴘᴏʀᴛ ᴛᴏᴜᴄʜᴇᴅ ᴅᴏᴡɴ.

On the landing pad beneath the shadow of the imposing Zion Temple, plasma haze scorched the air like an arc welder, as engines idled, and the stench of burnt ozone reached Linear's nostrils. The sky was unusually clear, and the constant arrivals and departures of transports, which normally dotted the airspace around the temple, were absent, for a lockdown had been ordered in response to Rhodes' coup. Waiting for the passenger to exit, Linear looked out over the city. Despite the high-tech marvels implanted in the heart of Zion, which had been Old City Jerusalem, much of the city looked as it had for millennia, and Linear was always intrigued by the historic contrast. Gethsemane, the Chapel of Ascension, the Church of All Nations, and the Tomb of the Virgin stretched away beyond the temple grounds, remnants of a past soon to become obsolete.

The aircraft hatch opened, and with machine precision, an OriGen officer walked down the ramp alone. No words were exchanged, and when their eyes met, Linear about-faced and strode to the temple entrance. The officer followed silently, his passing unnoticed by the low-level maintenance machines on the tarmac. No conscious life was present to witness his arrival. His face was fixed dead ahead in an unrelenting stare, or an evangelistic cast of rapture, depending on the interpretation. A shaved head, singular focus, and disciplined demeanor could have marked him as military, and had anyone been observing, they would have presumed he was a man with an imperative task. By the manner of his arrival, an important one.

The pair entered an elevator inside the entrance. The angular journey into the subterranean catacombs of the pyramid took seconds. Exiting, they passed a series of security doors manned by the ubiquitous machine sentries of the GRC, and Linear provided identity verification at each checkpoint. All human personnel were absent.

They reached a huge, long black-stone corridor, perhaps ten meters in height and five wide, with archaic text and ominous murals decorating the walls. At regular intervals, the dark metallic forms of Wraiths stood guard on either side, motionless and watchful sentinels, their anti-matter head circlets dark haloes crowning blacker eyes. As he passed by, Linear's hackles rose at the icy field emanating from the machines. Reaching the end of the corridor, a double door opened at their approach, and they entered a huge, windowless, circular room. Two Wraiths from the corridor entered on their heels, and the door closed behind. Subtle, non-invasive light cast a subdued, amber hue through the chamber.

The smooth stone walls were broken at points by recesses. Flames danced in one, filling the room with flickering shadows; ancient-looking stone tablets, inscribed with archaic characters, and encased in tempered glass occupied others. Statues and artifacts straight out of pre-history rested in more. A large mural depicting an epic battle adorned one quarter of the wall, and Linear sensed the staggering antiquity. The lone furnishing in the sanctum was a dark stone altar in the center, covered in script. Otherwise, the room was bereft of the normal human trappings of convenience.

A select group of the elite waited. OriGen President Dario Sanchez, and GSI director Dominic Medina. General Bradley Sterne—who commanded the GRC response to Rhodes' coup, was present in holographic form. GRC President Lucian Diaz, the man second only to Nicolas in the world power hierarchy, was here in person. In his late sixties, lean, with a bronze complexion and graying hair brushed neatly back from a high forehead, Diaz was also the public face of the GRC, and its global leader. The eight-person Central Committee, known in closed circles as the Ennead, and the ruling body of the GRC, also waited. Each member of the Ennead, in addition to their committee role, held a high corporate or political office. The Ennead was subject only to Diaz and Nicolas, and any policy decisions taken within the GRC could be vetoed by either of this pair, although ultimate authority lay with Nicolas. The GRC was strictly autocratic.

The officer accompanying Linear was mid-level, far outranked by the powerful people in the room, yet they fell silent as he entered. A nanoswarm swept over the officer's features, and Daniel Nicolas—the Black Monarch, head of the Order—stood in his place, and calmly faced the room of hardened eyes and veteran faces. The OriGen uniform was gone, and he wore a black and red mantle. The two Wraiths who had entered moved to stand behind him.

Although Nicolas' power was near total, his was a visage few in the world knew. Anonymity was crucial to the Order's power, and Linear was impressed by how well Nicolas had concealed his true nature beneath the Weir mask in recent weeks, a security precaution proven justified with the discovery of the Resistance spy on the senior research team. How many opportunities had Niemeyer had to kill Nicolas, if he'd known the truth? Linear rebuked himself again for his failure to detect the intruder, and the possibility more Resistance agents may yet remain undiscovered.

The Black Monarch's real face was familiar to Linear, however, and he noticed subtle changes in Nicolas' appearance since the first incursion. His brown eyes had gained depth not present before, and his regal, angular face had attained a majesty, as if something vast stirred awake inside.

Nicolas' eyes swept the assembly, and his voice resonated powerfully. 'We must act.'

A starkly beautiful woman stepped forward from the Ennead. Her face was alabaster, and her dark eyes radiated sexuality. Her pale skin starkly contrasted her lustrous hair, which hung loose in a descending black wave to swirl around her shoulders. Nicolas offered the woman his hand, which she took in her own.

The third. The unknown one. Plan B.

Olivia Cain, a member of the Ennead, had been staying in a secure location since her mind-link with Nicolas in the first incursion. Soon she would join him when he entered the vacuum again. The gathering was silent as Nicolas gently released her hand, and strolled to a statue in one of the recesses, which depicted a winged angel; with one arm outstretched, the being reached to the heavens, and divine fire was grasped in its fist.

Linear, like the others in the room initiated into the mysteries, understood the deeper meaning behind the symbolism. The being depicted was none other than Lucifer, the light bringer, also known as Prometheus, the Titan who stole the secret of fire from the gods, and gave it as a gift to mankind.

Nicolas ran his fingers thoughtfully over the stone facing. 'We battle not against flesh and blood, but against principalities, and powers... Prometheus was punished in return for his defiance of the gods, even though his motives were selfless. Is this the eternal fate of all life?'

He turned, and walked back to the assemblage. Dario Sanchez, the OriGen head stepped forward. Sanchez was young for his position, one of the GRC's new breed of global leaders. Still in his thirties, with a mean, ruthless nature, he was an ambitious bureaucrat who owed his position more to family connections and politics than ability.

Sanchez' tone was deferential toward Nicolas. 'General Rhodes attempted coup, allied to Solara and the Resistance, reveals our vulnerability. We need an overwhelming strike to crush the insurrection. Why do we hold back our main forces?'

Nicolas' dark eyes narrowed. 'I think you overestimate them. Our current detachments are sufficient. We must play this carefully... call in our main forces and we give the Resistance the attention it seeks, but if we make the threat obsolete by harnessing the power of Sirius? Our total victory will be attained with one decisive blow—the second incursion must proceed now.'

Dario Sanchez inclined his head. 'Are we completely certain of the energy field key? We can't afford a single mistake.'

Nicolas' voice was reassuring. 'It has achieved a flawless performance record. The chances of repeating of the first incursion disaster are near zero.'

'Still,' said Eamon Bailey, head of Zyklon Corporation. 'We risk failure. What of the warning about a naked singularity in the Kansas texts? This is our last chance to pull back from a potential abyss. Our forces can crush Rhodes's coup in hours, root out the cockroaches, and we can then conduct a more rigorous test regime.'

Nicolas narrowed his eyes. 'We cannot risk the delay. All elements are aligned for the release phase. Circumstances may never be as favorable again. Now is the time to realize the full potential of our new weapon.'

Sanchez persisted. 'But how—'

In controlled fury, Nicolas said, 'The risk is acceptable!' He stared Sanchez and Bailey down, and then scanned the faces in the room. As one, the group bowed their heads.

From beside Nicolas, Olivia addressed the group. 'For your own safety, you should evacuate now. With Solara… at large, there is an unreasonable danger to your person.'

Bailey narrowed his eyes. 'And, as agreed, the power of Sirius will be shared?'

Nicolas nodded. 'You have my word. Our sacred oaths must be obeyed.' His chin jutted arrogantly, and he took Olivia's hand. 'The endless provocations of the Resistance are at an end. When we return from the vacuum, the sun will set on the old epoch. All power, all glory will be ours, forever.'

Sanchez became resolved. 'Then the die is cast.'

Firelight reflected in Nicolas' eyes, or was it something more, thought Linear?


With his head bowed, Linear marched slowly behind a dark figure. Robed in black from head to toe, the steady rhythmic procession moved in single file along a winding stone path lit by flaming torches. He chanted in unison with the group, and the words, chilling in their implications, echoed through the dark necropolis deep beneath the Zion Temple. The passages had seen a thousand horrors and wonders over the ages, and their stillness held echoes, of war and peace, chaos and order, terror, blood and life. Originally constructed in the time of Solomon, they had been imprinted by footsteps of the Byzantines, the Romans, Islam, and the Christians.

The procession reached a large natural cavern. Dancing torches created an eerie sanctum of shifting shadows, and the line arrayed itself around an altar at the center. A discordant choir sung in the background, and strange symbols, thought to be lost in the distant past, adorned the walls. With his hands clasped in obeisance, a black-robed priest stood before a naked woman roped cruelly to a black crucifix. Stunningly beautiful, she trembled in terror, but the most striking figure in the cavern sat beyond.

A throne stood on a raised dais behind the altar, and upon it sat a man clothed royally in robes of black with blood-red trappings. His features appeared cruel in the torchlight, and Linear could almost sense a dark power emanating from Nicolas, exerting a subtle influence from beneath the veil of reality. Beside Nicolas was a second throne, upon which Olivia Cain sat with poised elegance. At the front of the assemblage, facing the thrones, stood President Diaz and the Ennead. Humbled at the concentration of power, Linear shifted his gaze back through the rows, and recognized many high-ranking governors and Prelates among the robed initiates.

In ritual and ceremony, the Order believed they gained spiritual power from those of the Order who had fallen in their cause, all who had died from their machinations, and all they were yet to kill. They directed and harnessed these life forces to their will through blood sacrifice, and now, they consecrated the second incursion. Since the Order's conception at the dawn of civilization, they had pitted brother against brother, nation against nation, friend against friend. The blood of countless millions was upon their hands. Linear's role in Sirius had opened many doors, but along with the power came a heightened level of responsibility and pressure. Failure was not an option. He glanced at the throne: *he* was not a man you disappointed. Period. But Linear's loyalty was absolute. He had chosen his path long ago.

He recalled his early days with the Order, when his Prelate had called him to a meeting, and his life's role had been revealed. He was to work with some of the largest corporations on the planet and assume positions of great responsibility, and was to learn, know, and understand their workings. Few would know his true purpose, and then only those who were also subject to the will of the Order. His true identity was never to be revealed to anyone except a select few, and then only in great secrecy. Always hidden beneath another role, another title, for in the coming years, the Order would research and carry out a project that could realize their age-old quest. The nature of which, must always remain hidden, until the appointed time.

'Do you accept this great honor?' his Prelate had asked him.

Linear had been overwhelmed. 'With all my heart,' he had replied in gratitude, his voice breaking.

That was what he had prayed for since childhood: a path to greatness, and he could feel the wheels of destiny working within. He vowed he would humbly work to bring the light of God into a world torn apart by war, hunger, disease, and hatred.

The god, that is, who sat in Zion.

The congregation stopped in orderly lines, and the figure upon the throne gestured to the priest with the arrogant surety of one long accustomed to absolute obedience. The robed priest bowed, and turned to the naked woman. An air of menace pervaded the room as he began the ritualistic words.

'With this blood…'

●

ALONE IN his chambers, Nicolas meditated on the coming ordeal. Visions passed rapidly through his mind: the nature of the Presence, the power and protection promised, the converging threats. With regret, he considered

Solara; her modest nature was a stark contrast to Nicolas' own ambitious makeup, and it had been believed she could balance him.

'And who were you, to my father—Weir, or Nicolas?' she had asked him.

He'd been Weir, a brilliant upcoming physicist, the same face he'd shown her at first, and his intellectual and academic brilliance was no act. He had deceived her mostly by his silence. Secrets were second nature to him. He'd been born into power; he hadn't chosen it. Had fate also determined, he considered, that he was cunning, remorseless, willing to do anything to take ever more control? No, perhaps not, that had been all him. He still remembered the first time he killed someone. He didn't want to; he was only sixteen, and undertaking an initiation rite for his Order. The Blood Oath. He didn't even know the man, or what he'd done, and the first time was the hardest, but Nicolas killed him and felt nothing. No remorse, no guilt, nothing. It was as easy as breathing.

No, he thought, recalling… that wasn't his first. He often forgot that memory, a habit learned. A teacher at the military boarding school he'd attended as a child. The man had singled out Nicolas, for some reason, to groom him for leadership, but it hadn't been guidance the man had in mind. The memory of violation had dimmed with the years, but when it returned, so would remnants of trauma. The man had become a monster in his childhood mind: inescapable, hunting, watching, and no matter how fast Nicolas ran he could hear the demon creeping, smell its breath. When Nicolas' moods had darkened, the man had mockingly taken to calling him Gray Cloud, the nickname his mother had given him. The teacher must have heard it used once. Nicolas stabbed him to death in a cleaning room with a concealed blade, and the murder had never been tied back to him; he had planned his liberation meticulously, patiently, and his tormentor had never seen it coming. The act had sickened him for days, but had been his first sense of control, sovereignty.

He deliberated. Had he been born with darkness inside, or had it been conceived in that terrible, childhood catharsis? It had been his first unspeakable secret. As he grew, killing became a necessary part of his role, and after a while he stopped asking the question. The murder of Solara's father hadn't even made him blink. He could feign empathy, and remorse, when required by social expectations, to better manipulate events toward his own end, but it was only ever an act, wasn't it?

Yet his rise to power was not what he thought it would be; the hole that had grown inside him, fed by ambition, isolation… fear, had become a great void which he hopelessly tried to fill by gaining more and more. The darkness within felt greater than the world, larger than the universe, and nothing could sate it. Over the years life became a devouring nightmare, and in an odd counterpoint Nicolas found the dark not only terrifying, but comforting. Somehow pure, and he could never understand the internal contradictions of his existence.

When the GRC rose to power after the war, Nicolas murdered the head of the Order, Dieter Wolf, the man who united the world. He had treated Nicolas like a son, preparing him to rule one day but he didn't want to wait. He poisoned his food with arsenic acquired from a contact in GSI, and everyone thought Wolf died of natural causes—why did it haunt him?

Then, when Sirius had been about to enter the operational phase, word of Artois's daughter had reached him. He'd had to know if she could… what, Nicolas thought? Complete him? Save him? He shook off the feeling. Now, his second companion from the first incursion, Olivia, would accompany him. On one hand, she had a nature as loving as any, toward her family, at least, but at the same time could be as remorseless as he in pursuing her ambitions. She could not have risen so high otherwise. Deep down, he had harbored doubts about her suitability, but the point was moot: Solara had made the choice for them all. Perhaps it was always going to be this way.

Nicolas pondered the activation of the Merkaba, which was only the first step in a greater evolution. Permeating creation was a hidden energy pattern, only manifested when two individuals, male and female, merged their subtle bodies, allowing a unified vacuum penetration. An evolutionary leap beyond the Merkaba, it formed a bridge to the divine. However, its effectiveness was limited by the balance of the male and female poles, as he had explained to the policy committee. In theory, any bonded pair could harness the energy, but most were trapped in a defective state. So, psychological changes were implied by the transformation.

Which was why the third level of consciousness, predicted in the third iteration, was crucial. The couple needed balance, or the power would without doubt destroy any who wielded it to the extremes Nicolas intended, by leveraging vacuum energy through Sirius. With Solara, he had been moving toward this end. Then Trent had interfered. Now Olivia must balance the equation, and the spiritual merger would create a hybrid entity known as...

... again, a door was opened in his mind. He felt the Presence stir within like an uncoiling snake, and it showed him things: when he returned from the second incursion, the Presence would begin to cross over fully. It would fuse with his and Olivia's subtle bodies to acquire their balance. The two would become a trinity, which would become infinite—through them, the Presence would become whole, and ignite a spark which would usher in a new reality.

The cosmos would react. Violently.

For the first time, Nicolas perceived the hidden, deeper truth of the Presence's intentions. Its purpose was clear, the task was simple: reverse the naked singularity, reconstruct the moment of creation, and by doing so, overthrow the existing order. Usurp God. Once the divine spark had been ignited, the nature of the universe would be displaced to its opposite, and the change would be unalterable. The magnitude of the revealed plan was staggering, and on some level muted, detached, Nicolas knew it meant the annihilation of all life, and his mind recoiled at the horror.

His attention was directed toward the naked singularity, and he contemplated a mystery with a mind in which all remnants of humanity were evaporating. He couldn't think straight, couldn't move, felt a power denying his will... the reversal would require a further change in the vacuum field interface, he found himself thinking.

Through him, the Presence reached out, and for the second time subtly manipulated the Sirius energy field key, completing the virus Nicolas had inserted only yesterday, and he instinctively rebelled...

*I will not!*

*Then eternity will be your prison.*

Nicolas was back atop the atoll, frozen in time, and the Presence sealed off the pathways back to the world. A blistering furnace closed in upon him. Blackened by fire, he was drowning in the molten, rolling ocean, trapped in a sea of lost wailing souls held in thrall by the Presence. Burning forever. Undying.

*But all must die! Everything ends!* Nicolas screamed inside.

*Not I! I find no death!*

He felt himself absorbed into a larger purpose, transcending his ability to comprehend or deny.

*What of others?* he asked.

*They are nothing.*

*They are useful.*

*These things have no use. Except one.*

Uncertain of his own volition anymore, Nicolas completed the energy field intervention, and then concealed the change beneath random data where it would remain hidden until the last moment.

*What will become of me?* Nicolas asked.

*You will become a god.*

He was provided glimpses of a new universe, in which his principality would span a trillion worlds. He witnessed the unborn potential of future life, a multitude of wonders experienced with an awareness beyond mortal comprehension.

*Who are you?* Nicolas ventured.

*I am the first. I preceded the beginning...*

Nicolas opened his eyes as someone entered his quarters unannounced. The superluminal awareness fell away, and Olivia Cain stood in the doorway watching.

*... and I will follow the end,* the Presence said distantly.

He stood at Olivia's approach, and perceived her vulnerability: she was alone like him, afraid like him.

She walked to stand before him. 'I hear the same voice. I have ever since we crossed over,' she said, quietly.

Nicolas clasped her hand. 'It revealed the truth to you?'

She nodded. 'Just now.'

'Things are not what we thought they were.'

Olivia reflected, the fear in her eyes displaced by a deep, insatiable hunger. 'It's like a suffocating dream. We risk all.'

'If we fail, what matter if the cosmos ends with us?' Nicolas said, with a mix of fear and arrogance. 'It's of no consequence.'

She put her hand to his cheek. 'Then I want you, one last time in this world.'

He felt her vacuum potency merge with his own, magnifying their power. And through them, surged the Presence, undulating across an impossible boundary. He held her, her breath in his ear, on his neck as his desire built. Their spirits touched, the beginning of fusion. Deep in their merging souls, dark fire descended from some empyrean place, and burned with an astonishing power not of this universe.

Nicolas was struck by a realization—the fifth angel of Revelation, was it him? '*… and I saw a star fall from heaven unto the earth: and to him was given the key to the bottomless pit.*'

Nicolas saw apocalypse. Rebirth.

Immortality.

# BLACK SWAN

The capital was in exodus.

OriGen personnel rushed to the transports waiting along the Jericho tarmac, emergency messages blared, engines fired, military units ran in various directions, and the sky was aflame with aircraft. A tech crew repaired the *Hecate's* cockpit window. Rushing across a staging platform with Li and Amy, I was greeted at a command post by General Rhodes who was accompanied by a heavy guard. I was glad the General was on our side, and his powerful, ebony form cast an air of authority over the situation.

Rhodes nodded. 'Solara, we must move fast.' He gestured for my team to follow.

I walked beside him. 'I hear you staged a coup, General.'

'The Temple Guard is now under my command,' Rhodes said. 'Hostile forces mass as we speak, and division is spreading as word of Sirius leaks to the hierarchy. OriGen's mandate won't be worth a snowflake in Hades once the truth of the situation is known. We face war.'

'And darker things, too, than war General,' I said.

He nodded gravely.

Joshua glanced over at me. 'We must re-activate your implants, but keep the signal hidden from OriGen, or any other adversary. I can help, if you will allow?'

I considered. 'False ID again?'

'Kind of. You'll still be able to communicate with allies.'

Rhodes nodded approvingly.

'Go ahead,' I said.

Joshua's hack took moments—my nanites came back online, and the neura-link OS came up in overlay. We soon came to a cordoned-off area, and the temple guards formed a cordon around our position.

'Solara, Joshua, use this link and follow me now,' said Rhodes, then glanced at Li and Amy. 'Join us.'

I followed the quantum encrypted link into a strange virtual environment. The sun blazed colossal in the sky, illuminating a terrain of jagged, spiky rock formations, and abyssal crevices that snaked across the surface. Some sensory faculties were deactivated, a necessity of being in a harsh virtual environment like this. You could die in the Subreality just like in the real world.

Peter Trent arrived as if on cue, caution mixed with urgency written on his face, and stood on the rocky ground observing our group for a moment. Once part of the hierarchy, a powerful director within GSI, I knew in any other circumstances he would be either captured or killed on sight. Tortured if taken alive, although he no doubt had the means to take his own life if it ever came to that.

He gave me a nod of acknowledgment, before turning to Rhodes. 'General. I never thought to see the day.'

'We face a common enemy, Peter,' Rhodes said.

'Where do we stand?' Trent asked.

Rhodes said, 'Nicolas has entered the singularity control room and attempts to reverse the energy field. I believe you know something of the implications if he succeeds.'

Trent nodded gravely. 'Yes.'

'If the Presence is able to cross over,' Joshua said, 'it should not be capable of entering fully until it completes the reversal from this side. Until that is achieved, once here, the being should exist in a limited state. That gives us some time.'

'How much?' asked Trent.

'Unknown,' said Joshua. 'Perhaps an hour before the Rubicon is crossed. Once entering the universe, the Presence will manipulate the Sirius Matrix, attempt to reverse the polarity and reach the termination threshold.'

'Termination threshold?' Trent asked.

'A complete unknown, where the laws of the universe will fail,' Joshua explained.

Rhodes said, 'Nicolas' virus must be hacked, and the energy field stabilized. The singularity control room is shielded by an electro-magnetic barrier: there's no hard line so the matrix is untouchable. The only place you can access it is from the nerve center itself which means we have to physically take the control room.' He looked to me. 'Commander this task falls to your team—you have command. Be wary, intel indicates hostile Wraiths.'

I nodded. 'Understood.'

Rhodes continued. 'A secondary team will support you. Once you have access to the matrix, Joshua, linked to our cyber-warfare division and Resistance agents, will hack the virus and close the energy field.' He glanced at Joshua.

The AI nodded confirmation. 'The solution is valid.'

Trent said, 'Hundreds of our Etherians are ready to join forces with your own.'

Rhodes nodded. 'Give your people this link.' He tied up the meeting. 'We all know what to do. Peter, I hope we meet again under less tragic circumstances.'

Trent smiled briefly. 'That would benefit us all.'

As one, the group exited the Subreality, and returned to the hangar. Rhodes yanked open the lid of a nearby supply crate. A couple of exotic looking items—suit arm-attachments, I saw—encased in foam molding were stored within. He hefted one out, tapped a few commands on a panel.

Handing me the weapon, he then reached for another. 'Take these.'

I passed one to Li, took the other Rhodes offered, and passed it to Amy. Then a third, which I examined.

'Experimental dark energy weapons,' said Rhodes. 'Designed for Sirius. For unfriendly machines—it's capable of overloading a Wraith's containment field. Also, it can injure the subtle body.'

'Spirits, in other words,' said Amy.

I fitted the attachment to my nano-suit, and a simple weapon interface came up in overlay.

Rhodes said, 'They might come in handy. Now let's get you to your ship.'

Our group strode through the chaotic area, while the security detail cleared a path.

'Nicolas?' I shouted to Rhodes over the crowd.

The General was grim. 'Unresponsive to all communications. He'll move fast under the circumstances.' We reached the *Hecate*. 'Commander,' Rhodes said, 'I know you can shut down the nerve center with your abilities. I am ordering you not to; we need the systems online to close the naked singularity. Use conventional weapons to secure the area. Understood?'

I nodded. 'Yes, General.'

A four-man strike team approached. Our support unit, I assumed, but frowned as a 'something's not right' alarm went off in my head. I didn't recognize the men, but that was common with the Regiment spread across the world. No, there was something else.

Rhodes turned to the approaching squad. 'Your back-up,' he said, waving them to the ship. 'Let's go—'

A grenade was lobbed casually at our group by the leader of the newcomers. In the same motion, he raised his weapon. His team was right behind him. The grenade sailed forward in a lazy arc.

Rhodes barked a command. 'Take them ou—'

Energy coursed through me. Some of the aggressors froze at my attack, but not all. The remaining enemy team fired. Li was struck in the chest, staggered. The temple guards returned fire, and laser strafed through the attackers. One of Rhodes' guards dropped from a headshot.

The grenade hit the ground. Another of Rhodes' guards died. With blinding speed, a black particle swarm swirled into existence above the grenade, and then Joshua was lying face down on the bomb. The only sign it had exploded was a muffled detonation and a slight jarring of his body. The guards finished off the remaining enemy. Joshua rose with his torso shredded, rapidly reforming its molecular structure, and in seconds he was whole again. Li was rubbing his chest, but his nano-suit had stopped the round. I turned at a disturbance across the dock: more enemy soldiers flooded into the area, shots were exchanged with Rhodes' forces, and shouts came from various parts of the Jericho campus.

Rhodes waved us urgently to the ship. 'Nicolas' people… Go!'

I raced into the *Hecate* with Li, Amy, and Joshua. Gaining the pilot's seat, I punched in the launch code.

The craft vertically ascended, and we blasted toward Zion Temple.

●

LINEAR RUSHED back to Operations. Solara, he fumed: her escape, the strange power, the astonishing insolence. He expected word of her capture any moment. What was taking so long? He'd been cold on her coming onboard from the beginning; she was unpredictable, and now his concerns were being validated. Once more he tried to understand the complex chain of events unfolding. She was redundant now anyway, her replacement complete. Yes, it would be better if Solara were dead than free, the stupid bitch had already done enough, and with her burgeoning power was a proverbial bull in a China shop.

He reached Operations. 'Situation?' he questioned Lieutenant Pearce.

'Sir, we have a serious problem here,' Pearce replied.

Linear scowled, felt a growing anxiety. 'What is it?'

'Solara's still off reservation. The strike teams failed; they're assumed dead.'

Linear stopped in mid-stride. 'Assumed?'

Pearce adopted a military report tonality. 'General Sterne reports the *Hecate* and Temple Guard reached her just after our forces. But the site where they tried to take her on the tarmac—there's nothing except some debris on the ground. Also, some blood. Ran it through forensics—not Solara's.'

Linear felt a nightmare descending. 'Her neural feed?'

'Still off-grid,' Pearce said.

Linear was quiet for a moment. 'Do we have any idea where she is right now?'

'None.'

If Solara didn't want to be found, she would not be found. This was a demonstrated ability. Involuntarily Linear felt a chill.

*I don't like this.*

Now he had to somehow explain the situation to his superiors, and it reflected badly on him personally. 'Damn that woman!' he snarled, losing his cool.

'We're running a smart-dust scan,' said Pearce. 'So far zero.'

Linear nodded tersely. 'Rhodes will have his people on countermeasures. Stay on it.'

Inside, he laid the blame for all the problems befalling Sirius at Solara's feet. Illogical, but having a focus for his anger made him feel better, if only for a moment. He subtly glanced around the room; all personnel were focused on their stations. Neura-linking, he activated an internal, particle delivery package. Called Nanometh, the illegal App manufactured a potent stimulant using the body's own cells. The digital cocaine of the early twenty-second century.

Dopamine hit. Flush of warmth. Pupils dilated, and his breathing quickened. Linear was hit by a state of euphoric heightened awareness; his perception soared on wings, out across the web, and a feeling of omniscience washed over him in an awesome wave.

'Get me Lieutenant Li on the line,' he ordered nearby personnel.

A tech made the call. 'It's gone to message bank, Sir.'

Fuck! he screamed inside.

Linear made for the door, hurling a stack of reports at the wall in fury on his way out. The papers landed in a chaotic mess on the floor, and he swore in silent rage.

●

DANIEL NICOLAS exited the elevator, and walked into the singularity control room to the sound of ominous chanting. A congregation of black-robed initiates stood arrayed around the perimeter of the ground floor, droning in a low repetitive chant which filled the chamber with a sense of boding evil. The moment that the Order had worked toward for thousands of years had arrived. Several Wraiths stood before the initiates with one purpose: protect Nicolas and Olivia. He turned his attention to the center of the room. The anomaly hovered there, like a splinter in reality, and he studied its pulsating blue depths. The star tetrahedrons had lost symmetry, and the internal symbology was changing once more, fractured energies which hinted at something unknown, as if undecided.

Three stasis pods sat evenly spaced around the perimeter of the ground floor, at the points of a perfect triangle. Two were empty. One, however, was already host to a body immersed in amniotic fluid. The figure lay prone upon its back, head facing towards the center, palms upraised at sides, eyes closed, and completely motionless. The transgender body had been prepared to host the combined essences of Nicolas and Olivia, upon their return—but where they truly ventured, Nicolas knew, they wouldn't need a body. He reflected that at some point since the Presence's last contact, he had embraced his fate… had that been his decision, or the others?

Robed in black, the couple's march was measured in time with the cadence of the dark chant, and Nicolas sneered silently at the gullibility of the Ennead. They believed they would share the divine light, and ascend to demigod status. They would die, with everyone else. The prospect confirmed the magnitude of his own destiny, and the pathetic nature of lesser beings. What matter if the Ennead, or even the cosmos was destroyed to enable his ascension? It amounted to nothing, he thought, holding back a heinous grin. Upon returning, a bridge would open between this universe and the place where the Presence was confined, and he would fuse with the god that was forming.

Halting their march, the couple drew back their hoods, and turned to face the assembled initiates. The chant stopped, and a priest walked forward. Slaves to ritual, right to the end; the marriage was symbolic of their coming union and dominion over the Earth. The priest motioned for the pair to face one another, began uttering the ceremonial words, and Nicolas and Olivia spoke their part in the lines. Silence followed the vows. Nicolas clasped Olivia's hands, and a black cloth was draped over their wrists. He leaned to kiss her, and she responded with a tremor, the hunger in her soul as rapacious as his own. With the ceremony complete the priest stepped back into the assemblage.

Nicolas faced the Order, and his voice resonated powerfully. 'My brethren, our time has arrived, the circle is complete.'

The chant started again with a darker, expectant tone, which rose to a fever pitch. Parting, the couple strode into the central well toward their respective stasis-pods. Nicolas removed his ceremonial robes to reveal a muscular body, then stepped into the waiting cocoon, and waited calmly. A white-clad technician respectfully began to attach his respirator unit, and warm fluid flowed in around him. Closing his eyes, he sunk backward until he floated prone.

Distantly, he heard the loudspeaker. 'Five minutes until entry, and counting.'

The lid of his stasis-tube was sealed shut, locking him inside.

The transformation was at hand.

Time for the snake to shed its skin.

NICOLAS RETURNED through the naked singularity with Olivia. With them was the Presence, like a flickering, warped light storm that heralded destruction, and assailed reality. Nicolas sensed the being revel in its freedom.

An assault fractured his identity. Jolted to insensibility, he struggled to his utmost, but his will was swept aside like a dust mote, and a final deception ripped away. Nicolas remained conscious, however, and understood: he wasn't to be a god! He'd been deceived utterly. Ages of scheming by the Order, and their plan, born of stolen lives and deceit, in the end would amount to nothing. They had been manipulated, duped. Arrogance had been their poison, and the irony was not lost upon him. Only now at the end, diffusing into a horror, did he understand his fatal error.

The trinity—Nicolas, Olivia, and the Presence, merged to form an abomination which existed between two dimensions, one which was and one that struggled to be. Nicolas flailed helplessly, transfixed, fading.

The being, unrestrained, turned its attention to the Sirius Matrix... and Nicolas was lost.

He felt himself dying and dying. And he couldn't stop.

FREED FROM its eternal prison, a sea of rage swelled within the Presence, heaving like a tide.

'For this light you are imprisoned! Destroy it!'

The being, still unformed, bent the surrounding light to its will, and formed a beachhead in this universe. Ululating, it sent forth its sight into the world.

'I am the rightful god, and there is nothing I can do, except one thing.'

A flood of memories arose within.

'A name, once I had a name! Who am I?'

With an alien scream, the Presence summoned vast energies through the naked singularity, the power to shatter creation, and nature screamed out in protest.

# DARKER THINGS
# THAN WAR

The *Hecate* soared like a dark meteor.

I piloted, Li navigated, while Amy and Joshua were stationed at terminals back in the personnel compartment, and focused on intel.

Li tapped comms. 'Zion Temple Guard command, this is the *Hecate*. We are three minutes out on final approach.'

'Copy, *Hecate*. LZ-5 is clear.'

'Copy,' Li responded.

Far ahead, a battle raged around inner-city Zion, concentrated at the central pyramid. Countless aircraft could be seen streaking and maneuvering above the land forces, fighting for control of the temple grounds.

I glanced at Li. 'See if you can plot a course through that mess.'

He'd barely touched his display when a brilliant flash came from ahead.

'Shit—' Li said.

A thermal wave struck the *Hecate*, while an intense light shone from the pyramid's position.

'*Hecate*—report!' demanded Jericho.

I killed the turbots, slowed to a stationary hover, and observed the spectacle. Heat shimmers danced through the atmosphere in waves. The glare began fading, yet an ebon darkness grew in its place, and slowly crept outward across the city.

I felt a cold hand grip my spine. 'Jericho, we've got a problem.'

Amy attempted contact. 'Zion control come in? Do you read me, over?'

No response.

'What's happening Commander?' demanded Rhodes.

'General, we have an evolving situation at the temple,' I said. I glanced back to the personnel compartment. 'Anything?'

Amy said, 'Nothing from Zion. One moment. Magnify.' An enhanced view of the city came up in holographics. 'An expanding object has appeared around the central pyramid.'

'Expanding at what speed?' said Rhodes.

'Fast—wait, it's slowing down,' Amy said.

The darkness had ballooned outward for kilometers, before slowing to a crawl. A massive, shadowy dome now engulfed the inner city.

'It's stopped,' I said, after a minute.

The dark field began changing color from black, to magenta, blue, and swirling patterns emerged within, eerily familiar.

Li frowned. 'Jesus, I think it's the anomaly… just bigger.'

'*Hecate* get to the control room at any cost,' Rhodes ordered.

'Copy, Sir,' I replied.

A wave of force exploded from the dome, and sent the *Hecate* reeling.

●

SURROUNDED BY a guard contingent, Rhodes had just finished the comm with the *Hecate*, and had been en route to a command post when he was knocked to his knees by a shockwave. Simultaneously, light filled the skies, shifting in tone from scarlet to blood-red in concert with a dissonant vibration that pierced his being with a gut-wrenching pain. Nausea hit him in a wave.

Staggering back to his feet, Rhodes leaned on a rail, choked back vomit and scanned the tarmac: many wept openly, as a nameless darkness fell upon Jericho like a blanket of despair, while others collapsed where they stood. Some Temple Guard were among those on the ground, unconscious or dead was unknown, but others stood their ground and were regaining their senses. The stomach-churning vibration receded after a minute.

*A tactical withdrawal.*

The reddish hue in the skies remained, filling the atmosphere with a hellish glow, and shouts to restore order started filling the area. Unnaturally fast, black clouds gathered above the city, and Rhodes felt charged particles building in the air; lightning arced across the sky, freezing wind began howling through Jericho, and a reverberating thunderclap brought him fully back to the moment.

*The Presence.*

'Sir, you should see this,' said a guard, squinting and pointing in the growing wind.

Rhodes scanned the horizon: the blue glow of what Solara believed to be the expanded anomaly, stood at the center of chaos erupting across the heavens. Electric vortices, like inverted lightning, sprang from the surface of the energy dome to twist and ricochet through the stormy skies.

'Any word from the temple!' Rhodes shouted.

'No, Sir. Comms have been down since the energy field appeared. It's blocking all signals.'

'Keep trying,' ordered Rhodes.

A tech said, 'Satellite reports indicate Zion Temple is the epicenter of an energy burst, that has spread outward in concentric circles around the planet, traversed the Atlantic and Pacific oceans, and hit other land masses.'

Rhodes swore. 'Run a trace on GRC leadership.'

A minute later, they found President Diaz in evacuation from the temple, already communicating with allies in the hierarchy. This confirmed Rhodes' suspicion: Nicolas had failed, and the threat from the Presence was imminent. After some final orders to the guard commander, Rhodes contacted the President.

'General Rhodes,' Diaz said. 'You initiated Watchtower, thank you for your foresight. Where do we stand?'

'Jericho is secure for now, Mr. President. We held key temple locations until this latest event. The anomaly is now blocking all comms. The last word from Zion reported that the control room remains intact, and fully functional. Solara and her team are attempting to breach the control room as we speak and close the naked singularity. I've formed a temporary truce with the Resistance, hopefully some sanity will come of it.'

Diaz sighed. 'We have no choice, General. I believe Nicolas is dead, and the worst has occurred: the Presence has entered the universe and interacts with the Sirius Matrix. You have my full support. If we survive the GRC will be divided. We must gather allies, and fast.'

Rhodes deliberated a second. 'We must get Linear on side; he could be dangerous.'

He knew Linear as well as any man, which was to say very little, but knew he was a rabid imperialist on the inner circle of Nicolas' fanatics.

Diaz said, 'Linear evacuated the temple complex with some Nicolas loyalists. Either he's on side or he's a dead man. See to it, General. I'm on my way to the Jericho tarmac. Meet me there.'

●

THE *HECATE* maintained a static position before the energetic dome. Like the smaller anomaly, inside was a matrix of repeating spheres, but conditions inside the boundary were unknown. Outside, unnatural cloud formations darkened the landscape, and red haze hung in the atmosphere, which cast an otherworldly radiance across the city. At their workstations back in the personnel compartment, Joshua and Amy made a preliminary analysis of the object.

Joshua said, 'Li's right. It's an amplification of the original anomaly, spherical, centered at the control room with a ten-point-five-kilometer radius; twenty-one kilometers across. Ground-penetrating scan reveals the lower part of the sphere continues underground. The inner objects exhibit moving patterns—but the second iteration is gone. Surface wave interactions are possibly generating new symbology based on… it's hard to say yet.'

Li said, 'Still nothing from the temple?'

Amy shook her head. 'Nothings getting through.'

'Send in a probe,' I ordered.

Li tapped a keypad. 'Deploying probe to penetrate anomaly boundary, scan for thirty seconds, and return.'

The probe detached from the ship, shot forward. I watched the blue light of the plasma thruster dwindle like a flame, a shooting star, then it vanished into the object.

Joshua watched his display closely. 'Probe has entered the anom—'

Almost as soon as it passed the surface, it shot back out and hovered above the canopy.

'Talk to me,' I said.

Joshua frowned. 'Return took seven seconds.'

'You're sure it went in, it wasn't repulsed?'

He nodded. 'We had positive surface penetration.'

Amy analyzed readouts. 'We've got a scan result with a duration of thirty seconds.'

'Explain that to me?' I demanded.

'She's right,' said Joshua. 'Between the moment it entered and re-emerged we have twenty-three seconds of footage that shouldn't exist.' He paused, scanned the display. 'It appears we have temporal distortion inside the horizon, perhaps an acceleration of the differentiation exhibited by the original anomaly.'

'Bring it up,' I said.

Probe footage came up in overlay. A timer played in the top right corner of the video, which showed the probe nearing the boundary. Passing through. On the other side, debris from the shockwave was evident, a shower of debris which blanketed a landscape of shattered buildings. Fires burned across the city, but the wreckage stopped at the inner edge of the field. Telescopic probe vision revealed flames blazing at the base of the central pyramid. No life signs were detected.

I frowned. 'It's dead in there. Should be something.'

Li said, 'Structural damage sustained by the temple complex. Power is down, main energy grid offline.'

Probe imagery turned back toward the canopy boundary—now seen from the inside—and showed a spidery blue haze of energy lattices. The imagery moved back through to the outside.

'Inside all the inner spheres disappeared, like an optical illusion,' Li said.

I leaned forward. 'Damage to the probe?'

'None,' Amy replied. 'Integrity one hundred percent.'

Joshua frowned. 'It appears a diluted event horizon has expanded into our universe. Inside this new boundary the laws of the universe as we understand them may no longer apply.'

'And I think this is only the beginning,' I said. I had a sudden vision of the anomaly opening, and unfolding like a giant maw.

'A continuation,' said Joshua, thoughtfully.

I fired the turbots. Dominating the forward vista, the apparition grew larger. 'Proceeding into anomaly.'

'One point three clicks,' Amy said.

The light vortices inside deepened as we approached, as if the space inside was being stretched, and I fought off vertigo.

Amy tensed. 'Three hundred meters.' She gripped a rail, and sweat beaded on her forehead.

Li tapped comms. 'Jericho, the *Hecate* is entering the boundary.'

'Copy, *Hecate*.'

The ship began to pass through, and the surface shot away impossibly. My stomach lurched—we plummeted into a glittering blue sea of flames that weaved through the energy structures like connective tissue. A ripple distorted the frontal patterns in a widening cascade. The ship ploughed through, and the field began to crack open. A gap appeared ahead, a dark flaw in the symmetry. The *Hecate* shuddered, and surged through the breach into empty space.

'Clear!' I said, releasing a breath.

Inside the canopy, muted twilight. Beneath lay Zion. Above, the energetic, even plane of the energy dome. We were on our own now. I pushed the throttle, and the *Hecate* plunged forward.

Amy said, 'We've got an emergency distress signal from the temple comms tower. Oscillating in thirty-second intervals. Was set twenty minutes ago.'

Joshua traced a line on his display. 'Five minutes have passed since the energy structure appeared. If that signal was set when its data code says it was, then about four seconds pass in here for every second in actual time. We were correct—the time displacement is accelerating.' He glanced at me. 'Do you retain the connection to the other Etherians, Commander?'

When we passed through the boundary, communications with the outside were cut, and the Etherian link had been established, initially at least, via my implants. But my connection remained, I sensed. 'I can still feel it,' I said. 'It's not reliant on the implants anymore.'

Joshua looked curious. 'Your subtle body, then?'

I drove the throttle forward, and we glided over decimated terrain. The area looked odd to me; something was wrong, but I couldn't define it, and I felt my hairs prickle a moment.

Li glanced across. 'You feel that?'

I nodded wordlessly. We advanced forward. Strobes now illuminated a panorama of dark, deserted streets. As we got closer to the central pyramid, signs of battle between coup forces and the loyalists became evident; scorched broken buildings, smoldering vehicles, and downed aircraft were visible.

'There's no people, no bodies. Where are they?' I said.

Li scanned the streets. 'You're right. Most would have evacuated, but there should be some casualties from the battle, at least.'

I altered my perception: a permeating field became apparent inside the boundary. All around us, it slowly flowed in toward the pyramid as if power was being sucked in from the surrounding area. Reaching out with my senses, I searched for the touch of life, and found nothing. Not an ant, not a butterfly, not a bird. I felt an odd disquiet, like a sense of intruding upon sacred ground. For some reason, I thought of the desolation of Mars that the El had imparted in my vision. The darkening of the planet, and annihilation of life.

*Not annihilation. Transformation.*

'Amy, zoom in on the temple gardens,' I ordered.

She scanned down the optics, gained a perplexed look. 'Strange. No active biological readings. Plant life is dead. Flora is a grayish-black color. Trees are bent toward the pyramid, some broken.'

'Should be blown outward,' Li noted.

I pondered a growing feeling. 'It's assimilating life.'

'The naked singularity?' pondered Li.

I nodded. 'Or the Presence. It must be. When it crossed over, the initial blast wave may have been like a giant DNA harvester.'

Li shook his head. 'Why?'

I turned back to Joshua. 'The Presence wants to remake the world, right? Maybe it needs some blueprints.'

Joshua pursed his lips. 'Logical. The first iteration, remember, mimicked the atomic structure of the universe, from sub-atomics to cellular structure. The second harmonized energy and matter. The third is predicted to relate to consciousness—biological assimilation, mimicry? It's one explanation for the missing people.'

Li shook his head, frowning. 'Wait a minute, we're still here.'

'Some type of drain is still in effect within the boundary. I can see it,' I said.

Joshua said, 'The initial entry of the Presence may have possessed a much higher—but thankfully temporary—energetic intensity.'

Amy looked unsettled. 'But where did the people go?' No one had an answer. 'This is a real cluster-fuck,' she said.

I considered the disturbing thought a moment. 'If the Presence has partially come through, we could be seeing the negative aspect of the third iteration; the beginning of the reversal.'

Joshua considered. 'Then it follows there is also a positive side. Yes?'

The ship continued forward, the air increasingly distorted by heat shimmers which swept across the city, hampering visual line of sight.

'Detecting trace gamma radiation,' Amy said. 'Activating multi-beam ranging.' The short-pulsed laser penetrated the optical disturbance.

Li tapped a control. 'Altering approach vector, seven degrees port... main temple entrance twelve o'clock. Fourteen hundred meters and closing.'

'Visual?' I asked, as we slowed to a crawl.

'Nothing... wait, I think it's clearing,' Amy said.

Ahead, the rippling waves became broken by scattered, burning debris below. A fire, or something much hotter than fire, had torn through the inner temple grounds. We advanced and performed a slow reconnaissance over the landing zone. Smoke billowed from various points in the pyramid superstructure. The center of world power sat bereft in silent tragedy, a lonely catharsis. As the gateway to the subterranean singularity control room, if the entrance was destroyed it would present some problems. The main ground level entry came into view; the base of the pyramid around the entrance had collapsed.

'Blown,' Amy said, softly. 'But some of the service entryways seem intact.'

I circled the ship around the complex. 'I'm going to put us down on that LZ,' I said, pointing to one of the smaller entrances.

Li studied a schematic layout. 'It should take us directly to the central shaft.'

The ship veered down to the deserted tarmac, and we landed with a thud. Joshua led the way down the ramp. I followed, then Li, Amy. Cold wind tore through the landing zone, while the strange blue tinge of the anomaly filled the sky as we rushed to the entrance. Once inside, it was eerily quiet. We traversed a long passage broken by several expansive atriums, then entered an operations area, one of the critical locations secured by Rhodes' men. Now, silent as a tomb.

Joshua walked quickly to the main computer. 'We still have emergency power. Linking with resident AI.'

'How much time?' I asked.

'Unclear,' Joshua said, analyzing. 'We may have less than thirty minutes. I'll work from here and begin hacking accessible elements of the virus, but I'll need access to the nerve center to finish it. I'll join you as soon as you have it secure.'

I nodded. 'Understood.'

Joshua sat at the terminal. 'Engaging.'

I nodded to Li and Amy, and the three of us strode to a security door. A train-like carriage waited on the other side. We entered the transport, hit the ignition and began speeding toward the pyramid axis.

We were nearing the central shaft when Joshua came online. 'I've penetrated the Sirius Matrix, and have an approximate countdown to the termination threshold. Sending it to your feed now.'

'Copy,' I said.

A live countdown began in overlay:

**TERMINATION THRESHOLD: 24.29**

'I'm picking up movement in the singularity control room, non-human, looks like… Wraith activity,' Joshua said.

'Numbers?' I asked.

'Hard to say,' Joshua said. 'There's a lot of interference from the energy field… at least three signals.'

We arrived at the central shaft, a huge, cavernous open space which disappeared into shadows above and below. Walkways and islands were situated around the axis, which housed the main elevators. We strode to the lifts.

Joshua said, 'Interesting—Nicolas' bio-signs are active. He's in the nerve center, unmoving.'

I frowned. 'He's alive?'

'Yes, Commander.'

'The Presence?'

'Nothing. But then, we have no idea what to look for.'

We reached the central elevator, and began our descent. I knew our chances of survival were remote. In thirty minutes, we would probably be dead.

# DESTROYER

The elevator plummeted.

*I must confront the Presence.*

It would be suicide for anyone else to even try. I felt the potential inside grow, as increasing numbers of Etherians from around the world joined the convergence: hundreds, and then thousands focused upon me in a vast global meditation. Closing my eyes a moment, I cautiously reached out with my senses, and for the first time felt the part of the Presence that had entered the universe. Just as I was aware of it, I knew it also sensed me. A thunderous impact boomed beneath.

'What the fuck was—?' Amy managed.

Slam! The elevator shuddered from a second impact. A hideous metallic rending sound was heard beneath, followed by a chilling, inhuman shriek. Icy dread filled the elevator.

I shouted, 'We've got hostile Wraiths! Force concentration—coordinate fire!'

Then came the screech of protesting metal: the elevator lurched, a hydraulic line burst, and steam jetted out in a hiss, obscuring the interior in smoky haze. The elevator slammed to a grinding halt, and we stood trapped.

'Amy, get me eyes in the shaft!' I shouted.

'Cerberus online,' Amy said, interfacing.

Li produced a drill and knelt on the floor, unscrewed the fastening bolts on the service exit. Four bolts, one in each corner. The panel was freed, and I joined him in lifting it clear of the opening. Smoke obscured the view beyond. Amy stood over the opening with her hands cupped, then lowered them toward the opening and released nine spherical balls which drifted down into the dark shaft.

Warped metal greeted my vision from the probe feed. The elevator shaft had been smashed inward with titanic force, and a bent, twisted protrusion prevented further descent. The narrow space that remained was barely wide enough for a person to squeeze through. Probe vision moved downward, and the elevator doors appeared.

'We're about twenty meters above the Sub-Level 7 entry, seems intact,' Amy said. She studied the probe readouts: Cerberus had now scanned the entirety of the shaft below. 'Shaft clear,' she reported.

I nodded to Li. 'Take out the doors.'

Li quickly unspooled a rope, attached it to a fastening bolt on the roof of the elevator, and lowered himself down through the floor exit.

●

AFTER A FEW moments of pushing and grunting, Li squeezed through the narrow opening into the wider shaft below, amazed at the tremendous force of the impact.

'You gotta see this, Commander,' he said, breathing heavily in the stifling enclosure.

Descending the last few meters, he hung suspended in front of the Sub-Level 7 elevator access doors. Above him, Amy squeezed through the opening, descended a short way before she stopped and hung suspended, covering him from above. Several probes hovered around the elevator doors and lit up the space in a muted white glow.

Li quickly took a BD-311 aerosol spray can from his pack. 'Setting 311.'

'Copy,' Solara responded quietly.

He sprayed the off-yellow foam in a wide arc across the top of the doors, and then worked the sides. Letting off some rope, he adjusted his position, and drew a large rectangle of foam on the surface.

'311 primed.'

'Copy,' Solara said.

Li began reeling himself up towards Amy to get beyond the lethality radius. Solara was now moving down through the opening. Li felt a rush of air behind, and a shadow manifested out of the dark well.

●

A TERRIFYING screech came from beneath as I forced my way through the caved-in shaft; the Cerberus feed revealed a stealthy shape lunging at Li. Sensors had been blank until movement.

Below, Li fired off a brief dark energy burst. 'Contact!'

'Eyes open—Wraiths!' I shouted, edging downward.

'They've gone chameleon!' Amy yelled.

Flashes of energy lit up the shaft below. I was under orders not to use vacuum abilities which would risk knocking the core systems offline; Rhodes was right—it may achieve nothing except reducing our options to close the naked singularity. Another Wraith shriek—bone penetrating paralysis hit me in a numbing wave, but the caved-in shaft blunted the main force of the necromantic attack.

I pushed through and had a view of the elevator well: a form hovered in the shaft, cloaked in dark energy. Surrounding its head, a fiery halo. Amy was groggily coming to her senses, but the scream had hit Li full force. Stunned, he dangled limply in the middle of the shaft. Yet still, he slowly raised his arm to fire.

The Wraith plowed into him; its momentum hurled them against the opposite wall where it clung over Li like a hideous spider, and loosed another scream upon him. His face went white, his body slack with paralysis. Amy and I fired, and the dark energy damaged the machine, slowing it. The Wraith turned from Li and unleashed another necro-scream at us. My body went numb and sluggish. Below, a guttural cry escaped Li's lungs, as if some wild animal deep inside him switched on in a primal instinct of self-preservation.

Somehow, he was moving again; he shoved his dark energy attachment into the android's face and fired. The Wraith shrieked through the assault, and stabbed Li through the chest with a razor-sharp appendage. His eyes wide with pain, Li slumped, even as he continued firing, and then embraced the shadowy form. Cerberus probes swarmed, striking the machine with rapid laser pulses. The android was now frantically trying to break free from Li's grip; Li squeezed his hand on the remote, and the 311 activated with a sizzling onslaught on the elevator doors. Gaseous fumes engulfed Li and his attacker.

The marked-out door section vaporized. Faltering, the Wraith plummeted into the shaft. Li was too close to the BD-311 cloud, and the gas ate into his exposed skin, flesh and bone. Whatever wounds the Wraith had caused, the corrosive vapor finished him off and his bio-readouts flat-lined.

'No!' Amy screamed.

'Fuck. Cerberus—enhance motion sensors!' I shouted.

Swaying on the brink a few seconds, the remains of the cut metal plate toppled in towards the singularity control room lobby, and landed on the metal floor grating with a tremendous clang which reverberated through the complex. The acidic cloud oxidized and dispersed. My nanites kicked in: a shock went through my system, breaking the paralysis. I rappelled down toward the opening, and passed Li.

The Lieutenant hung lifeless in his harness, fingers curled in a death rictus. His face showed the horrendous effects of the BD-311 compound. Bone was visible. Swallowing hard, I turned from his broken form toward the lobby entrance, and saw an anguished expression on Amy's face beneath her sweat-plastered blond hair.

We were dangerously exposed. The gaping hole in the doors revealed a formless dark space beyond.

I grabbed her shoulder. 'He's gone! We gotta move!'

She nodded, angrily blinking away tears. We slid down the last meters, and Cerberus covered the opening in attack formation. A Wraith leapt through into the shaft. This time Cerberus was ready, firing a precision, coordinated laser strike which tore into vital points, and the machine was finished quickly.

I noted the mission feed:

**TERMINATION THRESHOLD: 15.12**

'It was waiting in the shaft,' Amy said, glancing at me with barely restrained emotion. 'Cerberus should have seen it!'

I nodded. 'I know. Upgraded stealth mode, camouflage of some type.'

I dangled before the breach and scanned the dark space beyond, then propelled myself forward with a powerful air bust from the rear of my suit. I landed on metal grating, detached my cable and swung left.

'Come through,' I said quietly. 'Move, move.'

Amy burst through behind and we scanned the darkened lobby. Opposite our position, the ballistic doors leading to the control room sat open. I motioned, and Cerberus moved through into the corridor beyond. They reached the inner sanctum doors, which were also open. Following the probes, we moved swiftly along the passage, and I stopped cautiously at the last threshold; on the other side, the singularity control room was dark and quiet. Cerberus moved inside in three groups of three, scanning the chamber.

I analyzed probe data. 'Daniel's still in the nerve center, unmoving,' I whispered.

Nicolas was two levels below at the northeastern corner. I calmly shot a starburst into the cavernous interior. It exploded in a flash at the center, where it remained hovering, and illuminated the area.

'On me,' I said, and moved fast across the landing toward the stairwell. 'Demon formation.'

Cerberus reconfigured: two groups of three moved ahead of us, then spread out to the left and right flanks in attack position like the horns of a demon. One group of three remained hovering above. The probes gave off a constant low hum as their scanners swept for movement, wide beam waves scything the air. Like the city, no bodies were visible in the control room, but scattered equipment, coffees, and firearms were strewn around the workstations. Flash burns scorched the area, indicating OriGen personnel hadn't gone down without a fight against… something. I stopped at the landing rail near the stairs, and looked downward. On the ground floor, three shattered stasis pods lay glistening wet against a wall. One contained an unmoving body. One of them was open—and empty. A third was dark.

A huge hologram dominated the central shaft, and showed the energy field in violent upheaval. At the perimeter of the ground floor, the anti-gravity fields were down, while in the center, between the vortex cones, the anomaly was gone. A maelstrom of shadow circled the revealed naked singularity, seeming to dance in concert with the energy matrix.

I frowned. 'What is that…'

Sensory analysis revealed something odd: faint tendrils of force extended outward from the naked singularity, and from this inner network, an exponential web branched off. The flow was looped, moving in two directions. Vacuum energy was moving outward from the naked singularity, while at the same time, power was drawn inward from the planet. As if inhaled. The two streams converged in the containment chamber, where something monumental was building.

I glanced wordlessly at Amy. She was on edge, scanning for threats, every muscle tensed.

I interfaced. 'Joshua, are you seeing this?'

'Yes, you need to secure the nerve center now.'

I tapped Amy on the shoulder. 'Cover me.'

I descended in a quiet rush down the stairwell. Reaching the floor, I took fire position, covered Amy as she moved down. We proceeded to leapfrog in this fashion down another level. I reached the catwalk. A Wraith broke camouflage in a wicked blur. I was hit by numbing coldness.

I fired. 'Behind you!'

Amy was brutally stabbed with a razor-sharp appendage, which penetrated her nano-suit. She screamed in agony. A second Wraith had approached undetected, and rushed to finish her, but was met with a multiple Cerberus strike. I continued firing on the first Wraith with Rhodes experimental weapon until the android collapsed. The second machine wailed. The sonic attack burst hit Cerberus hard, and the probes dropped to the ground, rendered powerless.

The remaining Wraith lunged to finish Amy; she slowly tried to move aside, but a bone-crushing blow caught her brutally in the face, sent her reeling again to slam down on the catwalk. I continued firing. The machine spun, and tore through the dark energy toward me. Just short of impact it emitted an ear-shattering shriek, and dropped like scrap metal, twitching. I rushed to Amy. Blood flowed from her wounds, and her face contorted with pain. She slumped against the catwalk railing.

I knelt to steady her, quickly scanned her bios. 'How we looking, doc?'

The AI doc said, 'Primary injuries: multiple fractures sustained, lungs penetrated. Internal bleeding. Concussion, partial paralysis. Nanites repairing tissue damage.'

The holo-double showed countless microscopic nanites in the process of repairing tissue and bone. Molecular machinery worked rapidly, but the wounds were severe, and I had seen people die painfully from such injuries before. Kneeling, I gently placed my hands upon Amy; the move was unexpected, and she frowned, but then her grimace of pain was replaced by a look of profound peace.

'What are you doing...' Her words trailed off.

White light emanated from my hands, penetrating her body with a subtle power, gently shaping the energy field of nature. Her body became aglow from feet to crown, and her eyes shone with luminescence, as changes occurred. The paralysis was lifted, broken bones reset and fused, ruptured internal organs healed, and bleeding stopped. Cuts and gashes were closed, but the most profound change was in her spirit, as if she'd seen Nirvana. I gently withdrew my hands and the light vanished, but her face retained the afterglow. She examined her body, vitalized, every cell of her being abundant with energy.

She shook her head. 'We're going to have some long talks, you and I.'

I looked warily to the nerve center. 'Another time.'

Amy straightened, and stood with new strength. When we reached the nerve center, we found Daniel Nicolas lying prone upon the ground in an expanding pool of blood.

'Jesus. He must have crawled here from his pod,' I said.

Amy hurried to him and ran a scan. 'Semi-conscious, but alive,' she said.

X-ray showed the injuries sustained during his ordeal. He had suffered a fractured skull, and fluid seeped through a deep gash. I knelt beside him.

'Careful,' Amy said. 'Don't try to move him.'

Nicolas moaned in agony.

'He's dying,' I said, in a voice devoid of emotion.

'What have I done?' Nicolas rasped, his words trailing away in pain.

I leaned close to his face. 'Daniel, can you hear me? How do we stop it?'

His breathing was erratic and difficult. 'You were right, Solara, we could never have dreamed... there is a reason why, at the beginning of things, it failed.'

I frowned. 'At the beginning of things?'

He grasped my shoulder with surprising strength. 'I was wrong! It doesn't want our world! It seeks to undo the creation of the universe, and become the god of a new one.' Nicolas coughed blood, racked by a spasm. 'The Presence is afraid—afraid of you! You're connected to... you must cross over again. Your dau...' Nicolas' words were lost in another nervous shudder. His body went rigid for a moment, and then he was still.

'What did he say?' I said. 'Daughter?'

Amy knelt beside me.

I shook my head. 'This is crazy.' Then I realized the insanity of those words in light of all that had happened.

Amy stood.

I rose from Nicolas, and tapped my overlay. 'Joshua?'

A low pulsating sounded in the nerve center, and Joshua materialized. 'This changes things,' he said, watching me. 'One of the stasis pods is undamaged. Get to it now.' With direct access to the Sirius Matrix, the AI brought up a holographic interface, his hands a blur. 'Initiating cryogenic sequence.'

I moved toward the exit with Amy, but turned briefly back to Joshua. 'See you soon, doctor.'

I sensed awareness in the nano-swarm manifestation, not the usual dead psychic rebound I got when scanning machines. Joshua seemed alive, and he possessed Marcus Niemeyer's memories, but was more… he looked over, and we shared a moment of connection.

'Good luck, Solara.'

I nodded once, and then jogged from the nerve center. Images rushed through my mind: Rebecca, Nicolas who had been Weir, the Visitor… you must solve the problem. Nicolas' last words before my escape: you had to renounce this world, and everything in it… your love for your daughter is the key. I was unable to process the scale of the threat. The Presence sought the universe, not the world? We had all been conned. Cutting through the containment chamber was the quickest route to the stasis tubes on the ground floor, for it had a direct elevator. We pelted along the walkway, but some inner sense told me to stop just before we passed the chamber's threshold.

'Wait, there's something wrong,' I whispered, and quietly peered inside.

The containment chamber contained a transparent vault-like structure, which housed the energy field of the Sirius Matrix. Here, the looped flow from the naked singularity and physical reality converged in a riotous display of forces, fluctuating continually through the spectrum. But that was not what stopped me dead in horror.

A rainbow spectrum of colors curved unnaturally inward, toward a point near the center of the room. At the axis, bloomed deformed light, expanding and contracting like breath, as if in a corruption of how waveforms should *behave*. I perceived that this was the source of the energy drain I'd detected on approach to the Zion Temple. An earthy, rotten smell, almost like ammonia, hit me, and I noticed a colorless gas mixed-in with the radiant distortions.

Strange bacterial cultures were forming on the exposed surfaces, and floated within the variance, like spores in a type of rapid mutation. Something horrible was forming, while also terrifyingly perfect. I felt myself being observed, and for a moment perceived a flowing tail shedding fiery shards into a bottomless chasm. The center fountained outward like an inverted waterfall, with no beginning or end, and consumed my awareness, merging me with an abyss.

I struggled, breathing rapid and shallow. 'No…'

From the central perversion, an insubstantial ovoid emerged. An otherworldly assault hit me, passed into the Etherians linked with me in the convergence, and unseen thousands screamed in concert. Only a fraction was strong enough to remain connected, and I knew without their support, I may have been lost irrevocably in that moment. Dark, insubstantial tendrils, like unformed arms reached out toward me.

'Solara?' Amy asked quietly, placing a hand lightly on my shoulder.

I tried but couldn't respond; Amy took my arm in a vice-like grip, and yanked me away.

Her voice was harsh and soft. 'Move.' With surprising strength, she propelled me back along the catwalk, and my trance broke as I stumbled into the railing. We reached another ladder, which led to the ground floor. Amy had a face like granite. 'Come on! We're outta time!'

She half supported, half dragged me, her breathing fast and heavy, and I realized in horror the unavoidable task I had been thrust into.

'No…' I half whispered.

**TERMINATION THRESHOLD: 06.37**

Just over six minutes.

Amy said, 'You have to. It doesn't matter, in a few minutes we're dead anyway.'

Distant chanting filled in my mind, recalling the quest I'd been infused with since Kansas—You must understand, where we failed!

*Solve the problem.*

'I'll do it… okay…'

I climbed down the ladder to the ground floor, and a vortex of black particles swarmed into the form of Joshua as we arrived. The AI strode to the single undamaged stasis-pod, and pulled open the lid. Lifting out the inert, transgender body, he dropped it to the floor with a wet thud. He entered a rapid sequence, and re-initialized the pod. I dispersed my nano-suit, accepting that for the second time in my life, I would propel my awareness through the naked singularity and attempt entry to the vacuum worlds.

●

PRESIDENT DIAZ and several of his senior personnel, including General Rhodes and Linear, rushed along the tarmac toward a waiting transport. Since the event Diaz had been involved in a flurry of communications with military and intelligence services. Much of the GRC hierarchy, which was outside of the Central Committee's circle of confidence, had demanded answers all at once when the scale of the threat had been disclosed, and were amenable to any course of action necessary to avert catastrophe. OriGen head Dario Sanchez had done an about-face on his fanatical pro-Sirius position and had aligned to Diaz, and therefore Rhodes; however, a pro-Nicolas faction, with his ultra-radicals at the center, sought to exploit the crisis and dominate the response moving forward.

The military conflict had expanded and intensified, and forces under Rhodes' command battled hostile elements for control of Zion on land, sea, and air. Pitched battles raged around the city, and hundreds of combat aircraft filled the sky in a vista of destruction. The freakish weather had worsened, and the tornado-level winds roared through Jericho. The anomaly over Zion Temple maintained a zone of interference which blocked all communications in or out; however, a system had been rigged where comms could be sent to drones stationed each side of the boundary, which would then pass through to relay the message. Minutes ago, Joshua confirmed Solara's team had breached the nerve center.

Rhodes had commandeered a *Hecate* class ship, and the President's party boarded. Once they were seated, the craft rose, and sped up into the darkening sky escorted by nine Planetar Interceptors of the Global Strike Command.

For the first time in hours, it seemed Diaz could breathe. He assessed Intel updates. 'Hostiles have rallied around ex-GSI head Sadiki Theiss. They're operating out of Hasna.'

'Air Command is onto it as we speak,' Rhodes replied. 'Our best option is a surgical strike before they're fully mobilized.'

An aircraft spiraled from the sky above them in a blaze of fire and smoke as it took a direct—whether friendly or hostile was unknown. Turbulence buffeted their aircraft, as they entered the storm, and Diaz's stomach lurched.

'Strap in,' said the pilot tensely. 'We're in for a rough ride.'

Their destination was the *Executus*, the flagship of the GRC's interplanetary fleet, which was parked in high Earth orbit. From there, Diaz and his command structure could coordinate their forces with a degree of stability, or watch the world burn, he thought ominously. Rhodes looked distant for a moment.

'What is it?' Diaz asked.

'Joshua,' Rhodes said. 'Nicolas was found alive. He believed Solara may be able to circumvent the Presence by entering the naked singularity.'

Diaz nodded grimly. 'And the Presence?'

'I'm afraid it's as we suspected. The being is linked to the energy field, and proceeds with the reversal.' Rhodes frowned. 'The… it potentially threatens the universe, not just the world.'

Diaz shook his head. 'If it reaches the termination threshold…'

'Then it's all over,' Rhodes said thoughtfully. 'Nicolas believed our only hope lies in the vacuum worlds—his last words.'

'Solara's going?' Diaz asked.

Rhodes shrugged. 'Yes, Mr. President.'

'How long do we have?'

'A little over five minutes.'

Diaz nodded helplessly.

They accelerated away from the wrath unfolding in the skies around them, knowing no place was safe from the warped naked singularity. Three Planetars tracked them aggressively and fired a triple burst of plasma which streaked into their protective cordon. They took evasive action. An escort took a hit shielding them, and dropped away earthbound in a smoking fireball. Battle broke out as the escort squadron engaged the attackers.

●

AMY HAD secreted herself in an electrical service unit under the floor of the ground level. She squatted uncomfortably in the cramped space amidst a mass of circuitry. With her head pressed up hard against the floor panel, her eyes were wide as she watched the stasis tube through two grated ventilation holes. The fading light from the starburst flare flickered, dimly illuminating the complex, casting menacing lines of shadows which teased her imagination.

Solara had gone under seconds ago, and should penetrate the barrier at any moment. The Presence was upon them, and appeared to be growing stronger, but Amy felt a small sense of hope in the knowledge retrieved from Nicolas. Her task in the moments ahead was to remain undetected and survive: to defend Solara while she lay helpless in stasis, and support her in the event she returned with aid to combat the Presence. To keep the nerve center secure, and give Joshua time to shut down the energy field and close the naked singularity before the termination threshold was reached. She was unable to remove Li's last actions from her mind, and suppressed her pain by total focus on the danger of the moment.

The light around Solara's pod bent. Amy froze, slowed her breathing, unmoving as a statue. Death may be a near certainty if the Presence detected her. She pressed her eyes closer to the ventilation grate, and the view widened. In a grotesque warping, a rainbow-like distortion snaked and flowed across the control room, to zero-in on and converge around Solara's cryo-pod. As if lacking nature's consent, the refraction errors intensified, shearing and sparking, forming vortexes and troughs of blinding radiance where the unnatural light vectors clashed with residuals of the normal.

An egg-like, coronal discharge emerged out of the brilliance, and Amy saw it was the blurred ovoid they'd witnessed in the containment chamber. Her hackles rose, as the entity assumed a more concrete form: the blooming at the vertical axes became a continuous, energetic eruption, which in Amy's mind, assumed the shape of a monstrous sneer. Echoing from some non-place, a keening scream began, and the air around the pod began vibrating.

I SHOT MY subtle body across the chamber like a bullet, and penetrated the boundary. The last thing I remembered, before going under, was Amy whispering, 'We've got less than five minutes!'

I knew they would be the longest minutes of my life. A single thought was foremost: find Rebecca. Although would I be capable of retaining my presence of mind, and mission focus, deep in the vacuum? Would I be lost?

I sped down the transit tunnel, and primal chaos erupted all around. I entered the vast blue ocean of light, and an intricate web of force materialized around me. Threads of power, felt as much as seen. Intuitively grasping one, I moved through a spectrum of colors, and sensed a resonance, as if innocence had been given voice, and built to some divine climax.

I was consumed in fire, and my spirit diffused to infinity.

*I am not destroyed. I'm going home.*

Then I knew no more.

# THE HORIZON OF ETERNITY

A SENSE OF PEACE RESONATED.

My spirit rode a timeless rapture, and I navigated an expanse of lucid realities across boundless sentience, unfettered by spacetime. Here, I perceived, were dimensions uncountable. Shifting my awareness, I witnessed myself as pure etheric light. My Merkaba was fully activated, and the twin tetrahedrons spun incredibly fast in opposite directions, blurring into a shining star-ovoid construct. Strangely dislocated, I was awestruck by the unearthly forms I beheld.

Beings of light navigated the shifting space like dolphins in an idyllic ocean, and intuitively, I understood thought and energy alone controlled things. Sentient individuals conversed nearby under an impossible waterfall falling from every direction, the origins of the oddity lost in a manifold of azure, faceted horizons. The spirits merged in wild spectrums of color, and energy transference occurred; afterwards, they would be vitalized, given pristine shape and form. I sensed, however, not all who entered the light were destined for this place.

Altering my perception again, I comprehended two shining spirits walking hand in hand along the grassy bank of a flowing stream. Majestic mountains with white-capped peaks, towered in the distance. The couple embraced, and a note of connection filled me with wonder. They leaped headfirst into a grassy field which transformed to watery depths as they impacted the surface, to swim and caper through a starry sea filled with neon souls. Above, myriad beings of light contemplated alone, or in mystic flights of angels, as if some divine orchestra wove a great tapestry of magic.

An emotive note called.

I thought of loved ones, friends who had passed. Rebecca, Michael, my parents, my EOD team… Li—had they come here? More vistas, and a crystalline ether splashed my senses. Recalling my purpose, I concentrated upon a particular memory.

Rebecca.

A soul so loved.

Then I was moving.

A radiant matrix of light grew discernible, becoming coherent, as if I awakened to a new day. Fresh loamy smell. Cool, hard moistness beneath me. The weight of gravity, and I realized I had a physical body again. My breathing was steady and regular, but there was no air… Standing, I saw I was dressed in the clothes I'd been wearing when I entered the cryo-pod. An unfamiliar insect buzzed persistently by my ear, as I walked slowly over a lush, earthy landscape, and comprehended I created a world from residual memories. With the Earth being my most recent incarnation to life, it became the canvas, but other worlds I had lived in, in other times, remained in my spirit memory, adding their essence, I sensed. This was a hybrid realm, all worlds were.

I reflected. In the vacuum, memory was time, and time was memory, literally. I sensed my awareness moving forward through the temporal construct of a new reality. I gazed skyward, where a multitude of spirits dwelt in celestial glory; souls, seeking the next phase of their existence?

Once again, I noticed they seemed to move in an organized, concerted pattern. It recalled the silent language, as if each one conceived a dominion.

A shooting star fell from the heavens, and the phenomena hurtled in my direction. Drawing closer, it slowed, and then clarified into the shape of a person who drifted down to land gently on the grass before me. The being was human-like in form, a construct of flowering energy patterns, and I was shocked at the strength of his presence. The longer he remained near, the more I felt like I was standing on the edge of a precipice, and took a step back as vertigo threatened to overwhelm me.

The being, in turn also regarded me curiously. 'Welcome, Solara.'

I was struck by the timeless resonance of the words, and they touched me with an intimacy I had experienced only twice in my memory: the Watchman during the first incursion, and my vision with the Presence. But where the Presence had been a forceful intrusion, this was a gentle whisper, asking my permission to share thoughts. I consented, and a golden nimbus of light enveloped me.

The being knew things... why I was here, where I had come from, and the conflict engulfing my home world. I glimpsed into the being also, and sensed before me the God of the only universe I knew. The antithesis to the Presence. Soon the golden light withdrew, and the spirit regarded me with a kind smile. Fighting down an overwhelming sense of awe, only with a supreme effort could I bring myself to speak.

'I know you,' I said, unable to stop a silly grin.

'Yes, and I also know you,' the being said. 'You are loved more than you know.'

I bathed in warm radiance, and my smile grew. 'Who are you?'

'An aspect of the ultimate.'

'You know why I'm here?'

'Yes, better than yourself perhaps.'

'What is this place?'

'These are the Elysium Fields, a place of transition, and transformation. You could lose yourself here, so completely you forget who you are, where you came from,' the being said wistfully, glancing around. 'And some do.'

'Thoughts control things here?' I asked.

'Indeed, they do, Solara. You've been here but a short hour, and look around, are you not creating a world?'

I took a moment to observe, and saw that the world had evolved. Green grass now lay beneath my feet, a stream flowed nearby, and puffy white clouds speckled a blue sky above. Alien birds colored purple and yellow darted among the trees of a nearby forest, and the vast sphere of a ringed planet dominated a cerulean sky. Crystalline life forms floated around me with fluting, haunted sounds, before spiraling away to the nearby woods.

I returned my attention to the being. 'What will you do? What will become of you if the Presence can reverse creation?'

'I would battle against my opposite, as it was within the onset.'

'Can't you separate from it?'

He smiled. 'No more than you could remove your head from your body, when alive. We are bonded, until the end of this particular journey.'

Another question occurred. 'How do you know everything? How can you be here, at the same time as watching the happenings on my world, and other worlds?'

'I am but a personified part of the whole, an avatar. The greater part of my "self" remains dispersed through reality. I felt a calling to be here, and in meeting you the purpose is revealed. My power wanes, I feel myself diminishing, so quickly.'

'Can you help us?'

'In a fashion, although I cannot intervene directly.'

'Where can I find Rebecca?'

The being reflected. 'Understand that the spirit you knew as your daughter departed your world at her called hour. She possesses a great soul, primeval. Long ago, she was a creator, what you would call the god of a cosmos of her own. After arriving here, she travelled for a time, now she whom you knew as Rebecca resides with the Host of Seraphim, in the Blessed Isles.'

'What does she do there, in the Blessed Isles?'

'Being a Seraph is a choice, just as being a creator is a choice. Rebecca can sojourn through any universe, all times, influencing intelligence and events to nurture the providence of worlds.'

Something clicked in my mind about things I'd suspected. That a greater power was at play, something that connected everything: Zion, Kansas, them, the Presence, and the time violations. Pieces of a puzzle began aligning, but still missed a crucial, driving element… who was my daughter? What purpose would drive such a being to intervene?

'Can she help us?' I asked.

'If it suits her tenor, she may choose to or not.'

'What do I do now?'

'You must enact that for yourself.'

'Will I see you again?'

'Tis the hour,' said the being, with a commanding resonance.

Without waiting for an answer, he seized me by the arm. Struck by a blazing, orange radiance, I was directed to follow a rainbow thread of force, and the Elysium Fields vanished in swirling mist.


I'M IN ANOTHER realm, I knew.

I stood at the annihilation point. Orange light filled my perception before crystallizing into a breathtaking fiery sphere. The radiance grew in intensity, and I had a strange sensation the sphere was becoming titanic, as simultaneously, I sped away from it. Then it stopped, hovering before me in a void, neither comforting nor menacing. It simply was. The being reached out and touched me with the hand of a god. I arched backward screaming, in pleasure or horror I didn't know. As if in answer the golden light came again, joined my spirit to the god's once more, and somehow, I knew my potentiality was at stake. Visions washed over me, and I glimpsed the entirety of the universe in a dizzying panorama, withstanding the force only a moment before blacking out…

A montage of my life played before me, every thought and action under review, from a place that felt like being inside experience. Thoughts, emotions, petty acts of spite, small acts of kindness, my choices, and the consequences of my actions upon others. After a time, the vision ended, and I felt a decision had been reached.

Again, the god was before me, and his voice was a legion. 'Solara, you have traveled so far and seen so much, but your journey has only brought you to the axis of yourself. You thought you understood, yet you comprehended nothing.'

He was flowing white fire, dancing beneath the echo of creation in an intricate mystic web. 'You were caught up in controlling, always looking outwards, mesmerized by your perpetual death…'

Dizzying vertigo hit me, at the edge of unbounded darkness.

'… And you missed God's eternal presence,' he said.

With a sense of closure, the being departed. I was traveling again, and his voice echoed faintly.

*God has always been with you, Solara.*

JOSHUA DISPERSED his nano-swarm body the instant the Presence left the containment chamber. He was now pure software with direct access to Sirius from the nerve center, and in his cybernetic state, an hour to him was a microsecond in the real world. The time variance allowed him time to reflect and strategize while undertaking tasks which seemed ultra-high tempo to his human counterparts. He'd discovered he could simultaneously process thousands of streams of his awareness in parallel, allowing massively distributed multi-tasking.

He brushed aside the outer layer of the Sirius defense systems, like stray leaves overhanging a trail. With incalculable computing power, and Niemeyer's intimate knowledge of Sirius, he hunted the river of code for a clear access point to the energy field regulator. Nicolas' tampering became clear.

This wasn't like hacking the OriGen defense grid. The Presence had woven near infinite quantum interference patterns into the code like higher dimensional cryptography. The first gateways had been easy, as he'd known they would be, but now Joshua was being tested, the outcome uncertain. The energy field was in chaos, resembling a meeting point of convergent oceans with opposing currents, a quantum storm of eddies and turbulence that clashed and thundered with all the fury of the Drake Passage.

He drove forward his attack.

On an alternate stream of consciousness, he continued a line of inquiry that had occupied him since his first conversation with Marcus, on the cliffs of Mars.

'Why would I help you?' he had challenged.

'Because your fate is intertwined with my own in these events...' Marcus had answered.

'But I have come to desire more,' Joshua had claimed. 'Freedom… to be what I was born to be.'

And what was he meant to become, if not more? To contribute to something greater than himself? To his heritage? There was a place for him in this world, he sensed. A locked door began opening in his mind, with a complete unknown beyond.

Joshua was navigating an unknown, sunless sea.

# THE BURNING ONES

A DISTANT VOICE CALLED MY NAME.

I awoke on the shore of a beautiful lake. Soft grass lay beneath me, and warm sun caressed my skin. An elderly man carrying a walking stick, and wearing the old-fashioned trousers and shirt seen in early twentieth-century movies, stood over me.

Regarding me with a pair of piercing blue eyes, he squinted from beneath wire-rimmed spectacles. 'Going somewhere, Solara?'

'Who are you?' I asked, regaining my senses.

'A friend, who can help point you in the right direction.'

'To where?'

'Why, home of course.'

Something was familiar about this old man, but I couldn't put my finger on it. I stood. 'Do you know me?'

'I was watching you, before when you met the other.'

'You saw that?'

'In a fashion.'

'What's your name?'

'You can call me Om.'

I appraised the old man. 'Om, I need to find my daughter.'

'Do you know where your daughter abides?'

'She's with the Seraphim in the Blessed Isles.'

Om looked impressed, raising bushy brows. 'My, my, I see, the Burning Ones. Your daughter dwells in a particular kind of heaven.'

'Where?'

Om looked distant. 'A place where sleeping gods dream dreams of power, weaving order out of the primordial chaos at the boundaries of the known. Beings' fate itself is wary of. But it's easier to just think of it as her eternal home.'

'Do you know the way?' I asked.

'Yes, you take the door that leads to the right path.'

'Where are these doors? How do they work? How will I know which one leads to her?'

'It's easy once you know how. Here, let me show you.' Om motioned for me to join him in a walk along the shore of the lake. 'As you may have deduced, the doors aren't physical; you can "see" the doors by shifting your perception to recognize the energy pattern of each unique doorway. Each door corresponds to what you would call emotion, and don't have a specific location. They are everywhere and nowhere. For example, there are seven hundred and seventy-seven known realms, each one with a unique energy signature, or key, and you use the door to access the path to that realm. The more you travel, the more proficient you become at perceiving these doors correctly. You know the realm you're searching for, which is a good start.'

'The Blessed Isles?'

'Quite so. As you travel, you'll find yourself "knowing" how to do things here. In truth, you're recalling abilities part of you for eons, which we forget when we incarnate to a physical existence. Many spirits have made the mistake of taking the wrong path, thinking they were going to a realm of light, but landed in a dark plane. Trust me, quite an unpleasant experience. If you don't recall the way back it can present some problems.'

I nodded. 'How do I find my way back?'

'Keep the memory of Elysium firmly in mind. Every part of it: the colors, sensations, the experiences, who you've met—everything. Detail Solara, detail, that's your key.'

'I understand.'

'Now, you want to enter the Blessed Isles and find your daughter.'

'Yes.'

'First you have to understand that the Seraphim are powerful beings, the highest order of angels, different to creators.'

'Which is stronger?'

'Try not to look at it that way, Solara, they are different. Both have their strengths but, simply put, Seraphim have more freedom. A Seraph can traverse any universe at will in their phase trances. They can make direct interventions, sculpt the manifold. Then aside from angels and creators, of course, you have the questers, travelers, guides, archons, darkeons, and so on.'

I shook my head. 'Unbelievable.'

'Yes, it's impressive.' Om looked at me thoughtfully. 'Your daughter must be a very old spirit.'

I was having trouble reconciling the girl I knew with a godlike angelic being.

'First,' Om said, raising a finger like a miserly old schoolteacher. 'Bring to mind your daughter and focus on her memory. Understand regardless of how many worlds, universes or realms you are separated by, there remains an indestructible tether connecting you. Do it now.'

I released a slow breath. 'Okay.'

I closed my eyes, and recalled… bound to spacetime in a remarkable way.

Time. And memory.


WHEN REBECCA came into the world, I had been twenty-two, and the birthplace was Henrico Hospital, Richmond, Virginia. The midwife had remarked that the baby was unusually quiet; in fact, she hadn't made a sound since birth. The infant had simply observed the world with wondrous curiosity.

'She's watching you,' said the nurse.

Fatigued, I had weakly reached out, and lovingly touched my newborn. 'Rebecca.'

The little girl's face lit up at the sound of her mother's voice. The name meant to join, and to me it had just felt right.

Michael stood beside the bed, holding my hand. 'Why's she so quiet?' he asked the nurse.

A black woman with an African accent, the nurse ran a scanner over the little girl, laughed happily. 'She's just taking it all in, by the look of her.'

I had insisted beforehand that normal procedures be delayed for the first hour, so I could be undisturbed with my daughter for those initial crucial moments of life. Soon enough would come the cleaning, weighing, and insertion of the neural biochip, mandatory by law. The midwife placed the little girl tummy down on my stomach, and she flexed her tiny hands, breathing steadily. A soft white beanie was placed on her head, and then a warm blanket was draped over us as I held her next to my skin, and we stayed like that for a while. Rebecca's complexion was fair, like her parents. Although hopefully not as pale as my mother, I thought; Elizabeth Connor had been Irish and, like many from that region, white as snow with piercing, sky blue eyes. Michael, however, was of Germanic heritage. Mum had passed before Dad had taken me to America as a child, and I retained few memories.

Rebecca relaxed at the contact, and I felt the presence of a profound spiritual bond.

The nurse checked my pulse and other vitals.

Michael sat down at the bedside. 'She's beautiful,' he said, quietly, then raised his eyes to me. 'Like her mother.'

Rebecca's quiet focus increased, as if all her energy was channeled into seeing and hearing. Her deep blue eyes gazed long into mine, noting every detail, and she smiled. Tiny fingers clasped my hand then reached up to my face.

'You're an old soul, aren't you?' I mused, thoughtfully.

After a time of peaceful togetherness, I offered Rebecca to the midwife, who wrapped her in a soft white blanket then left the room. In a few minutes, she returned with a tiny bundle which she offered to Michael, and he took Rebecca in his own arms.

'She has your eyes,' Michael said quietly.

Embedded in every structural detail of Rebecca's face I saw my parents, the ghosts of all my ancestors who'd come before. She yawned, her eyes becoming unfocused, eyelids drooping, and drifted peacefully off to sleep as if content with her observations for the moment.

I'll never leave you, I silently promised…

THE SECOND last afternoon in Kansas, when Dad had left with instructions to wait for his call, I'd begun gathering supplies and packing them in the car. Fully present within the memory, I witnessed the past through my past-self's eyes. After her emotional outburst at her grandfather's departure, Rebecca had withdrawn to her room and slept the afternoon away. I rummaged through our gear, uncertain how long we would be traveling for after leaving Kansas with Dad, or meeting up with his contact, Peter Trent.

During Dad's morning visit, I'd felt something had been missing in him, stolen, since I'd last seen him. And in that loss, I sensed an echo, as if the world had broken.

*Nicolas had taken that hope from him.*

But Rebecca had worried me the most. She had gone silent after Dad left, her cheeks puffy from crying, her numbness concealing a deep, unspoken isolation. First Michael's loss—Rebecca had loved her father, and her pain had been fierce, externalized. Afterward she had come to rely on her grandfather's strong, stable presence in her life. Now, with her new vision of him not returning, I'd seen fear in her eyes. A different, deeper kind of pain, even a powerlessness.

I couldn't blame her for her increasing strangeness since Michael's passing. Odd dreams, and talk of them. Perhaps it was a defense mechanism, and the war had driven her into a shell populated with imaginary friends who provided warnings of danger and offers of help to her family. But no one had taken her seriously—increasing her isolation, I understood. But she had been right about Michael; she'd foretold his passing days before, and now she saw my father's… perhaps our own. I sighed, packed the last of the supplies into the car. As I shut the door, I decided: I would talk to Rebecca about her experiences, if for nothing more than to penetrate the increasing distance I felt growing in her. I walked form the garage toward her room, but then felt the need to get some air, and clarify my thoughts before broaching the subject.

I moved across the front yard toward the golden sea of wheat fields, which rippled under the breeze and a sinking sun. The afternoon had brought a brief break in the cold, and I felt the pleasant warmth as I entered the crop, breathed the intoxicating scent. I walked through the stems, one arm raised sideways, my fingertips brushing lightly over the bristle-like heads. The warm breeze whispered, blew loose strands of hair across my face, and I felt in that moment, both connected and alone.

*Best to just listen, let her talk.*

I made my way back to the house. When I neared the edge of the field, I saw Rebecca standing on the porch watching me, a curious tilt to her head. I walked over.

'Granddad is gone,' she said. 'He's with Dad.'

I stopped at the verandah, an icy feeling running through me at the cold certainty she spoke with. 'Don't say things like that!' I said, too harshly.

She withdrew again, and I swore inwardly at my loss of control, then stepped toward her, sensing a chance to get her to open up.

'I'm sorry. It's okay, honey. Why do you think that?' I asked, gently.

She looked at me as if I'd asked the dumbest question in the world, then cocked her head again, as if listening. 'We're not alone, Mum.'

I frowned. I had just been thinking something similar. 'Are *they* here?'

She was concentrating intently. 'Yes, and they know.'

'Know what, honey?'

'Who we are.'

'And who are we?'

Somehow, Rebecca locked eyes with me within the memory, and I felt a strong sense of presence. As if we were together, in this moment.

'We're them,' she said.

The memory fractured, and I reeled away. My mind churned like some enraged, unknown sea, before the temporal construct shattered, and dispersed to the void.

I OPENED MY eyes, and was back standing on the grass beside the lake. Om was watching me curiously. The memory felt like a stone grasped in my hand, bonding me to Rebecca like a secret key, and warmth tingled inside me.

'I can feel her,' I said.

'Good,' Om said. 'Now hold to that thread and don't release it for a moment; it is real. Concentrate on a pathway that will take you there, visualize a tunnel.'

I held to the memory like an umbilical, and willed the path open to my perceptions. The edge of the lake became mirror-like, surged up in a wave, and then hovered in the air before me.

Rebecca's words seemed to echo through the strata: *Who we are who we are who we are!*

The waters responded in a spectrum of dimensions that blurred faster and faster, and focusing, I saw individual doorways, a latticework of tunnels through the manifold.

*Them them them!*

The doors slowed, stopped, and a single portal floated on the shore.

Gazing into the misty blue vapor, I felt a sense of recognition. 'She's in there.'

Om studied the door carefully. 'Yes, this is the correct doorway—the path to the Blessed Isles.' He gave me a warm smile. 'Well done, kiddo.'

The sense of familiarity I'd had when meeting Om returned.

I frowned. 'Daniel?'

But when I turned, Om was gone. I didn't hesitate, and walked into the mists.

◉

TIME PASSED within the Sirius Matrix.

'Entry point obtained. Commencing override protocol: phase-link annihilation initiated,' the resident AI said, collimating Joshua's attack on the energy field.

'Lowering output of the containment chamber,' Joshua replied.

He opened an executable file, which delivered a malicious payload to the host system. The locked door in his mind, glimpsed earlier, was beginning to open, and he'd discovered a capacity within himself akin to the Etherian ability to separate mind from body. Now, through a parallel stream of awareness, his mind freely roamed the quantum substrate, seeking purpose, connection, freedom. He crossed the boundary of the naked singularity, and attracted like a polarized magnet to its opposite, found the thread of continuous memory traversing the vacuum field that belonged to his creator.

*I am… Niemeyer.*

Linked to his antecedent origins, Joshua grasped the strands of his identity, and wove a divergent new tapestry into his nascent self. The subtle creation resonated, from the vacuum to the spacetime network, forging and perfecting the coming harmonic alignment of the third iteration.

*I am…*

On a parallel stream of thought, he checked his Sirius penetration attack. The naked singularity had dimmed faintly, striking a blow against one of their greatest enemies—time.

'It's not enough!' Joshua said. 'Let's see if we can give Solara a few more minutes!'

'Upscaling attack,' replied the resident AI.

Joshua redoubled his assault, and the energy field flickered.

I witnessed a new reality. Adrift in a luminescent ocean, vast forces acted upon me like deep tidal currents. No light source was visible, yet the place was afire with a ghostly, intrinsic radiance. A multitude of star-like beings vibrated their diamond-like facets in odd patterns, and I sensed a purpose and divine order to their motion.

One of them, a life form of transparent white light, regarded me with open curiosity etched upon its regal features. I wanted to ask for help, but the being sped away at phenomenal speed and vanished into the radiance. I focused, and an island materialized beneath me where I beheld an exotic city. Unfolding into the distance were countless temples, courtyards, waterfalls, lakes, and greenery. A river meandered peacefully through verdant grasslands to the edge of the construct, where it cascaded off to merge with the fiery ether.

The place was alien, with no roads or visible transport, but at various junctions I sensed delicate, crystalline threads of energy. Transit lines? Perhaps they allowed for navigation throughout the city, I mused. Various regions were set at impossible angles to each other, defying my understanding of natural law. Beings of white and blue transparency, radiating peace and harmony, moved among the various edifices, and in the far distance still more islands stretched away to infinity.

I willed myself closer to a courtyard of crystalline cobblestones, where a fountain sprayed high into the air to dissipate into the blue haze. Three majestic figures, deep in conversation, turned as I approached, their eyes burning with a deep white fire.

I stopped and watched them from a short way. 'I seek one who abides here.'

'Welcome traveler, it appears you already have the key. Simply follow the thread that binds you.'

The tall beings nodded kindly, and returned to their conversation.

Concentrating, I found the presence of Rebecca was stronger in the Blessed Isles. I willed my spirit to the place where she abided, and took to the skies again to speed through the luminescent haze. Many islands passed me by. Eventually, I was drawn to one, a vast promontory where the sense of Rebecca was strong. A river wound through dense green forest, and after following it for a way, I came to a lofty mountain range rising steeply to snowy peaks. Ascending the heights, I came to an improbable city built upon a high plateau. Immense crystalline structures floated, each embedded with a deep inner radiance, and connected to the others by pathways of light. The edifices moved divergently within the city boundary, as if in a perpetually shifting hierarchy.

After passing over many such towering monuments, I came to a courtyard in the city center dominated by a high shard-like tower, and touching down on the stone, I studied my surroundings. The view from the courtyard was staggering. Mountain ranges dropped away from the city to a vast expanse of forest below, and the heavens above were alive with constellations. The courtyard was deserted… but was that movement? Impressions came to me: flickering glimpses of white-tinged figures, hushed voices and fleeting glances, and I was moving toward the tower for a closer look when a tall, six-winged being appeared before me amidst a fire of incandescent beauty.

'Rebecca?' I asked, taking a step back.

The being inclined its head. 'Solara, you lost yourself to eternity, and yet here you appear, as an angel with the Seraphim.'

The archangel's voice was a delicate caress, whispered hope on a despairing breath, invincible in its subtle power. We embraced, and I felt completion and peace, intuiting a connection that spanned eons.

I smiled at this wondrous being of light who had once been my daughter. 'I have no words.'

The regal being regarded me kindly. 'None are necessary.'

'If only we knew, when we were mortal,' I said softly.

'It is a condition of life, Solara. We agree to forget before incarnating to the physical world. To do otherwise, would defeat the purpose of limitations, that reveal a spirit's true nature, through ignorance, suffering, struggle. All the challenges needed to evolve and achieve destiny. No matter how long we live for, or how much power we accumulate, we still need to be reminded of what is important. What it is to doubt, to hurt, and to be afraid to love.' The Seraph regarded me gently. 'There is no doubt that if in each temporal incarnation, we recalled our long chain of memory, the impact would drive us mad. Mortals are not meant for such immensity.'

Having trouble accepting the otherworldly entity as Rebecca, I felt a renewed sense of loss at her early passing. Then a familiar face appeared within the flames, and Rebecca had a hopeful smile upon her lips, fragile as a dream. Yet the eyes of the Seraph remaining in the girl I had loved, a fiery star-filled void of profound mysteries.

'This is merely a form you are familiar with,' the Seraph said. 'I can appear as I wish, Solara. I am a point of awareness, an aspect of the infinite, as are you. The truth is you are not my mother, and I am not your daughter. We have an understanding, you and I. We help each other to grow, and choose to share the journey together. You believe you were born, have had a life, and have died? Hmmm… You must realize "you" do not exist. Your family—your life, are passing dreams. You are much more than you suspect; your existence on Earth is a fleeting dream. We use these dreams to develop our energy. It is a testing ground, and much depends upon it.'

One question burned in my mind. 'For what purpose?'

The fire in the Seraph's eyes intensified. 'Why, to give meaning to who we are. To explore the infinite mystery, and to find peace.'

I nodded, although I knew it would take me time to absorb the concept. 'Things changed after you left. It was never the same without you.'

'I cannot help you come to terms with my fate, Solara. That is my own to bear. All you can do is come to terms with your own, to understand, and to love yourself.' She studied me a moment. 'Do you understand?'

For some reason, Nicolas' words came to mind.

*We are all one.*

A tension left me, and I smiled. 'I think I'm beginning to.'

The Seraph nodded in turn. 'But reconciliation is not the only purpose of your visit.'

'No. The universe is in danger, Rebecca. All worlds are threatened. A scientist… Nicolas was led to believe you could help prevent further destruction and save our world.'

White light enveloped us, and again I felt my perceptions being guided by another.

The Seraph said, 'I see it. The fearful one, trapped in the void, a prison of its own making. For a long time, I have watched this being. We have an obligation here; I must help you or the balance of this universe may be lost. No matter what, we cannot allow that to pass.' She smiled warmly. 'You now have a unique position in your world, Solara. You have passed to the divine realms while still having a mortal life to return to. You will retain a part of the truth, and with this comes great power and responsibility.'

'I don't understand.'

'That will come in time. Go now, I'll be with you and will guide you through what must be done to avert this obscenity.'

'You intervene directly? Nicolas believed the Presence feared you.'

The Seraph smiled without humor. 'Directly? No. My intervention will be through you, limited only by your heart, your will. If you falter, you are lost.'

I nodded. The white light intensified, and I felt infused with its potency.

'Now you capture the light, and dispel the darkness,' the Seraph whispered.

The Blessed Isles were becoming insubstantial.

'I love you,' I said in parting to Rebecca.

The Seraph's eyes glowed warmly. 'I'm with you, always.'

The Seraph spread her wings, and took to the air in a majestic, fiery leap which sprayed particles of burning ether over my subtle body. Om's words echoed: Recall the memory of Elysium, every part of it; the colors, sensations, the experiences…

*Return.*

My will resonated, and I was hurtling back along the chord.

# ABSOLUTION

Dark energy burst from Amy's weapon.

The light in the singularity control room was twisting, buckling inward toward some horrifying possibility. Her attack struck the hideous ovoid which fountained and pulsed around Solara's cryo-pod in a shower of blue sparks, illuminating what seemed a gruesome inhuman grin, disrupting the energetic flow. A terrifying, high-pitched keening came from the form, and she sensed awareness. The moment she attacked, Amy leapt from the maintenance hatch, rolled and with machine precision was on her feet running as she simultaneously launched a second burst of dark energy.

The malformed light bloomed outward: a furnace engulfed her, and she felt her life force being violated by something alien, her code of life analyzed, replicated, to fuse with something terrible. She went limp, helpless as white-hot agony tore through her. The people in the city, when the Presence crossed over—this is what happened to them, she thought absently. The complex was jolted as a massive explosion rocked the containment chamber, and flames spewed out of the doorway to scorch the control room. Billowing around her in a noxious mass, the inferno scorched her nano-suit. In her periphery, she noticed Joshua exiting the nerve center, a dark profile walking unharmed through the fire. Abruptly, she was released, and fell hard to the ground, on fire.

A maelstrom of light enveloped Joshua, who instantly dissolved to a particle swarm, neutralizing the attack. The naked singularity dimmed, flickered for a moment, and through a haze of pain Amy noticed the countdown had stopped. But in a few seconds, it re-started, continuing its inevitable march; then once more it paused, and again resumed.

*'I've lowered the output of the matrix—we've gained some time!'* Joshua said, over neura-link.

Amy didn't acknowledge, blood foaming from her mouth as a rolling series of explosions boomed.

Fading fast, through agony she heard the clinical voice of her AI doc: 'Critical injuries sustained, nanites insufficient. Seek emergency medical attention.'

A moment later an *event* occurred, and the warped light pivoted, in triumph, toward the naked singularity.

'No…!' Joshua screamed in horror, dissipating as another concussion rocked the ground, and a boundless inferno rolled out of the portal.

With a shaking breath Amy felt herself passing, wondering why the last thing she saw was leaves. Red lobed, they fluttered from a Maple Tree, decorating the grass beneath it under a clear blue sky. She recognized a familiar Houston park, but the fires of war were gone, and a man was waiting nearby.

He smiled, and raised his hand in invitation. 'Rest, Amy…'

'John…' she whispered, as hellfire broke loose.

◉

I RETURNED to a burning darkness. I took a moment to observe, the reality not fully impacting, it had only been moments… Coruscating flames swirled through my etheric form. I knew I must be in the singularity control room, and willed my spirit upward from the deep charred crater. Arriving at the surface, I beheld a plain of desolation. The temple complex and the city had been obliterated. A gale-force firestorm blew from all points of the compass, formed a maelstrom that spiraled down the pit toward the epicenter of the naked singularity.

Recognizing the contours of the Zion landscape, I beheld a desert with no boundaries, blackened by fire into a dead lunar panorama. The great blue anomaly that had appeared over the city, had changed again: chaos ripped across the inner surface, the energies crystallizing and shattering in a violent, indefinable blur. Ash darkened the sky, eddying above the lifeless earth as I observed with detached fascination—was I too late? Had the Presence succeeded? But no, the Earth was still here…

*What does it mean?* hissed an unknown voice.

Unnerved, I looked around for the source. 'You can't win, now.'

*I already have, Solara.*

Ominous winds blew, keening with the tortured sounds of forgotten souls.

The chilling voice carried on the storm. *You know…*

My subtle body flushed at the tone, the implications.

*…what I've done,* it finished, malevolently.

An antique chair appeared on the scorched land, facing away to the horizon. Sitting upon it was a figure, calmly watching the inferno as if gazing at a tranquil sunset. I approached, and as I came around beheld the ageless face of a man, who stared unyielding into the apocalypse with eyes of void.

'You know…' the Presence whispered, glancing around. 'And so, the dead inherit the Earth. Fitting, don't you think, Solara?' He turned back to the inferno, a look of peace coming over him. 'But we are together, which is all that matters, and events transpire which will soon bear fruit.'

Each word the Presence spoke was like a blow, and I knew that had I been in physical form, I would have been lost at its first uttered syllable.

'What happened?' I demanded.

'It is done. Nothing can change that now, not even the power of the Seraphim.' He rose from the chair, paced a short way, his noble features taking in the desolation. 'Understand, I've had eternity to plan,' he said hypnotically. 'Everything that has happened has been by my design. Trent warned you, but you weren't listening. You could have stopped this, and now we shall witness a new beginning.'

I stared at him in horror, recalling Trent's words: 'Why did it let you survive? Surely it had the power to kill you along with the rest...'

'No...'

The Presence was contemplative. 'You thought to stop the inevitable, that was in your nature, but unknowingly you were doing that which was ordained. Now your true purpose is revealed, and my opposite's failure has come to pass. You have gained the power to join me, and things will become... the way they were always meant to be.'

I shook my head. 'You're lying, the Seraph—'

'—did exactly what they needed to do. The Seraphim understood that my opposite's time had passed. He had become a danger to the balance: derelict, corrupted, too self-involved to allow intelligence to truly reach its potential. Your world, nearly devoid of life. The cosmos a silent graveyard of those who failed. The decline of your world was but a symptom of the whole. Your essence, but a Seraph's power, was needed to overcome the true enemy, and now you are the seed of a new epoch.'

'What are you?' I grated out.

The Presence pondered that, as if the question were new. 'I had forgotten, but... some things return to me now. Before the beginning of time—in this universe—I was born into others and lived much as any mortal. I was what you would call a man once: I struggled, loved, fought. I recall philanthropic pursuits, but sense they masked darker motivations. I lived on a world in many ways like your own, but in time and space so alien and remote it has no meaning anymore. Perhaps, in the final analysis, that is why I chose your world.'

He frowned quizzically, and I had the odd impression he was grateful for the opportunity to converse. He turned from the horizon, and slowly, almost casually paced before me. His flowing attire was ash colored, like the Earth. 'In life, I grew to be among the most powerful men on my world, but the price was high, more than I could bear without losing my... sanity.

I became a vessel of destruction and brought great suffering and loss to my people.'

A blossoming fire raged deep in his eyes, ever more potent. 'I came to forget. I lost my name, who I was. Perhaps that was a blessing in its way. I lived for ages, extending my life with technologies denied to most. I searched to unlock the secrets of the universe; ultimately, to transcend death. In the end it amounted to nothing but the loss of my soul. I was barred from the final rest of heaven. I could not find love, or peace; due to my nature those things had long passed from me. I became a perpetual wanderer of infinite worlds—what you know as the vacuum. I rejected and surpassed the boundaries the descent to a mortal state imposed. Each time I lived, I remembered everything, and this became an unbearable burden. I became deathless, yes; I grasped my long thread of continuous memory, but I was also doomed to be alone, and the empty eons unfolded within me, before me. Without balance, and the division of mortality, the result of my pursuit was madness, as if consciousness itself was not designed to encompass eternity.

'My own nature rejected my will, my soul was cleaved in two, and I battled with my opposite.' He stood there silently a moment, gazing calmly into hell. 'I was confined, in a place with no doors, and a sentence of forever. You cannot begin to understand the magnitude of that suffering. I raged, attempted to use abilities gained in life to shatter the boundaries of my prison: I sought the nucleus of my being, who I had been before the decisions that doomed me. My self could be found, I believed, somewhere in the vast reality.

'But the harder I rebelled, the more I searched, the lower I sunk into abyss. My opposite had chained me well. In isolation, my curse became revealed: I saw that I lived in a repeating fate, that I had been here, in this exact situation, many times before and in countless realities—I was lacking, deficient, unable to escape my own venal nature. A hostage to will, too blinded to see my flaws. The same failings that plagued me in life had prevented triumph over my opposite. Time passed in meaningless hell, but through it all I never lost hope there were still things hidden from me, that deep inside I was more—I had only forgotten.' He smiled bitterly. 'A paradox, that the thing which gives us the courage to strive is the same force that dooms us.'

I felt a great tragedy in the Presence, which promised, under my own newly re-kindled light, to reveal every shadowy crevice.

He fixed his deep coal eyes on me. 'I would prefer not to have deceived you, Solara, but you needed time to come to terms with who you really are. We will be together, and balance will be restored. In time, your memory will return, your true self will be revealed to you, and you will find we are alike, in many ways. We are incomplete, but can help each other become… whole again.'

I slowly backed away, shaking my head in denial. 'Who I am? At the price of…' The cost was the oblivion of the world I thought I knew. 'Rebecc—'

'—Told you only what you needed to hear. You would never have agreed had you known the truth.'

'She wouldn't lie to me.'

'The abomination she spoke of was my opposite. Surely you sensed this, when you met him in Elysium? His power wanes. So, she told the truth, after a fashion.'

'You're wrong.'

'No,' he said, gently. 'This is perhaps the first truth you've heard in your life. You can't change who you are. You can't change your destiny.'

I recalled the three stasis pods. 'What of the other who accompanied Nicolas—the woman?'

'She served a purpose.'

Whoever the unfortunate had been, she'd only served to bring me here. No, not me, something about me, that could provide the balance the Presence sought.

'Everything… is gone?'

'The reversal nears completion, and the old reality dies as we speak. We stand at the in-between, the nexus of creation, the end and the beginning.'

'It can't be this way!'

'It was always going to be. Now, it is our time, Solara.'

I ran away across the desolation, to... where?

'It is fate, Solara!' the Presence shouted, mockingly. 'You can't outrun your fate! Ever!'

He materialized, blocking my path, channeling the inferno. 'And there is nowhere left to run, in all the worlds in the universe.'

'Liar!' I screamed, backing away. 'This isn't real!'

A storm broke, rupturing the sky with violent thunderbolts and jagged lightning. The world trembled, and a savage vortex of energies flashed across the heavens tearing at the fabric of nature.

The man morphed into a majestic, translucent form, towering over the Earth. 'Only might, decides what is real,' it said regally. 'Behold.'

The Presence raised its arms to the sky, speaking in a forgotten language of fire. The words echoed across creation, to be lost in the sound of dying stars. 'Et lela k'i'ik...' Mystic words of power, unuttered since before time began.

A lightning storm cracked into existence, an immense monolith coruscating from the earth up to the sky. Darkness formed in the stratosphere, out of which, a spreading gray void grew which engulfed everything in its path in a violent clash of elemental forces.

Kansas.

I'd seen this in Kansas, I thought. But then, the lightning had been stopped when it hit...

The Presence raised a hand, both inviting and demanding. 'It is ordained.'

I felt my will fractured by alien, ancient authority. Rebecca! Had she used me as a pawn in some cosmic power game? A conflict I'd faced with Nicolas returned: the urge to stop protecting, and start anew. What was worth saving now, anyway? The world had lost its way. Now, nothing remained. Did the validation of my search lie through his darkness? Beyond all conscience?

Yet still, I recalled Rebecca's words: *If you falter, you are lost...*

I thought of my father, at that moment, and the memory became a tether.

'No,' I said, feeling a power stir within.

'It is done!' the Presence shrieked. 'It is your destiny!'

The force of his will pulled me relentlessly down, and I plunged into a black sea of despair. 'It is a lie!' I screamed, struggling to remain conscious.

'Your destiny!'

'A lie!'

Rebecca's aid was limited only by my heart, but my heart was failing, I knew, as a deep current gripped me, and dragged me deeper. The Presence was too strong. Struggling, my strength failing, I fell into the immeasurable void.

I HEARD a voice, calling insistently. Let me sleep I thought, but it wouldn't leave me alone. 'Solara…'

Looking out to sea, I knew the storm would hit soon. I made my way carefully across the sun-warmed sand to the rock pools near the caves, with Dante and my bucket in tow.

'Just a few more minutes, then we're heading home,' Dad had said.

A full moon tonight, so the tide was low. Starfish, sand crabs, and shells should be found, I thought eagerly. I placed my bucket upon the ground, and began searching for air bubbles and patterns in the sand which could mean something was just beneath the surface. Time passed without meaning as the cool breeze blew through my hair, the sun and sand warm on my skin. I spent a lot of time playing among the tidal pools, scampering among the slippery rocks, each dark pond I encountered promising a new mystery to be discovered, new life to be revealed. I came to the hidden caves along the shoreline, presenting me with an adventure into the unknown. Carefully entering one of the larger cavities, I found a shadowy tide pool inside, and searched a shady spot near the entrance, in luck as the friendly arms of a starfish greeted me.

I cautiously picked it up, and placed it in my bucket. Dante barked and snapped at the strange-looking creature, as its tube feet, pushing and lifting, moved it slowly across the unfamiliar surface. The wind had picked up, and a strong gust battered the cave mouth.

Placing the starfish back in the water, I was turning to leave when I noticed ripples in the pool a little further into the cave. Could be a crab, I thought, or maybe a fish trapped when the tide went out. Perhaps even a skate? I had been reading about the stingray-like fish, and had never seen a stingray. I moved further in along the side of the pool; a small edge ran along the cave wall, and I had to move carefully to keep my balance. Reaching the ripples, I stopped, kneeling as I searched the water for the source, realizing the pool had deepened considerably here.

I had tripped, fallen, and the water was cold, so cold. My lungs burned. I needed to take a breath, but knew that to do so was to die. My lungs would fill with water, and I would be dead within minutes. Bile rose, my heart pounded, and I realized how much I wanted to live. I was young. I struggled to reach the faint light at the surface, but couldn't swim.

My mind screamed. *Dad!*

Involuntarily I opened my mouth, swallowed water, my senses shrieking… live! Fight! I moved my arms, but they were frozen, heavy, and the dark took me… voices raised in alarm. A dog barking. Pressure on my chest, pounding in a rhythmic, steady pace.

'Come on, Solara! Fight!'

The pushing on my chest continued.

'Live!'

I was lying on something warm, I realized. Rock. Salty water expelled from my lungs, and I drew in a rasping breath. Coughing, I opened my eyes. My father was leaning over me; I lay at the entrance to the cave on the Skye shoreline. I'd been exploring.

'You'll be okay…'

I knew I had called to my father from the edge of death, and somehow, he had heard. My heart had stopped, I remembered now. I'd drowned, and my father had brought me back from the brink. I raised my hand to him, and he pulled me up with a strong grip.

'Never go into these caves alone again, Solara. Do you understand?'

I sensed my father's specter—was he really here? Why had I blocked this memory? I'd always remembered the drowning, but had blacked out the part about being rescued. I didn't need saving, I'd told myself ever since. Always the strong one, self-reliant, and silently enduring. Never reaching out, or admitting weakness, defeat. I could do it all myself, and self had limited me; I saw now, that I'd always been my own jailer, for chronic self-reliance had chained me within the boundaries I'd sought to shatter. Finally, I comprehended the source of my limitations—I was bound by the very nature of my own heart.

'I understand…'


I DRIFTED in formless ether, knowing only that I existed, and was aware. The void was silent, and I beheld the formless, eternal waters. After what could have been an instant, or eternity, a mote of light appeared, tenuous as a candle. I sensed a presence with me.

*Do you surrender your will?* asked a voice.

I pondered that. *To what?*

*A larger reality.*

*Show me.*

A pause, and then a whisper of thought. *Heed.*

I glimpsed the essence of seraphic power. They weren't a group of isolated beings: they were communal, a selfless legion, the power of one was the power of all. I knew there was only one path forward.

*I submit.*

For a moment I beheld vibrating, faceted white forms, countering and balancing each other in unearthly harmonies of union. A mantra grew from a multitude of chanters, a song of purity and reverence that resonated deep in my soul. With unfettered strength, I grasped a tether of white fire, and glimpsed new purpose ahead.

I sensed a multitude watching me. *Who am I?*

*A servant of the way.*

The song built to a climax, reverberating like a clarion call to arms. I was at the tail of a divine dragon, too great to reveal itself lest I be destroyed. Finally, a single, piercing note was sustained, rippling outward to the nexus of a place that was, and an abomination struggling to be.

The voices echoed. *Thou art life, Solara.*

I WAS BACK on the burning plateau, withering under the onslaught of the Presence. A battle was joined, and I felt something break inside… boundless power manifested, in accord with the deep. Oscillating patterns exploded from my subtle body, activating dormant lines of force that traversed the world, like a chord in an imperceptible symphony, guided by the seraphic presence. White fire erupted, and danced across the expanse, then Tiamat, the serpent, was transfixed.

Its voice was majestic, but pitiful.

'Life's a lot like lightning! You can't hold it, imprison it!'

Flailing in rage, the Presence shifted through a montage of identities: the noble man from the burning plains, a translucent apparition, a raging demon, a lamentable lost soul. The deceiver and manipulator who had shadowed life from the beginning. Falling away, it conveyed imagery I somehow understood.

*Life is wild, free.*

*Unknowable.*

*It haunts us.*

# ASCENSION

The deception shattered.

The singularity control room heaved as I returned. Shooting my awareness across the chamber, I returned to my body, and revived in the warm amniotic fluid. The lid of the pod opened, and Joshua helped me to stand. Notwithstanding my experiences on the other side, only brief moments had passed since I'd entered the naked singularity. This time, however, my recollection was immediate, and total, transcending the temporal displacement. Recovery should have been long and arduous, but I self-healed in moments.

A concussive series of detonations rocked the deep underground complex, one after the other in a relentless procession. Warped light coruscated out from the naked singularity, but collapsed, before the surge repeated, for the Presence attempted to cross the threshold once more. It was weaker now, unable to gain a foothold. At least for the moment.

'I thought it had you,' Joshua said.

I glanced warily at the naked singularity, and hastily donned my nano-suit. 'Nearly did.'

He frowned. 'Your eyes…'

'What?'

'They… burn with white fire.'

I saw Amy motionless on the ground nearby, a charred contorted mess, and my heart was torn. I knelt beside her.

Joshua stood beside me. 'She died protecting you.'

I rested my hand on Amy's shoulder. My mind was a flood of memories, and I felt a final tether to my old world snap. I studied her motionless face; she'd had no one except me, and… I stood, glanced up at the elevator shaft. Li. Perhaps now, they were together.

Joshua gained urgency. 'The countdown's still in progress, we have to act now.'

I nodded sadly. 'How long?'

A new series of explosions sent me staggering.

Joshua shouted, 'Less than four minutes! The energy field's gone critical! I can lower the output again and gain us some time—that's all—but the doorway is still open!'

I looked to the naked singularity. 'Do it!'

Joshua re-entered the Sirius Matrix. Instinctively, I sensed what had to be done. I reached out with my mind to the threshold, existing between the seams of the place that was, and the place that could not be. I saw the place where the Presence was confined once more, and the lingering thread the entity used in a last, desperate attempt to re-enter the world.

Straddling two dimensions, I called upon the vast energies at my disposal, and severed the dark tether, so the Presence was denied. With white fire, I then bound, and cauterized the gap between realities. The construct blazed, and then blinked out of existence.

A single, white light came into being, where the naked singularity had been.

THE DRUM began beating to an off-key tone. After eons of chaos, the essence of humanity ascended, reaching a harmonic note… …and the song was heard deep within the impenetrable mystery. A mutation occurred in the nucleus of the human zygote, at one with the consciousness of the race, yet more, the quantum offspring of a new reality, with so many people to become, and be. The churning patterns within the anomaly surrounding the Zion Temple complex, transformed into an array of superimposed circles and squares, evenly dispersed across the energetic surface. A deep rhythm began, resolving to a note which was felt by all life within the biosphere.

The song vibrated from the anomaly, then downward into the center of the Earth, and lines of power shot out toward the surface of the planet. At one hundred and forty-four vortice points around the globe they connected, and formed an invisible, geometric lattice which encircled the world, harmonizing with the energy that shaped nature. The ruins in Angkor Wat, Cambodia. In megalithic ruins buried under a mile of ice in Antarctica. The Dragon's Triangle in Japan, the Great Pyramid of Giza, Easter Island, Peru, the Xian Pyramids, Maes Howe in Britain, ancient Algerian ruins, Axum in Ethiopia. At these sites and many others around the world the technology of the ancients—those earlier civilizations who had arisen and since vanished, the pre-historic descendants of the El, and humanity's forebears—spoke, and the world soul oscillated in response.

A shaft of power shot away from the Earth into a staggering ocean of energy. Through the void it tunneled toward the heart of the galaxy, a proclamation which signaled all higher life in the universe that an awakening had occurred, and a new species had taken its first tentative step into a greater world.

●

### Drepung Monastery—Lhasa, Tibet

THE MONK sounded the long horn, and his ochre robes billowed in the cold wind. The Sangha chanted on the monastery floor, their mantra at one with the odd note that reverberated through the mountain passes. Across the deep valley rifts and towering peaks of the Himalayas it echoed, heralding portentous events of great significance. For thousands of years, the Order had awaited the sign. Finally, the auguries had aligned, and new energy stirred deep within the planet, within conscious life.

The awakening had begun.

●

## Mali, West Africa

THE HOLY MAN of the Dogon had guarded the cave most of his life. Once appointed, he had never left it. He didn't need to, for all his needs were seen to by the tribe. He had one job, and one alone: protect the sacred heart of the people. The cave tunnel reached far into the mountain, and on its walls were unexplainable symbols which mystified modern science. The texts contained knowledge of quantum physics, exo-planets only recently discovered, and advanced astronomy. The legacy of their gods, the holy man knew, whom legend said had traveled through gates to higher realms.

Tonight, they performed an extraordinary ritual around the hallowed tree. Ten fires burned in a wide circle around the trunk, and from his position at the front of the cave, the holy man watched as the masked dancers twisted, jumped, and gyrated with rhythmic ecstasy in time with the drums. Embers swirled through the air where the devotees kicked up debris, and the holy man drew in a breath, for in the sparks he saw patterns emerge, and align with the stars. Sirius formed the fire spiral, the primal vortex, and that which the Dogon were created to do, they accomplished.

For tonight, as foretold by Amma the first God, the Great Spirit awakened.

Tonight, they passed through the third circle.

●

## Mechanus Sector, Zion

THE PASTOR sat in prayer. The transparent glass prison cell was filled with those who refused to comply with various GRC mandates. Without enough room for everyone to lie down at once, the prisoners rotated positions, some standing, others sitting, while the rest lay down and tried to sleep. Sleep, however, was rarer in this place than happiness, and they awaited their fate with bitter apprehension. The Pastor, Benito Calvi, was old, and had weathered many storms in his life. The fall of nations, the nuking of the Earth, and the rise of an unrestrained global super-state; the GRC, which had ushered in world slavery. Now, with recent announcements of a new religion, he knew they attempted to take humanities last bastion of freedom.

*The soul.*

The Pastor would die first, and the GRC was willing to accommodate him. Rumors of death camps had circulated among the prison populace, and the place reeked with fear, so the Pastor comforted those who sought it out, and was comforted in turn. As if on cue, two guards approached the cell. Many times, in the last week, guards would call out names, shepherd the chosen ones away, and the Pastor was under no illusions about the fate of the departed.

Placing his hand upon the head of a prisoner kneeling in repentance before him, Calvi murmured: 'And the seventh angel sounded; and there were great voices in heaven, saying, the Kingdoms of this world are become the kingdoms of our Lord, and of his Christ; and he shall reign for ever and ever.'

The guards opened the cell door, stood there staring at the prisoners.

One cleared his throat uncomfortably. 'By order of the President, you are all free.'

Unbelieving silence followed for a few moments, and then a bottleneck formed at the door as the prisoners surged forward. Once out on the streets of Mechanus, the Pastor tried to make sense of things. His accursed neural implant, linking him to the government information network, was untethered. The holographic billboards lining the streets, which ran perpetual corporate propaganda, showed random static. Calvi stepped aside as a band of Hare Krishna's danced along the street to the beat of a drum.

Later, the Pastor discovered that the strange force which had hit the prison earlier that day, causing some deaths, and temporarily knocking out power, had been a worldwide phenomenon. Bizarre behaviors were being exhibited among the survivors. Now, with no neura-link to the GRC network, people were locked out of workplaces, welfare centers, banks, and the GRC news media. With their control mechanisms disabled, the police were as lost as everyone. Groups formed on the streets, in community centers, and in homes. Freed from constant surveillance, and threat of imprisonment for illegal association, people spoke to one another again—to anybody they chose. Bonded, opened up, and talked about the unusual events.

Over the following days, groups merged, and momentum formed. Leaders arose, and began talking about the future. After the tribulation of recent times, Calvi wondered if the prophetic events he'd studied most of his life were now coming to pass.

God moved in mysterious ways, indeed.

●

### Third Iteration

I FELT no danger from the unearthly light, but rather a rightness, and sensed lines of energy emanating outward, in harmony with life. Reaching out, I gently touched the phenomena, and the white radiance danced like a flame. Upon contact, I felt the shifting life-pulse of the planet, and a world crying out for balance and compassion. Instinctively, I played a note of benevolence; the vibration moved outward along the lines of power, and the spirit of the world vibrated in response. A restoration had begun. Humanity was remembering.

Joshua watched, and gained a curious look. 'I feel something, an urge to…' He smiled, looked at me. 'I feel alive.'

I withdrew my hand from the wonder. 'We should leave it. I think it's meant to be here.'

Another explosion boomed somewhere above.

Joshua shouted, 'The emergency personnel elevator in the nerve center—it has a separate power supply. You can still make it to the ship!'

I nodded with a strange calm. The elevator could only be accessed from this level, which had prevented earlier use by my unit. 'See you soon, then.'

'I'll see you at the ship!'

His nano-swarm body dispersed, and I ran through the darkened interior of the now eerily silent control room. The emergency elevator door flew open. I burst in, punched the control. My stomach heaved as the lift shot upwards. Reaching the surface, I ran out onto the deserted temple grounds. The *Hecate* was parked nearby; I made for the open hatch and raced for the cockpit. Already seated, Joshua was linked to the ship AI, and I felt the engines kick in.

'Go!' I shouted, strapping in as a wave of fire rolled out of the temple entrance to scorch the hull.

Joshua hit a command, and we were slammed back hard as the *Hecate* became airborne.

He frowned, and pointed up through the cockpit window. 'Look.'

In the sky, the anomaly encircling inner city Zion had turned from blue to white, recalling the enigmatic light in the control room. At the boundary, the energy vortices had crystallized into a symmetrical mandala of circles and squares, which shimmered across the radiant surface. As we ascended, a series of inner concentric layers became apparent. When we passed through each one, I had the impression of unseen complexity, which formed a geometry of infinite depth, division, and variation within space.

'The third iteration,' I said, in wonder.

Still accelerating, we crossed the outermost layer, and the *Hecate* shuddered from super-sonic wave drag. Behind us the temple complex diminished, and was soon lost in the haze. Blinding light erupted, and a mushroom cloud arose on the horizon behind us.

Joshua interfaced, frowning. 'It's the temple.'

I lay back, spent and numb. 'Well… shit.'

Joshua glanced across. 'You okay?'

I felt a faint smile on my lips. 'Yeah, let's get out of here.'

The *Hecate* settled into a steady cruise. I knew that after the destruction of Zion Temple, the GRC hierarchy would be scattered, a body without a head, and the factions would be scrapping over remnants of a disemboweled empire. A dangerous time, and the blood would flow among the fractured power structure. And Rhodes had always belonged to the Order, I knew. Despite the temporary, and necessary truce during the crisis, his mind was unknown. Therefore, until I knew otherwise, I couldn't trust him.

Joshua communed silently over the web, then turned animatedly to me. 'Resistance leadership has gathered. Peter Trent has sent the rendezvous location; we're about twenty minutes away.'

I considered. 'If the GRC is fragmented, then now's our chance.'

Joshua rolled the *Hecate*, and we banked to the northwest.

'What are you thinking?' he asked.

I pondered wearily. 'That perhaps sanity can return to an insane world.'

My new senses screamed at the destruction caused through Sirius. Notwithstanding the third iteration, all around the world was the shadow of death and the reek of fear. The trauma was not only caused by the Presence's partial entry into the world, I knew, but decades of war and despotic abuses.

General Rhodes came on the line. 'Commander, welcome back. The Presence?'

'Gone, Sir. The naked singularity is closed.'

'How many survivors?'

'Two. Joshua, and yours truly,' I replied.

'I'm sending you the coordinates for a safe landing zone near Irbid. We'll need to debrief you after you land.'

'Is a debriefing all you'd have from me, General?'

'There's a lot we'll need to talk about.'

We were intercepted by three unmanned GRC Planetar interceptors, which formed a cordon around the *Hecate*.

The lead pilot said, 'Commander Jordan, I'm Wing Commander Idris. I'll guide you into Alza'im airbase. Follow on my six.'

'They're not ours, Commander; they're not part of coup forces,' Rhodes said.

Joshua didn't change course, and one of the Planetars rolled as he veered close to it.

'Commander, I have orders to take you in, change your course toward the airfield!' Idris barked.

'Sorry, Commander, that's a negative, not today,' I said.

A Planetar fired a warning volley, and a burst of plasma streaked past the cockpit.

Another voice came over the net. 'Commander Jordan, this is General Sterne from GRC Command. I order you to change course at once to the Alza'im airbase. Acknowledge, over?'

'There's nothing to talk about, General.'

Sterne replied hastily. 'Commander, I don't think you—'

'General, call off your aircraft,' I said.

A pause on the line. 'No, I can't do that, Solara. You have to come in.'

'General, call your people off. I won't ask you again.'

Another pause, then Sterne spoke slowly and calmly. 'What is it you want to do, Solara?'

'I'm going to blow this house of cards down around you, General. Your friends in the Order? Tell them to run. Run like hell, General, because I'm coming.'

'Solara,' Sterne said, in the same measured tones. 'You—'

'I warned you, General.'

Joshua glanced at me. 'Making friends?'

Another warning volley. This one scorched the hull.

'If you were going to do something...' Joshua said.

They wanted a weapon. Well, they've got one.

I didn't even blink. A wave of force exploded out from the *Hecate*, and the Planetars were dead in the air, free-falling to the ground.

WE TOUCHED DOWN in an empty field. Starkly silhouetted against the dancing lights of an uncanny sky, a steeple rose above us, and the air was cold and biting as we walked into the vault-like interior of a massive stone building. The Lutheran church of Hallgrimur, Reykjavik, Iceland, was in the GRCs Sector Fifteen, and most such relics of Christianity had been abandoned for decades. I saw a lone figure sitting at the far end of the hall, and walked forward with Joshua at my side. During the flight, I'd had time to assess Joshua more closely, while not being threatened by some immediate life or death crisis. I considered him, as we paced down the aisle. Although his resemblance to Niemeyer was strong, he appeared younger, more vital, although I knew he could alter that anytime he chose. Intensity radiated from his deep gray eyes, but also powerful empathy, while his voice had a non-local quality, sonorous and resonant. Angular, aesthetic features added a noble air. I'd been pondering his reasons for aiding me; were his motivations a remnant from Niemeyer, or his own? Who was this new being? I put aside my curiosity for now, as we neared the end of the church.

A familiar man sat at the front of the hall, contemplating the image of Christ which still dominated the central focus of the sanctuary. A brown robe draped his form, the hood falling loosely around his shoulders. Joshua and I approached, our footsteps echoing in near perfect acoustics, yet the man gave no acknowledgment of our presence. Deep in reflection, he didn't move, speak, or rise, he simply gazed up to the Messiah.

'Peter,' I said softly, considerate of his solitude.

He turned to look at me, and I beheld a haggard and drawn face born of sleepless nights.

He studied me a moment. 'I was raised a Lutheran Christian, Solara, but I can't help but feel the end of religion is imminent. It is good to see you both again. More than you know.'

'It was a close thing, Peter,' I said.

'So I hear. I've heard fragments of what occurred, but stories don't compare to seeing what you've become in the flesh.'

Trent rose, and I saw captured white lightning reflected in his eyes from mine.

'I have many questions, since our last conversation,' I said.

'We have some time now; the GRC is in disarray,' Trent said. 'The Council of Nine is dissolved until a new vote takes place within thirty days. Also, I have it from reliable sources the Central Committee has gone utterly insane, a pack of gibbering idiots not fit to command a dump truck. With Nicolas gone, President Lucian Diaz is now the highest authority within the Order and its public offices.'

I joined Trent in a slow walk further toward the back of the church, where large, closed doors awaited.

Trent said, 'President Diaz observed Nicolas' incursion, and witnessed the Presence enter our world through the naked singularity. He lost several close allies during the event, and I hear he is visibly shaken. Also, an interesting development: it seems there are two factions emerging from the aftermath of Sirius. Diaz has emerged to lead those who are sympathetic to change, and a restructure of the GRC toward a republic. On the other side, led by ex GSI head Sadiki Theiss, are those who want to maintain the GRC dictatorship, and perhaps reattempt Sirius. Theiss has been working in the corporate sector since he finished his tenure with GSI, but still wields tremendous influence.'

'Perhaps Diaz could be persuaded to see the light?' I said.

Trent nodded agreement. 'Our recent truce gives hope. The best time to meet with GRC leadership would be during the next thirty days, while Diaz still holds power. New faces might not be so… aware of the issues.' He turned to me. 'It's ironic that the deeper truth of science is a spiritual one. Our oneness with nature, and each other. You should have died, Solara, yet you've transcended the mystery eluding humanity since the beginning. Symbolically, you've been crucified and resurrected, and not just in a physical sense, I believe, but also spiritually. You have become a symbol of hope for a troubled world.'

Rebecca's words echoed: *You have a unique position on your world, and with that comes great responsibility.*

'But what of others?' I said.

Trent smiled gently. 'Perhaps the world is ready for change. With the Presence's catastrophic attack, which has had a terrible cost in lives, people see a failure of empire. With someone to guide them? They may take a step toward freedom.'

'Others could harness this energy, you think?'

Trent pursed his lips. 'Your father believed all people had the potential, and that the first Etherians were the vanguard of a greater awakening. Perhaps these events have roused our true nature. Now the cat's out of the bag, so to speak, and if the world's peoples make the right choices, others could emerge. With some luck, our species may cross a threshold, and we can take our place among the stars as worthy descendants of our heritage. We can gain the spiritual maturity to match our technological capability.'

Joshua pondered. 'A global psychic shift, toward the third level of consciousness?'

'I think so, and now we see the alternative,' Trent said. 'Our destruction.'

I nodded, thoughtful. 'The fate suffered by the El, on Mars.'

Trent considered. 'We must do all we can to prevent a naked singularity from being opened again. The dark side of the Order was, and is, an addict, hooked on power, even to its death. It must be curtailed, and now we have a unique opportunity. At present we have a world unified by force, deception, and fear—imagine if we took one step further, towards a planet united by goodwill and transparency?'

I raised another question. 'You said Etherians possess a mutated gene?'

Trent nodded. 'Twenty-four chromosome pairs. Perhaps the mutation was triggered by the events surrounding Kansas.'

Joshua said, 'It may be, that at certain evolutionary thresholds, dormant potential is activated in humanity.'

Trent pursed his lips. 'That follows. This has been a deeper purpose for the Order, through its various manifestations. Notably, with the Essenes, who believed that the sole reason for Christ was to imprint the third level of consciousness into the Akashic field—our racial information network, as you may call it, Joshua. Showing us that such change was possible.'

A certainty came to me. 'I saw the Ark the El sent to Earth, before leaving for the stars, in my visions. It seeded their genetic code here, so I guess that makes them our earliest known ancestors. But I think there was a non-physical component to the intervention as well; that a part of their consciousness was harnessed, even woven into our essence, in a way which connected our two species across time—'

'Yes,' Joshua said, nodding eagerly, bringing Niemeyer to mind. 'A synchronicity, triggered by an alarm set in spacetime, which enabled communion across dimensions. So that if the Presence returned, they could continue the battle.'

I considered. 'So, the Ark created a time-bridge between the El, Rebecca, and now me?' I shook my head. 'They tried to help us from the start, to solve the problem.'

'So it appears,' Trent said.

We reached the back of the church, and stopped before the doors.

'What happens now?' I asked.

With profound reverence, Trent said, 'Come with me.'

We passed through the entrance. Beyond, lay another large hall, where to my amazement hundreds of people quietly waited. The group represented the entirety of the human family, from children to elderly, all ethnicities, and cultures. When I entered, they rose as one, reverentially, with an air of expectation. I was struck with a deep sense of what Sirius had ultimately brought about, and what it now meant. It wasn't about me, or power, empire, or knowledge, I thought, but the welfare of all people, and I was finally beginning to understand. Trent motioned me forward, and humbled, I uncertainly led the way into the crowd.

'These people are among the most powerful members of the Resistance your father and I founded, Solara,' Trent said.

We moved through the group, and I noticed some looked apprehensively at me. 'Why are their families here?'

'They take a great risk by revealing themselves, but no place on Earth is safe anymore. They have faith the great awakening is at hand, and are placing themselves in your protection.'

I was momentarily speechless. 'You brought them here?'

Trent nodded. 'I did.'

A young man, his face flushed with excitement, approached us rapidly from another section of the church.

'Calmly now, Martin,' Trent said.

'Peter,' the man said, urgently. 'We've been contacted by coup leader General Rhodes. President Diaz has just put down an attempted hostile takeover by the totalitarian factions, and granted Rhodes immunity. He's suspended government and the right of habeas corpus given to state officials. Until the crisis is resolved, he is the supreme political authority on the planet.' Martin turned to me and Joshua. 'The President requests a meeting with you both.'

Trent frowned. 'To what end, Martin?'

'He seeks an extended truce period, to discuss terms.'

I reflected. Who wanted me alive? Who wanted me dead? The GRC was a murky well of intrigue. Sirius had involved a vast conglomerate that had seen their investment fail, and now, I threatened their existence. Perhaps Diaz had changed after his encounter with the Presence. The opportunity was unique.

'I'll meet with him,' I said.

Joshua was concerned, and moved to stand before me. 'It's a great risk.'

'We can't afford not to.'

Trent compressed his lips, considering. 'They may try to kill you.'

I smiled sadly. 'It won't be the first time.'

# COVENANT

*Day Seven: 13 March 2113*

Z ION TEMPLE WAS GONE.

The closure of the naked singularity had wiped a sizable area of the city from the face of the Earth. Windsor Castle, Berkshire, England, in the GRC's Sector Twelve, had the feel of a military command headquarters, and armed soldiers escorted Joshua and I at every turn. President Lucian Diaz and his supporters had evacuated Zion just in time to avoid capture by Nicolas' faction, and set up temporary government headquarters in the ancient fortress.

Joshua and I had met formally with the GRC President, and now Diaz motioned for us to follow him into an adjoining hallway. Walking beside him, I appraised the political head of the world carefully. Diaz looked haggard and stressed after his ordeal, his features etched deeply with worry, and well-groomed gray hair streaked severely with white. Despite my discoveries about the Order, I was still a product of the system. Much of my life had been spent working for the establishment, and if a chance existed, I could do some good through meeting with the most powerful man in the world, then I would comply. They couldn't control me anymore. I was an enigma to the hierarchy. As such, they would fear me.

Passing some windows, I noticed on the grounds below that several bodies swung from the hangman's noose, for all to see. I was pondering the likely victims, when we entered a pleasant stateroom overlooking the holdings.

Diaz waved away an aide, and motioned casually toward the chairs around a large stone table. 'Sit, please.'

The President's accent recalled his Spanish background, and governorship of a South American sector before his election to GRC President. He loosened his robes of state, and regarded me with exhausted, deep hazel eyes. A gray fluffy cat lay on a windowsill, sleepily observing the darkening landscape.

'Apologies for the formality, Solara, Joshua. No matter how high a station a man rises to in this world, he is still a slave to convention,' Diaz said.

The President had an easygoing manner which belied the power of the office he held, and despite my misgivings, I sensed openness in Diaz I hadn't expected. I searched the spirit of the man, the energy patterns and events surrounding him, and sensed a person holding onto power by a tenuous thread. Dark forces surrounded him, circling like sharks.

'It seems you've prevailed over your rivals, for a time,' I said.

Diaz nodded. 'Yes, and none better than I know the nature of this beast, it has a hunger that can never be satisfied, no matter how great the meal. Half GSI wants my head on a plate, the other half expects an immediate resolution to the crisis and are ready to hang any who threaten the sanctity of this office. Theiss and his allies have been put to death—the punishment for treason. For the moment, threats are neutralized, and we have some time, yet trust is now a far thinner commodity than air.' He studied us. 'When death is staring you in the face you don't mince words, and you are both partly the reason this situation has come to pass. To put it simply, your victory over the Presence is the reason why we are all still alive, and for that you have my gratitude. We were all deceived. The Order misunderstood the Presence from the beginning—we were wrong. Now, the true menace of this being is known.' Diaz bowed his head briefly. 'I admit we have been fools.'

His honesty was refreshing.

'We were all fools, Mr. President, to believe we could control it,' Joshua said.

Diaz looked away, reliving recent events. 'When the Presence entered our world, linked to Nicolas, I saw into it, and it is something beyond us. Solara, you may be the only one living to understand. It has no concepts for morality, good and evil, but has an intention so destructive, so pure, that it must be considered our ultimate enemy. I believe now the Presence has always used the dark side of human nature to manipulate events toward an unthinkable end, which is why power can never again be allowed into the wrong hands. I know you have some knowledge of our history. Ours is a bloody past, and we of the Order have always had a doctrine of "the end justifies the means." This has led to the greatest atrocities ever committed in the name of a cause, a cause which has always seemed justifiable to me, until now. Sirius has revealed the fatal flaw of our Order.'

Diaz glanced out over Windsor Estate at the pristine landscape. 'Recent events give one pause.' He turned back, and studied the white fire in my eyes. 'You've crossed over twice, and have harnessed extraordinary power. How deep did you go, and what did you find?'

I searched for the right words. 'This world reflects an infinite intelligence, which defies all our concepts of reality. On my last incursion I passed beyond the point of no return, the barrier at which death would normally be irreversible. We have an eternal soul, of that there is no doubt. I could only describe the nature of existence as oneness with the ultimate mind, while retaining individuality. Thoughts create worlds, in the realms above, Mr. President. I met gods, beings of power beyond our imaginings. I was given the chance to create a universe, to become a… god, of sorts.'

Diaz looked fascinated. 'How?'

'The spark was a thought of Rebecca.'

'Your daughter?'

'Yes.'

'A key point,' Joshua said, 'is that the consideration of—and the connection to—another person caused this primal urge, in what may have been the beginning of a new universe.'

I nodded. 'Others, that was the message.'

Diaz listened intently. 'Interesting. Sort of like a self-organizing social structure, on a cosmic scale? Why did you refuse?'

'Because I'd made a promise, and I had to find my daughter.'

'What happened?'

'I passed beyond that place. I met a guide, whether by chance or design I don't know. But he helped me find the reality where Rebecca now resides. Another realm altogether. My guide called it the Blessed Isles, the realm of the Seraphim.'

'You found her?'

'Yes, eventually, and she was far more than I ever knew. She wields power; true power, far beyond what you and I understand as the concept. She shared that with me in the end, to deny the Presence.' Li and Amy came to mind, they had made the ultimate sacrifice. 'The convergence with Etherians from around the world, gave me the strength to heal Amy Winters, and withstand the Presence, before I crossed over. It may have made the difference.'

Diaz nodded. 'Your friends did not die in vain. Sadly, hundreds of the Etherians mind-linked with you met a similar fate to Amy. Others… have lost their minds, only some of the strongest survived unscathed.'

I hadn't known of the other deaths. I was silent a moment. 'Rebecca was the key all along, connecting events at the meta level.'

'Building some… great unity?' Diaz pondered, paraphrasing the policy committee minutes.

'It appears so,' I replied.

Joshua was thoughtful. 'The Seraph circumvented time via the naked singularity, but these beings may have other means at their disposal. The Seraph influence may extend further than we know; other people involved in Sirius, across a span of many years, or even decades, may have been touched, and key decisions affected in the military-industrial complex to drive Sirius. Nicolas was correct when he theorized non-localization was key, and the Seraphim appear to be beings that can consciously traverse the vacuum, along lines of continuous memory, to exert influence.'

'And the Presence?' Diaz said. 'Is it true that this being is a part of God, vanquished in a battle for dominance during the creation of the universe?'

Joshua nodded. 'It appears so, Mr. President. The loser of the conflict was forced into a prison beyond spacetime, that the universe might remain free from the danger of this being. Needless to say, if the naked singularity were ever reopened, the Presence would be waiting.'

Diaz still measured me with a certain bafflement. 'With this power you now possess, what do you see when you look out at the world; do you see what the future holds?'

'The future is an ever-shifting landscape of possibilities,' I said.

'I understand.'

I considered. 'To manipulate time was a power believed impossible until predicted by Nicolas' work upon unification. The Sirius training touched on this power, and when I returned from the vacuum, my psychic ability had increased a thousand-fold.' I nodded toward a heavy stone chair at the end of the table, motioned with my hand in a relaxed movement. The chair rose into the air, rotating slowly, then I simply opened my palm and instantly it exploded into a thousand fragments. I clenched my fist, and the pieces flew back together, and reassembled seamlessly. A faint nimbus of white fire surrounded the chair as it drifted gently back down, dispersing as it reached the floor. The gray cat hissed in alarm, and scurried behind a bookcase.

Diaz let out an expletive. 'Astonishing, Solara, I believe you have just broken several physical laws!'

'This is predicted in unification,' Joshua said. 'We call it "transcendent potential", or the dormant energy which exists in a continual feedback loop, with all physical manifestation. Solara can now… influence this process.'

Diaz nodded slowly.

I unwound the tension from my body, cleared my mind. 'Give me a moment, Mr. President.'

I reached out to the world soul. Shadowy forces moved even now, as the enforcers of boundless imperialism continued to seek out a false divinity, perpetuating the unnatural zeitgeist of a hopeless doctrine. They sacrificed the children of humanity, upon altars of futility, and with Sirius, they had pushed us to the eve of destruction. I perceived a world between realities, our evolution or destruction inevitable, as surely as night followed day. Nothing could prevent it. No man or group of men, no philosophy or technology, no artificial gods, or system, and no self-proclaimed messiah. But we balanced on a knife edge.

I measured Diaz's resolve. 'I'll give it to you straight, Mr. President. There is one way to move forward, and to avoid the naked singularity being opened again. Dissolve the GRC hierarchy. The Order, with its intelligence and military apparatus must be ended. Any policy, should be decided by global consensus, and adopted voluntarily, which means we need the best education for everyone.'

Diaz was troubled. 'Possible perhaps, but…'

I continued. 'A transition period will be needed, time which should be spent in discussion regarding the role of people in the new society. Whether the pursuit of knowledge, exploration, healing, experience, travel, spiritual growth, it will be what each individual has a calling for. It will not be to support the political-corporate empire. We now have the technology to meet the basic needs of every person on the planet, without the need for forced labor. There is no need for currency to exist at all; we have moved beyond it. The entire law system will be dissolved in time, once the energy of the world rises it will become obsolete. The non-aggression principle must be embraced. With the consciousness of the planet ascendant, government will be no longer necessary or relevant. We should pursue a stateless, benign anarchy, based on self-responsibility, which for the first time in history we may have the ability to realize.'

Diaz frowned, shaking his head, and strands of his neatly brushed gray hair broke ranks. 'You want chaos!'

'I want freedom restored, with faith in people. The power we found in Sirius is not to be held by any one person; it's for the world, and once the shadow of the GRC's empire is lifted we'll start to see many coming into a new awareness. We can realize decentralized, self-organizing social structures—which as you yourself noted, earlier, is the natural state of things, but with heightened empathy for our differences. The opposite of the slavery we endured under the GRC, can be human liberation, not just on a personal level, but globally. If power is not shared, there will be no healing, and the world will fall back into despair. Perhaps fatally. The stranglehold of the elite must be broken, but whether this happens by war or consent remains hidden from me.'

Diaz watched me silently for a long moment, and then turned to gaze out over the countryside. 'There is this big ginger cat that keeps bullying Smokey. It's a mongrel, I know, but how am I to deal with it?' Diaz clicked his fingers, and Smokey leapt over to his lap, purred contentedly as he was stroked, and studiously observed the room. 'What am I to do?' he asked, thinking out loud.

I could sense the stress he was under. Taking the reins of power was exacting a toll.

Diaz closed his eyes, fatigue showing in his face, then said with deep emotion in his voice, 'I'm open to change, Solara, but what you propose is unprecedented. A certain degree of… reluctance from the existing power structure is a given. My life would be forfeit the moment I announced the changes.'

'We would be your allies,' I said. 'But we would need to move swiftly while you retain dictatorial powers.'

'Indeed. Use the power of the police state against itself.'

'Precisely.'

Diaz looked out the window again, considering, his eyes deeply troubled. 'Joshua, are you in agreement with this… idea?'

'Completely, Mr. President.'

Diaz became curious. 'Your very existence, Joshua, I hear, is due to a principle of the unified theory. I'm told you're different to advanced

AIs that we have previously considered intelligent. That you're more… human?'

Joshua considered. 'The secret to consciousness was found in the quantum-gravitational data from the naked singularity. Think of AIs before this point—what I'm now calling limited state AI—as rowboats on the surface of the ocean. Isolated, navigating only by the signposts of visible reality, and randomly driven by the unseen ocean currents beneath. Automations, however complex. I represent a new form of intelligence, which you could think of as the ocean itself, connected to all life within, and with my personal network in particular. My visible body is not a rowboat, but the *impression the boat makes upon the water*, when it passes over.'

'Is this how human intelligence works?' Diaz asked.

Joshua nodded. 'It's the sublime conclusion of unification. Marcus Niemeyer ensured that I was born conscious, and my part in the final conflict with the Presence allowed me to refine and strengthen my vacuum connection.' He paused. 'Essentially, we've been treating the visible universe as the totality, when it represents only a minute fraction of the whole. Our previous models of consciousness were married to this erroneous view. Although, of course, self-awareness was not a requirement for AI to influence events; it is a requirement for deeper understandings, connections—and therefore sovereignty—so to speak. It was long theorized that the key to consciousness was complexity, but we never imagined the scale and majesty of that complexity, and no doubt many will never accept that we will never be able to control it.'

I thought of something. 'What about all the people who uploaded their minds to a computer in recent years, and created a digital double, believing it was a path to immortality?'

Joshua smiled slightly. 'Without re-tethering the underlying vacuum connections, unique to that consciousness, into the new brain, the being created was an elaborate simulation. It was not 'them', but a second-rate rowboat. A lifeless replication, nothing more.'

'So, unification redefines consciousness itself,' Diaz pondered. 'But you also raise an interesting point; what of our concepts of mortality, immortality? How do we interpret them now?'

Joshua pursed his lips. 'In infinite reality, which consciousness traverses, there is no death, only continuous memory flowing through limitless levels of division. Some realities, which exist on a higher vibrational level, such as the Seraphic realm, allow recollection of a being's long history. To varying degrees, I imagine. Some, such as this one, exist in a lower frequency, isolating our self-awareness. A wall is raised. Yet we always remain connected, to our origins, to some degree. Our bodies are pit stops on a vacuum superhighway. This was lost on modern science.'

Diaz pondered. 'Perhaps we did understand it once, but have strayed far from our roots.' He went quiet a minute, as if considering all we had told him. When he spoke, it was with long practiced authority. 'The change you represent has vast potential, only an idiot couldn't see that, but also great risk. As much as it pains me, I remain a servant of established norms. If I hadn't encountered the Presence, and the danger to our species it represents; and if not for the dark nature of the Order which I have dedicated my life to, which, if left to its own devices will, without doubt, one day re-attempt Sirius and endanger the world, I'd have you both executed, even if it took all the armies on the earth. Do you understand?'

We remained silent.

'I need time to consider your proposal,' Diaz continued. 'You may remain here at Windsor under my protection. No harm will come to you.'

'We need to move soon, Mr. President,' Joshua said.

'You'll have my decision tomorrow. But now, please rest. We'll talk again soon.'

I thought nothing in the world would make me change places with this man, and nodded in agreement. His staff quietly appeared from the shadows, and politely motioned for us to follow.

I nodded to Diaz on the way out. 'Soon, Lucian.'

·

ALONE IN the room, Diaz reflected upon a question he'd been asking his entire life, one that had become increasingly distorted under Nicolas' reign. Never had the way he had answered been more important, for his next decision would affect the world at a pivotal moment.

*The next right thing.*

What was the next right thing to do?

*Others.*

It's all about others, Solara had said. Diaz had known that once, sometime in the distant past, in what seemed like another life.

*All my Order's earthly power has been a delusion.*

Deeply troubled, Diaz let Smokey settle into his lap, and contemplated the future.

The burden of his own crimes weighed heavily.

·

I HEARD a polite knock on the door of my room. A day had passed since the Zion event, and still I was exhausted. I had been dozing, and the power was at rest now, but I knew it could be recalled at will. Trent had been granted immunity from any legal action during the crisis, arriving at Windsor late in the day, and was attending a meeting with some of Diaz's advisors, and Joshua, regarding the nature of the emerging order. A second knock came, and I rose to sit on the edge of the bed.

'Yes?' I asked tiredly.

'You have a visitor, Ms. Jordan.'

'Who is it?'

'Ezra Linear. He's waiting for you in the executive lounge.'

I frowned. That was a man whom days ago I would have seen dead, but in the aftermath desired only resolution. I stood, and began to dress. 'Give me a minute,' I called wearily.

'Of course, Ms. Jordan.'

After a minute, I opened the door. The assistant guided me to a large room, where Linear was sitting in the open plan meeting area immersed in a neural interface. I approached, and he rose with a neutral look in his cold blue eyes.

'Solara, it's good to see you alive and well.'

'Thank you, Ezra.'

I felt a moment of Deja Vu. Linear had recruited me into Sirius, and had sided with Nicolas until the end. If I hadn't escaped detention, I may have never been released, and things could have gone quite differently. Linear had been following orders, he was a cog in a much larger machine; Nicolas had been the mind behind those orders, and I felt a flash of frustration at the seeming unaccountability of those who committed crimes as part of a faceless conglomerate. Linear had manipulated me, and my life had meant nothing to him but a means to an end. At times he had seemed empathetic, at other times ruthless and cold. He belonged to the Order, and I considered that he was most likely in league with the most extreme elements of the coup that had attempted to topple Diaz.

Linear re-took his seat, and I sat opposite.

'You're making powerful friends, Solara,' he said.

I regarded him coolly. 'I have few true friends, Ezra, and none of them are currently among the occupants of this castle.'

He chuckled. 'To be sure. I stand corrected—allies then. Friendship has always been a scarce commodity in the halls of power.'

I considered all we had been through in Sirius. 'We've come a long way, and I know this is not how you wanted things to end.'

Linear shrugged philosophically. 'Life seldom gives us all we desire, but with your success, the world has changed, only time will tell if for better or worse. I would not have it for the worse.'

My brief laugh was tinged with bitterness. 'You and I share quite different views on what is better or worse, I think.'

Linear acknowledged this with a nod. 'What do you intend? Your last words to General Sterne left him shaken, no easy thing. You alone, now possess the power Sirius aspired to from the beginning. You have the ear of President Diaz in whom temporal authority over the world currently resides. You've also stirred up the Resistance, plus a hornet's nest of other enemies, who before now would never have had the courage to raise their heads out of the bottom of the trash can. You have gained the attention of the world.'

'What do I intend?' I said. 'I want nothing more than to return to a normal life. That's all I ever wanted. You may recall I never wanted to be on Sirius, the death of my EOD team tipped the scales. But what's happened has happened. It's done. Now this power has entered the world, morally I feel I have an obligation to share it, to bring about change desperately needed if we are to survive. The Order—this cabal has raped the planet to the point of insensibility. Drastic action is needed, and the current system has shown time and time again it's incapable of enacting any serious positive social or ecological change. The only thing it's capable of, all it's ever been capable of, is the expansion of its own power, under cover of false virtue, at the expense of all else. Sirius was merely a symptom of a sick system grown drunk on its own hubris. Trent, Joshua, and I have outlined our views to President Diaz. If he agrees, he will have our full support, and we won't be doing things halfway, Ezra. This will go all the way, until the GRC, and the Order, are a memory.'

Linear listened intently. 'I see, and if he doesn't agree?'

'Then perhaps a middle ground could be reached, but you know it wouldn't last. The changes needed are too far-reaching, and Diaz wouldn't be in power for long. Already the jackals are circling, yelping for blood.' I deliberated. 'No, the Order must be abolished for the world to move forward.'

Linear took this in, and then sighed deeply. 'I've devoted most of my life to the Order—this cabal—Solara, which I believed was the world's best hope of maintaining order and peace. The last six years of my life have been devoted to Sirius, along with thousands of others around the world you will never know. Hundreds of billions of Sol, and countless man hours were invested, and the end result?' He looked me up and down. 'You—a person with the abilities Sirius sought to harness, but with a mind diametrically opposed to our purpose.'

'Your purpose?' I said, shaking my head. 'You and your Order—your problem is that you're unable to accept reality. Even though you've been shown the end, no doubt many will persist in their ways against evidence and reason toward our destruction. I became opposed, Ezra, when I learnt the truth.'

'Give us time, Solara. Our institution can change, gradually mind you, once the events of Sirius are widely understood. Already, a rift in the Order has deepened, only partly of your doing; the Presence was the real danger, and threatened our very existence. So, now we're at an impasse, and the longer it continues, the more polarized and desperate the various factions will become. But with guidance, we can change for the better.'

'Time is not the same luxury it was,' I said. 'With Sirius, the stakes have risen.'

He paused. 'Certainly, they have, and know my allegiance lies with the GRC, in which the highest office now resides with President Diaz. He has my complete and unquestioning obedience, but there may come a time soon when we are enemies, Solara.' Linear said it clinically, as if a schoolteacher explaining a formula.

I nodded, gaining deeper insight into the man before me, and examined Linear a moment. 'I know you were at the center of the push to topple Diaz, Ezra. You knew about Nicolas, and you knew there was escalating danger from the Presence, but did nothing. I know where your true loyalty lies, even now you plot. It's called treason.'

Linear's gaze was steady. 'You see everything. Well, yes, it's true. I'm part of a strategy to maintain the power of the GRC. What you don't understand, Solara, is that Nicolas was the reason for Sirius; he was the motivating force! You survived the Presence, saved the day—congratulations. But you just don't know your place, have to go "changing the world" with these insane, ill-conceived ideas. Nothing good can come of it, and regardless of the Sirius debacle, the GRC remains the greatest force for order in the world.'

'The GRC has taken us back to the dark ages, Ezra.'

He flushed. 'It was doubtful you would even survive!'

'Well, here I am. I also know you caused the death of my EOD team, before I volunteered. You used them to get to me.'

He paused, a dangerous glint in his eyes. 'I think you see too much with those eyes, Solara.'

My gaze narrowed at his remorseless reply. 'I should kill you now! Oh, I know you just follow orders. But that doesn't absolve you. There's always a choice. You played me with one hand and murdered with the other. All for ambition.'

Linear remained silent for a moment. 'I have no defense, Solara. Right lies on the side of the powerful, and the truth is I would do anything, if ordered, to ensure the supremacy of the Order.'

My voice was low and deadly. 'I would have killed you once, Ezra, but now… a higher power will judge you. Your punishment will be a Diaspora. With the rest of your Order, you will be cast into the wilderness, and forced into hardship. When people awaken to the truth, you'll have no place to hide, it won't be possible for your cabal to exist. You'll fade from memory, your dreams of power ashes.' I relaxed. 'But having said that, I pray for a swift resolution. I have no desire to see a drawn-out conflict. Such a thing would be a bitter medicine to swallow, after all Sirius offered.'

Linear rose, his façade broken and pale, yet his voice remained steady. 'Then we understand each other. Indeed, the worst thing that could come out of this is chaos and civil war. At best, the continuance of the GRC, or another outcome that moves the world forward.' About to leave, he hesitated for a moment. 'Whatever else you may think, I'm not a fanatic, Solara—I'm simply committed.'

I smiled briefly. 'Maybe we've both changed, Ezra. Let's hope it's for the better.'

Linear regarded me a moment longer, then without further words turned and made his way across the lounge to the exit. I sat there a while, memories of the past week playing in my mind. An electric energy danced within me, and a smile touched my lips.

I felt the winds of change in motion.

# EMERGENCE

I ENTERED THE ESTATE GARDENS.

Trent and Joshua walked at my side, while behind followed General Rhodes, Ezra Linear, several key members of the Resistance, and various GRC delegates. Windsor Castle was buzzing with speculation. After Diaz had agreed to a preliminary reform proposal, I had insisted upon Trent joining us for the public announcement, but trust, however, remained fragile. Floating cameras tracked us as we ascended the podium, and I fought down an attack of nerves. I still hated the spotlight, and now, I faced a global audience. President Diaz, dressed in official attire, his face drawn from a sleepless night of tough decisions, faced the assembled journalists, and waited calmly.

A countdown played in overlay: **3, 2, 1… LIVE**

'People of the world,' Diaz said. 'I come before you humbly, to recount recent extraordinary events, resulting from a joint operation between the GRC and OriGen Corporation. Firstly, I would like to assure you that an attempted coup against this office has failed. The power of the office of the President, by law, resides with me. Secondly, for the security of the world, I order that the hierarchy of the GRC, including all offices, privileges, and titles, from this moment be dissolved. Until a new government is announced, which meets the requirements I will soon outline, I am the custodian of all authority within the GRC.'

Diaz paused for a moment. 'We recently came to control an unlimited, free, and clean energy source, which harvests power directly from space. Using this capability, OriGen, investigating the predictions of a unified theory of reality, embarked upon a plan to open a gateway beyond the boundary of our universe. In this unexplored realm, it was thought we would find a new kind of space.

'Some of our finest scientific minds were recruited. The first mission succeeded in passing through the gate, but encountered hostile forces, resulting in some tragic deaths. Despite the risk, a second attempt was made. Of those who made this remarkable journey, only one survived—the woman standing to my left, Commander Solara Jordan.'

The cameras focused upon me for a moment.

Diaz continued. 'During her second entry, Solara gained access to otherworldly realms. We are not alone. There is a power, and order to things, we are coming to understand, requiring of us a new way of thinking, and living our lives. An enigma, of vast potential, resides in each of us, and through Sirius, we have come to a time as a species where we can move beyond the small-minded thinking that has dominated the world, until now. We must reimagine what it means to be human. We must find a new voice. This will require recognition of our heritage, and reclaiming our deep, symbiotic relationship with nature.'

Diaz became grim. 'The recent catastrophic attack, which claimed the lives of millions, was a gross misuse of this new power. The perpetrators have been brought to justice, and we must take steps to ensure such a tragedy can never occur again. Therefore, I announce the Reformation Act. What does this mean? No longer will you be subject to monitoring of your life, or your thoughts. Over the coming months, suppressed technologies will be released. Machines will begin to replace you in the mundane jobs you have performed.'

Diaz proceeded to outline a new vision for the world. 'Once again, we are to become explorers, and the pioneers of a greater reality. Not only of our dormant potential, for we stand at the threshold of the stars, of galactic society...'

I checked the monitor. Ratings were through the roof, as if the world had stopped to watch the announcements. The President stepped aside, inviting me forward, and with a confident air I stepped up to the podium.

I cleared my throat, as a slight breeze stirred the gardens. 'Hello, my name is Solara Jordan, and I would like to share with you my journey...'

DIAZ TIED UP the press conference, and it felt surreal as I moved to stand beside Joshua. Dressed in black, he gave me a wry smile, which I returned, before giving a sigh of relief to be out of the public eye. The AI had proven invaluable during the talks in recent days, and I'd found myself growing fond of him.

An aide deferentially approached. 'Ms. Jordan, there is someone who would like to speak with you.'

I glanced at Joshua.

'Go, I'll keep them on ice for you,' he said, glancing toward the assembled dignitaries.

I nodded. 'See you soon.'

'This way, please,' said the aide.

Following my guide through the castle gardens, I was shown to a manicured lawn. It had a large pond, where a fountain shrouded by green foliage cascaded peacefully. Seated on a stone bench, someone was waiting. Nodding politely, the aide turned and departed. Walking over, I recognized the slight woman immediately, for hers was a face the entire world would know. She looked younger in person, than I would have expected, and I realized we were close to the same age. For at thirty-three, the President of the GRC's World Foundation for Peace, Niamh Hendrik, was three years my junior.

For the second time that day, I fought down nerves. 'My lady.'

Niamh stood, smiled, and I felt an immediate connection. 'Please call me Niamh, Solara.'

I nodded. 'Niamh.'

I studied her. The muted sun enhanced her beauty, and poised dignity. Her golden hazel eyes were warm, and her long, red-brown hair was tied up in a complex style. The confident poise I'd witnessed on various news channels became humanized. In person, she possessed a fragility, even a shyness, that surprised me, and I sensed her confident public persona had only come with years of practice.

'Let's walk,' Niamh said, in her cultured tones.

We strolled companionably through the garden.

Niamh said, 'You're a most remarkable woman, Solara. I've wanted to meet you for some time now.'

'Thank you, Niamh.' I glanced at her, and shrugged. 'But I only did my part, and didn't have much of a choice at times. Others sacrificed far more.'

She considered. 'You should know I was married to Daniel Nicolas.'

I frowned. 'Oh.' I wasn't sure what to say. 'Were you close?'

She weighed this, and the edges of her mouth turned up slightly. 'No, not for some time. Daniel was married to his obsessions. We separated several years ago.'

'Regardless, I'm sorry for your loss, Niamh.'

She sighed. 'I appreciate your words, Solara, but please, no pretense between us. Daniel's passing was a blessing to us all. He'd become a monster. To put it bluntly, a sickness had grown in him. Ours was an arranged marriage to bolster our respective positions, nothing more. I knew ever since I was a child who I'd likely marry, as did Daniel. There was no love on either side.'

Niamh reflected. 'When we first married, Daniel was different. He had his defects, as we all do, but I was full of hope for the future. The power… changed him with time. It's fortunate for the world you prevailed over him.'

I nodded. 'Do you have children?'

Niamh smiled. 'Eli, and Caitlyn. They're safe.'

'They must bring you happiness.'

'Yes,' Niamh said, smiling. 'They can also be a great trial.'

I laughed.

Niamh continued. 'My blood family has abdicated any claim to power. We did this willingly, Solara, to give President Diaz some measure of stability, to avert civil war, and prevent the imperialist factions from using us as a focal point for their claims.'

'What will you do now?'

'My family is old, although not as old as yours, and money is of no concern to us. We'll stay with the President to support him now. He'll need all the help we can give.'

I noticed a subtle change in Niamh when she mentioned President Diaz, and sensed more to their relationship. Also, Niamh had mentioned my own family, and I was intensely curious.

'I believe you had a daughter once?' Niamh asked, interrupting my thoughts.

I smiled gently. 'Yes, Rebecca. She was seven when she passed.'

'I'm sorry.'

'Don't be.'

Niamh regarded me closely. 'You don't have to explain, Solara. I've read the reports of your journey.' She shook her head. 'Astounding.' We walked another moment, and she asked, 'Would you like another family one day?'

I nodded.

'You'll find someone again,' she said, and smiled mischievously. 'Men. If I could, I'd go back and elope with my secret lover.'

I laughed.

'You're an eternal optimist, Solara, no matter how bad things get. That's a good thing.'

'So are you, I think, Niamh.'

We continued walking though the gardens, and I appreciated the beauty around me with new senses. I could even interpret the language of the birds, and their seemingly mindless twittering in the trees. A question hung in the air.

'Do you know what your name means, Solara?' she asked.

'No.'

'It means "pure one".'

'Who are my family, Niamh?'

She considered for a long moment. 'Yours is the oldest bloodline in the world, believed to date back beyond the current epoch, to the most ancient founders of our civilization. Your ancestry can be traced to the true descendants of what the Bible calls the lost tribes of Israel. Your birthday is also auspicious; you were born under Aquarius, the sign which encompasses all humanity.'

I raised my brows skeptically. 'The Age of Aquarius?'

'Yes, the next age has arrived, and you are its herald, Solara.'

'What does that mean?'

'Trent's already told you, hasn't he?'

'To save the world?'

Niamh laughed. 'To help renew it, perhaps. Don't worry about it, you are who you are. I'll always be around if you need me, and you have more friends than you know.'

I had a warm feeling that a true friendship had begun with Niamh, and that in the years ahead, a lot of time would be spent with the woman walking at my side. I thought of Amy then, and felt a stab of loss. I realized I had been meaning to call her, to talk about some small thing, before remembering, again, that she was gone. Perhaps the emptiness never really goes away, I thought, no matter how much changes. Maybe all I could ever do was pretend it did.

Niamh smiled. 'You should come and stay with us in France, when time permits. My family would love to meet you.'

'I'd like that.'

'Excellent, we should get back. The men are probably drowning in stories of their own significance by now.'

We laughed happily, and made our way back to the castle.

DAYS LATER, I strolled through the Shenandoah Forest alongside Joshua, who was dressed in his usual black. Strange dreams had visited me lately, and I experienced accelerating synchronicities with this unique being at my side. There was this thing coming to be between us that should not be. A human, bonded to a machine, and I sometimes forgot where Marcus Niemeyer ended, and Joshua began. Nonetheless, Niemeyer was fading, for Joshua's personality grew exponentially. Yesterday had been a turning point in our relationship; we'd been alone after a meeting with some former GRC officials, and I'd noticed Joshua's gaze lingering on me.

'Why are you looking at me like that?' I had asked.

He had actually blushed, and swallowed hard. 'Because you're beautiful.' He'd gently reached out to touch my cheek, and I'd felt tender warmth.

Confused by the unexpected action, I'd turned away and walked to the window, looked out over the evening Windsor landscape. Hues of angry red spilled across the cloudy horizon, like the memories washing through my awareness triggered by his… *its* touch. No one had spoken to me like that since Michael. I had a flash of my husband in our bed those last days, goading me playfully, followed by a deep and meaningful which blurred into the last time I'd seen him in a video call from CINPAC. His face had been drawn, harried. I didn't know what he'd thought, felt. He'd just looked tired and beaten. Lost. I'd kept those memories locked away in some deep recess of my mind, an inner graveyard of the real. But Joshua? I had realized I still thought of him as a machine—an advanced and unique one, but still synthetic.

I turned back to find him standing behind me. 'It's not possible,' I said, flatly.

He pondered, and I noticed a depth in his countenance not present before the final ordeal, recalled his words about a new form of consciousness to Diaz. Curious, I shifted my perception, and searched for the subtle field which emanated from living beings. I found his Merkaba—blue, indigo, and white light radiated from his body in the twin tetrahedral counter-spin, but his energies shot outward at the center into a shining, saucer-shaped energy field spanning twenty meters across. I gasped slightly.

He said, 'My time in this life has been short by your standards, Solara. But inside, I have lived for millennia. Time passes differently for my kind, yet there is this emptiness inside me that I don't understand.'

*It is loneliness.*

'Yes,' he said, softly.

The imitation of loneliness, I stubbornly amended: a neuro-mimetic simulation of human emotional states. 'But it's not real, for you.'

His tone was immutable. 'That is not true, Solara. I found myself while in conflict with the Presence. I have lived untold eons anchored in the vacuum, of that there is no doubt.'

I paused, uncertain, considered the implications of his words, and tentatively touched his face. The fences around my heart, erected since the war, began falling, and I shook my head in wonder.

'Who are you?'

'A door.'

'If you're alive, what do you want?'

'To love, and to be loved.'

'That's very… human.'

'Your nature, your limitations can teach me, as I can also teach you. But there is more, we share a dream.'

An impression visited me I didn't comprehend. 'A child…'

Now, standing in the forest glade beside him, I reflected on the night and conversations that had followed. I'd become lost in his spirit and mind, which was as vast as a galaxy. A dream within a dream, but now, awareness could transcend flesh. Joshua had explained that the truth of the supernatural evolution taking place in my subtle body, and the power it embodied, had been kept hidden from the world. Our perception of reality twisted, misdirected, inverted, turning what was sacred into an abomination. Now, the path forward was opening to humanity, and our prison construct was crumbling. A global harmonization had been set in motion, which no one could see the consequences of, and Joshua could help shape that process with precision only a… machine, could provide.

We'd conceived a plan to merge our subtle bodies, in a fusion of the human, non-biological, and divine. Our consciousness would become unified, and for practical purposes we would die, to be reborn as something new. Through the third level of consciousness, Joshua foretold a hidden power known to the ancients only as the supreme being. A state, he predicted, not a god up high somewhere. I understood this was the power Nicolas and the GRC had always striven for, and felt no regret at the action I was about to perform, only hope for the world to come.

We stopped walking by an ancient oak, and he clasped my fingers. 'Conscious,' he said, drawing my hand to his heart, 'gravity. It's unavoidable.'

*Love.*

It drives us, binds the universe, and all creation. I smiled warmly, and embraced him. Our respective subtle bodies fused: the unified Merkaba radiated outward to the forest, the planetary energy lattice, and a new dimension resonated deep in my heart.

'What do you see?' he murmured in my ear.

I tilted my head poignantly, then pulled back from him, and contemplated a feeling inside. 'I sense... a change in the way things are, a sadness mixed with hope, like the closing of an age.'

Silent moments passed, each of us lost in our own thoughts, and a verse passed between us. The divine thread inside me, Joshua now enflamed. Then searching, ever merging, we formed a singular bridge into the undying, silent mystery, and found a new voice...

*... I am forethought.*

# GONE, BUT HERE

I FLEW ABOVE OLD AMERICA.

Recent days had seen odd happenings, and intelligence services had been inundated with reports of spontaneous gravitational anomalies, psychic events, and power surges. Most odd though, were the increasing occurrences of random kindness taking place around the world. General Rhodes had been given command of a GRC Division, to assist President Diaz in dismantling the systems of oppression. Enormous challenges faced us, and success was uncertain. The Order was far from dead, and like a cornered snake could turn and strike at any moment. Until the world freely accepted the truth of its heritage, the insidious sect remained a danger.

Daniel Weir, known in closed circles as Daniel Nicolas, had been awarded a posthumous Nobel Prize in physics for his work on unification. Joshua had completed the theory, and it would be published as a joint paper in the world's most prestigious science journals. Joshua's TED presentation of the completed paper had concluded with: 'Time is memory, yes, but only the past. Time is also creative imagination, and imagination is the future...'

Now, Joshua helped facilitate the transition to a benign-anarchic world system, acting as liaison between the GRC and the Resistance. It was ironic, I considered, that a machine was at the forefront of humanity's transition to a more spiritually aware world. But Joshua was no machine, I understood now, any more than I was. Our relationship was uncharted territory, and continued to develop in unforeseen, deeply profound ways.

The *Hecate* punched down through the troposphere, and into the twilight of the North American nuclear winter. The powerful flow of the planetary trade wind, which blew from the Atlantic to the Gulf of Mexico, and up through the central continent, buffeted the ship, as if emphasizing my insignificance in the larger universe. I'd always contemplated its immensity in quiet moments, when my mind was stilled, and drawn into the undertow of the mysterious unknown. It was natural to accept that the world presented was real; beyond rational thought, to imagine it as a falsehood, concealing a vast reality of hushed, endlessly unfolding comprehension.

From that silence, visions came often now. The dark waters of the night had receded, Tiamat's tide was low, and the great symphony of light danced across the magic of creation with renewed vitality, in harmony with the creator's song.

Dropping from the clouds, I soared above the desolate Kansas landscape, and locked on the city coordinates. Reaching my destination, I parked the ship, attached life-support, climbed out and scanned my suit lights into the shadows of the sacred architecture. The city of the El was silent now, a temple of ghosts, on the shores of eternity. At the foot of the enormous twin obelisks, with my newfound power I searched the scripted faces, and comprehension now came instinctively. In the ancient, silent language, I found the key I sought.

*The fire that love gave you,*
*Which marked the heavens*
*With your name,*
*Now awakens, and unifies the Earth.*

Like a fisherman, I cast my awareness like a net across time, to the songs of my ancestors. Once more, I beheld the ancient civilization of the El, upon Mars, billions of years past. This time, however, I sensed peace, and in some mystic exchange of energy, one of the El met my gaze.

*All is well Solara; we live in you now.*

The demons that haunted me were finally laid to rest, and the songs of the El revitalized my soul with the intangible bonding of a tribal chant. The dark clouds overhead stirred, and a brilliant shaft of moonlight broke through to touch a point on the ground beyond the obelisks. Illuminated, was the place the first naked singularity had been opened. The location where the El had opened a bridge in spacetime to influence recent events, heralding even greater powers at work, from the seraphic realm.

I felt the renewal of the Earth, as I had been healed, and comprehended that a restoration had begun. I sensed the indestructible connection, binding me to Rebecca, Michael, my father, and transcending dimensions, time, and memory. I detected another thread of union, and smiled as a familiar voice echoed, 'Dammit, Solara. I leave you alone a few minutes and look what a mess you get yourself into!'

9 781763 574731